The Tinder Chronicles

The Complete M/M Paranormal Trilogy
Tinder / Hunted / Destined

by Alexa Land

Dedicated to every Tinder fan who reached out to me and asked for more.

Table of Contents

Book One: Tinder

No, my parents didn't actually name me after a handful of combustible twigs. They named me Tyler, but no one ever called me that. The nickname was my older brother Eddie's fault. The story went that when I was a kid, just about anything would make me mad. So Eddie started calling me Tinder, because it was so easy to ignite my temper. Eddie was long gone, but the nickname lived on. I didn't mind it so much. It was kind of my brother's lasting legacy.

Eddie died the same way the rest of my family did, by hunting vampires. And no, I don't need you to speed-dial the county mental health department for me. Vampires are all too real, and I've got the battle scars to prove it.

Even if I hadn't been born into this line of work, I would have done it anyway. When I was four years old, I watched a vamp tear my mother to shreds right in front of me. She was a hunter too, just like five generations of our family before her. And after witnessing something like that, I understood better than anyone the need to wipe those remorseless killing machines off the planet.

Right now though, I was on a different kind of hunt. After tossing back the last half-inch of whiskey in my glass, I scanned the crowd at Silvio's, a dive bar in Long Beach's gay ghetto. Normally this place was pretty low-key. But since it was a Friday night, the crowd was young, loud and exuberant. To make matters worse, Silvio's had live music on the weekends. The band was currently massacring a Queen song I used to love, but that now was ruined forever. Christ. I seriously needed to get what I came for, then get the fuck out of here.

I'd lived in Southern California all my life, but still managed to feel like an outsider pretty much all the time. Like now, for example. I scanned the faces of a group of college guys and fought the urge to roll my eyes. I was the same age as most of them, barely twenty-one, but they felt like a different species, so shallow and frivolous. They had no concerns beyond getting good grades and getting laid. Well, okay, maybe I could relate to the second half of that.

One of the college guys, a big douchey football player type, saw me looking and came up to me with a cocky grin. "Hey sexy. Wanna dance?"

I pushed my black hair out of my eyes and frowned at him. "What do I look like, your fuckin' prom date? Hell no, I don't want to dance."

His expression went from cocky to annoyed in point-oh-two seconds. "Okay! You don't have to be a dick about it."

I slid off the barstool and looked him in the eye. We were the same height, a little under six feet tall. I told him, "I'm here to get laid, not to dance. Do you want to take me in the back and fuck me? If so, let's get to it. Otherwise, you're wasting my time."

Douchey jock boy mulled this over for a couple seconds, then said, "Yeah, okay."

He followed me to the restroom at the back of the bar. A big sign on the door spelled out the fact that sex in the restrooms was strictly prohibited. Uh huh.

As soon as I bolted the stall door behind us, jock boy tried to swoop in for a kiss. "Oh come on," I said, dodging the kiss effortlessly. "Just fucking. None of this romantic kissy face bullshit."

10

"You're really a piece of work, you know that?" he said. "It's a good thing you're cute."

I turned my back to him and unbuckled my belt, then unzipped my jeans and pulled them down to mid-thigh. "I'm also easy," I said, pulling a compact bottle of lube from the pocket of my leather jacket and squirting a little on my fingers. "So quit complaining and enjoy it." I worked a little lube into myself, then bent in half so I was leaning over the toilet, my hands splayed out on the back of the stall.

Joe College rolled on a condom, then fucked me hard and fast. He was kind of pissed off at me, so he wasn't being gentle. Good. I hated it when my sex partners treated me like a girl. After cumming in record time, he pulled out of me and threw the condom in the toilet. He zipped up and swung open the stall door before I even got my pants back up. Like I said: douchey. I got dressed and left the bathroom, staring daggers at an older queen over by the sinks that had started to smirk at me.

Oh, quit judging me. Yeah, I let myself indulge in sex with strangers. And I did that kind of a lot. But why the hell shouldn't I? I could be dead tomorrow. Hell, I

11

could be dead five minutes from now. The fact that I'd even made it to twenty-one was kind of a miracle. None of my four brothers or sisters made it past twenty. My job was stressful as hell, and this was one of the only things that took my mind off of it, even if it was just for fifteen minutes at a time.

Or, in the case of douchey jock boy, one minute and twenty-five seconds at a time.

Brief as that was, I'd gotten what I needed and could go to work now. I left the bar without a glance at Douchey or his college buddies and stepped out into the balmy spring night. Despite the warm weather, I kept my leather jacket on as I slid behind the wheel of my beat-up Camaro (yes, a Camaro. Are you judging again?). I was packing enough weaponry to overthrow the government of a small nation, so the jacket stayed on almost all the time.

It was time to find a crowd and go fishing. I pointed the car toward Shoreline Village, which would be hopping on the weekend. More people meant a greater chance of sniffing out a vamp.

No, I didn't literally sniff them out, like some sort of supernatural bloodhound or some shit. Actually, I was able to see this kind of energy signature that everyone gave off. The glow around a vampire was pure white, while humans put out a nice, rosy, pink hue.

Yeah, yeah, I know that sounds like a big, steaming pile of new-agey bullshit, like reading auras or something. But what can I say, I saw it. And that was what separated true hunters from any random asswipe with a stake: this special ability we were born with to recognize vampires. Since both my parents had been true hunters, my sixth sense was more pronounced than most. I could spot a bloodsucker up to a quarter mile away.

It was an incredibly useful tool in my line of work, because vamps didn't exactly go around wearing big black capes. They didn't sparkle either, in case you were wondering. Most of those sons of bitches even filed their fangs down so they could blend right in to the general population, and no, that didn't impair their ability to feed from humans. Think about it. Any moron with so much as a ballpoint pen could open a vein if they really wanted to.

Vampires also pretty much never bit people on the neck and left two perfect puncture wounds. What, like they were *trying* to get hunted to extinction? That'd be like leaving a calling card announcing their existence and bringing the wrath of the clueless masses down on them. They just weren't that stupid.

*****

Shoreline Village was even more crowded than I'd anticipated, because it turned out to be spring break. I overheard a couple high schoolers talking about it. It wasn't like I had any reason to keep track of that sort of thing.

The cluster of colorful shops and restaurants surrounding a little marina were a big draw with everyone from tourists to local families to partying college kids. The Queen Mary was docked nearby, and the Long Beach skyline sparkled in the background. In other words, the Disney factor in this place was turned up to Maximum Sugar Coma.

I stuffed my hands in my pockets and wandered the half-circle boardwalk around the marina, weaving through the crowd. Despite my efforts not to attract attention, I got a lot of looks from people. High school girls tended to be attracted to the bad boy thing, which was how they interpreted my dark clothes and leather jacket. Their parents read the way I was dressed as shorthand for *criminal* and shot me warning looks to make sure I stayed away from their daughters. I often failed to stop myself from rolling my eyes at them.

A touch on my shoulder made me whirl around, my right hand immediately on the weapon inside my jacket as someone said, "Seriously, Tinder? You ready to stake me right here in the middle of all of this?" I relaxed at the sight of Lee Halstrom, a fellow hunter that I crossed paths with now and then. He was only half true hunter, on his dad's side, so his senses weren't as strong as mine. But he was good in a fight and we'd teamed up a couple times.

"What the fuck are you wearing, Lee?" He looked like a frat boy in a tight yellow polo shirt and pastel plaid shorts, a backpack slung over one shoulder. Lee was maybe twenty-one, six-two and muscular with short sandy blond hair, so the frat thing wasn't much of a stretch.

"It's called blendin' in. You should try it some time." Lee was originally from Katy, Texas and spoke with a slight drawl. I normally found it kind of hot, though the outfit was neutralizing his sex appeal in a big way.

"And when you have to get to your weapons quickly, then what? You gonna say 'y'all please excuse me for a moment' and then go digging in your backpack? Sounds like a good way to get yourself killed."

"Come on," Lee said. "You know as well as I do that we won't have to pull our weapons here."

He had a point. Vamps used places like this as a grocery store, they picked out their next meal and then compelled the human to go home with them. It wasn't like we were going to have to bust up any spontaneous feedings in the middle of the boardwalk. No one would be dumb enough to jump us here either, in front of a thousand witnesses. Vamps had a really strong survival instinct and they'd never draw attention to themselves in a situation like this.

"Well, you still look like an idiot," I said.

"Said the guy who's sweltering in a leather jacket in this weather." Lee grinned at me, then slowly ran his gaze down my body. I knew what was coming next.

"You look good though, Tinder. What do you say we once again violate our 'we're never doing that again' pledge and sleep together when we finish up here?"

Lee had fucked me half a dozen times over the last year and every time we swore we'd never do it again. It was a bad idea, mixing business with pleasure. I already liked him and didn't need any extra emotions clouding my judgment when I was trying to do a job. Getting attached to someone to the point where you became concerned about their safety was a surefire way to get yourself killed. "Not tonight, Lee."

"Meaning you already got laid."

"Meaning not tonight, Lee."

He watched me for a beat, then grinned. "Fine. So, I better make this a quick hunt. I'll have to hit the bars before they close tonight, since you're shootin' me down." Lee thought of himself as bisexual, by the way, which was a nice way of saying he'd fuck absolutely anybody.

"You should've cleaned the pipes before work, Lee. You don't need that kind of distraction throwing you off your game."

"I'm not off my game, and I'll prove it to ya. Two vamps, eleven o'clock." He grinned smugly.

I glanced where he'd indicated and then it was my turn to grin. "You mean *five* vamps, eleven o'clock. So much for being on your game."

"Five, shit," Lee muttered. "They been travelin' in packs more and more lately."

"Yeah. I don't know what to make of it," I said as I leaned casually against the railing at the water's edge and glanced at the group of bloodsuckers. There were four males and one female, all dressed in expensive-looking clothing.

"They're making their move," Lee said quietly, leaning against the railing beside me. The vamps had fanned out, two of them targeting a young couple, the others approaching a group of three college girls and compelling them with just a few words. All of them headed to the parking lot, spread out in little groups of two so as not to attract attention. We followed at a distance.

They ended up piling into two Mercedes and a BMW. The flashy cars were so predictable. I had yet to meet a vamp that didn't use their ability to compel

18

humans for monetary gain. I mean, think about it: as long as a human was under your control, why not take a stroll past the ATM? Or hell, why not have them sign their sports car over to you on the spot?

I slid behind the wheel of my car and followed them, Lee's beat up Ford pickup in my rearview mirror. I kind of expected the vamps to head toward Belmont Shore or one of the more upscale neighborhoods in Long Beach, a flashy home to go with the flashy cars. But instead, they caravanned to an industrial area near the Port of Long Beach. That wasn't good. For one thing, our tail would be much easier to spot, since at night that part of town was deserted. I also didn't like the unknown factor, having no idea where they were headed.

Eventually they pulled into the loading dock of a brick warehouse and someone lowered the big metal doors behind them. This whole situation made me uneasy, both because of the unusual number of vamps involved and because this setting deviated from their usual playbook.

I parked on a cross-street, my vehicle hidden by another building, and went around to the trunk. I was arming myself to the teeth when Lee pulled up behind me. "What the fuck are they doing in a warehouse?" he asked as he got out of his truck.

"Hell if I know."

"I don't like this."

"Neither do I."

"I wish there was someone we could call for backup," Lee said as he stepped into a dark grey jumpsuit and pulled up the zipper.

"Hate to break it to you, but *we're* the cavalry. Nobody's coming to our aid," I told him as I grabbed my crossbow, then paused to look at him. "Why the fuck are you dressed like one of the Ghostbusters?"

He knit his brows at me. "That shirt's brand new. I don't want to fuck it up first thing."

"You sure? You'd be doing the shirt a favor by destroying it."

"So how do you want to do this?" he asked, ignoring my wisecrack.

"I'll go in the front, you go in the back. Assuming there even is a back entrance. Stake first, ask questions later."

Lee slung a leather strap over his torso, lined with ammunition. He held a shot gun in his left hand and had strapped a big stake to his right forearm. "Give me about sixty seconds head start so I can get around to the back of the building."

"Okay."

"Oh, and Tinder?"

"Yeah?"

"If we both live through this, forget what we said. I'm bending you over the hood of your Camaro and fucking you right here." He grinned at me and took off running.

I grinned at that too as I did a final weapons check. About half a minute later, I jogged across the street and up to the warehouse. The main door was solid-looking metal, so I figured my chances of kicking it in were slim to none. After weighing my options for a couple seconds, I went up to the door and knocked.

"Yeah?" a deep voice called from inside.

"Candy-gram."

The vampire manning the front door was clearly not the brains of this operation. He swung the door open and said, "What?"

"Didn't your mother ever tell you not to open the door to strangers?" I fired a thin wooden stake into his heart with my crossbow and he instantly turned to dust. That was the only good thing about vampires: they didn't leave behind pesky corpses that needed to be explained to the authorities.

I stepped over his clothes, which had fluttered to the ground (what, did you expect them to turn to dust, too? Come on!) and immediately fired another stake into a vamp that was coming out of an office to my right. Bullseye! I would have thought I was off to an awesome start, except for one annoying little detail: neither of these fine Undead Americans had been among the group I'd followed here. Apparently, I'd struck the vampire mother lode.

Damn. I was definitely toast.

A long hallway stretched before me and I jogged into the heart of the building, reloading my double-sided crossbow and listening carefully. A few faint voices could be heard up ahead. I wondered if Lee was inside yet.

I paused outside a closed door and listened, my heart racing, adrenaline coursing through me. There

22

were several people on the other side. I flung the door open and did a split-second assessment. There were eight people in the room, including all five humans that had been taken from Shoreline Village. I dusted a vamp to my left with my crossbow, but didn't have time to aim before the other two came at me.

Hand-to-hand combat with vampires was an incredibly bad idea. They were much stronger and faster than humans, so they really didn't have to rely on expert fighting skills like I did. All they had to do was catch you. Then they could snap your neck like a twig, or tear you limb from limb, or whatever sounded fun to them at the time.

Fortunately, I had quick reflexes. I managed to dive under the lunging grasp of one vamp, barrel-rolling across the floor and knocking the second vamp off her feet. I flicked my wrist, extending the big stake that was strapped to my forearm and dusting her before she even knew what hit her. This enraged the first vampire and he threw himself at me in a blind fury. I raised my arm and the stake to meet him, closing my eyes and turning my head as he disintegrated all over me. Gross.

I jumped up and looked around the room. The humans were all wide-eyed and totally stunned. Damn it. It really sucked when anyone in the gen pop got a first-hand look at this shit, because it meant a lot of extra work for me. For now, I ignored their panicked questions and went up to the person who seemed least like she was about to crap herself. "There are probably more of them in the building, so as soon as I leave this room, I want you to barricade the door behind me," I told the skinny redhead. "Use all this furniture and those crates, then don't open the door for anyone but me. Do you understand?"

"They just turned to dust! How is that even possible?" she stammered.

"Look," I snapped, "do you want me to stand around answering questions, or do you want to live through tonight? Barricade the door behind me! I'll come get you when this is over."

I ran out the door and pulled it shut, then paused and listened as I reloaded my crossbow. The redhead was barking orders at the others and I could hear furniture being dragged across the room. When something heavy hit the door, I took off running. I rounded a corner and almost smacked directly into another vamp. Fortunately, I was able to drive my stake into him before he had a chance to rip my head off. Beyond him, four more vamps at the far end of the hall began barreling toward me. I didn't like those odds.

I got a shot off with my crossbow but only winged one of them, so I did the only thing that made sense: I turned and ran like hell in the other direction. The corridor dead-ended in a metal staircase and I started to climb. The fact that I was working my way further into the building worried me. By going up, I was cutting myself off from possible escape routes. But facing off against four vamps at once was pure suicide.

A big, burly vamp was coming down the stairs toward me, who I recognized as one of the fab five from Shoreline Village. I shot at him with my crossbow, but he managed to dodge the shot. Damn it! He lunged for me and again my agility worked to my advantage. I avoided his grasp and he stumbled down a few steps before righting himself. That gave me a chance to reload my crossbow. I didn't miss the second time.

The other four were closing fast and I sprinted up the stairs. On the top floor, I continued my mad dash. When the corridor ran out, I ducked into a big, drab office and slammed and locked the door behind me, a split second before one of the vamps reached me. It was a metal fire door and fairly solid, but I knew it wouldn't keep a bunch of vamps out forever. I shoved the big desk across the room and up against the door, then leaned against it, gasping for breath, my heart pounding like it was trying to bust out of my chest. Shouts could be heard out in the hall. It sounded like the vamps that had been chasing me were calling for even more reinforcements. Awesome.

I looked around the room. Besides the desk, all it contained was an office chair and a big metal file cabinet about five feet wide and six feet high. There were no windows, only a single skylight in the center of the fifteen foot ceiling. Yeah okay, I could make that work.

The file cabinet was a bit problematic, because it weighed a ton and I couldn't budge it. I folded the top door of the cabinet up and back and swore vividly as I began grabbing armloads of files and flinging them out of the cabinet. As I worked on emptying it out so it was light enough to drag under the skylight, I wondered what had happened to Lee. There'd been no sign of him since I entered the building.

It took for-fucking-ever to empty the cabinet. Meanwhile, it sounded like the vamps out in the hall had located an axe and were trying to chop their way through the door. I rolled my eyes at that. If they'd been smart enough to hack through the wall instead of the metal door, they'd be in here already.

Even with all the paper out of it, the steel cabinet was still crazy heavy. Lucky me to find the one file cabinet in the universe built to survive a nuclear blast. I crouched down, grasped it by the edges and threw my weight into it. The cabinet slid about half an inch. I tugged on it again and again, painfully making my way to the center of the room and completely wearing myself out in the process. That sucked, because as soon as I got myself out of this room, I was going to have to run right back into the ground floor of this building and get those civilians to safety.

The chances of living through this were not looking good.

When I very nearly had the cabinet in position, the skylight shattered. I held up the edge of my jacket and hid under it as glass rained down on me. A light thud alerted me that someone had just jumped through the skylight and landed beside me. I lurched to my feet and grabbed a stake from inside my jacket as I whirled around, but was immediately grabbed, transported across the room and slammed up against the wall, my wrists pinned to either side of my head.

I looked up into pale green eyes and a permanent smirk. "Which just goes to prove," I said, my voice a low growl, "that no matter how bad a situation is, it can always get worse."

"Hello, Tinder. You're looking well."

"Hi Bane. Hey, do me a favor. Let go of my right wrist for a second, so I can jam this stake through your heart."

Bane was the most aptly named vampire ever, because he was, in fact, the bane of my existence. I'd gone up against him several times over the years. It somehow always ended with him getting away, despite my best efforts to reduce him to something I could suck up with a Dustbuster.

And now he had me pinned to a wall, his big, powerful body pressed against mine to keep me immobile. This was seriously not good. I threw everything I had into trying to break free. Failing that, I tried to head-butt him. He pulled back, just out of range, then changed his hold on me, grasping both wrists with one hand and holding them to the wall above my head while wrapping his other hand around my neck. It fucking pissed me off that he was so much stronger than I was.

"So, I don't suppose if I asked nicely," he said, "you'd be a love and stay in this room for the next half hour." His English accent made his odd request sound downright civilized.

I knit my brows at him. "I think that's about as likely as you jamming this stake through your heart yourself, just because I said pretty please." I still grasped the big wooden spike in my right hand.

He sighed and said, "It's such a bother that you can't be compelled. Makes everything just that much more difficult." He pushed down the cuff of my jacket with a fingertip, revealing the beginning of the incantation that was tattooed all along the inside of both of my arms. My body was a canvas of spells and symbols, all of which provided me with various protections. Several, including the one he somehow knew to look for, made me immune to compelling.

"I live to annoy."

He grinned at that. And then he said randomly, his voice low and seductive, "You smell like sex. That's quite often the case, is it not? And yet, you never smell like the same bloke twice. You really should have more respect for yourself, Tinder."

"Eat me."

His grin erupted into a full-blown smile. This was slightly unnerving, because Bane was in the minority of vampires that had elected not to file their fangs down. Blending in with the general population was apparently of no interest to him. "Thanks for the oh-so-tempting offer, love, but I haven't the time, I'm afraid." In a lightning fast move, he grabbed the stake from my hand and drove it through my right shoulder. I cried out as pain shot through my body. "Rain check," he said with a wink.

He stepped back from me. I started to collapse but was held up by the stake, which had passed all the way through me and embedded in the wall. "Son of a bitch," I muttered through clenched teeth.

Bane scaled the file cabinet using the empty drawers as a ladder. He jumped up effortlessly and hung from the frame of the busted out skylight, then kicked the file cabinet over. "God damn it," I hissed.

He hung by one hand and pointed at me. "Stay," he said, like he was talking to a dog, then used both hands to easily pull himself up and out of the skylight.

I threw every swear word I knew at him as I grasped the end of the stake with my left hand and tried to pull it out of my shoulder. It wouldn't budge. Just then, the axe finally broke through the metal door. I took hold of the stake again and tugged frantically. My chances of escape where nonexistent since that asshole had knocked the file cabinet over, and no way did I have the strength to pull it upright again. But when the vamps finally busted through that door, I wasn't going down without a fight. I'd probably be able to take at least a couple of them out before they killed me.

Since the stake was embedded too deeply in the wall to remove it, I knew what I had to do. I gritted my teeth and lunged forward. The stake was a lot thicker at the handle end and the pain was so intense as it tore through my shoulder that I almost blacked out. I dropped to my knees, panting and shaking, but for only a few moments. Soon I pushed myself up and staggered across the room to my crossbow. I pointed the weapon at the door as I sat down, leaning against the upended file cabinet, and waited for the vamps to finish breaking through.

Only, they never did. Some kind of commotion in the hall interrupted them, the blade of the axe embedded in the door so deeply that I could see a few inches of it on this side. For several minutes, some kind of battle raged. I thought at first that it might be Lee, but that would have been over quickly given how many vamps were out there.

Eventually all fell silent. I gave it an extra minute, then pushed to my feet, holding my right arm against my stomach to try to stabilize my shoulder. I leaned back against the desk and used my legs to shove it out of the way, then paused and listened at the door. Nothing. When I flipped the lock and peered into the hallway, the only thing out there was six piles of clothing. What the fuck?

Maybe they'd all turned against each other. Who knows? I really didn't have the time to contemplate that right now and ran back downstairs to where I'd left the civilians. The door was ajar, the room empty. "Damn it," I muttered, falling back against the wall.

Just then, Lee caught up to me. "Dude, where were you?" I asked.

"Lying unconscious in the back alley."

"What happened?"

"I was climbin' the fire escape lookin' for a way in when two vamps came after me. I managed to ice both of 'em, but right before the second one turned to dust he shoved me. I landed in the alley, whacked my head on the concrete and blacked out." He touched the back of his head gingerly and winced. "What does a concussion feel like?"

"Are you dizzy? Confused?"

"Nah. I just have a raging headache."

"You're fine. Come on, let's sweep the building so we can get out of here," I said, pushing off the wall with a slight grunt.

"You're hurt too." Lee looked me over, then pulled aside my leather jacket and the collar of my t-shirt. "Shit, what happened?"

"A stake happened."

"You're bleeding pretty heavily, we need to do something about that."

"We will, right after we sweep the building." Lee pulled a bandana out of his pocket and handed it to me, and I pressed it against the wound.

As we went floor by floor, Lee said, "Nice work in here. I don't know how you wiped out a ton of vamps and freed all those people, but I gotta say, I'm impressed."

"I didn't free anyone, they were gone when I got back downstairs. I assume they were all taken somewhere else by the remaining vamps."

"No, they got out, all five of 'em. I passed them as I was coming into the building," he said. "Their memories from tonight had been wiped, neat as could be, and they'd all been told to hurry home. I was gonna ask if you'd somehow learned a memory spell that could be used on more than one human at a time."

I stuck my head into a room along the corridor we were travelling, then said, "Man, I *wish* I knew a spell like that. But I didn't do anything." (Though yeah, I did actually practice witchcraft. Long story.)

"This night has been weird as hell."

"No shit," I muttered as we climbed a back staircase. "I ran into Bane, by the way."

"God I hate that evil son of a bitch. Please tell me you killed him."

"Nope. He did this to my shoulder."

"What the hell was he doing here, and why were there so many vamps in this building? I mean, I've heard of a few of 'em teaming up, but nothing like this. It was practically a fuckin' vampire convention."

I really didn't have any answers for him. Lee leapt around a corner, gun drawn, like he'd seen one too many reruns of TJ Hooker. "Clear," he announced. No, a gunshot wouldn't kill a vamp, but it often slowed them down enough to then get a stake into them.

We finished searching the building and found no signs of anyone, living or undead, so we headed to our cars. "Take your shirt off, let me see your injury," Lee said as he retrieved a big Army surplus medical kit from his truck.

I sat on the hood of the Camaro and took off my jacket, then peeled off the t-shirt, which had stuck to my skin from all the blood. Lee poured a bottle of water over the wound, then took a look at my back. "Christ, it went all the way through. Doesn't it hurt?"

"Of course it hurts! How the hell would this not hurt?"

"You're not acting like you're in pain, though," Lee said. I shot him a look. I'd been a hunter since I was a kid and had sustained more injuries than a hundred normal people combined. Like I was going to make a big deal out of this one.

He dumped some alcohol onto a gauze pad and pressed it to my wound, and I flinched just a little. "Oh look, you *are* human, tough guy," he teased. That earned him the finger. He repeated the process with the exit wound on my back. This time I made a point of not flinching.

I also didn't react as Lee did a piss-poor job of sewing up the injury. When he'd taped clean squares of gauze over the stitches front and back, he gently ran his hand down my arm and smiled at me as he said, "This isn't what I'd intended to do to you tonight over the hood of your Camaro."

I jumped off the car, grabbing my jacket and t-shirt. "I know what you intended and I wasn't going to let you do that anyway." I changed the subject by saying, "Do you have any injuries that we need to triage before I take off?"

"Nah, I'm okay. I'm just gonna put an ice pack on my head and take a fistful of aspirin."

"See you around, Lee," I called as I got behind the wheel and fired up the engine.

*****

I was moving slowly when I got back to the house I was renting, probably from the blood loss I'd sustained. I trudged inside, dropped my jacket on the floor and bolted the door behind me, then picked up a piece of chalk and redrew the protection symbol that was already on the back of the door. I had to do that every time I came home, because its potency wore off quickly.

The house was empty, except for an air mattress in one corner of the living room. I sank down on it and tugged off my boots, then pulled the blanket over me. I shook a little as some of the adrenaline drained from my system and pain radiated from my shoulder. After that, I'm not sure if I fell asleep or passed out.

Tinder: Chapter Two

I awoke well past noon, showered and changed the
bandages on my shoulder before getting dressed and
heading to the diner. A huge breakfast was definitely in
order to build my strength back up.

As far as I knew, the diner was just called Diner.
That's all it said on the faded, hand-lettered sign outside
the shabby, formerly white building. It was owned by a
tiny Yugoslavian man named Guy, who still manned
the grill every day, even though he had to be in his late
seventies. He was mean as hell to everyone except
Mimi, the plump, fifty-year-old Latina that comprised
the entire wait staff.

I slid into my usual booth by the window,
sunglasses still in place. I was such a regular here that
there was no need to place an order. Mimi breezed by
with a cup of coffee and raised a drawn-on eyebrow at
me as she said, "Looks like another rough night, chico.
You keep partying that hard, you ain't gonna live to see
thirty." I smirked at her, but I did it affectionately. I

liked Mimi and didn't mind that she acted like a mother hen sometimes.

Not five minutes later, she set a huge, greasy plate of food in front of me and refilled my empty coffee cup. She plucked off my sunglasses and set them on the table before going off to attend to her only other customer. I started shoveling eggs and hash browns into my mouth, silently giving thanks for places that served breakfast at all times of the day.

The meal helped rejuvenate me a bit. When I finished I left a few bills on the table, then walked half a block to the post office and unlocked my P.O. box. As predicted, a single slim envelope was waiting for me.

Every two weeks like clockwork, I was sent money from my benefactor. Not everyone that knew about vampires was young and able-bodied enough to fight, so those that couldn't take up a stake helped out in other ways. Fortunately for me, there were people willing to fund the war on vampires. Over the years they'd organized, forming secret societies, gathering donations for those of us on the front lines. These organizations had helped my family for generations.

For the last three years, my checks had been sent to me by a man with the odd name of Arthur Primrose Matlin, whose address was a P.O. box in San Diego. I had no idea who he was, but I was damn grateful for him. It'd be pretty hard to do what I did while having to worry about things like keeping a roof over my head. And God bless Art, he was reliable as the day was long, never once missing a payment.

I tore open the envelope and removed the thin stack of checks. Each was made out to T. Reynolds (that'd be me) for a small amount, just a couple hundred dollars each, so they could be cashed just about anywhere without drawing attention to myself. I folded the envelope and stuck it in my pocket, to be burned later. Yeah, okay, my line of work made me a bit paranoid. I was always careful not to leave a trail back to my benefactor. It would really suck if some vindictive vamp ever tracked down Arthur, or any of the people working to fund the war on vampires. And ugh, yeah, I really needed to stop using the words *suck* and *vampire* in the same sentence. Every time I did that, it felt like a bad unintentional pun.

Because I still had a million questions about last night, I went home to get my car and drove back to the warehouse to do a little investigating. Since it was Saturday, the industrial area was quiet, even in broad daylight. I watched the building for a while from my parked car, just to make sure there weren't any humans going in or out of that place. There wouldn't be any vamps, of course, because they'd go up like a struck match in the sunlight. I just loved that about them, almost as much as I loved the fact that they turned to dust when you staked 'em. They may have the advantages of speed and strength, but fortunately they had their weaknesses too, and the burning in sunlight thing was a doozy.

After a few minutes, I got out of the car and checked the clip on my .44, then slipped it into the back waistband of my jeans and pulled my leather jacket over it. I jogged across the street and went up to the same metal door that I'd entered through last night. It was slightly ajar and I tried to remember if Lee and I had left it this way. I pushed the door open and stepped through, the rubber soles of my Doc Martens soundless on the concrete, then returned the door to its original position.

Once again, I went through the building floor by floor and room by room. Why had the vamps been here, of all places? There was nothing notable about this place, no reason that I could see for maybe a dozen vampires to congregate here.

When I returned to the room where I'd trapped myself, the fire axe was still embedded in the door and the bloody stake was still driven about eight inches into the wall. Fucking Bane.

Why the hell hadn't he killed me? He'd certainly had the chance. And what the hell was that shit about waiting in the room for half an hour? What was he playing at? If he had some kind of scheme going in this warehouse and wanted me out of the way while he carried it out, surely killing me would have been a more efficient way to go.

This place looked like such a bizarre crime scene that I felt compelled to destroy some of the evidence. As far as I knew, we hunters had no supporters on the Long Beach Police Department, and weird crime scenes brought questions and inquiries, both well avoided in my line of work. I grasped the stake with both hands and pulled. It didn't budge. I braced both feet on the wall and again pulled with both hands. It still didn't move. Christ, just how strong was that son of a bitch?

I went and got the fire axe from the door and hacked at the wall until the stake was free, then tossed the axe on the floor and returned the stake to the inside pocket of my jacket. I didn't have to worry about leaving fingerprints on the axe, since I'd burned mine off when I was ten.

Next I took a quick look at the files that I'd scattered all over the floor. It turned out this warehouse had been used by some small-time furniture importer, bringing in cheap chests from China (say that ten times fast) through the Port of Long Beach. That information helped me not at all.

As I went back out in the hall and kicked the piles of clothes and shoes into one big, less suspicious pile, I decided that the warehouse itself probably wasn't important. Maybe the vamps had just happened upon it by chance, compelling it out from under some poor shmuck, and then decided to hold a party here. Well, except for the fact that they basically *never* gathered in big numbers like that.

I went downstairs and into the main bay of the warehouse. The three luxury cars were still in there and I took a quick glance at their registrations. This didn't tell me anything, beyond the fact that they'd all been procured from rich, compelled people in Newport and Huntington Beach. I left the warehouse and returned to my Camaro.

Because I tended to be a bit obsessive at times and just couldn't let this go yet, I decided to retrace the vamps' evening and drove back to Shoreline Village. I did this knowing full-well that this little exercise was pointless. It was daytime, so there weren't going to be any bloodsuckers around. Also, it wasn't like the ones from last night had left behind any big, obvious clues, like accidentally dropping an envelope in the parking lot labeled *What We Were Doing at That Warehouse*.

But hey, it wasn't like I had anything better to do anyway. At least not until nightfall, when I could hunt.

I found a bench in the shade and watched the crowds, just to pass the time. My thoughts kept coming back to Bane, probably because my injured shoulder was throbbing like crazy. As I said, I'd tangled with him many times in the past, beginning when I was about sixteen. He'd been toying with me back then, he hadn't considered me a real threat. Actually, he still didn't. Maybe that was why he hadn't killed me. As far as he was concerned, I was just a harmless kid, so why bother?

Something caught my eye all of a sudden and I sat bolt upright, a cold trickle of fear sliding down my spine. I'd engaged my hunter's sight just because all the pink around me was kind of soothing...was I really seeing what I thought I was seeing? I yanked my sunglasses off and stared at a group of people leaving the carousel. All of their energy signatures were a nice, normal rosy tone, except for one. His energy was pure white.

Vampire.

It really threw me off. It was early afternoon and the sun was beating down relentlessly. Yet here he was, strolling right along, chatting happily with a family. He was with a short, balding man of around fifty and a woman of maybe forty with bleached blonde hair. With them were three little boys ranging in age from about eleven to six and a guy around my age. He was maybe 5'10 with sun-streaked hair and a slim runner's build. The vampire slid his arm around this guy and gave him a little squeeze before leaning in and saying something to him that made him laugh.

What. The. Fuck!

I trailed behind this group at a distance, studying the vampire. He was really big and broad-shouldered, maybe 6'3 and muscular with longish, jet black hair and pale blue eyes. He was unusually attractive, as was often the case with vamps. I always figured that was because vampires were hand-selected. Their makers picked who they wanted to turn and spend eternity with, and it's not like anyone went for the scrawny kid with acne when they could have Mr. Universe.

Bane, for example, looked like a movie star, tall and classically handsome with thick dark hair and unusual green eyes, pale mint rimmed in deep emerald. The fact that he was so good-looking pissed me off. It just made it that much easier for him to get close to his victims. Asshole.

I kept following and observing. Obviously, the vamp had compelled this entire family, but why? And the burning question (ha!) was how he'd gotten hold of a talisman to let him walk around in broad daylight. Those items were so rare that this was the first time I'd ever actually seen a daywalking vamp in person.

My kind had been collecting and eliminating talismans like this for millennia. Often the bespelled object was a ring or a coin, something small, portable. Fortunately, there was a finite supply. Only a full-blooded witch could pull off a spell like that, and there was no such thing anymore. The witch gene had gotten diluted down after centuries of breeding with Muggles (shut up, the Harry Potter movies were awesome). For the last two hundred years or so, no one'd had enough power to create an item that would allow a vamp to do what that one was doing. So, given the rarity of these talismans, I had to wonder how one of them would have come into the possession of an unknown vamp in Long Beach, California of all places.

And what that vamp was doing with the Brady Bunch, I couldn't even begin to guess.

The family had gotten a table at an outdoor café. It was between mealtimes so the patio was fairly uncrowded and I was able to get the table right beside them. The adults ordered margaritas (no thank you, nothing for Mr. Tall, Dark, and Undead), and the kids got strawberry smoothies. The waiter came to me next and when I ordered a beer, he carded me. I glared at him as I handed over my ID. He looked unimpressed.

The littlest boy at the next table grabbed the vamp's hand. I very nearly leapt out of my seat and staked the bloodsucker on the spot. "Uncle Nikolai, you guys need to stay one more night," the boy said. "I don't want you to go home yet." My eyebrows shot toward my hairline.

The guy that was around my age said, "We have to go home, Ryan. I have to work tomorrow. But we're going to come back next weekend so we can celebrate Easter together."

"Come early! I want Uncle Nikolai to make more nana pancakes," the little boy said. I felt like whacking my head against the table.

"I can make you banana pancakes," the woman told him.

The boy insisted, "They're not as good as his, Mom."

"They're exactly the same," one of the older kids said.

Dear God, I was living in freaky bizarro world, where vamps walked in daylight and had discussions about pancakes with little kids! I dragged my hands over my face.

I continued to listen in on their conversation, and the only conclusion I reached was that I definitely should be drinking something stronger than beer. I accidentally groaned out loud when the vamp started having a discussion with the little boy about the Easter Bunny, and had to cover it with a cough. That got a couple glances in my direction from their table.

Finally, happy vampire bonding time drew to a close. They paid their bill and headed for the parking lot, and I followed. After hugs all around (my staking hand got downright twitchy during that) the parents and three little boys got in a minivan and drove out of the lot.

The guy my age, who I'd heard referred to as Nate, and the vampire climbed in a beat-up old Jeep and paused for a long kiss before starting the engine. My car was nearby, and I got behind the wheel and trailed the Jeep out of the lot. Traffic was heavy (as usual) when we got on the 405 north but I stuck with them, keeping a couple cars between us. Eventually, they got on the 101 north. I wondered just how far we were going. I glanced at my gas gauge: less than half a tank. If I lost this daywalker, I'd never forgive myself.

After a solid couple hours of driving, they took the turn off for Santa Barbara and began winding up into the hills above the city. For some reason, the pain in my shoulder had been intensifying all afternoon and it was aching sharply by now. I really wanted to stop driving and was so relieved when they finally pulled up outside a tiny cottage.

The house was light blue with white trim, pots of flowers dotting the little porch, and it probably clocked in at around a thousand square feet. It was so ridiculously Disney-cute that I expected the seven dwarves to come marching out. Really? This was the home of a daywalking vampire and his human…what exactly? Pet? Compelled minion? Delusional nut job that had read Twilight one too many times?

They went into the house hand-in-hand and I swung out of the car, which was parked halfway down the block. The houses were few and far between, and the opposite side of the street was undeveloped hillside. I ducked into the brush and climbed the hill to give myself a good vantage point, then settled down in the tall grass to do some surveillance.

The scene of domestic bliss before me induced an instant eye roll. The vampire had gone into the kitchen and had started preparing a meal, while the human sat on the counter right beside him. Every minute or so, the vampire paused what he was doing to feed the human a little piece of whatever he was chopping. Every other minute, they stopped to kiss. At this rate, the meal would be done a week from Tuesday.

I was completely baffled, on every level. First of all, what were these two doing with each other? Vampires thought of humans as nothing more than livestock, a means to a meal. On the rare occasion that they actually found something desirable about a human, they turned them into one of their own kind. What they *didn't* do was play house with them.

Vampires might start out as human, but they became a different species once they were turned. Sometimes they even forgot everything about their human lives after being transformed into vampires. So what I was seeing was very much the equivalent of a mountain lion dating Bambi: it violated all the laws of nature.

The even bigger head-scratcher was the talisman. An object like that was so rare and so valuable that this vampire should be constantly on the run, hunted by other vamps who wanted it for themselves. Or if he was going to try to stay put somewhere, he should be living in a fortress with an army of sired (and therefore loyal) vamps standing guard.

Retrieving that object was hugely important, and the reason this vamp wasn't already a pile of dust on the linoleum. I had to take my time with this and figure out what was going on here. Were the twin oddities of the amulet and the human consort somehow related? There had to be more to this vamp than met the eye and I wanted to learn his secrets.

I settled in for a long, dull evening. After the human ate the dinner that the vamp prepared for him (that right there was so fucking weird), the two of them snuggled on the couch and watched a movie. Patience had never been my strongest attribute, so I was bored out of my mind and really restless. But hey, at least I had the constant, intense pain in my shoulder to keep me company. It was steadily getting worse, which was a bad sign.

After a while, I began to wonder what exactly I was watching for. Maybe I kept waiting for the vampire to *act like a vampire*, to slaughter the human (yes, of course I'd try to prevent it), then steal the guy's car and drive to his *real* life, the one in the big fortress-like mansion with the Ferrari in the driveway. I mean really, if you were completely amoral, as all vamps were, and could compel humans to give you anything you wanted, why would you settle for a tiny house and a Jeep older than I was?

When the two of them started kissing, I felt like a peeping Tom. The one positive was that at least this vamp was gay. If I had to watch a hetero couple making out, that would have just been awkward.

Oh, but then this too took a turn for awkwardville, because they soon started doing more than just making out. This had definitely escalated to foreplay. Even that was all backwards and unexpected, because the much smaller human had clearly taken the lead, pushing the big vamp onto his back on the couch and parting his legs. As soon as the human stripped off the vamp's jeans, I felt like a total degenerate for watching and pivoted around so my back was to them.

I sighed, resting my arms on my bent knees and my head on my arms. I was probably in need of a hospital, given the way my shoulder felt. Not that I was about to go to one. I'd learned first aid as a kid, right along with how to fight, because hunters looked after themselves. If we sustained an injury bad enough to require medical assistance, chances are it would be something suspicious-looking, like a gunshot or a stab wound. Or, you know, getting pinned to a wall by a wooden stake. Flying under the radar was vital in this line of work and going to a hospital where they'd call the police if it looked like a crime had been committed was completely unhelpful.

Since I'd been trained in medical care, I knew without even looking at it that my shoulder was becoming infected. I needed to find a drug store and flush the wound thoroughly with alcohol and change the bandages. I also needed to start myself on a course of antibiotics, which was problematic. Actually, all of this was problematic, since I was worried about that vamp slipping away and taking the talisman with him. I really didn't want to let him out of my sight.

After several minutes, I glanced over my shoulder. *Oh holy shit.* The two of them were going at it hot and heavy on the couch. The big vamp was on his hands and knees, with what looked like a belt binding his wrists together as the human fucked him. I looked away quickly. The fact that my dick got hard from that little peep show pretty much made me feel like a total pervert.

I crept out of my hiding place in the bushes and returned to my car, reclining the seat part-way but keeping their front yard in sight. If that vamp went anywhere, I wanted to know about it, though it really hadn't looked like they were leaving any time soon.

*****

God damn it to hell son of a bitch! I'd fallen asleep in my car. What a rank amateur move! You'd think I'd never done surveillance before. I popped the seat into an upright position and rubbed my eyes. Oh man, I felt like shit. I was weak and kind of shaky, and the infection must be progressing fast, because I clearly had a fever. I had to go and take care of myself, but first I wanted to verify that the vamp was still in that house.

I wondered what time it was as I got out of the car and only partially closed my door so I wouldn't make any noise. It felt really late, a fine mist hanging in the air and making a halo around the street lamps, the neighborhood perfectly silent.

The Jeep was still parked in front of the house. That was a good sign. I was just going to do one lap around the house, play peeping Tom again at the windows, and then go and fix myself up and come right back here.

These people really didn't believe in curtains. I could still look directly into their living room, which was now dark and empty. The backyard was surrounded by a six-foot-high wooden fence with a locked gate. When I went to climb over it and tried to use my right arm, the pain from my shoulder brought me to my knees. I took a couple deep breaths and tried again, getting over the fence with just the aid of my left hand this time.

The backyard was small and tidy, with orange trees and a deck just big enough to hold a table and two chairs. The first window I looked through revealed the kitchen, which was also visible from the front of the house. Heavy curtains were drawn over the next window, but they were slightly askew. I put my face right up to the screen and squinted into the dark interior. I could make out a bed…were there one or two people in it?

That answer came a moment later, when a big hand closed around my throat and bashed my head against the side of the house.

When I came to I was chained to a chair, barefoot, my coat on the kitchen table with all my weapons laid out next to it in a neat display. The big vamp was standing over me, his arms crossed over his chest, a murderous look in his eerie pale blue eyes. Beside him, the little human was nervously chewing on the edge of his thumbnail.

"He's awake," the human said.

"No shit, Sherlock," I muttered.

That earned me a low growl from the vampire. I could practically feel the anger rolling off of him.

"What are we going to do with him?" the human – Nate, I think – asked.

"No idea." The vamp's voice was low, dangerous. He was more animal than person right now, completely lethal. I'd seen it a million times and was kind of surprised I was still sucking air. Once vamps went over to their dark side like this, they pretty much started killing everyone in sight.

59

"How would a vampire hunter find us here?" The human's voice was a bit shaky.

"He was sitting beside us at that café in Long Beach where we had drinks with your family. He must have followed us."

"But how did he know what you are?"

"I suppose we could ask him," the vampire said, leaning down so he was eye level with me and staring at me intently, like he was trying to decide which body part to rip off first.

The human reached out and rested his hand on the vamp's forearm and I reflexively yelled, "No!"

"No what?" Nate asked me.

The vampire answered for me. I hadn't noticed before that he had a very slight accent, slightly more pronounced now that he was angry. "The hunter knows I'm dangerous right now, so he was trying to warn you away from me. He thinks I might hurt you." Then, probably just to mess with me, he draped his arm around the human's shoulders. In response, Nate slid his arms around the vamp's waist and hugged him. That was kind of like mistaking a Grizzly for a big, cuddly teddy bear, and I stared at him like he was out of his mind (which he probably was).

"Why do you think you can't compel him?" Nate asked. Apparently I'd come in on the middle of this conversation.

"I'm pretty sure all his tattoos are wards and spells, protections to keep him from being compelled," the vamp said. "I've never seen it in person, but I heard about it from the other vampires when I was imprisoned. If this person's a true hunter, he's at least part warlock and is using magic to protect himself."

"Magic," Nate muttered. "Seriously?"

"For lack of a better word. It's really more the ability to channel energy, to call on forces that most humans don't have access to."

Nate took a moment to absorb that, then said, "Okay. So if you can't compel him, we really have a problem."

"I'll still give it a try, of course, but I'm willing to bet it's not going to work. Plus, there's another problem," the vamp told his companion. "He's really sick. His body is fighting some kind of major infection and his fever keeps climbing. Without medical aid, he'll be dead in a few days."

"But the good news is, you will have turned me into a corpse well before the infection can kill me. So at least that problem's solved," I said, glaring at the vampire.

The vamp ignored that and turned toward Nate, cupping the human's cheek with his big hand. "We're not going to solve this tonight and you're exhausted. Why don't you go back to bed, baby? I'll stay up and keep an eye on him."

"That's vamp-speak for 'you're going to realize I'm a monster if I slaughter this guy in front of you, so I'm going to do it behind your back.' Just FYI," I said.

Nate frowned at me, then said to the vampire, "No way am I getting any sleep now. Not when someone just tried to break into our home and kill you."

"For the record," I chimed in, "I wasn't breaking into your home. Yet. I was just doing some recon, trying to get some answers."

"What kind of answers?"

"Well, for starters, I wanted to determine whether you were compelled, or just enough of an idiot to voluntarily live with a remorseless killer." I held Nate's gaze levelly.

"He didn't compel me."

"So you're just an idiot, then?" I raised my eyebrows at him.

"You know," Nate said to the vampire, "I'm not normally a violent person. But this guy really makes me want to punch him in the face."

"I get that a lot," I said, relaxing my position. As we were talking, I'd been assessing my situation. I had chains wrapped three times around my waist, another set holding my ankles to the chair legs, and manacles binding my wrists behind me. The chains were thick, heavy, and had a patina of age. Nobody had picked these up at the Home Depot, they were old-school torture chamber-grade and I wasn't breaking through them. The chair I was chained to was my ticket out of here. As soon as the vamp left me alone, I could easily throw myself back and smash it, then just untangle the chains. I'd still be left with my wrists chained together, but I'd be able to run.

I'd also been assessing the vampire. The accent was probably Greek and the chains suggested he was possibly quite old. He wore a ring on his left hand, which looked fairly new, and which matched a ring on the human's left hand. That must mean that this moronic human had actually married a vampire. Christ, it made me want to grab him by the shoulders and shake some sense into him.

At the collar of the vampire's black t-shirt, I caught just a glimpse of a fairly thick silver necklace. I couldn't get a good look at it, but I could kind of make out the line of the chain through the fabric, and saw that it culminated in some type of big pendant in the center of his chest. I could swear the pendant was in the shape of a cross, but that would be excruciating against a vampire's skin.

Well, whatever it was, it was a good candidate for the bespelled talisman I was looking for. Of course, the talisman could also be something he kept in his pocket, a coin or some other object. But if it was me and if I could go up like a sparkler in the sun, I'd want an object I could wear to make sure I didn't accidentally drop it or lose it.

While I was taking all of this in, the two had been debating going to bed. *Oh yes, please go to bed so I can get the fuck out of here,* I thought as I gave them a pleasant smile. This made both of them knit their brows at me. Apparently my pleasant smile was less than convincing.

They reached a compromise. The vamp picked me (and the chair) up like I weighed nothing and carried me into the bedroom, then set me down in a corner. "I feel like I'm in time out," I said. I watched them as they got into bed, but after a beat the vamp got up again, picked me up, and turned me to face the corner. "Now I *really* feel like I'm in time out," I muttered.

Once back in bed, they had a hushed conversation. I couldn't quite make out what they were saying, but I got the gist based on their tone of voice. The human was really scared (because of me, not the vamp, ugh), and the bloodsucker was reassuring and comforting him. After a while they fell silent and I twisted around and looked over my shoulder. The vamp was sitting up in bed, watching me closely. His little human was curled against his chest, sound asleep, the vamp's big arms encircling him. It would have been kind of sweet if they'd both been human. But since one of them was a monster, it was actually fairly disturbing. I turned back toward the wall.

*****

A gentle touch on my forehead snapped me awake the next morning. Nate was eye level with me, a crease of concern between his eyebrows. "You're burning up with fever," he said. "You need to be taken to a hospital. But if I do that, we'll have to set you free, and then you're going to come back here and try to murder my husband. So obviously, we have a problem."

"What do you care if it's the infection that kills me, or the monster you were dumb enough to marry?" My voice was thin and raspy and talking was a huge effort, so I shut up after that.

He stood up and said to someone behind me, "Help me get him to the bathtub, we need to bring his fever down."

I felt the chains being taken from my body and then I was carried into the adjoining bathroom. When I tried to lash out at the vampire that was holding me, I realized just how bad off I was. I could barely raise my arm.

They put me down on the tile floor, and one of them undressed me as water ran into the tub. Keeping my eyes open was too much effort at that point, so I didn't bother.

"God, look at this," Nate said quietly. A hand brushed my collar bone. "The tattoos are all over his body." Gentle fingers ran across my rib cage. "I don't even recognize all the languages." He picked up my left arm and ran a fingertip from my inner wrist to my armpit, over the Latin spell that protected me from being compelled. The same spell was repeated on my other arm in Hebrew.

"There are two I don't recognize either, and I think some of the symbols are Native American. He's like a living Rosetta Stone of spells and incantations," the vampire said. One of them peeled the bandage off my chest, which had become stuck to my skin. "Shit. This really looks bad."

"What do you think happened to him?" Nate asked.

"He was staked."

"How do you know?"

"He was carrying the stake with him inside his jacket. It's soaked in his blood." Of course the vampire would be able to sniff out the fact that it was my blood on the stake. I was rolled onto my side, and the vamp said, "It goes all the way through," as he peeled the bandage off my back.

"He's probably had such a rough life. He must be my age, but look at this." Nate touched a faded scar on my stomach, one of several on my body. *Vamp with a knife, back alley in Los Angeles. I was ten, which is the only reason he was able to get a piece of me,* I wanted to say. But that would have taken way too much effort.

The vampire picked me up and lowered me carefully into the cold bath. Since I felt like I was on fire, it was an immediate relief. Someone brushed my hair back from my forehead and applied a wet cloth. They were being so nice to me, especially given the fact that they really had no choice but to kill me.

Nate's voice was close beside me. "Did he have an I.D. on him? I wonder what his name is."

"He had six IDs, all of them fake. The names were all characters from sci fi movies, including Rick

Deckard, James Cole, Richard B. Riddick and L.N. Ripley."

"L.N. instead of Ellen, he's funny."

"Did you get each of those references?" the vamp asked.

"Aw man, you're questioning my sci fi nerd cred," Nate said, a smile in his voice. "Of course I get them, they're characters from some of my favorite movies. You said he had six fake I.D.s, what were the other two?"

"Thomas Jerome Newton and Sam Lowry. I figured those two might be a bit obscure for you." The vamp's tone was light, teasing.

"Oh please. *The Man Who Fell to Earth* and *Brazil*. You so totally underestimate me."

The vamp chuckled and said, "I'm sorry, baby. I forgot who I was dealing with."

They both fell silent for a bit. After a while Nate said softly, "Those movie choices make me think this guy and I probably have a lot in common. Like maybe if we'd met under different circumstances, we might have been friends." After another pause he asked, "Nicky, what are we going to do?"

"This is going to be okay, baby. We can disappear if we have to. He's just one person, he can't track us around the world."

"But this is our home," Nate said quietly. "It's the first real home I've ever had, and we've been here such a short time. And what about my family, my mom and brothers and Irv? I don't want to leave them."

"I could go, I'm the one he's hunting. I could draw him away from you, to make sure you don't get hurt when he comes after me. I'll come back when I know the coast is clear."

"No chance, Nikolai. I love you, and you're not facing this alone."

"I just need you to be safe, Nathaniel."

"Same here, and we're dealing with this *together*. That's all there is to it."

As the vampire agreed with him, the now warm wash cloth on my forehead was removed and replaced with a cool one. "He's so sick," Nate said. "We need to take him to the emergency room. I'm afraid he might die."

"I may have an alternative. I could go find a doctor and compel her to come and help him. That would buy us some time at least, as opposed to turning him loose at a hospital."

"Okay. Why don't you do that now?"

"I'm not leaving you alone with him. He's dangerous," the vamp said.

"So, chain him to the legs of the bathtub. He can't hurt me then, even if he regains consciousness."

"He's not unconscious. He's listening to everything we're saying."

"How do you know that?" Nate asked.

"I can tell by his heart rate and the way he's breathing."

Nate got up and went into the other room and was back in less than a minute. I felt a thick band of metal encircle first one ankle, then the other. My left arm was raised up over my head and chained, and then he gingerly took hold of my right arm, moving it slowly so it didn't aggravate my injury. It too was raised over my head and chained. I was way too weak to struggle.

After the vamp left, Nate sat on the edge of the tub. "It's going to be ok," he said softly. "Nikolai's getting someone to help you. Can you hear me?" I kind of nodded, enough for him to get the idea. He left and was back a few moments later, sliding his hand behind my head and raising it up a bit. I felt something cool on my lower lip. "Here, try to drink a little." He tipped the glass and water drizzled into my mouth. It felt so good. I concentrated on swallowing it. Even that was an effort.

He was patient, giving me just a little at a time so I could drink it without choking. When he finally set the glass down, I whispered, "Thank you." It was barely audible.

"You're welcome." He replaced the cloth on my forehead with a cool one again and said, "My name's Nate. What's yours?"

"Tinder." I wondered if he could even understand me.

But he repeated it and said, "I don't know if that's really your name, or if you're making a joke because you're burning up, like a bunch of tinder."

"My name," I managed. "My jokes are funnier than that."

Nate chuckled a little and I pried an eyelid open and looked at him. He was watching me closely, the little worry line still between his eyebrows. He was really cute. Too bad he was going to hate my guts after I killed his husband. I let my eye close and exhaled slowly.

He got up and rummaged around the bathroom for a while. Eventually he declared, "There it is," and returned to his perch on the edge of the tub. "Open your mouth, Tinder." When I did, he slid the cool metal tip of a thermometer under my tongue.

I started to feel like I was drifting. After a while, the thermometer was removed from my mouth and Nate muttered, "Holy shit." I don't remember what happened after that.

*****

Next time I awoke I was chained to their bed, dressed in a clean pair of pajama pants with fresh bandages on my shoulder. "He's awake," the vampire said. He was in a chair across the room, a book on his lap.

Nate appeared and slid his hand between my head and the pillow. "Hey," he said. "Here, try to drink something." He held a straw to my lips and I did as he said. When he put the cup down he asked, "How do you feel?"

"Less like I'm on the express train to deadsville." My voice sounded scratchy.

"You were out for a full day," Nate said. "People must be worried about you. Do you want me to call anyone for you and let them know you're okay?"

"Nah, there's no one to call."

"What about Bane?"

"What?"

"Bane. You must have been having some intense fever dreams and you kept calling for him."

"Bane's the bloodsucker that pinned me to a wall with my own stake and brought on the fever in the first place. If I was calling for him, it was only so I could return the favor and use that stake on him."

"Bane's a vampire?" Nate looked surprised.

"For now. Next time I see him, he'll be a pile of dust."

"Ah."

I tugged experimentally on the heavy chains that bound me to the very big, very heavy iron bedframe, and said, "So, what's the plan here, Nate? Because just so you know, vampire hunters make lousy house pets. You can't actually keep me indefinitely."

"We're working on finding a spell to override the protections tattooed on your skin. Then Nikolai can compel you and make you forget us. It's been slow going. The fact that you used eleven different spells and symbols from a range of cultures isn't making it easy."

"You've been doing your homework."

"Yup. I have your whole body memorized," Nate said with a little grin.

I winked at him. "That's kinda hot. If I didn't know better, I'd think you were flirting with me."

He looked a little surprised again, and asked, "Are you gay?"

"Yes. I'm also a heartless bastard, by the way, so there's not much point in trying to bond with me over the things we have in common. I'm still going to escape and kill that monster that's sitting across the room." To the vampire I said, "Where did you get that alleged book of spells, the mall? I'll die of old age before you find anything useful in there." He glared at me before returning his attention to the book.

Five days later, we were still at a stalemate. I was well on the road to recovery, thanks to the series of powerful antibiotic injections that had been left for me by whatever random M.D. the vamp had found to manipulate. And I was still their prisoner.

Despite my earlier claims, I really was bonding with Nate. He was a great guy, I couldn't help but like him. While I'd been so sick, he'd taken time off from work so he could take care of me. He was kind and infinitely patient. I complained constantly about pretty much everything, especially about being taken care of, which I claimed to hate. He simply agreed with me, then went ahead and took care of me anyway.

It turned out we did have some things in common, most notably our love of sci fi movies, which we could both go on about for hours. Movies (like sex) were one of my few indulgences, a pressure valve for when my job got to be too much and I just needed to check out for a while.

Once I got a bit better, Nate went back to his job at a community center, where for a few hours each day he taught kids and old people how to draw. While he was gone the vampire steered clear of me, despite my ongoing efforts to goad him into a fight. I'd thought of fourteen ways so far to end him with items from around the bedroom, if only he'd take the bait and come close enough for me to deploy some of my tactics.

When Nate was home, he rented movies for us and played cards with me (he totally sucked at poker) and tried to show me how to draw. That was kind of a thing with him. He went to art school and it was easy to imagine him in a few years, working with little kids full time as an art teacher. You know, assuming his husband didn't have him for dinner first.

One night, in a move born out of desperation, I grabbed Nate and wound the chain that joined my manacles around his neck. "I'll trade ya," I told the big vampire, who instantly went into Incredible Hulk mode and looked like he was ready to detach my head from my body. "Nate's life for yours. What do you say?"

That plan failed spectacularly when Nate relaxed in my arms, then turned to face me. "You're not going to hurt me, Tinder, and everyone knows it. Including you." He patted my arm and stepped out from under the chains. It took him a long time to talk the bloodsucker down after that one.

The next day when Nate was at work and I was completely bored out of my mind, I yelled, "For Christ's sake, would you just kill me already? Just fucking come in here and *kill me!* You're never, ever going to find a spell that makes me compellable, so just give up already!"

The vamp filled the doorway and leaned against the jamb. "I'm not going to kill you. I know you think all vampires are murderers, but it's not true. I don't kill when I feed, and I'm not going to kill you just because it's more convenient than finding another solution."

"Really? Because you were ready to rip me to shreds last night."

"I love Nate, so it enraged me when you threatened to hurt him. But I was ready to beat the shit out of you, not murder you. There's a difference."

In a fit of frustration, I flailed wildly against the chains. "Save your energy," the vamp said. "Those chains held me for decades, so they're certainly strong enough to hold you. Though I did manage to escape from them after my master was killed. Seems you're really not that motivated to get away."

"I don't believe you. I've tried to pick these locks twenty different ways. It's impossible to escape from these chains."

"I didn't pick the locks, though I tried that many, many times."

"So how'd you get out?" I wondered if he really was dumb enough to tell me his secret.

"I broke my own hands and feet, crushing them to the point that I could slip them one by one through the manacles."

I must have looked fairly horrified, but then I composed myself and said, "Well sure, with your super vampire healing ability."

He shrugged and said, "It still hurt like hell, and it took me days to recover because I couldn't feed and heal myself. Like I said, you just have to be sufficiently motivated. Then anything's possible." The vampire was completely messing with me. Not that the story was made up, it really felt like he was telling the truth about how he'd freed himself. But he knew I'd never go that far to escape. He grinned and went back to the kitchen as I rolled my eyes and flopped down on the mattress.

*****

That night after dinner, Nate and I sat on the floor at the foot of the bed watching the 1950's sci fi triple feature he'd brought home, a huge bowl of popcorn between us. The current movie was called *Them!* It was about people being attacked by giant ants, and it was *hilarious*. The vampire sat in a corner behind us, another useless spell book on his lap, incessantly tapping the armrest of his chair with a fingertip.

I was laughing, shoveling food in my mouth, and making jokes about a giant can of Raid when a familiar voice from the doorway nearly made me choke on the popcorn. A jolt of panic shot through me as I leapt to my feet, knocking the bowl over, the chains on my wrists and ankles rattling.

"This is the very first time I've seen you acting your age, Tinder," Bane said, reclining casually against the doorframe. "It's a delightful thing to behold."

It took me only a moment to regain my wits, and then I vaulted over the corner of the mattress – even though I was chained to the bedframe, I still had plenty of slack so I could reach the bathroom. I smashed an upholstered ottoman and grabbed the little wooden leg to use as a stake (that was number twelve in the fourteen ways I'd identified to kill a vampire with common household objects).

Bane grinned at that. "Oh come on, love. Haven't you heard that size matters? Shall I go fetch you a hammer so you can eventually drive that little splinter past my sternum?"

"What are you doing here, Bane?" My voice was a low hiss.

"Isn't it obvious? I'm rescuing you. Actually, in a way, I'm rescuing *all* of you," he said, smiling at Nate and the other bloodsucker. He pushed off the doorframe and strolled up to Nate's husband, who was so on edge that he looked capable of tearing the newcomer limb from limb. Bane extended his hand and said cheerfully, "Forgive the intrusion, mate. I'm August Mayes, though a few centuries ago, I picked up the unfortunate nickname that Tinder is so fond of."

Nate's vampire crossed his arms over his chest and said in a low voice, "Next time, you might consider knocking."

"Please forgive my bad manners, I know that was terribly rude of me. But I didn't want to give Tinder time to go ballistic." Bane looked apologetic (yeah right).

After a long moment, the resident vamp relaxed slightly, shook hands and said, "I'm Nikolai and that's my husband, Nathaniel."

"My, how very progressive! A vampire married to a human. We could all take a lesson in interspecies harmony, could we not?" Bane raised his eyebrows at me as he said that.

"You have five seconds to tell me what you're doing here, Bane, or else I'm going to demonstrate that it's not the size of the stake, it's how you use it." I advanced toward him as far as my chain would allow, stopping just before it pulled me up short.

He reached into an inner pocket of the expensive looking black leather jacket he was wearing and pulled out a little amber vial with a white hang tag. "I told you love, I'm here to rescue all of you. I hold in my hand the solution to your problems."

"What is that?" Nate asked.

"A potion! Sounds so wonderfully *medieval*, doesn't it? I had it made for Tinder and had to go all the way to Nova Scotia to get it. All he needs to do is drink it and then he'll forget the last three or four weeks of his life, including – and here's the good part – ever having met the both of you." He gestured to encompass Nate and his vampire when he said that.

"How did you know where to find me? And why do you think you know anything about this situation?" I demanded.

"I installed a tracking device on your car, so I'd always know right where you are," he told me.

"*What!* When did you do that?"

"Three, four years ago."

"Are you *shitting* me?"

"Tsk, now there's a vulgar expression. No, love, I am not *shitting* you, and I feel debased just saying that. I knew you went on a little impromptu jaunt to Santa Barbara – lovely town, by the way, but God forbid you'd come here to relax. You don't seem to believe in down time. Anyway, when your car didn't move for a few days I figured something was up and came to investigate. I found it parked down the street. Unlocked, by the way – so careless. I had fun going through your music collection. Where on Earth you still find eight tracks for that relic you drive is a complete mystery." Bane smiled at me cheerfully, his green eyes sparkling.

"Anyway," he continued as I stared at him with a raised eyebrow, "while perusing your oddly old-fashioned taste in music, I listened in on what was happening in this house and quickly figured out the situation: they couldn't let you go because you'd kill Nikolai, you didn't want to kill that little human, they didn't want to kill you, blah blah blah. You were clearly never going to resolve that stalemate on your own, so I went out and found you a solution."

"Why?"

Bane shrugged his broad shoulders. "Why not? It was something to do. Heaven knows when you've lived as long as I have, diversions are few and far between. This was a fun little exercise in problem solving."

I knit my brows at him. "So you're saying you had nothing better to do than come to my aid. Why do I find your motives completely questionable?"

"Because you're a highly suspicious person, that's why."

"You show up with a vial of forget-me-juice and actually expect me to drink it. Are you insane?"

"Well, it can also be injected, but it'd be much more pleasant if you just cooperated. I'd prefer not to have to pin you down and stick a needle in your cute little arse."

"I'd love to see you try," I growled.

Nate chimed in, "So, last time Tinder saw you, you staked him to a wall and left him for dead. Now you actually expect him to trust you and drink God knows what?"

"I didn't leave him for dead. I was trying to keep him out of harm's way for a few minutes, but the boy *does not listen.* I told him to stay put and he refused, so pinning him to the wall was my only alternative. I'd also like it noted that I missed all major arteries and muscle groups when I staked him, on purpose."

"But you almost killed him with a massive infection," Nate said.

"Well, that was hardly my fault! It was Tinder's stake. You should ask *him* where it's been to get that dirty." Bane was camping it up, putting on this cheerful, light-hearted façade for some reason. I didn't buy it for a minute.

I couldn't begin to guess his end-game, but I did know one thing. Whatever he was playing at right now benefitted exactly one person: him. That was how Bane operated.

Nate's vampire had engaged Bane in a conversation about the potion's origin. Apparently he now thought he was a bit of an expert on that sort of thing, having read a couple completely mainstream books on witchcraft. Finally he turned to his husband and said, "This sounds like it would be a good solution, assuming Tinder was actually willing to take it."

I knew why he'd addressed Nate and not me. He now expected my friend to talk me into it. When Nate turned to me, I preempted him by saying, "I don't trust Bane. Whatever's in that vial is probably going to kill me."

"If I wanted you dead, I could have killed you six hundred and fifty two different ways by now," Bane told me. God only knew how he'd arrived at that oddly specific number.

"Like hell you could."

"Sweetness, you're chained to a bed. I won't lie: I like everything about that. However, it does make you a bit of a sitting duck. Allow me to demonstrate."

He moved so fast that he became a blur. I started to react, but in the next instant my back was pressed to his chest, his left arm tight around my torso, his right hand holding mine so that the stake was pressed beneath my chin. He said, his mouth right beside my ear, "I don't want to kill you, Tinder. I've never wanted that." He did something odd then and ran his thumb slowly down my jugular vein before letting go of me and taking a step back. He'd kept the stake in his possession, dropping it into a jacket pocket.

I was shaken, but wasn't going to let Bane see that. I squared my shoulders and said, "If that's really a memory potion, then there's some other motive at work here. What are you trying to get me to forget, the warehouse? I stumbled across something I wasn't supposed to, didn't I?"

"You really are completely suspicious," he said. "This *will* make you forget the warehouse and everything else that happened over the last few weeks, but that's neither here nor there. This is the least potent dose of this potion that anyone could fabricate, so it can't help but take that much of your memory. But what difference does it make? As soon as you run into your big, blond Texas playmate again, he'll get you right back up to speed. The warehouse is totally irrelevant anyway. I'm just trying to get you out of your current predicament."

"For all I know, you already killed Lee so he can't tell me about the warehouse."

"For fuck's sake!" Bane exclaimed. "Forget the damn warehouse! It's nothing! Just drink the potion so you can go home and these nice people can get on with their lives."

I sighed and glanced at Nate, who had a hopeful expression on his face. Damn it, see? This was why I didn't get attached to people. As soon as you started to like someone, you had to start worrying about *their* feelings, what was best for *them*.

"Give me the fucking bottle," I said, and when Bane held it out to me, I took hold of the little glass vial and glanced at the tag. It said *drink me.* I shot him a look. "Really?"

"A little levity. If only the contents had been solid, then I could have written *eat me.*" He gave me a cheerful smile.

"What's in it?"

"Oh, you know: herbs, roots, pixie dust."

"What's *really* in it?"

When he recited the ingredients (many of which were extremely rare), I decided he was telling the truth about what the potion would do to me. I could also see why it had required a trip to Nova Scotia. It wasn't like you could source any of those things at the local Safeway.

I glanced at Nate, who still looked so hopeful. If I'd really believed Nate's vampire was a killer, there would have been no question about me ending him. I wouldn't even be considering this. But from everything I'd seen, this one was an exception. If he was a killer, I would have been dead the moment he found me in his yard, no two ways about it.

The daylight talisman was still a concern. I knew I'd have to kill the vamp to get it away from him, which would be devastating to Nate. I reasoned that at least it belonged to a vampire docile enough to actually fall in love with and marry a human. I hadn't thought vampires were capable of that, but this one was an anomaly in many ways.

Still, I didn't quite have it in me to just walk away. The idea of purposefully leaving a vamp alive completely went against my grain. For Nate's sake though, I could get around my own rule. I could make myself forget I'd ever stumbled across this one particular vampire.

Besides, I really didn't see any other alternatives. This situation had already dragged on far too long, with no end in sight. I twisted off the lid and tossed back the contents of the vial before I could talk myself out of it, then exclaimed, "Ugh, it tastes like dead fish!"

"I think there's some herring in there for flavor," Bane said with a grin.

"That was for you, Nate," I said. "It's probably the stupidest thing I've ever done, trusting Bane like that. But if it works, then you and Nikolai have a shot at living your lives. It's probably the only way I wouldn't come back here to kill him."

Nate threw his arms around me. "Thank you, Tinder."

Nikolai unfastened the manacles on my wrists and ankles, then took a step back, watching me closely.

"One problem," I said. "I still remember both of you."

"It doesn't kick in until you fall asleep," Bane told me. "When you wake up tomorrow morning, all of this will be wiped from your memory."

I retrieved my clothes from the closet and got dressed in the bathroom, and when I came out I said, "Can I have my gun back?" All my weapons had been hidden from me.

Nate left the room and returned with a tote bag, which he'd slung over his shoulder. "How about if I walk you out?" he said with a little smile.

I grinned at that. He didn't trust me with weapons around Nikolai. Smart boy. "Give us a minute," I told the vampires, then took Nate's hand and walked out of the house and down the block to my car.

"How did you know what Nicky was?" he asked me. "I need to know how to keep him safe from other hunters."

"I can see the energy that people and vampires put out, theirs is a different color. Only natural-born hunters can do that and there aren't that many of us anymore. In all of California, there are maybe a dozen or so. There are also a few hundred idiots with stakes who like to *think* they're vampire hunters. The ones like me are all you need to worry about, but statistically speaking, you should be okay. Well, unless you run into me again in Long Beach."

"I'll keep an eye out for you," he said with a sad little smile. "I'm going to miss you, Tinder."

I glanced toward his house. Nikolai was on the sidewalk, his body language tense, and Bane was on the porch, both of them watching us. They obviously thought I might still pull something. I leaned close to Nate and whispered as quietly as I could so Bane wouldn't overhear, "That talisman of Nikolai's, the one that keeps him from burning in the sun, is really rare.

Every vampire on Earth would kill both of you in a second to get their hands on it. Keep it hidden and never tell another soul about it, no matter what. Got it?"

Nate looked startled as he nodded, then grabbed me in another hug. This one I could return, since my hands were no longer chained. "Thank you," he said. "You really are a true friend and I'll never forget you." He handed me the bag of weapons and kissed my cheek before turning and walking back to his house. When he reached Nikolai, the big vampire drew him into his arms and the two went inside together.

I got behind the wheel. A flashy silver Aston Martin was parked directly behind the Camaro and Bane gave me a little salute as he walked past and got in the sports car. On the long drive home he followed me, even stopping for gas when I did. I didn't bother to shake him. He already knew where I lived, since he'd been tracking my car for years.

When we both finally pulled to the curb in front of my house, he got out of his car and stood on the sidewalk. I walked up to him, one hand inside my jacket, holding the end of the stake that I'd returned to its inner pocket. There were cars driving by so I couldn't actually dust him here, but it was best to keep my guard up. I said, "For Nate's sake, I guess it's good that you stepped in."

"That's probably as close to a thank you as I'll get from you." He seemed uncharacteristically sedate.

"I still don't get why you'd help me."

He barely smiled, just a little upturn at the corners of his full lips. "No? I can show you why I'd help you. You won't remember it anyway." He stepped forward and took my face in both hands.

And Bane kissed me.

Kissed me!

It was fierce, passionate, and after a moment I sank into it. I let go of the stake and grabbed his shirt with both hands, pulling him to me, parting my lips for him.

In the next instant, the door of his sports car clicked shut and he revved the engine and pulled away from the curb. I braced my hands on my knees, my pulse racing, still feeling the sensation of his lips on mine.

Christ, what was wrong with me? I should have punched him in the face for that! I should have taken the opportunity to plant that stake in him. But instead, I let him kiss me. And holy shit, I actually *enjoyed* it!

And now he expected me to forget that ever happened.

I dashed into the house, locking up behind me and quickly retracing the protection symbol on the door. Then I ran to the kitchen and rummaged around for a pen and something to write on. I finally came up with a Sharpie and a flattened brown paper grocery sack, and wrote in big letters at the top: *Bane kissed me. What the fuck?!*

On the next line, I wrote: *His real name is August Mayes. He put a tracking device in my car. FIND IT.*

Next, I jotted down the address of the warehouse and every detail I could remember about that night.

And I wrote: *You took a potion to erase a few weeks of your memories. There were some things you needed to forget. Don't dig, don't look for answers. Just accept it, forgetting was for the best.*

I thought back over the last month, trying to come up with anything else that really shouldn't be forgotten. All I came up with was: *the air pressure in the right rear tire has been getting low.*

Really? That was all that was noteworthy about the last month of my life?

Well, okay, not exactly. There'd been Nate, the only friend I'd ever made. But I couldn't write about him, of course. That would defeat the purpose of this little exercise.

I carried the paper bag with me into the dark living room along with the pen and a flashlight, in case I thought of anything else to write down. After lining up everything beside the air mattress, I stretched out on the little bed and proceeded to lay awake for hours, staring at the ceiling.

It had been a stupid idea to take something to make me forget. I should have just had the willpower to stay away from Nate's husband on my own. But the fact was, I was driven to kill every vampire I came across. I wouldn't have had it in me to make an exception for that one, just because he was married to someone I'd come to care about.

After a while, I realized I felt really lonely. God was that irritating. It had been three and a half years since the last member of my family was killed. I was used to being alone. I was good at it. What happened? I spent a few days in a house with other people and made a friend, and immediately forgot how to be by myself? Come on!

I rolled onto my side and pulled the blanket over me. Then without even realizing I was doing it, I reached up and touched a fingertip to my lips, recalling Bane's kiss. Part of me wanted to rip that sentence off the paper bag and flush it down the toilet, to forget it ever happened.

But I couldn't let myself forget. It was too important, while at the same time completely confusing. I didn't understand why I'd let it happen, why I'd let anyone kiss me, especially *Bane*. And I didn't understand why he'd done it. He was incapable of actually having feelings for anyone, after all. Though now that I thought about it, it was probably just to mess with me in these few hours before I fell asleep and forgot all about it.

I also thought about Bane's motivation for helping me. Was I supposed to think he'd helped me because he cared about me? Was that how the kiss was meant to be interpreted? Come on, that was bullshit. He'd helped me because he wanted me to forget something. I kept

coming back to that warehouse, but I'd searched it top
to bottom and found nothing. I would have probably let
it go, in fact, if this hadn't happened and brought it
back to my attention.

Oh, and while I was on the subject of Bane, there
was the fun little fact that he'd been monitoring my
whereabouts for the last three or four years! That was
beyond aggravating. But then again, maybe it made
sense that he would want to keep track of me. I *was*
trying to kill him, after all.

It took a few more hours to fall asleep. My
thoughts kept circling around Bane, but I got no closer
to making sense of anything that had happened tonight.
The thin grey light of dawn had started seeping into the
room by the time I finally nodded off.

The potion hadn't worked.

Holy shit, I remembered everything. Nate, Nikolai, Bane, *all of it*.

Why hadn't it worked?

I sat up in bed and pushed my hair off my face. Immediately, I started to get suspicious. I had willingly drunk a concoction provided to me by my enemy. *Why the fuck had I done that?* And if it wasn't meant to wipe my memories, what had it been designed to do?

For one paranoid crazy-train moment, I thought, *what if it was meant to interfere with my abilities as a hunter? What if I've lost the sight and can no longer identify vampires?* But then I did a reality check. Nothing could do that to a hunter, no magic was powerful enough.

The right potion could easily slow my reflexes though, make me worse at my job and quickly get me killed. But again, I was being paranoid. Bane really could have killed me a dozen times over. He was

99

bigger, stronger, and faster than I was. He had no reason to want to handicap me.

Maybe the formula had simply failed. It wasn't like making a potion was easy. A little too much of this, not quite enough of that, and it wouldn't do what was intended. I knew that from first-hand experience.

And really, this was a blessing. Ok, so I was going to have to deal with the Nate situation on my own. But if I'd woken up this morning and read the part of the note that said *there were some things you needed to forget, don't dig, don't look for answers,* I probably would have blown a gasket.

Um…where was the note?

I leapt out of bed and looked around me. The note, pen, and flashlight were all missing. I tore apart my bed, looking in and underneath everything. It wasn't here. I ran to the kitchen and looked around, then pulled open one of the drawers. The flashlight was in its place. In another drawer, the pen was right where it should be.

Only, I hadn't put them away. I was sure about that.

Someone had been in my house, which should have been impossible with all the wards I had in place. A cold trickle of fear slid down my spine. I had gone to great lengths to make my home safe and secure, to make sure that when I was here, I was protected. This was the one place in the world where I could relax, the one place where I could sleep soundly, without one hand on a gun and the other on a stake.

I did a full perimeter search. The house wasn't very big, so it didn't take long. All the doors and windows were still locked and warded, so how the intruder had gotten in was a mystery.

It had to be Bane. Somehow, he'd gotten in here. Anyone else would have killed me in my sleep.

And what did he do once he broke in? He took away the things I was trying to remember, the kiss, the warehouse, his name, the tracking device – he wanted to make sure I forgot all of that. He'd even put away the pen and flashlight, so I wouldn't find any reminders that a note had ever been written. How creepy that he knew right where they belonged!

This told me three things: Bane had expected the memory potion to work (otherwise why destroy the note?); he somehow had access to my house; and he was owed *such* a beat-down next time I saw him.

Something else occurred to me all of a sudden. I had fallen asleep just as the sun was coming up. Did that mean Bane had a daylight talisman of his own? Whoever broke in here wouldn't have had the cover of darkness.

I had a million questions and no answers. I paced around the living room and thought back to last night. It seemed completely insane that I'd voluntarily drunk that potion. How the fuck did any part of me ever think it was a good idea to trust something given to me by Bane?

Unless....

Unless Bane had done something to me to influence my decision.

I was pretty covered (literally) when it came to protection against compelling, but possibly he'd figured out some other way to exert control over me, a spell or something similar. Vampires had been manipulating humans for millennia, after all. A vamp as old as Bane could have picked up a few tricks throughout the centuries.

I went over every detail from the night before and one thing stood out. It had been odd when he ran his thumb down my jugular vein. That wasn't just a random touch. Some types of spells worked through physical contact with the intended victim. I needed to do some research, figure out if that was what he'd done. If so, I'd have to learn how to protect myself so it could never happen again.

Clearly, I really needed to have a talk (and the aforementioned beat-down) with Bane. The problem was, I had no clue where to find him. I knew very little about him, actually. Before last night I hadn't even known his real name, assuming he'd told the truth about that.

Eventually, I stopped pacing and headed for the shower. I wasn't going to reach any big insights on an empty stomach. After I got cleaned up and dressed, I shrugged on my jacket, noticing the ventilation that Bane had supplied in the right shoulder area. He'd been so pissed when I hadn't listened to him in that warehouse, mad enough to stake me to get me to stay put after I refused to obey him. Maybe that incident had prompted him to find a way to control me....

Ugh. All this hypothesizing was getting me nowhere. I walked the few blocks to the diner, where Mimi greeted me with coffee and a smile.

I was halfway through my breakfast when someone dropped into the booth across from me. "Tinder, when was the last time you and I saw each other?" Lee was dressed like a cop in mirrored shades and a navy blue windbreaker (he really did have delusions of law enforcement). I was surprised to see him here. I'd only mentioned this place to him once, and that was months ago.

"Beginning of spring break, a Friday. We raided that warehouse that was crawling with vamps." I just knew what he was going to say next.

"I think I have amnesia. I don't remember anything from the last three and a half weeks."

"What's the last thing you remember?"

"Fucking you in the bed of my pickup truck."

"Yup, that was three and a half weeks ago."

His brown eyes looked troubled when he took off his sunglasses. "Do you know what's happening to me?"

"I think you were slipped a memory potion. Bane tried to give me one too, only it didn't take for some reason. It was designed to do exactly what you're talking about, to wipe the last few weeks from our memories."

"Why would he do that?"

"I'd guess it has something to do with that warehouse I just mentioned."

"A potion's a lot of trouble. Why didn't he just kill us?"

"No idea." I took a sip of coffee and said, "I need to do some digging, see what I can find out about Bane. What do you know about him?"

"Almost nothing. Do you mind if I snag some of that?" Lee was eyeing my breakfast.

"Knock yourself out." I pushed the platter toward him and he tucked into the food like it was his first meal in days.

"Thanks," he said between mouthfuls. "This is so good. Seems like all I ever eat anymore is ramen. I'm so damn sick of it."

"Why is that all you eat?"

"Why do you think? Because it's all I can afford." Lee reached for a little pot on the table and slathered the toast with about half an inch of strawberry jam.

"Has your benefactor been late on payments?"

"Benefactor! I haven't had one of them in like, three, three and a half years. I *wish* I still had a benefactor."

"So how are you getting by?" I asked.

"I work a part-time day job. How have you been supportin' yourself?"

"I'm still getting checks."

Lee looked surprised. "Damn. I figured all the money had dried up at the same time. I talked to another true hunter last year, and she said her funding got cut off the same time mine did. We kinda figured the backer organizations had gotten infiltrated and taken down by the vamps. But if you're still getting checks, then maybe they just cut back funding to only full-blooded hunters. Who knows? It's not like the backers were ever very big on communicatin' with us."

"Where have you been living since the money ran out?"

"I sleep in my truck most nights. A couple times a week, I stay at a residence motel downtown so I can use the showers and clean up a bit."

"Shit Lee, I had no idea. How come you never said anything?"

He shrugged. "What's to say?"

"A hunter shouldn't be sleeping someplace totally exposed like that. I can't believe you haven't been picked off by any vamps yet."

"I've been lucky."

"I want you to come home with me after we eat."

His eyes lit up. "So I can fuck you, even though we swore to never do that again?"

"No. Well…yeah, probably. But what I meant was, I have a spare bedroom so you might as well use it."

He raised an eyebrow at me. "Since when do you stick your neck out for other people like that?"

I frowned at him and said, "I'm not sticking my neck out. I have the room and you need a place to stay. That's all there is to it."

"Yeah, ok. I ain't gonna look a gift horse in the mouth." (I have never understood that expression.) He smiled at me hopefully. "At the risk of jinxing it, did you agree to have sex with me a minute ago?"

"Pretty much." I hadn't been fucked in days, and was ready to crawl out of my skin.

His truck was parked in front of the diner, and after breakfast we drove the few blocks back to my place. When we pulled up at the curb, his face lit up all over again. "Wow, you got a whole house? I was expectin' an apartment. You got a yard and everything!"

Kind of. I had a patch of dead grass in front of the house, and another one around back.

Lee slung his backpack over his shoulder and grabbed a bed roll that was stashed beneath the seat before following me inside. "This place is real nice," he said. I would have thought he was being sarcastic, but the happy expression on his face said differently. It was a 1970s ranch-style tract house, pretty indistinguishable from every other home in this lower working class development. It was nothing special. Well, unless you were used to sleeping in a truck.

The minute the door closed behind us, we started pulling each other's clothes off. "Hang on," I said, and locked the door and redrew the protection symbol. Then I pushed him against the wall and kissed him without even thinking about it.

When I let him up for air, Lee said, "Well hell, what all did I forget?"

"What do you mean?"

"You just kissed me. You never once let me do that in all those times we slept together. Did I forget that we started datin' over this last month?"

I knit my brows at him. "No, we didn't start dating. I just felt like kissing you. Could we not make a big deal out of it?"

"Forget I said anything." Lee kissed me again as he unbuttoned my Levis and slid his hand in them, cupping my ass and pulling me against him so that his hard-on was pressed against mine. He removed his hand long enough to stick his finger in my mouth, then returned both hands to my ass, one spreading me while he pushed his wet finger inside me.

I moaned against his lips as he prepared me with a rough finger fuck, and then he pulled down my jeans and spun me so my back was to him. He pushed me to my knees and grabbed his backpack, fumbling with the supplies that he kept in a side pocket. After rolling on a condom and slicking it, he squirted some lube onto his fingers and drove two into me, hard enough to make me bite back a yell. He was learning, that was just what I wanted. The first time we had sex, he'd tried to be sweet and gentle with me. I'd told him that if he ever did that again, it'd be the last time he fucked me.

Lee grabbed my hips, drove his cock into me, and immediately began pistoning in and out of me, his body slamming against mine. His fingers dug into my hips hard enough to leave bruises, his moans loud and jagged. Lee was absolutely pounding me – he really had learned what I needed. My body swayed with the force of his thrusts, my elbows locked to keep myself upright.

He took me deep, sliding into me up to his balls, then pulling almost all the way out before plunging into me again and again. When he finally came, he yelled and pulled me back onto him, and kept thrusting into me as he rode out the last of his orgasm.

We were both shaking by the time he finished, and Lee eased out of me and started to reach for me. "I swear to God, if you try to cuddle me right now, I'm taking back the roommate offer," I growled.

"Sex with you is like fuckin' a cactus. Not that I'm complaining," Lee said with a little grin as he stood up, took care of the condom and began putting his clothes back on.

"Don't you have to be at work today?" I asked as I got to my feet and pulled my jeans up.

"Probably. It would help if I knew where the hell the job site was. I'm at different locations every few days doing cleanup on construction projects, but with my memory gone, I don't know where I'm supposed to be. I'll probably need to find a new job now, since the foreman's probably already fired me for missin' work." He picked up his bedroll and pack. "I guess I was hunting last night because I'm exhausted, think I'll catch a few Zs. Which one's my room?"

"Take your pick. Both bedrooms are empty," I said, gesturing down the hall.

"Why do you sleep in the living room?" he asked, glancing at the pile of bedding in the corner.

"Habit. Though now that I have a roommate, I guess I'll stop doing that." I went and scooped up my air mattress, pillow and blanket as I said, "I'll get a key made for you. Until then, if you go out, be sure to lock the door behind you and I'll let you back in." Lee took the smaller of the two bedrooms, the one at the end of the hall, so I moved my stuff into the master bedroom and decided some sleep was a damn fine idea.

It was dark when I woke up, which was good. I'd gotten used to a regular sleep schedule after spending about a week with Nate and needed to get used to being awake at night again, since that was when I hunted.

When I went into the kitchen for a drink of water, I found a note Lee had left on the counter (written on the back of a receipt. I could really use a pad of paper): *Heading inland to hunt. See you in the morning.* I was glad he didn't automatically expect us to team up now that we were roommates.

Since I had slept in my clothes (as usual) I was good to go once I pulled my jacket on, and headed out the door. My top priority was tracking Bane down and getting some answers. Even though it might have been to my advantage to let him think my memories had been wiped, I didn't have time for games.

I slid behind the wheel of my car and just sat there for a few minutes, trying to figure out how to find him. I couldn't drive around randomly and hope to run into him. But then I thought of a way to bring him right to me.

I drove straight to the warehouse and parked directly in front of it. The tracking device somewhere in my car would let him know I was here, which would tell him immediately that the memory potion hadn't worked. I was willing to bet he'd come running when he realized that.

As long as I was here, I decided to do another sweep of the building. The main door was locked so I went around to the back, climbed the fire escape and smashed a window to get in. When I flipped a light switch nothing happened, so I pulled a penlight from my pocket and used it to go room by room.

The warehouse was completely empty. And I mean *completely*. Not so much as a gum wrapper had been left behind, from the ground level bay that used to house the cars to the top floor office where I'd been trapped (I didn't envy whoever had hauled that solid steel file cabinet out of here). Also, the broken skylight and hacked up door had been replaced and the wall where I'd been staked was patched and repainted.

It left me more confused than ever. There'd been nothing important here. Why bother to remove old furniture and useless files and a whole lot of junk, right down to every last scrap of garbage? If it had just been the legitimate owner of this place moving out, he wouldn't have been so thorough. No one would under normal circumstances, and that level of obsessiveness made it suspicious.

I returned to the main bay on the ground floor, sat with my back against the brick wall and armed myself, a gun in one hand, stake in the other. This might be a long wait. I had no idea how far away Bane was, or even if he monitored the tracking device in my car regularly. But I felt certain he would come, just as soon as he realized where I was. Call it a hunch.

Bane announced his arrival about twenty minutes later by kicking in the solid metal door at the front of the building. I stood up and squared my shoulders, gun and stake at the ready. It was fairly dark, a nearby streetlight casting only a little illumination through a couple filthy windows. But even without seeing him clearly, I knew for a fact that Bane was furious. The lines of his body were tense, his hands curled almost into claws at his sides.

I raised the gun and said, "We need to talk."

He started to run at me, and I reflexively pulled the trigger. But in the time it took me to do that, he'd crossed the room, faster than I'd ever seen a vampire move. Bane grabbed my hand and wrenched it upward, so that the bullet lodged somewhere in the high ceiling. He slammed me against the wall hard enough to knock the air from my lungs and growled, "Why the fuck didn't the potion work on you? It worked perfectly on that blond son of a bitch." He slammed my hands against the wall, forcing me to drop my weapons.

"Let go of me!" I fought him with everything I had. It was like a moth struggling to get away from a cat.

"I'll bet your parents did something to you, maybe feeding you barra root when you were growing up to make you immune to things like memory potions. That would be just like them, doing something that dangerous and irresponsible to you, those bastards."

"Don't you talk about my parents that way, you fucking asshole!"

"Oh come on, Tinder. Are you really going to defend them, after everything they did to you?"

"What the fuck are you talking about?"

"Do you think it's a coincidence that two true hunters got together and had five kids? They wanted an army to fight in their war against my kind, not a family. They put you in harm's way from the time you were old enough to walk. All they ever did was use you like a soldier and now you're defending them!"

I stopped struggling and stared up into Bane's eyes. "Why are you saying this to me? Isn't it enough that you can tear me apart physically? Do you really need to tear me apart emotionally, too?"

After a moment, he let go of me and stepped back. "I'm sorry. That wasn't my intention. It's just always enraged me, the way those people had so little regard for your safety."

Without even knowing I was doing it, I swung out, my right fist connecting with his jaw. "Don't you *ever* fucking talk about my parents! You don't know anything about them."

Bane barely reacted to being hit, and I'd put all of my strength behind it. "I do, actually, though I didn't mean to go off on that tangent," he said. "I'm just so fucking angry that the potion didn't work."

"Did you do something to me to influence my decision to take it?"

"I used the most powerful spell I could muster to make you think it was a good idea to take that potion," he admitted, "and it barely swayed you. You've protected yourself better than you realize with this particular combination of spells and symbols." He tugged the collar of my t-shirt aside to reveal the edge of one of my tattoos and I smacked his hand away.

"So you're telling me you're capable of working witchcraft. That's special."

"For all the good it did."

"What's so important about this place? Why did you need me to forget it?"

Bane smirked at me and said, "It would be rather self-defeating if I just went ahead and told you."

I sighed and pushed my hair out of my eyes. "Why do we have to keep going around in circles like this? Why the hell can't you just give me a straight answer?"

"Because I'm trying to protect you, you git."
Bane's English accent dialed up along with his
frustration.

"I don't need or want your protection, Bane."

He narrowed his eyes at me. "Don't be stupid,
Tinder. You're all alone in the world, fighting an
enemy you barely understand. You need all the help
you can get."

I pushed him, hard. It was like pushing a brick
wall. "You can take your help and shove it up your ass.
I don't need a fucking thing from you or anybody else.
And you're wrong anyway. I'm not alone."

"Oh no? Are you counting the new little friend you
made in Santa Barbara? The one you can't be around,
because you're too much of a mindless killing machine
to stop yourself from murdering his husband?"

I flung myself at him, going for his throat. That got
me pinned to the wall again. The minimal amount of
effort he needed to do that was absolutely maddening.
Bane leaned close, his voice low when he said, "Or are
you referring to that big, dumb Texan? I can smell him
all over you, you know. How long did it take you to
spread your legs for him after I kissed you? Was it even

twelve hours? You couldn't wait to use him to try to forget me, could you?"

"You fucking arrogant son of a bitch! That had nothing to do with you!"

Bane leaned forward and slowly ran the tip of his tongue over my lower lip. Then he locked eyes with me as he said, "So it's just coincidence that you let him kiss you for the very first time right after I kissed you? That wasn't you trying desperately to push our kiss from your thoughts and replace it with a cheap substitute?"

"Let go of me," I growled, pulling against his grasp.

His voice dropped another octave. "I fucking *hate* smelling him on you, tasting him on your lips. It's a good thing you didn't let him cum in you, or else I'd kill him."

I stared at him defiantly. "I *would have* let him cum in me. It's Lee's idea to wear a condom, not mine. Why the fuck would I care about safe sex? My days are numbered anyway, you know that as well as I do. It's a fucking miracle that I've even made it to twenty-one."

Bane grabbed me by the shoulders and shook me. "Stupid, stupid boy. You have absolutely no sense of self-preservation! And the fact that you've made it to twenty-one wasn't a miracle. It's because I've been helping you every step of the way!"

"You're completely delusional!"

He glared at me. "Really? What do you suppose happened to all those vamps that had you trapped in that office upstairs? Did they all spontaneously combust?"

"I was about to get out of there. I didn't need you to swoop in and save me."

"Oh, out the skylight? There were three vampires waiting on the roof, they knew you'd try to escape that way."

"Why were they waiting? Why didn't they come in after me the way you did?"

"Because the skylight was only wide enough for one at a time to fit through. They figured you'd pick them off if they came in one by one."

"They're right, I would have. And if I'd made it out onto the roof, I would have fucking killed them then, too!"

Bane shook me again, his hands almost crushing my shoulders. "And you call me delusional! You aren't a superhero, Tinder. You're just a boy. You never would have made it out of that situation alive, just like you wouldn't have survived the other predicaments I got you out of over the last few years!"

"Fuck you, Bane! I never asked for your help! I don't need it or want it, so just stay the hell out of my life!"

"And let you die? Is that what you want?"

"What difference does it make if I live or die? Why do you fucking care?"

He answered me the same way he'd answered last night. The kiss was rough and demanding, his mouth claiming mine. I hated the fact that my entire body came to life, responding to his kiss, hated the fact that my arms immediately wound around his broad shoulders. He pushed me against the wall, his big hands running down my sides. I closed my eyes and parted my lips, his tongue in my mouth as his hands ran back up my body.

Bane took hold of my t-shirt and tore it open all the way down the front, then slid his hands under the fabric, caressing my skin as he continued to taste my mouth. I couldn't even pretend I didn't love this, not when my hard cock was pressed against him. He took hold of the button fly of my jeans and pulled. The buttons gave way and then so did the thick denim, tearing like paper as he ripped the Levis off my body.

I muttered, "Damn it, those were my favorite jeans."

Bane grinned at me, then crushed my mouth in another hard kiss, his hands sliding down my nearly naked body. He reached behind me and grabbed my ass while skimming my cock with the palm of his other hand. A tremor went through me and I moaned against his lips. His response to that was to take hold of my cock and stroke me a few times, before reaching up and pushing the leather jacket and ripped t-shirt off my shoulders and onto the floor. I was now totally naked except for my boots, while he remained completely clothed. A shudder of pleasure slid down my spine.

When he picked me up, my arms and legs automatically encircled him. He reached between us, running his index finger over the sensitive head of my cock, then reached behind me and used my own precum as lubricant, pushing his finger into me. His other arm was wrapped around me, holding me securely.

"Hang on, love," he said and let go of me, so only my arms and legs held me to him. While he worked my ass with one finger, he began jerking me off with his other hand, both of us leaning back slightly to give him room to maneuver. He watched me as he did this and I held his gaze, my breath coming in short, fast gasps, my heart racing.

I cried out when I came, bucking into his hand, and he caught every drop of cum in his palm. It had been a long time since I'd found release, so there was a good amount. He reached behind me and spread me with one hand, then worked my own cum into me with two fingers as I moaned and let my eyes slide shut. "Yes," I murmured as he began massaging my prostate, my cock snapping right back to attention.

And all of this, it turned out, was just the appetizer.

As I continued to hold onto him, he tugged down the zipper of his dark jeans and freed his huge erection, then used the remaining cum on his palm to slick himself, which I found deeply erotic. He raised me up, his hands gripping my ass, and positioned me so my hole was pressed to the tip of his cock. He was going to take me raw. I shivered in anticipation. Part of me almost wanted to make a sarcastic remark about safe sex, but of course vampires couldn't catch or pass on human diseases, so there was no point in a condom.

Bane paused for a frustratingly long moment, kissing me again. And then he drove his cock into me.

He became something else then, something wild, bestial. He gave himself over to his vampire side, a low growl rumbling in his throat, his green eyes flashing with a dangerous light as he took me. All I could do was hang on, my arms and legs wrapped tightly around him, my head on his shoulder.

He was completely in control and I felt small and fragile in his powerful grasp. But even as wild as he was right now, he took care of me, fucking me hard enough to make us both feel so good, but not crossing the line to where he'd really hurt me. I clung to him tightly, lost to the pleasure, surrendering myself to him.

When he bit me I cried out, his teeth tearing into the top of my shoulder. But instead of struggling to get away, I just held on tighter. I said his name, his real name, as he drank from me, his cock in me so deep, his arms holding me securely. When he finally released my shoulder, he whispered in my ear, "You're mine." In that moment, it was absolutely true.

He'd been fucking me standing up and suddenly switched our position, laying me on the floor on top of my leather jacket. He held my gaze as he pumped his big cock into me, taking hold of my ankles and raising them to his shoulders so he could push even deeper inside me. My hands shook as I struggled with his clothes, pulling his shirt up so I could get to his body. His skin was smooth as I ran my hands up his broad back.

After a few minutes, he removed my ankles from his shoulders and rolled us over so I was on top of him. I fumbled with the buttons on his shirt as I rode his cock, then ran my gaze up his strong, flawless body before looking into his eyes. He was watching me closely, a little smile on his full lips, and said, "You're the most beautiful thing I've ever seen, Tyler."

It was odd hearing my real name. I had no idea how he even knew it. It made me feel vulnerable somehow and I broke eye contact, still riding his cock as I laid down on him and put my head on his shoulder.

Finally we were skin to skin, and the contact was electric.

He sat up, holding me to him, thrusting up into me. I was sitting on his lap and wound my legs around him as I hugged him tightly. He bounced me on his cock, in me so deep, and I moaned and gave myself over to the pleasure.

Bane reached between us and took hold of my cock. "Look at me," he said as he began to stroke me. I did as he asked, sitting up a little and looking into his eyes as he whispered, "My beautiful boy." He worked my cock hard and fast, then flipped me onto my back on the ground again and increased the force of his thrusts into me.

He brought us both to orgasm at the same time, throwing his head back and yelling as he came in me, his fangs exposed. Again and again he shot his seed deep inside me as my own orgasm tore from my body, cum spraying my stomach and chest. He kept thrusting until he was completely satiated, and then he rolled us over so I was once again laying on his chest, trembling and gasping for breath, his cock still inside me.

I was beyond exhausted, but after a minute I pulled off of him and dragged my shaking body to the wall, sitting against it so it was propping me up. My hands were shaking so hard when I picked up my gun that it was surprising I didn't shoot Bane by accident. I held it with both hands and steadied it on my bent knees. My voice was rough when I said, "This doesn't change anything. Not a single goddamn thing."

Bane sat up, his expression dark, dangerous, his voice low as he asked, "What are you doing, Tyler?"

"Stop calling me that. You don't have the right to use my real name." Anger shook my voice. I knew it didn't really have anything to do with what he'd called me.

"Okay *Tinder*, what the fuck are you doing?" He zipped up and rose to his feet slowly, his body tense.

"Coming to my senses, though an hour too late. I fucking hate you and I hate your kind, Bane. I hate myself too for being so weak, so ruled by my libido that I let that happen. It is *never* happening again. I'd rather blow my brains out than let you back inside me."

"Are you fucking kidding me? You loved every moment of that!"

"I was an idiot. Get the fuck out of here, before I put a bullet in your heart and follow it up with a stake."

Bane stared at me incredulously and then his eyes went dark. "This isn't over. Not by a long shot." He strode from the room.

Once I was sure he was gone, I lowered the gun and curled up on my side on the floor, pressing my eyes shut. I really must have been out of my mind to let that happen. And I couldn't even pretend that Bane had done something to influence me. I'd *wanted* it at the time with every part of me. The blame was all mine.

After a while, I sat up and tugged my jeans over to me. They were torn completely in half. I was going to be such a mess going home, and hoped Lee would still be out so he wouldn't witness my walk of shame. My legs shook as I pushed myself to my feet. My whole body was sore and would be for days, a constant reminder of what I'd let Bane do to me. A shiver of pleasure ran through me as I remembered him thrusting hard into me, which in turn made me want to punch myself in the face.

I tied the ripped denim around my waist like a crude sarong and pulled on my leather jacket, grabbed what was left of my t-shirt, then pocketed my gun and stake. My energy was completely depleted and I walked slowly out of the empty building, feeling like I needed to sleep for days.

When I reached my car, I paused to look at the warehouse. There was so much I needed to sort out, beginning with the mystery of that place. I needed to learn to protect myself against whatever magic Bane had used to get me to cooperate back in Santa Barbara, I was vulnerable until I did that. I also needed to figure out what I was going to do about Nate and Nikolai. I really couldn't in good conscience let a vamp with a daylight talisman live, but Nate was a friend, so the whole thing was a problem.

The back of my neck prickled as I stood there and I could practically feel Bane somewhere nearby, watching me. That made me incredibly angry. I had the overwhelming urge to run after him, to hunt him, to finally end him, though I was in no condition to do that now.

But soon, there would be another opportunity.

Book Two: Hunted

Stop being such a wuss and pull the goddamn trigger!

I sighted down the length of the homemade crossbow in my hands and lined up my shot. I had to adjust the angle slightly, because the slim wooden stake it fired would be smashing through glass before it reached its target.

Again, I hesitated.

Come on, what the hell are you waiting for? I chided myself. *He's a damn vampire. Not only that, he's a damn vampire that can walk in daylight. Just shoot him already!*

The vampire in question was named Nikolai. And the thing that was stopping me from reducing him to a snack for dust mites was the cute little human at his side. Nate.

During a recent prolonged hostage situation, Nate and I had become friends (I had been the hostage. And no, I wasn't totally bonkers and suffering from a raging case of Stockholm syndrome, but thanks for assuming that). Nate and Nikolai now incorrectly believed they'd been erased from my memory. They thought they were safe from me.

So there they were, in the kitchen of their tiny light blue cottage, cleaning up together after dinner. They did this every night, always with the curtains wide open. They were such creatures of habit, which made Nikolai an incredibly easy mark.

I was sprawled out on my belly, on the hillside directly across the street from their house. Since the breeze was blowing my scent away from them, the vamp didn't know I was here. That was kind of stupid, though. I mean, scent or no scent, I wasn't exactly invisible in the dark. Not to a vampire.

Oh my God, just end him! I'd been out here for about an hour and parts of me were going numb. Plus, I was pretty sure some ants had found their way up the right leg of my jeans, and it itched like crazy. It was so stupid that I was stalling like this. I shifted slightly, lined up my shot...and failed to pull the trigger.

I was going soft. That's all there was to it. The fact that I'd let a hundred perfect shots go by proved it.

What difference did it make that he was married to a human, and that I happened to like that human? The bloodsucker was dangerous, more so than most because of the incredibly rare daylight talisman in his possession. It was completely irresponsible of me not to dust him.

For the love of God, now the vamp was standing directly in front of the window, reaching up to put something on a shelf above it. It was like he *wanted* to be shot. I sighted down the crossbow. *Again.* And I didn't pull the trigger. *Again.* I sighed dramatically and whacked my forehead against the dry grass a few times. When I looked up, the vampire was smiling at Nate, saying something to him as he grabbed a set of keys and stepped out the front door.

Just shoot him! I visually tracked him all the way to the beat-up old Jeep they shared, my shot lined up perfectly the whole way. He got behind the wheel and started the engine, and I rolled onto my back and stared up at the night sky. What the hell was my problem? I'd ended hundreds of vamps in my lifetime. Since when did I let sentimentality get in the way of doing my job?

The Jeep pulled out of the driveway, then rumbled down the street and disappeared around a corner. I sighed again and sat up, then scratched my right leg for a solid minute. Finally, I trudged down the hill, the big, heavy crossbow still in my hand, and knocked on the front door of the little cottage. Well, if I wasn't going to kill Nate's husband, I might as well say hello.

When Nate swung the door open, his expression changed from cheerful to horrified in an instant. "Oh God, Tinder," he stammered, his eyes darting to the big weapon I was holding. "No. Please, no."

I raised my hands – and the crossbow – in an 'I surrender' position. "Hey Nate. Don't panic, I'm not here to kill Nikolai. Well, I *was*, but it didn't work out. So I thought, you know, I'd come over here and say hi instead."

He staggered backwards into the foyer and bumped into a little table, which sent a ceramic dish heading toward the floor. I lunged forward and caught it, crowding Nate in the process. He pressed against the wall, completely panicked, and mumbled, "But you drank that potion. It was supposed to make you forget we'd ever met."

I handed him the dish, which he took from me hesitantly as I said, "A lot of times, stuff that's supposed to work on me just doesn't." I had various spells and protection symbols tattooed all over my body, and sometimes they worked in unexpected ways.

He looked like he was about to hyperventilate, so I told him, "Nate, please calm down. I'm not here to hurt you, and I realized tonight that I just don't have it in me to kill your husband. You're both perfectly safe."

"But you intended to kill him when you came here."

"Well, yeah. He's a vampire with a daylight talisman for Christ's sake, so of course I came to kill him! But like I said, I couldn't go through with it."

"Why not?"

"Because of what that would do to you," I admitted.

He watched me for a long moment as he returned the little dish to the table. Then he stepped forward and drew me into a hug. I leaned the crossbow against the wall and wrapped my arms around him, and we held each other for a while. When he pulled back to look at me his eyes were still wary, but he offered me a little smile. "Thank you, Tinder."

"I'm afraid that one day he's going to lose control and kill you, Nate."

"I know you're concerned about that. Nikolai used to worry about it too, he didn't really trust himself when he first met me. But he knows now that he's in control of his vampire side, he's not just a slave to his instincts. I think you know that too, and I think that's why you agreed to leave us in peace when Bane offered you a way to forget us."

"I guess deep down I do. Although, Bane did something to manipulate me when he came here, he used a spell. That's what made me agree to forget you two."

"He can do that?"

"Not anymore. At least, not to me." I raised the hem of my t-shirt to reveal a very new tattoo on my ribcage. "Just a couple days ago, I found a protection symbol that makes me immune to suggestion spells." I poked the tattoo gingerly before dropping the shirt over it.

Nate paused before asking, "Is there something going on with you and Bane?"

"He seems to think there is. For some reason, he has this crazy idea that he should look after me. Like I need a vampire guardian angel."

"There's more than that between the two of you."

"Well, kind of. I…um…accidentally slept with him," I admitted. Nate's eyes went wide, and I blurted, "It was totally stupid, and I fully realize what a hypocrite that makes me. I gave in to lust over common sense and I'm not proud of it."

"Come into the living room," he said, taking my hand.

"You don't want me in your home, Nate. I totally freaked you out tonight. It was kind of crazy to come up and knock on your door, I don't even know why I did that."

He squeezed my hand gently. "You did it because we're friends. I was sad to say goodbye to you, Tinder, I thought I'd never see you again. I'm actually glad you're here."

"No you're not. I scared the crap out of you by knocking on your door."

"I was afraid that you were going to kill Nikolai. But I see now that you're never going to go through with it, not just for my sake, but because you know Nikolai isn't dangerous. You really can't justify killing him."

I sighed and said, "My job used to be so black and white. Vampires are monsters and I kill them, end of discussion. I really don't know what to do about these grey areas, like Nikolai."

"And Bane."

I frowned at him. "No, not 'and Bane.' He's an evil son of a bitch."

"From what little I've seen, Bane obviously cares about you. You can't really think he's evil."

"He doesn't care about me. He's incapable of that."

"Why? Because he's a vampire?" I nodded and Nate said, "Nick not only cares about me, he loves me with all his heart."

"Nikolai's a total freak of nature."

"I don't know about that. I really don't have much to go on since I've only ever met two vampires in my life," Nate said. "But I tend to think, if those two are peaceful, there must be more. I mean, you must have gotten to know other vampires. Weren't at least a few of them like my husband?"

"Hell no, I haven't gotten to know other vampires. I really don't make a habit of cozying up to the enemy, aside from the one time I got way too cozy with Bane."

"So, maybe you really don't know what you've been hunting all these years."

That annoyed me and I dropped his hand. "I've been hunting the things that dismembered my mother right before my eyes when I was four years old. The things that also killed my brothers and sisters, and my father, and my grandfather, and every single person that I ever cared about."

"Oh God, Tinder, I'm sorry."

"See, most vamps aren't big, fluffy, love bunnies like your husband. Your perspective is really skewed," I told him. "And they don't just target hunters, by the way. I've come across *way* too many slaughtered civilians in my lifetime. Hell, there were a couple times when I found bodies piled up by the dozens in vampires' lairs." Nate flinched at that.

I continued, "That's why I hunt and why I think I have a pretty good handle on my enemy. It's not just some personal vendetta because they wiped out my family, it's because vampires are remorseless killers. So you found an exception. Probably. And okay, *maybe* Bane's an exception, too. But most vamps are nothing like them."

He said gently, "I'm sorry for all the horrors you've seen in your life."

"It's just part of the job." I picked up my crossbow and reached out and squeezed his shoulder. "I apologize for freaking you out. I just…I missed you. But I shouldn't have dropped in, that was stupid of me." I opened the door and stepped out onto the little porch as Nate trailed after me.

"Wait. Stay a while, Tinder. I think you really need someone to talk to."

I just kept walking, cutting across his tidy front lawn. "I'll see you around, Nate."

Just then their old, rusty Jeep pulled into the driveway. Nikolai leapt from the driver's seat, staring at me in near panic, clutching a carton in his left hand. I almost rolled my eyes. Vampy had gone on an ice cream run.

I didn't break my stride as I called, "Hi, bloodsucker. Don't worry, I'm leaving. You might want to learn to close your curtains, just FYI, because any hunter that wanders by here could kill you a hundred times over, just in the time it takes you to serve up a bowl of that rocky road."

"Yeah…okay," Nikolai mumbled, obviously rattled.

"By the way, if you ever harm a hair on Nate's head, you should know that I'm not just going to kill you. I'm going to make you suffer first, like no undead motherfucking vamp has ever suffered in the history of suffering," I told him. Then I cheerfully called, "Have a nice day," as I headed down the sidewalk.

My white rental car was parked a couple blocks from Nate's house. There were two other white cars parked along the same stretch of road and I had to pause for a moment. I had no clue which one was mine. My Camaro was currently in pieces in my garage, so I'd been puttering around in this generic P.O.S. for the last few days. I always had a hard time picking it out of a crowd.

When I finally figured it out, I left the hills above Santa Barbara and drove into the heart of town, eventually finding a place to park along busy State Street. No reason why this trip should be a total waste of time. After a quick, surreptitious weapons check, I pocketed my keys and stepped onto the broad sidewalk.

The night was warm, rows of palm trees rustling overhead in the light breeze off the Pacific. It was actually a really beautiful night, but I wasn't here to enjoy myself. I engaged my sixth sense as I made my way down the street. The one special skill of true hunters (and the thing that separated us from every

Buffy wanna-be out there) was the ability to see people's energy signatures. Humans produced a rosy pink glow, while vamps gave off a stark white light. Yeah, I know that sounds insane. Whatever.

As I walked, my thoughts drifted to Bane and that made me want to punch myself. Lately, I couldn't stop thinking about him. It had been epically stupid to have sex with him. I'd been so angry afterwards that I pulled a gun on him, but really I was mad at myself, not Bane. Sleeping with a vampire had been a huge lapse in judgment.

Still, he was constantly on my mind.

Even though I'd been encountering him on and off for about the last five years, Bane was a total mystery to me. All I knew about the vampire could be summed up as follows: I'd heard he was old to the point of being ancient, he had an English accent, and he was gorgeous (which pissed me off, because that was probably why I kept thinking about him). Oh, and he claimed to want to take care of me, which somehow justified putting a tracking device in my car and finding ways to break into my heavily-warded home. I suspected he was actually trying to manipulate me, not take care of me, but I couldn't figure out what he hoped to gain from that.

I tried to force him from my thoughts and concentrated on my surroundings. I walked the length of State Street's shopping district, then expanded my path out in a wide spiral before eventually circling back to where I'd begun. I was almost ready to give up on Santa Barbara after a couple deathly boring hours when a flash of white appeared in my peripheral vision.

The vamp was on the other side of the street, leaning casually against the corner of a fancy little wine bar, assessing the crowd on the patio. He was wearing a shiny suit and so much hair gel that if he rested his head against the wall, he'd slide right off. Oh man, I'd hate this guy even if he wasn't a vampire.

I jaywalked, determined to keep the oily vamp in my sights. The driver of a BMW honked at me impatiently as I cut in front of him. I didn't even glance at the douchemobile as I gave its driver the finger and continued across the street.

The honking caused several people to glance in my direction, including the vamp. Then, oddly, he did a double-take and pushed off the wall of the building, quickly disappearing around a corner. It was almost like he recognized me, but how could that be? Okay, sure, I blended in with this upscale crowd like a mangy cat at a pedigreed dog show. But there was no reason this random vamp in a city I rarely spent time in should become alarmed at my presence.

Then again, maybe I was totally misinterpreting the spot-and-scoot. Maybe something else entirely had set him in motion. I finally made it across the broad boulevard and ducked down the same alley the vamp had taken. He must have started moving quickly as soon as he got off the main street, because he was nowhere to be seen. I broke into a run.

Santa Barbara was a lot less attractive back here amid the dumpsters and service entrances. Some misguided attempt at hosing down the alleyway had resulted in stagnant puddles and a gag-inducing aroma, just to add to the ambience. A busboy stepping out of a restaurant with a bulging trash bag raised an eyebrow at me as I jogged past and I quipped, "What an incredible smell you've discovered." My geek reference was totally lost on him. He stared at me like I was insane as he jettisoned the trash bag and went back inside.

Now where the hell had that vamp gone? I slowed to a walk after a while, reaching out with my sixth sense. It only worked visually, it didn't locate vamps like sonar or anything (man, if only). So right now, it wasn't helping me much.

I had pretty good instincts though, and when the hair on the back of my neck prickled, I came to a dead stop. I tightened my grip around the wooden stake in my right hand and pulled it out of the inside pocket of my jacket, holding it against my chest. A couple pairs of footsteps were closing fast, making very faint splashing sounds in the damp alley.

I whirled around and assessed the situation in a split second, then lashed out with my stake. Two vamps were almost right on top of me. I drove my weapon into the chest of the one on the right and he turned to dust on the spot, his clothes crumpling to the ground.

I'd grabbed a knife with my left hand and swung it around in a wide arc, but the vamp with slicked-back hair ducked easily. I dropped to the ground and rolled out of the way as he lunged at me, my jeans absorbing some of a big puddle. Gross! Now I was going to smell like wet garbage.

Slick pulled a gun from inside his suit jacket and pointed it at me, and I rolled my eyes. "Come on," I told him. "You're a damn *vampire*. Carrying a gun on top of that is pretty much the definition of overkill." This made him pause for a moment, knitting his brows like he was trying to decide if I was totally crazy.

That was all the time I needed. I dropped the knife, pulled my own gun from the waistband of my jeans, and fired a shot into his forehead. That wouldn't kill a vampire, but it hurt like hell and definitely knocked them off their game for a few moments. While he yelled and raised both hands to his head, I jumped up and jammed the stake into him. He disintegrated before my eyes.

Before his clothes even settled on the ground, I was gathering them and his gun. These all went into a dumpster, along with a second armload of his buddy's clothes. Then I shoved my gun back in my waistband, grabbed my knife and the stake from the ground, and took off at a dead sprint, stowing my weapons as I ran. This particular handgun was a small caliber and the sound it made was little more than a pop, nothing like the sound guns made on TV. But still, someone would probably come out to the alley to investigate and I wanted to be long gone when that happened.

I tried to look casual as I returned to busy State Street, but I was failing to blend in a big way. I'd already resembled a homeless person before rolling around in a filthy alleyway, and now the upper-middle-class masses were giving me a wide berth, as if my lack of wealth might somehow be contagious. Fucking rich people.

I stopped short when I got to the block where I'd parked, down at the slightly less ritzy end of State Street. Half a dozen generic white cars were dotted along the curb. Gah! I pulled the keys from my pocket and took a look at the logo on the fob. It was a swoop...with another swoop through it. What the hell? Would it kill car companies to just use their damn name as a logo? Having 'Kia' or 'Toyota' or 'Mitsubishi' spelled out on the key chain would be a big help, especially since every car company seemed determined to produce totally nondescript boredom-mobiles these days. Okay, 'Mitsubishi' probably wouldn't actually fit on the little faux-leather tag, but surely they could do better than a pair of bent lines.

149

After unsuccessfully trying to unlock two other cars (and attracting even more attention, because I now looked like I was trying to commit grand theft auto on one of the busiest streets in the county), I finally found the right one and ducked into the (boring grey) interior. As I fired up the engine and pulled away from the curb, I watched my rearview mirror, half expecting the Santa Barbara P.D. to come rolling up on me. Attracting the attention of law enforcement when armed to the eyeballs was a very, very bad thing.

It was a relief when I finally turned onto first one and then another major surface street, losing myself in traffic. When I stopped at a red light, I turned the rearview mirror toward me and muttered, "Awesome." I picked a couple stalks of dead crabgrass from my shaggy black hair – probably a souvenir from the hillside across from Nate's house – and scrubbed at a dirt smudge on my right cheek. No wonder people had been staring. I looked downright feral.

After merging onto the 101 southbound, I settled in for the long drive home to Long Beach and played tonight's hunt over and over in my mind. None of that had gone according to plan. Well, except for the part where I dusted two vamps. Why had Slick acted like he recognized me? As I'd said, this wasn't even my usual hunting ground, and it wasn't like vampires were organized enough to put out an A.P.B. on me.

The fact that two vamps had teamed up to come after me was also unusual. Vampires were very solitary creatures – probably because they were so vicious that any contact usually resulted in them turning on one another. And yet vamps in Long Beach had started the same alarming trend of working together lately. The worst case was a warehouse I'd discovered with at least a dozen vamps on the premises. I still didn't know what they'd been doing there, but I'd been trying to find answers over the last few days.

I had a feeling Bane was involved with that warehouse somehow. But even if he wasn't, he probably knew why those other vampires had an interest in that place. He wasn't big on sharing information, though.

Oh yay, now I was thinking about him again.

God, why had I let him fuck me? I mean really, what a stunningly bad idea. And why the hell couldn't I get it out of my mind? Why did I have to keep remembering the feeling of his big hands on my body, the strength of his arms around me, the way he'd whispered, "You're mine," when he was inside me, and how much I wanted it to be true – just in that one insane, lust-crazed moment?

My cock got hard just thinking about it, which pissed me off. By the time I reached L.A., I was in such a state that I took a somewhat familiar turn-off and wound through one of Los Angeles' seedier neighborhoods, the kind of place where the buildings all had thick iron bars on the windows.

As I drove, I decided I might as well make myself useful and engaged my sixth sense. The few people I passed lit up instantly as soon as my sight was engaged, a warm, rosy color. As pink as the cheeks of a sinner in church, as my Grandpa Reynolds used to say. He'd been a hunter too, just like the rest of my family, and had died when I was eleven. The only reason he lived long enough for me to know him was because his hunting career had been cut short. He'd gotten injured in the line of duty and had been confined to a wheelchair the last half of his life. The fact that my grandpa was partially paralyzed didn't stop a vampire from slaughtering him, though. Our home was breached and in that same attack, I also lost my sister Meg. I'd had four brothers and sisters at one point. Not anymore.

I tried not to think about that now, concentrating instead on scanning the people I passed. The pink was comforting for some reason, almost literally a way of seeing the world through rose-colored glasses.

Man, what a stupid thought.

I parked in the cramped lot behind a black cinderblock building. The sign on the side of this place should have said Ed's Mineshaft, but half of it was burned out so only 'shaft' was illuminated. Well, that was appropriate enough.

I closed my eyes for a moment and took a few deep breaths as I leaned back in my seat, steeling myself for what I was about to do. Every time I came to this dump, I vowed it was the last time. But here I was again.

Eventually, I got out of the car and went around to the trunk. I offloaded my heavy leather jacket and about fifteen pounds of weapons, keeping just one knife and one stake concealed in my boots. On my way to the front door, I glanced at the garbage and a petri dish of a mattress leaning against the side of the building. I didn't even want to contemplate the stains on that bed.

Once inside, I scanned the crowd (pink, pink, pink) then disengaged my second sight. It was distracting in a place like this with wall-to-wall bodies. I'd barely downed my first whiskey before some random guy caught my eye. He cocked his head to the side, indicating the dark, dank room at the back of the bar. I gave him a small nod and slid off my barstool, leading the way. That was the good thing about this place: no one wasted your time with inane chit chat. We all knew what we were here for. Once he and I stepped behind the heavy black curtain, I dropped my pants and braced myself with my palms against the wall. Ugh, it was sticky. So gross.

The guy deployed a condom before pushing into me. Damn it, even though he pounded me nice and hard, it wasn't nearly enough. It wasn't *Bane*. That thought made me want to whack my head against the sticky black wall.

When that guy finished, another took his place, shoving his cock into me without a word. I let him. I'd always been promiscuous, but in the past week I'd become completely reckless, going out every night, losing count of the faceless strangers that I let use me.

I kept thinking, if only one of these men fucked me the way Bane had. If only one of them brought me to life, made me feel the things he did. If that happened, then maybe I'd stop thinking about him all the time. Maybe I'd stop craving him with every part of me. But no one even came close.

Sex had always been one of my only forms of release, a pressure valve against the overwhelming stresses of my job. And now, apparently, a goddamn vampire had ruined me for sex with anyone else. Fan-fucking-tastic.

I stayed there though, up against that wall, as stranger after stranger used me over the course of maybe an hour. Even though it wasn't all that satisfying, it still quieted a part of me, a lonely, desperate part that I hated to even acknowledge.

Eventually, a young blond was pushed up against the wall right beside me, rough hands unfastening his pants and pulling them down before a raw cock was shoved into him. He cried out as he braced himself against the wall, sorrowful blue eyes locking with mine.

No, that wasn't right. This guy couldn't be more than eighteen or nineteen. He didn't belong in a bar, especially this one. It attracted a really rough crowd, one that wouldn't let a cute little twink like that go willingly when he decided he'd had enough of his walk on the wild side. Tonight was going to end really badly for him unless I did something.

I started to stand up, but whoever was in me shoved my head against the cement wall, so hard that I saw spots for a moment. Asshole. I elbowed him in the stomach and yanked my jeans up when he doubled over. "What the hell?" he growled.

The guy screwing the little blond wasn't going to stop because I asked him nicely, so I physically pulled him off and told the teenager, "Get dressed, we're leaving."

The twink stared at me wide-eyed but did as I said. Meanwhile, the big, hairy dude that had been topping him took a swing at me, which I easily dodged. I grabbed the blond's hand and dragged him after me as a fight broke out, the bar's bouncer stepping in and immediately agitating the guy that had been in me.

Somehow, we made it to the parking lot unscathed. As we ran across the asphalt the guy asked softly, "Why did you do that?"

"Because you don't belong there. Do you have a car?"

"No."

"Come on then, I'm driving you home." I found the rental car on my second try and he got in the passenger seat, still staring at me a bit fearfully. "Where do you live?" I asked, and he recited an address in a cringeworthy part of L.A.

"He wasn't raping me," the blond said as I pulled into traffic. "I was letting him do that to me." His voice never seemed to rise above a whisper.

"That's crazy. What were you thinking? He wasn't even wearing a condom."

"But you were doing the same thing."

"Doesn't matter. I'm over twenty-one, what I do is my choice. You're what, eighteen? It's not even legal for you to be in that place."

"I'm older than I look." Still that soft little voice. He was quiet for a while, then said, "I'm Tyler. What's your name?"

"The same, actually," I muttered distractedly, reading the street signs and trying to navigate a part of L.A. I didn't know very well.

"Most people call me Ty," he said. "You can call me that if you want to."

"Promise me you won't go back to that place, Ty. If you want to get laid, there are dozens of nicer, cleaner, safer gay bars in Southern California. That place is a shit hole."

"Then why were you there?"

"In my case, it doesn't matter if it's dangerous. I can defend myself if I have to."

He admitted, "I was there because I want a new master and that seemed like a good place to find one. Mine was killed a few months ago and I hate being on my own." Oh man, so he was one of those D/s boys that thrived on abuse. He asked, his voice softer than ever, "Do you think…do you think maybe you might want to keep me?"

I glanced over at him. His huge blue eyes were so hopeful. It was absolutely heartbreaking. "Ty, you don't even know me. Do I really need to tell you what a bad idea it is to go around offering yourself to total strangers? That's a great way to wind up in the morgue."

"I know you're a nice person. You wanted to save me from that place."

"I could be a total psycho for all you know. You need to be more careful."

"I am careful. And I know I don't seem like it, but I can defend myself, too," he said, looking down at his hands, which were folded in his lap.

"No offense, but I really doubt it." After a moment I asked, "Am I going the right way?"

"Yeah. Just take a left at the next light."

When we pulled up in front of his building, I muttered, "You have *got* to be kidding me." It was a total dive. In fact, the word 'dive' wasn't nearly strong enough to describe it. Some whole new word would have to be invented to really capture the essence of this place, something like 'terrifying-hellpit-shithole-of-retched-fuckedupedness.' Okay, that was more of a phrase. And even that didn't cover it. I looked at my companion and said, "How have you not gotten murdered twice a day, every day, living in this place?"

He grinned, just a little. "Like I said, I can defend myself."

"Christ," I muttered. This had to be one of the roughest neighborhoods I'd ever been in – and I didn't exactly spend most of my time in Mayberry, if you know what I mean.

"Will you come inside with me? Please? I'll let you do whatever you want to me."

Man, this guy was one huge cry for help. "Oh come on!" I exclaimed. "It's like you're *trying* to get murdered! Never say that to a stranger. Never! Do you hear me, Ty?"

"You're really sweet," he said. "Thank you for caring about what happens to me."

I normally didn't stick my neck out for other people like this, but God, this guy was like a tiny newborn kitten playing in traffic. Not even the most heartless asshole could leave him out there to get run over. "Look," I said, "let me drive you to a motel, someplace where the murder rate isn't measured in deaths-per-minute. My treat. At least that way, I know you'll be somewhat safe for a night or two."

"You don't need to do that. But you can walk me inside if you want, Tyler," he said, his grin graduating to a very cute smile. He hopped out of the car and stood waiting for me on the sidewalk. It was surprising that he didn't get murdered in the four seconds it took me to jump out and come around the car to stand beside him.

"Okay. Let's not waste time out here." I shepherded him into the building quickly with a hand on his lower back.

His room was on the ground floor. It contained only a rickety twin bed and an old, beat-up backpack. When we stepped inside, he turned to me and put his arms around me. He was only about five-six and fit perfectly right under my chin.

"You're like a superhero," he said as I sighed and hugged him, "out there saving people. I didn't actually need saving, but I think it's sweet that you tried anyway."

"Maybe we both needed saving tonight," I murmured, and he looked up at me. I was kind of surprised I'd said that out loud.

He led me over to the little bed and tugged on my hand until I gave in and sat on the edge of the mattress with him. "I'm not going to fuck you, Ty," I said. "I'm actually a bottom. Maybe you noticed, given what I was doing back at that bar."

This guy was still holding my hand. And I was letting him, because it was kind of nice. "I was going to ask for something else," he said, a faint blush rising in his pale cheeks as he looked at our joined hands. "You're going to think it's really weird. I wouldn't even ask if I didn't desperately need it."

I hated to think what that could possibly be. "I'm not going to smack you around, or spank you, or whatever Dom/sub shit you're into," I told him.

He grinned again. "It's weirder than that."

"Awesome. So, I'm probably not willing to do that to you, either."

"It's not what you'd be doing to me. It's what I'd be doing to you," he said.

"Um...."

"Can I just show you? Please? I'll stop the moment you tell me to, I swear."

I knit my brows at that. "If I say no, you're going to go right back out there to another bar just as bad as that last one, aren't you?"

He nodded. "I really need this tonight."

"What is it?"

"I guess...I guess I shouldn't try to describe it. I just need to show you."

I stared at Ty for a long moment. He looked so incredibly innocent. What the hell was he about to spring on me? A torture device? A farm animal? What? I was curious, wondering what brand of depravity could possibly lurk beneath that angelic exterior. "Okay, show me. But if I say stop, we stop. Got it?" I told him.

"I will. I promise." He pulled the hem of my t-shirt up to my shoulder, holding it balled up in his small hand. "Wow, you have a lot of tattoos," he murmured, gently caressing my chest with his other hand before sliding it around my body in an embrace. Then he leaned in, took my nipple in his mouth and began suckling.

Was that it? This wasn't particularly weird. It was kind of pleasant, actually.

After a minute or two of this, Ty bit down. I gasped as he murmured, "Sorry," and went back to sucking on my nipple. Ok, that was slightly weird. He'd bitten me fairly hard, too...*probably hard enough to draw blood.*

Reflexively, I switched to my second sight and Ty lit up in pure white light. I froze, my breath catching in my throat, fear and panic flooding me. Oh God. *Vampire*. Seriously?

How was I going to get out of this? Could I reach my stake before he tore my throat out? He might be small, but he was absolutely stronger and faster than I was, all vamps were. His hold on me was relaxed now, but the moment I started to make a move he'd probably tear me apart.

He gently licked my nipple a couple times, then sat up and took my hand as he said, "I'm sorry. It got scary for you all of a sudden, didn't it? You stopped breathing and your heart began to race. Why didn't you tell me to stop, Tyler?"

I pulled away from him and jumped off the bed, then grabbed the knife and stake that were concealed in my boots, pointing them at him with shaking hands. "How the hell can you be a vampire?" I exclaimed.

Ty looked absolutely astonished, wrapping his arms around himself. "How do you know what I am?"

"Drinking my blood was the first clue."

"Most people have no idea, though. They just think it's some kinky sex thing."

"I'm a hunter, Ty. You brought a vampire hunter home with you."

"Oh God," he murmured, his eyes going wide and fearful.

I stared at him for several moments, then blurted, stalling for time, "The thing I don't get is why you didn't try to compel me. It wouldn't have worked on me, but it's weird that you didn't even try."

"I don't compel people. It seems really unfair."

"It…wait, what?"

"Well, if I compelled someone, then they really wouldn't have a choice about feeding me. That's not right."

I had been crouched down in a defensive position, but I straightened up a bit now and said, "Wow. You're really bad at being a vampire."

"No, I'm really good at it. I've never killed anyone, and never had to compel anyone, either. Granted, I've only been on my own for four months, but I'm proud of how well I've managed to survive."

"What's with living in squalor? Not to give you pointers or anything, but you understand that you can have anything you want, right? Most vamps compel humans to give them all kinds of things – cash, cars, houses."

"This is all I can afford and obviously I'm perfectly safe here." Well, he did have a point there, since it turned out the cute little kitten was actually the most deadly predator on the block. "Like I said, I'm not about to compel people."

"Who the hell sired you, Gandhi?"

He smiled sadly. "Not quite. My maker was a wonderful person, though. I miss him so much."

"You know there were no vamps at that bar, right? At least, not until you showed up. If you were looking for someone to take the place of your maker, you weren't going to find him there." I was still stalling because I somehow just couldn't make myself kill this guy. At least, not until he gave me a reason to.

Ty brought his feet up onto the mattress and hugged his knees to his chest. "I don't care if my new master is a vampire or a human. I just want someone who'll feed me and take care of me." He met my gaze and watched me for a few moments, then asked, "Are you really a vampire hunter?"

"Uh, yeah. Is the wooden stake not a tip-off?"

"If you're a hunter, why haven't you tried to kill me yet?"

"I really don't know."

He sighed and said, "Well, if I had to be stupid enough to bring a hunter home, I'm lucky that it was you and not the monster that killed Calvin. Otherwise, I'd be dead already."

"Who's Calvin?"

"My maker."

"Ah."

"That hunter literally gives me nightmares," Ty said with a little shiver. "A friend of mine happened to be watching from a window when Calvin was killed. He said this guy stabbed my maker in cold blood, when all Cal was doing was coming home from the library."

A fragment of a memory pushed its way into my consciousness, a dark side street, books spilling across the sidewalk.... Despite myself, I asked, "Do you know the name of that hunter?"

"Yeah. His name's Tinder. Have you heard of him?" I nodded, something cold and heavy settling in my stomach. "He's like the angel of death among my people," Ty continued. "You never know when he's going to strike and he's completely merciless. If he finds you, you die. So see, that's why I want to find a master and just drink from him. I won't have to go out at night to feed, not when Tinder's out there somewhere."

Christ, he made me sound like the boogeyman. Why was this upsetting to me? I should be thrilled that my name struck fear in the hearts of bloodsuckers. "If I try to leave," I said, "are you going to stop me?"

"No. I would never hurt you, Tyler. I promise."

"Back away from the door. Go over to that far corner," I said, raising both my weapons a little higher and gesturing with my chin.

He got up and did as I asked immediately, then said, "I'm really sorry I scared you, especially after you were so nice to me tonight."

I didn't reply. I just bolted from the apartment and out of the building, absolutely expecting Ty to come after me and attack me. But it didn't happen.

Surprisingly, the rental car was still parked in front of the building. It was so boring that not even criminals wanted it. As I got behind the wheel and tried to find my way back to the freeway, I kept thinking about Ty. I felt like I'd orphaned him. It was insane that I actually felt guilty for ending his maker. The only thing to feel guilty about was not finding and killing Calvin sooner. Then he never would've turned that sweet, beautiful boy into a monster.

"Oh shit," I muttered all of a sudden, pulling the rental car to a screeching halt at the curb. I leapt out and grabbed my big crossbow and a gun from the trunk, then took off at a run, backtracking half a block. I'd forgotten to disengage my second sight after leaving Ty's apartment and a glimmer of white had caught my eye.

I skidded to a halt at the mouth of a dark alley and found a vampire in mid-feed. Without a moment's hesitation, I raised the crossbow and fired, even though I knew I couldn't hit the vamp's heart from this angle. She let out a demonic shriek and dropped her victim, immediately whirling on me with a murderous look in her eyes. The vamp charged me as I flipped over the double-sided crossbow and fired again. The second narrow wooden spike found its target and she broke apart into a million tiny flecks of nothingness, just inches from me.

Now that the vamp (and the light she'd radiated thanks to my second sight) was no more, the alley was really dark. I pulled a silver lighter from my pocket and flicked it on, then went to take a look behind the dumpster. Man, how many times had I found myself in exactly this situation, in an alley just like this one? The sights, the smells, the circumstances were always the same. It felt like alleys only existed to host grisly murders like the one at my feet.

I crouched down and took a good look at the victim. The homeless man was quite obviously dead, his throat slit ear to ear so it would look like a random street crime and not a vampire feeding. The man's empty, staring eyes looked almost white in the flame from my lighter, cataracts probably having robbed him of most, or maybe all, of his sight. He must have struggled to survive on the rough streets of L.A., only to finally wind up as a meal for a monster.

I sighed and stood up. I'd failed this man. I hadn't gotten here in time to save his life. But at least the bloodsucker that murdered him would never find another victim.

And damn it, see? *That* was why I hunted. I'd let that little blond vamp get under my skin, let myself start to question my job as a hunter. Well, screw that. Just because I'd found a couple anomalies lately, vamps that managed not to kill, that wasn't how the world really worked. This was. How could I feel bad about hunting monsters that did things like this?

I trudged back down the street, feeling incredibly weary and not looking forward to the long drive home. Along the way, I contemplated the fact that not so long ago, I often went two, three weeks without encountering so much as a single vampire. Lately though, I'd been finding several a week. I didn't try to kid myself and attribute this to my awesome hunting ability. The vamps were increasing in number for some reason. I wondered how far this trend extended, if it was just Southern California, or all of the U.S., or hell, *everywhere*.

Ty remained on my mind as I drove home. I had a feeling the baby vamp and I would cross paths again someday. I'd probably wind up regretting the decision not to end him tonight. It might even cost me my life.

With every part I pulled out of my car, I got more
and more annoyed.

My Camaro was parked in the narrow garage
attached to my house. In order to get it in there, I'd first
had to drag all the landlord's weird crap out into the
backyard (he had fourteen barbecue grills hoarded up in
there. *Fourteen.* WTF?). Over the last few days, I'd
been systematically dismantling the Chevy, laying out
all the pieces on a blue tarp. It was hot and cramped in
the little garage, but I couldn't work in the driveway. In
this neighborhood, all the parts would get stolen the
moment my back was turned.

I'd been determined to find the tracking device that
Bane had installed in my car. I'd gone out and bought a
machine that was supposed to scan for trackers and
other bugs, but nothing had shown up. I knew the
tracker was in there somewhere though, so I'd
proceeded to do this the old-fashioned, long, boring,
stupid way.

So far, I'd found not one, not two, but *three* tracking devices. Seriously?

I'd almost stopped after I found the first one. But then, on a hunch I kept looking. I almost expected the second one. But a third tracker? Come on! Overkill much? Since I still didn't believe I'd found all of them, I kept going, taking apart the entire car piece by piece. Goddamn Bane and his insane notion that he needed to keep an eye on me!

I was bent over the front fender of my car, partially embedded in the engine compartment, when my roommate murmured in his Texas drawl, "Well, shit. Don't you look good enough to eat." After a moment, I felt Lee's hand cupping my butt. "Why don't you take a break, Tinder? You been at this for hours." By take a break, he of course meant *wanna screw?*

"I'm covered in oil," I pointed out, resting my elbows on the fender and glancing at him over my shoulder. Lee was a good-looking guy, tall and broad-shouldered, his sandy blond hair still a bit damp and spiky from a recent shower. "I can't take a break now, because I'd have to spend forever washing up and then come right back here and get dirty all over again."

"You can just stay dirty," Lee said, sliding his hands around my hips and rubbing his hard-on against my ass through our jeans. My dick immediately responded. "You don't even have to change position. Just let me do everything."

"Well, I suppose I *could* use a break...."

That was all the green-light Lee needed. He immediately reached around and unbuttoned my Levis, pushing them down before dropping his own jeans.

He had lube and a condom in the pocket of his t-shirt, and he squirted the cool liquid between my cheeks before working some into me with two fingers. I relaxed and spread my legs as wide as I could with the denim around my knees, sighing with pleasure. Lee was doing more than just prepping me. He was finger-fucking me roughly, just how I liked it, and I moaned and started rocking back onto his hand.

By the time he mounted me I was fully aroused, my cock leaking precum. I didn't always try to reach orgasm while being fucked, but this time I wanted release. Since I couldn't use my oil-covered hands, I ground out, "Stroke me," as Lee thrust into me, and his big hand wrapped around my cock. He established a steady rhythm as he jerked me off and pounded me, and minutes later I was painting the side of my car.

Lee wasn't quite there yet and grasped my hips, his body slapping my ass as he took me. I grabbed onto the front of the car, bracing myself, then yelled, "Son of a bitch!" I pulled out a little black tracking device that had been tucked up under the lip of the engine compartment and yelled, "*Four? Are you kidding me?*"

Lee laughed at that, not interrupting his thrusts into me, and came a minute later, yelling, "Oh shit," as he shot his load. He kept going until he was totally satiated, then eased out of me carefully. He pulled my pants back up and buttoned them, then gave my ass a playful slap.

"You know," he said as he tossed the condom and got dressed, "Bane's probably just gonna install new trackers the very first time you park your car in public."

"I know. But I still feel like I have to do this."

"You gotta wonder 'bout the level of obsession that'd drive someone to install so many devices in one car."

"Bane's not obsessed. He's just an asshole that enjoys messing with me." I threw the latest tracker onto

176

the growing pile in the corner and picked up my wrench, but then Lee startled me by taking me in his arms and kissing me, long and deep. "Damn it, Lee, what the hell are you doing?" I muttered against his lips.

He pulled back a couple inches and said, "I'm kissin' you, Tinder. That's what normal people do when they screw." His brown eyes sparkled with amusement and he swooped in and kissed me again, parting my lips with his tongue, pulling me against his broad chest. What he was doing actually felt really good, and I dropped the wrench noisily onto the concrete floor and grabbed his ass with both hands.

"That's better," he murmured before running a line of kisses along my jaw.

"Lee," I said, my voice a bit rough as he licked my earlobe, "I hope you're not getting the wrong impression about what's going on between us. You and I are just fuck buddies. You know that, right?"

"We're more than that, Tinder." He twined his fingers in my black hair and kissed my neck.

"See?" I pulled back from him as much as I could with the car right behind me. "That's exactly what I'm talking about."

He knit his brows and took a step back from me. "What's so wrong with this bein' more than just sex?"

"It's not what I want, you know that. I've been up front with you this whole time, perfectly clear that this was sex only."

"Sometimes I just don't get you, Tinder," he said as he turned from me and headed back into the kitchen. There were two clearly defined handprints on the seat of his jeans, and when I pointed this out to him, he called over his shoulder, "Good. I'm fixin' to leave 'em there as a reminder."

"A reminder of what?"

"A reminder that this is already more than just sex!" He disappeared into the house as I sighed dramatically.

My life used to be really straightforward. I just ate and slept and hunted. Occasionally, I had sex with someone I didn't know. Oh, and sometimes, I'd go see a movie. That was about it.

Until recently, I'd also been completely alone. After the last member of my family died about three years ago, I'd gotten used to solitude. Now that there were a few people in my life, things had gotten so damn complicated.

*****

I drove the rental car to the Port of Long Beach later that night. Lee had suggested we hunt as a team, but I pointed out that we'd cover more ground separately. Really though, this was just a continuation of our earlier discussion. It felt like he and I were becoming joined at the hip (okay, not the hip, exactly…). It was nice having him as a roommate, and the sex on demand was an awesome perk, but clearly he was starting to think of us as a couple. The word 'we' appeared in his vocabulary way the hell too often.

And he'd really been making himself at home in the few short days we'd been roommates. Not that there was anything wrong with that. But every time I turned around, there was a new piece of furniture or some miscellaneous item that he'd dragged in off the street.

This was weird to me. Since a hunter might have to pack up and move at a moment's notice, my family never owned more than would fit in the trunk of our car.

I'd mentioned this to Lee, but he'd just shrugged and said, "If we have to leave suddenly, this can all just stay here. It's not like I'll be out anything." Okay, he kind of had a point. Lee was perpetually broke and a world-class dumpster diver, he wasn't spending money on any of this stuff.

I was trying to do something about his financial situation and had sent a note to my benefactor asking if funds were available for Lee. I was still waiting to hear back. His theory was that because of budget cuts, only full-blooded hunters were getting money these days, since I was still receiving checks. His theory made sense. We were only guessing though, because the benefactors never actually bothered telling us what was going on.

Eventually, I pulled to the curb and parked. Though the warehouses down by the waterfront were really busy during the day, at night they were perfectly still. I got out of the car, picked a direction at random and started walking. Normally this wouldn't be my first choice of hunting grounds, but after stumbling across that mysterious warehouse with a bunch of vampires on the premises, I kept coming back here. I thought there was a chance the vamps might take over another warehouse after abandoning that first one.

Wandering the entire warehouse district twice over the course of a couple hours left me bored out of my mind. This was pointless. Nothing was going on down here, nothing at all. I gave up and headed in the direction of my car, my hunter's sight still engaged.

Suddenly, I got one of those feelings, the hair on the back of my neck bristling. I looked all around me, but saw nothing out of the ordinary. Impulsively, I climbed a rusty fire escape at the back of a condemned brick building. If there were any vamps in the area, maybe I could spot them from a higher vantage point. I picked my way across the torn-up asphalt tiles and peered over the edge of the roof.

My adrenaline spiked instantly. Moving this way from three directions were half a dozen vampires. They were lit up in the darkness, converging like planes on a collision course on an air traffic controller's screen.

I ducked down quickly, wondering if they'd seen me, then ventured a glance over the short retaining wall at the edge of the roof. Dread bloomed cold inside me. They were headed right for this building. All of a sudden, I realized what was happening.

They were hunting me.

There was no way to get inside this building from the roof, so I sprinted back to the fire escape. Two vamps were already halfway up it. I drew a big stake and a gun and fired a couple shots at them, but the vamp in the lead had thought to pick up a metal trash can lid and was using it like a shield to deflect my shots. I frowned at that and whirled around, frantically assessing my situation.

Oh man, this had been stupid! I'd totally cornered myself. But I'd had no idea there were a bunch a vamps on my tail. *And since when did they hunt in packs?*

I wasn't expecting the vamp that suddenly landed right in front of me, jumping onto the roof from the taller building next door. Reflexively, I thrust the stake into his chest, putting so much force behind it that I fell with him as he disintegrated.

Immediately, I was hauled to my feet by one of the vampires that had come up the fire escape. Another punched me in the stomach, so hard that several of my ribs shattered. The pain was intense, but I still struggled wildly as the vampire holding my arms tightened his grip and said, "Well, that was just too easy."

I looked around, my heart thudding in my chest as fear coursed through me. Several more vampires had joined us on the rooftop by now, ten in all. I'd only spotted a portion of them coming after me on the ground. The rest had leapt down from the adjacent building or had come up from the rear.

"Can this really be the mighty Tinder?" the red-headed vamp directly in front of me asked, his tone mocking. "Hardly the fearsome hunter I was expecting." He looked a little like he'd just stepped out of the Scottish highlands, his long, curly hair tied back in a messy ponytail.

"Bite me, Merida," I ground out. The Disney reference was totally lost on him. I had to question why I myself could come up with it.

The vampires closed around us in a circle, eyes gleaming in anticipation. Their spokesvamp continued as if I hadn't said anything, addressing the crowd. "It's disappointing, that's what it is. He was built up to be the stuff of legend, but look at him. He's more boy than man, really. Just another fragile little human." To illustrate his point, he circled behind me and took the place of the vamp holding onto me, then wrenched my arms upward. I yelled as bones snapped, the pain so intense that I would have dropped to my knees if he wasn't holding me up.

"How many of my kind have you killed, hunter?" The vamp pinned my broken arms excruciatingly behind my back as another yell tore from me. "Dozens? Hundreds?" He twisted my arms slowly, pain searing through me. "It's a shame that I can only kill you once. But at least I can drag it out, make you suffer for what you've done to my brethren."

Despite being in almost unbearable agony, I reached deep within myself and gathered my strength, then whipped my head back as hard as I could. The vamp wasn't expecting me to fight back, so when my skull shattered his nose, he yelled and let go of me. I flung myself forward and barrel-rolled across the rooftop, knocking down two vamps before leaping to my feet. I was near the edge of the roof and I didn't even think about it. I just jumped off.

I was ten stories up. The fall would kill me, I was sure of that. But it would be a quick death, so much better than slow torture at the hands of those bloodthirsty vampires.

The moment before impact moved in slow-motion, the only sound the rush of wind past my ears. I wasn't afraid to die. I'd never been afraid of that. I actually found myself letting go, accepting the end.

I was at peace.

Strong arms caught me effortlessly three feet above the ground and my eyelids flew open. Bane was staring at me incredulously, his green eyes troubled. Without a word, he took off running, moving faster than any vampire I'd ever seen as he cradled me carefully in his arms. In less than a minute, he'd put several blocks between us and the other vampires, loaded me into the passenger seat of his flashy Aston Martin, and gotten behind the wheel. The car took off like a shot and then the warehouse district was behind us.

Bane slowed down when he reached city streets and wound smoothly through traffic. I glanced at his profile as he drove. He was angry about something, a muscle in his jaw working as he ground his teeth, and he still hadn't said anything. Normally, I would have had an arsenal of sarcasm ready to hurl at him. But since I was in excruciating pain, all I could really muster were quick, shallow breaths.

Abruptly, he swerved into the driveway of a high-rise apartment building and punched in a code on a keypad, which raised a security gate. The silver sports car slid into an empty underground garage. After he parked, he retrieved me from the passenger seat, again lifting me into his arms. I didn't have it in me to protest.

We rode the elevator to a huge apartment on the top floor of the twelve-story building. Bane carried me through to the bedroom, where he placed me gently on the mattress. He sat beside me and stared at me for a long moment, and his silence was so unnerving that I whispered, "Say something," my voice thin and scratchy.

Instead of replying, he used his fangs to tear open his wrist. I flinched, both at the sight of those teeth and at what he'd just done. Almost all vamps filed their fangs down so they could blend in with the human population, leaving only hunters' second sight as a way to identify them. Not Bane, though. Apparently, he was out and proud.

I pulled back reflexively when he stuck his wrist in front of my mouth and demanded, his voice dangerously low, "Drink my blood, Tinder. It'll heal you."

"No."

"Do it, or so help me God, I will hold you down and force-feed you."

It was a well-known fact that vampire blood had the power to heal humans, but that was a line I really didn't want to cross. "No," I said again, trying to sound firm. "I don't want this. I don't want anything from you."

A low growl rumbled in his throat as he climbed on top of me, straddling my thighs, and held his slashed wrist right above my mouth. Even though he was furious, he was being really careful, arching over me so he didn't put any pressure on my broken ribs. "Stop being so stubborn, Tinder. You're minutes from going into shock, and I think you may be bleeding internally. Surely you must know I'm not bluffing about force-feeding you." Bane's English accent was normally slightly diluted from living in the States, but when he was angry it ratcheted right back up again, overshooting the Queen's English and teetering on the brink of Cockney.

I watched him for a long moment, the rage in his green eyes churning like a storm at sea. "Why are you so angry?" I asked.

"Because you fucking *wanted to die!*" He yelled it, then launched himself off the bed and stood over me. "I saw your face a moment before you thought you were going to hit the ground. And you bloody well looked happier than I've ever seen you! It makes me wonder why I've spent so much time trying to keep you alive when you're completely suicidal!"

"I'm not suicidal," I said quietly, the words punctuated by my fast, shallow breathing. "I've just always known this job is going to kill me. I accepted that a long time ago. So when I thought my number was up…I guess I was at peace. I felt like I'd done all I was supposed to do and could just let go. If I looked happy, that was why."

"Christ, Tinder," Bane muttered, pushing his dark brown hair back from his face with both hands. After a few moments he sat beside me, the mattress dipping under his weight.

My breathing was becoming more labored, and the relentless pain was really starting to wear me down. "Take me to a hospital," I whispered. Hunters almost never went to hospitals but I knew it was my only alternative, aside from Bane.

"No. Stop being so damn pig-headed and drink from me! You can't possibly spend weeks with both arms in casts, it would leave you completely defenseless."

He kind of had a point there. I stared at him for a while, brows knit as I weighed my options. Eventually, the pain wore me down, and I relented. "Let's do this quickly, before I change my mind."

His wrist had completely healed by now, so he tore it open again and held it out to me. "I can't believe I'm doing this," I muttered, then fought back my gag reflex and experimentally ran the tip of my tongue over his wrist.

The moment I swallowed, warmth and energy flooded me. It was an absolute rush, more powerful than any drug, and I found myself lunging for his wrist. He pressed it gently to my lips and I drank deeply, hungrily, my eyes sliding shut. It was so good, so nourishing and healing, its taste surprisingly palatable.

Bane let me do this for a long time, the pain easing and my body beginning to mend itself as I drank. When I finally ended it, he stood up and said, "You're going to need to stay in bed and rest. It'll take some time for my blood to fully heal you."

I felt slightly buzzed as I mumbled, "Where are we?"

"One of my safe-houses, it's the best place for you right now. The wards on your house aren't sufficient to keep out that vamp gang if they track you there."

"My wards are perfectly sufficient. They keep everyone out except you. And I'd like to know how you manage to get around all my protections."

"I was a full-blooded warlock before being turned into a vampire. My powers are a bit unpredictable now, but they're still more than enough to get around your piecemeal spells."

I frowned and said, "That's impossible. Warlocks can't be turned into vampires."

"It's not impossible, merely unusual. I meant what I said about getting some rest, Tinder. Your body needs time to mend." With that, he turned and started to leave the bedroom.

"Where are you going?"

"Far away from you."

"Why?"

He paused and glanced over his shoulder at me. "Because any minute now, you're going to have a powerful reaction to all that blood you consumed, and I don't want to be here when that happens."

I raised an eyebrow at him. "Define *powerful reaction*."

"Vampire blood is an aphrodisiac. Any moment now, you're going to be begging me to have sex with you."

"And…you *don't* want to be around when that happens?" I blinked a few times to clear my vision, feeling a bit dizzy.

"In some ways, drinking my blood is like drinking alcohol, it clouds your judgment. I'd never take advantage of you in that state."

I tried to roll my eyes at him, which just made the room spin. I leaned back against the pillow and muttered, "Oh no, of course not. But when I'm horny as hell in an empty warehouse, *then* it's okay to take advantage."

Bane grinned a little. "Entirely different situation."

He turned and started to leave, and I said quietly, "They were hunting me, Bane. It wasn't just random.

Those vamps knew my name, they came after me deliberately."

Again he paused, just inside the doorway. "I know."

"But vampires don't do that. They don't hunt in packs. It's just not how they operate."

"Not normally, no."

"Why are the vamps changing their behavior? What's going on?"

"Don't worry, I'm taking care of it. Get some rest." He left the room, and I leapt out of bed and ran after him.

"Come on, Bane! Why can't you just clue me in?"

"For fuck's sake, Tinder, I told you to rest!"

I put myself between him and the front door. "I know what you told me, and I don't give a shit. Everything's been changing, and I need to know what's going on. What are the vampires up to? Why are they hunting in packs? And what was up with that warehouse? Who went in and totally emptied that place? Was it you?" The room spun again, and I flung a hand out to steady myself against the door, which made me cry out in pain. My arm was healing, but it was nowhere near back to normal.

A wave of nausea crashed into me all of a sudden. "I really don't feel so good," I murmured as I dropped to my knees. In the next instant I was throwing up violently, my entire body heaving. Given what I'd just consumed, it turned the entryway of the apartment into a scene from a horror movie.

"What the hell?" Bane exclaimed as he dropped down beside me and held on to me.

It felt like my body was turning itself inside out. And it just went on and on, tears streaming down my face as my body purged itself of every last drop of Bane's blood and then kept going and going and going. Throughout it all, Bane clutched me tightly and I clung to the big arm wrapped around my chest like it was a life line. I shook violently as my body convulsed from the strain of what it was doing to itself.

When I finally passed out, it was such a relief.

*****

Apparently, I'd fallen asleep at some point. When I awoke, the room was dark, but a faint glow around the edges of the heavy curtains told me it was daytime. Bane's arms were around me. I burrowed deeper into them and he held me securely as he asked, "How do you feel?"

"Like shit." My voice sounded really raspy.

"No doubt." He brushed my hair back from my eyes and said, "You know, when I said you'd have a powerful reaction to my blood, I was *not* expecting you to vomit your guts out."

"I know. Why did that happen?"

"I have no idea, I've never heard of a human rejecting vampire blood like that. I'm going to look it up in my research library, right after I hunt down that vampire pack and tear them to shreds. I'd already be on their trail, but I didn't want to leave until I knew you were okay."

His hand slid down to rub my bare back gently as he was talking, and I asked, "Why am I naked?"

"Because you were covered in blood and vomit."

"Pretty. Did you bathe me?"

"I did."

"It's super weird that you feel the need to take care of me," I murmured, snuggling against him. My only excuse for that was that I felt miserable and was in desperate need of a little comfort.

"Shame that it takes nearly dying before you'll let me." He adjusted his hold on me and said, "I'm sorry you had such a violent reaction to my blood, but the good news is, it appears you kept it down long enough to mend your broken bones."

"Don't know if it was worth it," I mumbled.

I was starting to drift off again and he said, "Since you're doing better, I'm going to take off in a few minutes, before the vampires' trail gets cold. There's water at your bedside and your clothes are in the dryer."

"You did my laundry?"

"It was that or let you go about looking like an extra in a slasher film."

"Thanks, Bane."

"You're welcome, Tyler."

"I don't like it when you use my real name."

"I know. But you're too incapacitated right now to do anything about it."

I grinned at that before sinking back into sleep.

The next time I awoke, I was groggy and disoriented and had no idea how long I'd been out. I took a couple deep breaths and found that the pain from the broken ribs was completely gone. As I sat up, I pushed my hair out of my face and called Bane's name. The apartment was perfectly still. I grabbed the bottle of water he'd left on the nightstand and drank all of it before swinging out of bed. Then I went in search of the dryer, which I eventually found in a hall closet.

Getting dressed was far more exhausting than it should have been. After I put my clothes on, I laid down right where I was, on the area rug in front of the dryer. I kept my eyes closed for a few minutes, then forced them open and took a look at my surroundings. Bane had brought me to the Land of Beige. Beige, beige, beige, as far as the eye could see. The walls were beige, the curtains were beige, the furniture was beige (with dark wood accents, but still, the rest was beige). The rug I was laying on had a pattern of squares, all in varying shades of beige. God. It was enough to make me want to hurl again.

I pushed myself into a seated position and tugged on my boots, then stood up tentatively. My leather jacket was hanging from a hook in the little laundry closet, and when I put it on, it was a bit damp. I tried to picture powerful and elegant Bane with his sleeves rolled up, scrubbing the puke off my jacket, or for that matter mopping up the entryway, and failed miserably.

My weapons were neatly laid out on a (beige) towel on top of the washing machine. He'd arranged them in order of size, subcategorized by function. OCD much? It took a while to get all my weapons in place on my body, and when I finished, I needed to lay back down on the area rug for a few more minutes. Man, that vomitfest had really zapped my energy.

Eventually, I was back on my feet and propelling myself toward the front door. There was a note stuck to it, written in ornate cursive (that was such an old-vamp tipoff). It said: *Get back in bed. You're not well enough to be up yet.*

What a control freak. I opened the front door, which set off a piercing alarm. Ugh, great. I pulled the door shut behind me, clamping my hands over my ears (for all the good it did) as I hurried to the elevator. It also had a note stuck to it. It said: *NO.* Oh my God! *Total* control freak. I pushed the elevator button…about a hundred and forty-seven times. Nothing happened. The control freak had actually disabled the elevator!

The horrible, shrieking alarm was still going off. It was so loud that I felt like I was going to begin bleeding from my ears soon. I hurried to the end of the hallway and tried the handle on the big metal door leading to the stairs. Oh, here was a surprise: it was locked. And yes, there was a note stuck to it. It said: *Definitely not.*

"What the hell, Bane?" I yelled over the alarm, as if he could hear me. "You have some serious control issues, dude. Like, 'keep a team of psychotherapists employed for decades'-type issues."

If the alarm didn't stop soon, I was going to go completely insane. I returned to the apartment and was surprised to find I hadn't locked myself out. The control freak had probably somehow controlled that as well. I stepped back inside, closing the door behind me, and breathed a sigh of relief when the alarm stopped. I tried opening the door again, and immediately the alarm began wailing. When I shut it from inside the apartment, the alarm stopped. But when I was out in the hall and shut it, the alarm kept going. Really?

A faint ringing was coming from somewhere inside the apartment. Or maybe it was just the ringing in my ears after that auditory assault. It stopped after a minute. And then it started up again.

I followed the sound to the kitchen, where I found a slim black phone on the (beige) kitchen counter. God, even the kitchen was beige, who did that? The phone had a note stuck to it. It said: *Answer me.* That was the second vaguely Alice in Wonderland reference I'd gotten from Bane over the past few weeks. I wondered if it was intentional.

The phone stopped ringing. And then a few seconds later, it started up again. I sighed and answered it by saying, "You know what I hate?"

"Vampires?" Bane guessed.

"Obviously. But a very close second is the color beige. What the hell were you thinking with this place? It's like a baby had diarrhea over every square inch of this apartment."

"It came furnished and I never bothered to change it. That's a delightful visual, by the way."

"You need to get back here and let me out, Bane."

"No."

"Excuse me?"

"With that gang of vampires on the loose, it's not safe for you out there right now."

I busted out an impressive level of maturity and went with, "I can go home if I want to. You're not the boss of me."

He chuckled at that and said, "And you wonder why I treat you like a child."

"Up yours."

"You're only reinforcing my point for me." He sounded smug.

"Where are you right now?"

"Oxnard."

"Bullshit."

He laughed again. "Now why on Earth would I make that up?"

"What the hell are you doing in Oxnard?"

"Driving through on my way back to Long Beach."

"From where?"

"Points north," he said.

"Thanks for all that information, Captain Vague."

"I've been trying to track down the vampires that targeted you. I followed a lead that took me up to Pismo Beach, but it didn't pan out. Now I'm backtracking. Crikey," he said, and there was a soft thudding sound. I could hear him swearing in the background. After a few moments, he got back on the line and said, "Sorry 'bout that. I dropped the phone."

"You know who says crikey? Australians. Did you suddenly forget that you're British?"

"I lived in Australia for nearly three decades. Some of the speech rubbed off on me."

"When was that?"

"Latter part of the nineteenth century."

"Wow, you actually answered a question. Let's see if you'll answer another. How old are you, Bane?"

"Really fucking old."

"Oh look, we're back to vague again."

"Go back to bed, Tinder. You look like hell and will probably topple over at any moment," he said.

I raised an eyebrow at that. "Wait. Can you somehow *see me* right now?"

202

"Yes."

"Nothing creepy about that." I looked all around the room for cameras, but they were well-concealed. "I'm out of here and it's your call how I leave: the easy way, or the hard way." I put the phone on speaker and set it on the counter, then went over to the little beige breakfast nook, where I picked up a chair. "Do you see what I'm doing?" I asked him, carrying the chair over to a large window.

"That's not going to work."

I hoisted the chair over my head. "You know I'm not bluffing. Either tell me how to get out of this apartment by way of the front door, or else I'm going out the window."

"Don't throw that chair, Tinder. And when you fail to listen to me and throw it anyway, for God's sake, duck."

I sighed dramatically and swung the chair back despite the protests of both my sore arms, then launched it at the window. It ricocheted right back to me, striking me in the left arm. I cried out in pain and dropped to my knees, clutching my arm to my chest.

"Damn it!" Bane yelled. "Why can't you ever just *listen* when someone tries to tell you something?"

"You could have mentioned the windows were bulletproof, or whatever the hell they are," I ground out, taking a few deep breaths to manage the pain shooting through me.

"Did you break your arm again?" he asked.

"I have no idea. God that hurt," I mumbled, rubbing my arm gingerly. All of that had been completely exhausting, and I laid down on my side right there on the kitchen floor, curling into myself a little.

"You're not going to convince me to let you out by getting in a fetal position and acting pathetic," Bane said.

"Fuck you."

"Pithy comeback."

"Eat shit and die, vamp."

"It's cute how you regress when you're cross. Your temper always reminds me how you got your rather apt nickname." There was a smile in his voice.

I sat up and frowned at the ceiling, where the cameras probably were. "What if there's a fire? Did you think of that? You've totally sealed me in on the top floor of a highly flammable building. That's pretty irresponsible for someone who's allegedly trying to look out for me."

"There's not going to be a fire."

"There will be if I start one."

"You can't start a fire."

"Sure I can."

"You can't. I confiscated your lighter."

I patted my jacket pocket and swore vividly, then said, "You really raise being a control freak to a whole new level."

"Thank you."

"It wasn't a compliment."

"I know," he said. "But it's probably as close as I'll ever come to getting one from you, so I decided to embrace it."

I sighed and got up off the floor, scooped up the phone, and trudged back to the bedroom, where I collapsed across the mattress. "Good boy," he said, and I gave the ceiling the finger.

"I hate you Bane. I really, really hate you."

"No you don't. You want to hate me, but you're failing miserably at it."

"Now why would you say that?"

"Because you brought the phone with you when you went to the bedroom." I could practically hear his smirk.

I smiled sweetly at the ceiling and showed him the phone. Then I threw it as hard as I could against the bedroom wall, grinning with satisfaction when it broke into a hundred pieces. I flipped him off with both hands, then lounged against the pillows.

A muffled ring came from the nightstand. I sat up and pulled open the drawer. The phone was inside it. I pushed the speaker button with wide-eyed amazement and Bane said, "Oh, come now. I'm not *that* good. It's a second identical phone, not the first one reincarnated." I dragged my hand over my face and he added, "By the way, I'm glad to see you didn't re-break your arm."

"How do you know it's not broken?"

"You were able to flip me the bird with both hands."

"That's true. Let's see that again." I gave him the double-finger one more time, then pried off the back of the phone, removed the battery, and tossed it over my shoulder. I kind of expected yet another phone to start ringing somewhere in the apartment, but all was silent.

Too silent. After sitting there in the quiet for a while, I actually regretted ending our conversation. I was way too stubborn to put the battery back in the phone, though.

Apparently I'd fallen asleep yet again, and awoke feeling slightly less out of it than the last time. I got up and unconsciously did a quick weapons check, my hands going to all the spots on my body where I kept them concealed. Everything was in order. Then, because my mouth was really dry, I went to get a drink of water.

When I reached the kitchen doorway, I stopped short. Bane was seated at the little table, sunlight spilling across his broad shoulders. I'd never seen him in daylight before, for obvious reasons. It suited him in ways I could never have imagined. Warm chestnut highlights were brought out in his otherwise dark brown hair, and his pale skin was luminous. He looked up from his thin, silver laptop. The sun added incredible depth and sparkle to his green eyes, making them practically iridescent beneath their dark lashes.

He was so incredibly gorgeous, more beautiful than anything I'd ever seen. I didn't even know what to do with the overwhelming attraction I felt for him in that moment, so I went with muttering dumbly, "So, you own a daylight talisman."

"Of course I do." He was watching me closely, his expression guarded.

"Am I free to go?"

"No."

"I feel a lot better."

"It doesn't matter."

"Excuse me?"

"You saw what's happening out there, Tinder. The vampires are organizing, they're working together," Bane said, leaning back in his chair. "You're perfectly capable of taking on one or two at a time, but not five or ten. So until I figure out a way to make you safe out there, you're not going anywhere."

I stared at him incredulously. "So, you're actually proposing keeping me prisoner here, locked up in the Tower of Beige until you think it's safe enough for me to venture into the outside world? Are you *insane*?"

"I'm not *proposing* anything. I'm telling you how it is." He turned back to his laptop, tapping a few keys. Arrogant bastard.

"Screw that," I said, pulling my gun on him. "I'm leaving. You can either hand me the keys that'll get me out of here, or I can fill your skull with lead and get them myself."

"Your gun's unloaded," he said, still looking at the screen.

I checked the clip and growled, then threw the gun at his head. He caught it without even glancing up and set it on the table, then clicked a couple more keys.

This infuriated me, and I pulled two stakes from my jacket and flung myself at him. In the next instant, I was flat on my back on the tile floor, my hands pinned to either side of my head. Bane frowned down at me as he straddled my hips. "I don't have time for this right now, Tinder. I'm trying to figure out a way to help you, and it'd go a lot faster if you could stop trying to kill me for five minutes."

I glared at him. "I don't need or want your help. Besides, you're not helping anyway. What are you doing on that computer? Did you type *how to help Tinder* into Google? Nothing on there's going to do any good."

"If you feel you can cooperate, I'll let you up and show you what I'm doing. I think you might actually find it fascinating."

Despite myself, I was actually getting a bit turned on by being pinned underneath him. That was the *last* thing I wanted right now, so I muttered, "Fine. Get off me." He plucked the weapons from my hands and got up, tossing the stakes on the table before sitting down in front of his computer again.

"It's annoying that you don't take me seriously," I said. "You don't see me as a threat at all."

"What makes you say that?" His eyes were back on the screen.

"You're not even trying to keep those stakes from me."

"That's because I know you have no real interest in killing me."

"Oh really? Then why did you take the bullets out of my gun?"

"Because while you won't kill me, you *might* shoot me. I happen to like this shirt and didn't want it riddled with bullet holes." He adjusted the cuff of his dark blue button-down shirt as he said that.

I rolled my eyes and came to stand behind him, looking over his shoulder. A scan of an old, handwritten text was on the screen. "Yeah, that's fascinating," I said. "Look, I'm really not going to let you imprison me. So how about if you – hey, what is that?" He'd scrolled down in the on-screen document, revealing an elaborate symbol, concentric circles containing text framed by six smaller symbols.

"It's a protection symbol, but not the one you need."

"I don't know about that," I said, pulling up the other kitchen chair right beside him and spinning the computer to face me.

He swiveled the laptop back toward him, but only partway, so we could both see it. "No, look here. See this part?" With a few graceful flicks of his fingers, he enlarged part of the symbol. "It's all wrong. It says—"

"I know what it says." When I read the Greek incantation out loud, he looked astonished. "It says that it protects the bearer of this symbol from all things supernatural." I read a little more and added, "Oh, I see. It specifically only protects females." He was still staring at me like an alien had just popped out of my

212

chest and I rolled my eyes. "You think I'm a total moron, don't you? You can't even believe I read Greek."

"I hardly think you're a moron. But your parents never bothered sending you to school, so it does surprise me that you can do that."

"I may not have spent my childhood rotting in a classroom and learning shit like Algebra, but my parents taught me plenty. For one thing, I learned to read six different languages proficiently and three more passably by the time I was twelve. And really, once I knew how to read, a formal education was pointless. Everything I'd ever need to know is in books."

"It's shocking that your parents took the time to teach five children so many languages. I always assumed they just taught all of you how to fight and then shoved you out into the field, from the time you were old enough to hold a stake."

I admitted, "Actually, they only taught me all those languages. I picked them up easily. Plus, I was the only one of their kids…well, with a need to read ancient texts." I looked back at the computer, sliding my finger across the touch pad to bring more of the document into view.

"You're referring to your ability to work magic," he said, and I nodded, not looking up. "Why are you embarrassed by that?"

I shrugged and said, "I dunno. Maybe I figure I'm enough of a freak already, without also admitting I'm part warlock. I mean, you want to totally alienate yourself from the human race? Go around telling people shit like that."

"It's always bothered you," he said gently, reaching out and brushing the hair from my eyes. "Not fitting in, living a life so separated from the rest of society. I hate the fact that you were never given a choice, or the chance to lead a normal life. I always wished I could change that for you."

I met his gaze. "You don't know me, Bane. This, right now, is the longest conversation you and I have ever had. Why do you always act like you have me all figured out?"

Bane smiled at me, which revealed his fangs. I almost flinched. It was easy to forget what he was as he sat there bathed in sunlight. "Oh, I don't have you all figured out, love. Far from it. But I've seen enough over the years to know your parents did you a real injustice."

"I hate it when you talk about my parents. You didn't know them either, and have no clue how they raised me."

"On the contrary, Tinder, I knew both of your parents. Not well, but I knew them. I actually have a long history with your mother's side of the family, going all the way back to Portugal. In fact, I was an acquaintance of Duarte Sousa, your great, great grandfather."

"You're kidding."

"He was the last of your ancestors to display a strong proficiency in magic, that's how I knew him. Magical ability at the time wasn't as rare as it is now, it hadn't been totally diluted yet by cross-breeding with the general population. So there was a small fellowship of warlocks in the parish of Alvor, including Duarte and me. He was an exceptional fellow. You're like him in many ways."

"Did he know you were a vampire?"

"Of course."

"So, why didn't he kill you? He must have been a hunter, all of my mother's family were."

"Oh, he tried. Many, many times. But he stopped after a while, when he finally realized I wasn't his enemy."

"Now why the hell wouldn't he see you as the enemy?"

"Because I don't kill people when I feed."

"But still. You're a vampire."

Bane said, "You and I are having a civilized conversation right now, despite being hunter and vampire. It was no different for your ancestor and me."

"Yeah, well, all that proves is that I'm kind of a dumbshit." A thought occurred to me then, and I asked, "Did you sleep with him too? If you say yes, I seriously think I'm going to puke."

He laughed at that. "God no. Duarte was hardly my type."

"Why not?"

"He was straight, for one thing."

"Well, thank God. That would have been really creepy."

Bane was still grinning as he turned his attention back to the computer and scrolled down a little farther. I watched his classically handsome profile for a few moments before turning my attention to the screen as well. After a while, he said, "I'm proud of you, Tinder. I really expected you to go ballistic, maybe try burrowing your way out of here with a soup spoon after I told you I was keeping you here. But you're handling this remarkably well."

"I'm just waiting for my moment. If I try to escape while you're here, you're liable to stake me to a wall again. Thank you for that, by the way."

"You're welcome."

"I was being sarcastic."

"I know."

I knit my brows at him. His attention was still on the computer. "Are you even a little sorry you did that to me?" I asked.

"Not in the least. You refused to listen, just as you always do, and I really needed to keep you in that office for a few minutes. What choice did I have?"

I rolled my eyes and commandeered the computer, turning it toward me and flipping quickly through the document. Bane watched me for a moment, then pushed back from the table. "I'll leave the laptop with you. There are over two hundred texts on witchcraft and alchemy saved to that hard drive. Should keep you busy for a while."

He started to leave the kitchen, and I asked, "Where are you going?"

"A team of my people are looking for the vampires that came after you, but they don't seem to be making any progress. I should get back out there and keep digging. I just stopped by to check on you and decided to do some research while I was here."

"You have a team of people?"

"I do."

"What, like minions?"

That earned me a smirk. "Like employees."

"Uh huh." I got up from the table and stood beside him. "Okay, let's go."

"You're staying here, Tinder. I thought I made that clear."

"No, I'm coming with you to hunt those vamps."

"Like hell you are."

"Try and stop me." That was an idiotic thing to say. Bane was at least four or five inches taller than me and maybe sixty pounds heavier – all solid muscle. And, of course, he was a damn vampire, which automatically made him much stronger than I was. We both knew he could stop me with no effort whatsoever.

Still though, when he headed for the front door I went with him, saying, "Don't do this, Bane. Don't lock me in here. All that's going to accomplish is pissing me off."

"It's for your own good."

"I'm going to do whatever it takes to escape, so you might as well save me a lot of trouble and just let me go."

When he opened the front door, I tried to slip out with him, and he picked me up and put me back in the apartment like an errant puppy. After we did this a couple times, I ended up fighting wildly, trying to get out the door. He scooped me up suddenly, tossing me over his shoulder in a fireman's carry, and took me to the bedroom. As he deposited me on the mattress, I misinterpreted his actions and growled, "I don't want to sleep with you, Bane."

"Oh, don't flatter yourself, love," he said, grabbing a pillow and tugging off the pillowcase. "Last time we had sex, you ended up pulling a gun on me afterwards. I believe you told me you'd rather blow your brains out than ever let me back inside you. Do you really think I'm in a hurry to bed you again after that?" Bane was ripping up the pillowcase as he spoke, and the expression on his face made me pause. He looked hurt, and for some reason that surprised me. Why had I thought he was incapable of that?

My sympathy was short-lived, though, canceled out by the fact that he grabbed one of my wrists and quickly bound it to the slatted headboard with a strip of fabric. "Oh, hell no," I exclaimed, and began struggling like a man possessed. This made it only slightly harder for Bane to tie me to the bed, spread-eagled and cussing at him for all I was worth.

When he finished (that had taken him all of about ninety seconds, even with me fighting him with all my strength), he sat beside me for a few moments and watched me. I was sweaty and panting, totally spent. He wasn't even slightly affected. "I'll be back in a few hours to untie you," he said, "though you'll probably free yourself before then. I didn't bind you very tightly. Once you do get free, please try not to hurt yourself in your futile attempt to break out of this apartment. It was built by a drug lord, a man even more paranoid than I am. All the walls are reinforced with concrete, and you already learned about the windows the hard way."

"Damn it, Bane, don't leave me like this. What if that vamp gang tracks me down here? I can't even defend myself."

"It's absolutely impossible for them to find you here."

"No it's not. They found me on top of a random building in the warehouse district, for Christ's sake."

"I have so many wards and spells surrounding this building that there's not a chance in hell of them tracking you here." He tilted his head slightly as he reached out and brushed my overgrown hair back from my face. His touch was oddly gentle for a man that had just forcibly tied me up.

"What if my nose itches? Or what if I have to pee?"

"You probably should have thought of that before trying to defy me and slip out the front door."

"I love how you make everything my fault," I grumbled.

He smiled at me, then stood up and headed for the door. "Everything *is* your fault, Tinder. It's your own stubbornness that gets you in all these situations."

I yelled and swore at him as he left the apartment, only stopping when I heard the front door click shut behind him. Asshole. I turned my attention to my right wrist and went to work on my bindings.

"I see you made good use of your time," Bane said, leaning against the kitchen doorway.

I was seated at the table, scrolling through yet another document that he'd scanned into his laptop. His collection of books on alchemy and witchcraft was truly astonishing, better than any I'd ever seen. I'd found a pen and paper in a drawer and had been taking notes feverishly, filling two legal pads and starting on a third. I'd learned more useful spells and wards in the past few hours than I had in the last five years combined.

But before I'd resigned myself to my imprisonment and sat down with the computer, I'd practically destroyed the apartment. I'd ripped off drywall (there really was concrete behind it), torn up floorboards, dismantled window frames and attempted to pry open the plexiglass windows. Despite all that demolition, I'd obviously failed to escape. But at least I found the surveillance system, which I'd torn out of each room and heaped in a big pile on the kitchen counter, right where Bane would be sure to see it.

"Can I leave yet?" I muttered, not looking up from the screen.

"No."

I knit my brows and picked up a pen, quickly sketching an ancient Phoenician protection symbol. He came up beside me and flipped through my notes. "You know," he said, "you're going about this all wrong."

"Go to hell."

He ignored that and told me, "Every tattoo on your body and all the wards protecting your home concentrate on defense, not offense. Instead of merely making yourself immune to, say, being compelled, or impossible to detect with a locator spell, why not employ some spells and symbols that make you stronger? That way, you wouldn't be totally outgunned by your enemies."

"I would if I could, Captain Obvious," I murmured, putting the finishing touches on the symbol I was copying. "But I've never seen anything that can do that. I'm not even sure symbols like that exist."

He pivoted the computer to face him. I protested and tried to take it back, but he caught my flailing hand by the wrist as he clicked a few keys. "Oh, they exist.

You just haven't had access to the right resources." He swung the laptop in my direction as he let go of me.

The symbol on the screen made me catch my breath. It was totally unique and beyond intricate, written in a language I'd never even seen before – and given how many ancient texts I'd perused over the course of my life, that was pretty remarkable. The closest thing I could compare it to was a Celtic knot, the lines of text interwoven in elegant arcs and swirls, the whole thing coming together into a roughly oval shape.

Since the writing was tiny, I tried to zoom in as much as I could, then ended up having to cursor left and right, up and down, looking for patterns in the symbols. "Definitely more than twenty six letters in this alphabet," I murmured.

"There are thirty," Bane said.

"What language is this?"

The guttural sound he made was something like, "Varsrescht."

I turned to him and raised an eyebrow. "What the hell was that, Klingon?"

He grinned a little. "Not exactly."

I looked at the symbol again, running my fingers over the screen, getting frustrated because it was so hard to follow the twisting and turning lines of text. "Damn, I wish I could get a better look at this," I muttered, mostly to myself.

Bane considered that for a moment, then said, "Well, you can if you want to." He began to unbutton his shirt.

"What are you doing?" I asked suspiciously.

"You'll see."

He stripped himself to the waist, tossing his dark blue shirt onto the tabletop. Desire spiked in me immediately at the sight of his muscular chest and huge shoulders and arms. That earned me a smirk. "You forgot to tell your body that you never want to sleep with me again," he said. "I can smell it the moment you become aroused, you know. Don't think I failed to notice your arousal when I pinned you down earlier, either."

"You're such an ass."

"I'm merely pointing out the obvious, love."

"So am I."

Bane grinned at me, then said, "Bear with me a moment, please." He closed his eyes and began speaking quietly in what had to be that same rough language. It almost seemed like he was praying, though most likely he was reciting some sort of incantation. When he opened his eyes, he took both my hands in his and said something else. It felt as though a mild electrical current passed between us.

I pulled my hands back and asked, "What are you doing?"

"Giving you an all-access pass."

"Huh?"

"Taking down a few of my wards," he said, then spun around in his chair, turning his back to me. "Run your hands over my skin and you'll see what I mean."

That request sounded odd as hell, but I gave it a shot anyway. I swiped my palm quickly down his back and for just a moment, his skin lit up like a Christmas tree. Something big and dark appeared and then disappeared in the wake of that light show. I gasped in surprise as he said, "Slower, Tinder."

I lined up both hands, fingertip-to-fingertip, and ran them very slowly down the expanse of his skin from shoulder to waist, light spilling out between my fingers. A huge tattoo became visible in their path, the exact symbol I'd been studying on the computer. "Oh wow," I murmured, running my fingertips along the lines of text. "Where does it start?"

"Try to find dead center and trace it to the left."

I looked closely, then touched my index finger to a spot on his spine. I traced the pattern a few inches, then returned to the center and said, "Can you please tell me what it says, so I can get a feel for the language?"

He began to speak, slowly and distinctly, and I followed along for a few minutes, learning which sounds to assign to the letters. After a while, I asked him to start over in English and began to get a sense of how the language translated. I sounded out a few words under my breath, and he chuckled a little and said, "I feel like the Rosetta Stone. And you really do have an amazing gift for language, I can't believe how quickly you're assimilating it."

"How can there be a language I've never heard of?" I asked. "Well, unless it's a dorky made-up one, like Esperanto or something."

He glanced over his shoulder at me. "Oh, it isn't made up. It's part of a rich culture dating back many, many centuries."

"A rich, never-heard-of culture. Why can you speak it?"

"Because it's the language of my people."

"Your people? I wasn't aware that East-Enders had started speaking Klingon."

He chuckled at that. "Not the culture I was born into, the culture into which I was reborn."

"The culture…wait a minute, is this some kind of vampire language?"

"It is exactly that."

"There's no way," I said, leaning back in my chair. "If there was such a thing, I would have heard of it before now."

"No offense, dearest, but all you really know about vampires is where to shove the stake. We were a grand society, once upon a time. We not only had our own language, but also many beautiful customs, traditions, and celebrations. They're almost all forgotten now."

"A vampire society is pretty hard to believe, given how solitary they are."

"When my kind became hunted and our numbers dwindled, we disappeared, scattered to the far corners of the earth to avoid total extinction. That became the norm after a while, never gathering in groups to avoid attracting attention, blending in with the human population so we wouldn't be slaughtered. We wiped out every written record of our history, tried to be forgotten. To some extent, it worked. Most humans don't even think we exist these days. Only hunters remember, since their history is woven with ours."

The tattoo had almost completely faded out by now, only faint traces of it remaining on his smooth, pale skin. He started to reach for his shirt, but I put my hands on his back, light immediately spilling out between my splayed fingers. "Wait. Please? Just a little longer."

"One more minute," he said and I ran my hands over his back, again making the tattoo visible. Starting at the beginning of the inscription, I repeated the incantation once more, quietly, trying to commit some of the language to memory.

He actually let me do this for another five minutes before grabbing his shirt and pulling it on, saying, "Ok, enough of that."

"So, what exactly does this symbol do for you?" I asked.

"It amplifies my strength and speed considerably. I'm not suggesting this is the symbol for you, by the way. It only works on vampires. I just wanted to show you that symbols like this do in fact exist, and I know we can find you a human equivalent."

"Can you teach me more Varsrescht?"

"Not now. We're wasting too much time on this."

"It's fascinating, though. Can I please have just a few more minutes to study that symbol?" I asked, lightly touching his chest. The skin beneath my fingers flared with white light, and when I pulled my hand away, a portion of a tattoo appeared and then began to disappear. "You have more," I exclaimed. "Can I see them?"

"No." He turned his attention to the computer.

"Why are your tattoos concealed from view?"

"Because if my enemies can't read my protections, they can't counteract them. You should consider doing the same with your tattoos."

"Yeah, I'm pretty sure that kind of spell is beyond my pay grade."

"I can show you how to do it sometime."

I watched him for a few moments, then asked, "What are you doing?"

He concentrated on the laptop, then said, "I don't know where exactly you'll find the right thing to make you stronger, but I have a few guesses and am pulling up some documents for you. Promise me, though, that before you start randomly inking symbols all over your body, you'll check with me first. Half your existing tattoos are either unnecessary or completely redundant."

I sighed at that, then watched Bane's profile for a few moments before saying, "Can I ask you a question?"

"Just did."

"Don't be an ass."

"Sorry. Go ahead."

"Why are you so willing to turn on your own kind?" I asked. "I mean, here you are, waving your vamp pride flag and going on about your race's rich history and culture. But then you're also helping me, aiding and abetting the vamps' Public Enemy Number One."

"Number two, actually."

"What?"

"Vampires are systematically targeting everyone in California that they consider a threat. Since you're one of the few purebred hunters out there, and a bit of a legend, you're near the top of their hit list. But you're not quite in the number one position."

I raised an eyebrow at that. "There's literally a hit list?"

"There is indeed. It's like the FBI's ten most wanted, with photos, descriptions, bits of information. They've been distributing it all over the state." That explained why the vamp in Santa Barbara seemed to recognize me, he must have seen my photo.

"Is Lee on that list?"

The question seemed to annoy him. "Why yes. Your big, dumb playmate is number seventeen."

"I need to see that list, so I can warn the other hunters that are on it," I said. "Can you get it for me?" He clicked a few keys and pulled up a file, then turned the computer toward me. "Really? Is that it?"

"It is."

The document was entitled 'Seek and Destroy.' Subtle. It began with a brief paragraph explaining that the list included the biggest threats to the vampire race in California, and made it clear that everyone it named should be exterminated with extreme prejudice. I scrolled down and revealed the photo of the person at the top of the list. It was a picture of Bane.

"Oh God," I muttered, reading the physical description and the few facts about his known whereabouts that followed. When I scrolled a little further, a picture of me came up, the number two beside it. It was actually my old driver's license photo. It had been taken about four years ago, but I hadn't changed much. Since I'd used a fake name and address, I really wondered how the vamps had identified that as me. I read what little information they had on me, then said, "I'm five-eleven, not five-ten." Bane grinned, and I asked, "When did this list come out?"

"A couple weeks ago. I'm not sure if it's been very effective. Even with their photos and descriptions out there, hunters tend to slip under the radar."

"But we're not used to being hunted, it caught me off guard when those vamps came after me. I need to figure out how to contact the people on this list and warn them." I had no idea how I was going to do that, though.

I went through the rest of the document quickly. The list included thirty-six names, not all of which had accompanying photos. I had either met, or at least heard of, almost all of them. The people at the top of the list, except for Bane, were all full-blooded hunters. Those farther down in the rankings were for the most part partially sighted, like Lee. Fortunately, his photo was grainy and out of focus, and his location was listed just as Southern California. "Now how on Earth do the vamps know who has the sight and who doesn't?" I murmured.

"They don't. The people on this list are ranked according to how big a threat they're perceived to be. That just happens to correlate with the second-sight gift that true hunters have. A few people on that list aren't natural-born hunters at all, just amateurs that have gotten good at killing vampires."

"So, why are you at the top of this list?"

He said, "Because there's only one thing vampires hate more than hunters."

"Traitors?"

"Exactly. When I turned on my people, I signed my own death warrant. I knew that would happen."

"If you knew it would happen, why did you turn on them?"

"Do you really not know the answer to that, Tinder?" Bane asked quietly, pivoting the computer toward him.

"No, not really. I mean, you're clearly some kind of vigilante, but I have no idea why you fight other vamps."

He kept his eyes on the screen as he said, "Once I fell in love with a hunter, I really had no choice."

"Do you mean me?"

Now he turned his head to look at me, brows knit. "Who the hell do you think I mean?"

I stared at him, totally dumbstruck. No one had ever told me they loved me, not once in my entire life.

Not my parents or grandparents, people that really should have. Not any of my brothers and sisters. Certainly not friends or boyfriends, since I never really had any of those. "You love me?" I said dumbly, and he nodded. After a moment of letting that sink in, I asked quietly, "Will you say it to me?"

"Seriously?"

"Please?"

He looked like he wanted to protest, a sarcastic remark right on the tip of his tongue. But after a moment, he released the tension in his shoulders and sighed. Then he said, "I love you, Tyler. I absolutely, totally, unequivocally love you."

He seemed defeated somehow. When he met my gaze, there was both sadness and raw vulnerability in his beautiful green eyes. It dawned on me that he completely expected me to reject him, that he was just waiting for me to throw his confession back in his face.

But no way would I do that, not when those words meant so much to me. I climbed onto his lap and wrapped my arms around his shoulders. I really didn't know what to do, this was all so new to me, so I just whispered, "Thank you," because that felt right. Bane pulled back to look at me. Most likely, he was searching for sarcasm or insincerity. He wouldn't find either one. After a moment's hesitation, his arms came up to embrace me.

We held each other for a while and then I kissed him gently. When Bane deepened the kiss, it felt like an 'on' switch had been flipped inside my body, every part of me awakening. It was far more than just arousal. I spent so much time with my emotions disengaged, just doing what I had to do – hunting, surviving, and the next day, repeating the process all over again. I usually didn't allow myself to feel, not really, because if I did, loss and sadness and loneliness would just swallow me whole. But I let myself feel everything now and it was amazing, like waking up after a dark winter's hibernation.

"Please fuck me, Bane," I said softly as I tangled my fingers in his dark hair and rested my forehead on his.

He kissed me tenderly before pulling back to look at me and saying, "You'll just regret it if we have sex again."

"No I won't."

"It's a bad idea," he said, lifting me off his lap and setting me on the kitchen table as he got up. "You really will regret it and you'll end up despising me as a result. I think it's best if I go."

"No!" I hated how pitiful and desperate that single syllable sounded. But still, I grabbed onto his sleeve as I jumped off the table, then put my arms around him, holding on tightly.

"What are you doing, Tinder?"

"Begging you not to leave."

He grinned a little. "You're going to hate yourself for that later."

"I don't care."

He kissed the top of my head. "I'll call you in a few hours and let you know if I've made any progress tracking down the vampires that came after you." He untangled himself from me and left the kitchen.

"Please stay," I said as I trailed after him.

"No. I'm not going to add to your regrets."

"I *wanted* to regret it last time we slept together, Bane. And it really did throw me off at first, maybe because it was just so far from anything I'd ever imagined myself doing," I said as I followed him down the hall. "But since then…since then it's all I can think about. I haven't been regretting it, I've been *craving* it. I've been going out every night, giving myself to whoever will have me, chasing that feeling I had when I was with you. But it's never right, it's never enough. None of those other men could give me what I needed, because none of them are *you*."

He'd reached the front door and turned to look at me, brows knit. "You said you'd rather kill yourself than sleep with me again."

"I'm so sorry I said that." Conflict churned in his eyes. I could practically see his rebuttal building, and pre-empted it by saying, "Please let me make it up to you." I dropped to my knees, still maintaining eye contact, and quickly unfastened his belt and his jeans, then mouthed his bulge through the thin fabric of his sexy black briefs. A moan escaped him and I tugged down the front of his underwear and took his heavy cock in my mouth.

The moment I started sucking him, Bane visibly relaxed, exhaling slowly and reaching out to touch my hair. I kept looking up at him as I worked his cock with my hands and mouth, feeling him swell between my lips, the connection between us so powerful as I held his gaze.

When I slid my hands to his butt and deep-throated him to his balls, that was enough to turn him from controlled and calm to fiery predator. He actually growled as he grabbed me and pulled me up to him, crushing my mouth in a demanding kiss as he shoved my leather jacket off my shoulders and onto the floor.

He carried me to the bedroom and threw me on the mattress, then started to reach for my waistband, but I said, "Wait." He paused, watching me warily. I fumbled for the buttons on my 501s with shaking hands, saying, "I don't have that many pairs of jeans, I want to keep these." Last time, he'd torn my clothes right off of me. He grinned and grabbed one of my feet, then untied my boot and yanked it off, tossing it over his shoulder before doing the same with the other one.

I stripped myself naked, then got on my back on the mattress. My body was shaking with anticipation, my cock throbbing and leaking precum onto my belly, and he watched me closely, hungrily, as he undressed. God, he looked good. He was pure power and strength, so incredibly beautiful.

241

Despite my intense longing, I remained perfectly passive, laid out for him on the bed. As soon as he was naked, he grabbed me by the shoulders and pulled me to the edge of the mattress, so far that my head hung over the edge. He wrapped a hand around my throat and I opened my mouth, completely giving myself over to him. I knew this was going to be violent. I knew it was going to push me to my limit. I welcomed it.

He slid his cock all the way into my throat as I concentrated on relaxing and taking every inch of him. He growled again as he began thrusting into my mouth. It started to feel a little scary and out of control, but I just let go, putting myself completely in Bane's hands. The moment I surrendered to him was pure bliss, all fears and anxiety falling away. All that was left was Bane, and me, and such intense pleasure.

And then it got even better. Bane lifted my hips off the bed effortlessly, flinging my legs up over his shoulders, and took my cock between his lips as he continued to fuck my mouth. I gasped as he easily swallowed me to the hilt, then wrapped my arms around his waist and held on tight.

He changed his focus after a while. I moaned around his big dick as he let my hard cock fall from his lips, then ran his tongue between my legs. He began doing something to me that had never been done before. I gasped when his tongue probed me, opening me up. He stopped thrusting into my mouth, concentrating instead on fucking me with his tongue, and I actually laughed nervously at the overwhelming intimacy of what he was doing to me.

When he'd prepped me to his satisfaction, he spun me around so I was right-side up again. He pushed me up against the wall of the bedroom before driving his cock into me, his spit all the lube we needed. I cried out, but it was a cry of pure pleasure. Bane thrust into me fast and hard, his big hands around my waist, using the wall for leverage to really pound me. It was so damn good, so exactly right. I flung my arms and legs around him and held on, burying my face in his shoulder.

"Look at me." His voice was low and forceful, much different than his usual tone. I obeyed instantly, raising my head up and locking eyes with him. My breath caught. There were two distinct sides to Bane, the guy with a sparkle in his eye and a smirk always at the ready – and this one. He was pure vampire right now, his gaze sharp and predatory, totally focused. A little tremor went through me, but I didn't try to pull away – not that I would have been able to anyway. I just held on tighter.

After pounding me against the wall for a few minutes, Bane picked me up and swung me around, then deposited me on the floor on my hands and knees. I locked my elbows as he mounted me from behind, trying to keep myself upright underneath his big body. He took me even harder in this position, driving himself into me so deep, one hand holding the back of my neck as I swayed and rocked beneath him.

His other hand slid down my torso and he began stroking my achingly hard cock, in time to his thrusts into me. "Oh God, Bane," I moaned.

"Cum for me, Tyler." My body actually obeyed him. I cried out as the orgasm tore from me, shooting clear across the floor. I thrust into his hand as hard as I could, impaling myself on his cock each time I rocked back. The orgasm just kept coming and coming and coming. My yells were hoarse, primal, and my body shook violently. The only thing holding me up was Bane.

"That's it, sweetheart." His voice was soft, and I realized as I came down from that blinding orgasm that his thrusts into me were slower, more controlled now. I whimpered a little as yet another shockwave pulsated through me, my hips bucking automatically. He still held my cock, but his touch was different now too, gentle and soothing as he brought me back down.

When that huge, devastating orgasm had finally reached its conclusion, he eased his cock from me and I scrambled around and desperately tried to grab onto him. "No! Please don't stop. I don't want it to be over."

He picked me up and kissed me deeply as he cradled me in his arms, then said, "It's not over, love. We've barely gotten started."

I smiled at that as he put me on my back on the mattress, then climbed on top of me. I parted my legs for him, and he pushed his cock inside me again. The sound I made was embarrassingly close to a sigh of relief. He laid down on top of me, propped up slightly on his elbows, and went back to thrusting into me, slowly, deeply. It was so good, totally different than the

245

hard, fast pounding he'd been giving me earlier, but still so pleasurable.

I reached up and touched his cheek, and he turned his head and kissed my fingertips. "This is the first time I've ever had sex in a bed," I admitted. He knit his brows and studied me closely. There was a note of sympathy in his expression. I rolled my eyes and said, "Come on. I was just mentioning it as a side note. There's no need to look at me like I'm pitiful."

He grinned a little and said, "That wasn't a look of pity. It was a look that said, I am absolutely determined to take care of you, far better than you've ever taken care of yourself."

I had to grin, too. "I'm never going to make that easy for you."

"I know." He leaned down and kissed me again, pumping into me slowly, steadily.

When he broke the kiss, I asked, "How old are you, Bane?"

He threw his head back and laughed. "So, you figure this is a good time to get information out of me, do you?"

I smiled at him, reaching up and lacing my fingers with his. "Maybe."

"Why do you want to know?"

"I've just always been really curious."

"I'm five hundred and sixty-three."

"Holy Christ."

He laughed again and said, "Anything else you've just been dying to ask me?"

"Why have you never filed your fangs down?"

"Because they're who I am."

"They must make life fairly difficult, though. It means you can never blend in with humans, you always have to remain in hiding."

"Far from it. Humans can't see my fangs because I cast a concealment spell centuries ago. One of the many perks of being born a warlock."

"Then why can I see them?"

"Because I built a loophole into that spell."

"What was the loophole?" I asked.

"I specified that anyone I fell in love with would be able to see me for who I am. I never wanted to hide my true self from whomever I loved."

"But I've always been able to see them, from the first time I met you."

"That's not possible."

"The first time we met, I was sixteen. You were already in love with me back then, you big perv," I teased, grinning at him.

He laughed at that. "Not true. I fell in love with you about three years ago."

"Uh huh."

Bane laughed again, then flipped us over abruptly so that I was now on top of him. He slapped my ass and I yelped in surprise. "You've obviously regained your strength," he said, "since your brattiness has rebounded considerably. No more going easy on you."

Bane began thrusting hard up into me, wrapping his hands around my waist and bouncing me up and down on his cock like I was a sex toy. "Oh God yes," I ground out, reaching for my cock and stroking myself.

His eyes were again sharp and focused. They were normally pale jade green rimmed in deep emerald, but the color had intensified somehow, become richer, brighter, almost lit from within. I steadied myself with one hand on his big bicep, feeling the powerful muscles

248

flexing and contracting beneath his smooth skin, and murmured, "I think you're absolutely gorgeous, August. I've never told you that. But you're the most beautiful thing I've ever seen."

He did another one of those lightning-fast moves that only a vampire could pull off, flipping us both around so that I was now sitting up against the headboard, my legs up over his shoulders as he pistoned into me. "Oh no," he said. "I'm not going to forgive you for being a brat. Not even if you compliment me and use my real name." He smiled at me and leaned in and kissed me. And then he began absolutely pounding me.

It was pure ecstasy. I was so lost to it that I could barely form words, though I think I did manage to mumble something along the lines of, "Fuck yes, fucking fuck me." Oh, give me a break, I wasn't exactly coherent at this point.

He'd really been holding back. Actually, he still was, because if he didn't, he'd probably snap me in two. But he began taking me much harder now, each thrust actually raising me a foot or two up off the bed. I cried out and flung my arms around his neck, holding on tightly. God it was good.

Bane's voice was low and forceful when he growled, "You're mine." I clutched him desperately and he pulled me up off the headboard and onto his lap, still pistoning into me mercilessly.

"Yes," I murmured, clinging to him. I would have agreed to anything then, absolutely anything.

He bit down onto the top of my shoulder, fangs tearing flesh, marking me, showing me just how completely he owned me. Acting on pure impulse, I bit him, too, my teeth bruising and piercing the skin of his shoulder, and he moaned with pleasure.

After a few more hard thrusts into me, he released my shoulder. Then he threw his head back and *roared*. There's no other word for it. It was unlike anything I'd ever heard before, strength and power transformed into sound. He flipped me onto my back as he began cumming in me, and it was so incredibly arousing that I came too, yelling and arching up, my cock pressed between his belly and mine.

Another bestial yell tore from him, every muscle in his shoulders, arms and chest starkly defined as he thrust into me with barely contained violence, filling me with his seed, showing me I was his yet again. He kept thrusting into me until every last drop of his cum was inside me, slowing his pace gradually before finally going still. By this point I was sweating and shaking, my body totally depleted, hugging him to me with the very last of my strength.

He kissed me gently before easing out of me, and rolled us over so I was laying on top of him. "You okay?" he asked.

"So much better than okay," I murmured, eyes shut. I was still shaking and he pulled the covers over both of us and held me securely.

"Under vampire custom, we'd be three-quarters of the way to married right now." There was a smile in his voice.

I raised an eyebrow and one lid, and asked, "How so?"

"You bit me during sex, right after I bit you. All we needed were a couple lines of verse after that, and you'd now be my lawfully wedded husband."

I chuckled at that. "Your wedding ceremonies involve sex?"

"Absolutely."

I closed my eyes again and nestled against him. "Your language sounds like Klingon and you screw while getting married. You know, if it wasn't for the whole murdering people thing, I'd almost think vampires were a fun bunch of guys."

"We're not all murderers, you know. I never kill when I feed, and the same goes for the vast majority of vampires."

"The vast majority? I don't think so. In my life, I've only met a couple exceptions. You're one of them."

"And have you spent much time getting to know many vampires?"

"Well, no, because if I'd ever tried, I *would have been killed.*"

Bane considered that, sliding an arm behind his head. "Well, in your case, perhaps. You *are* a hunter, after all. Most vampires probably really wouldn't give you the benefit of a doubt, just like you've never given us one, either."

"Why would I give the benefit of a doubt to a group of creatures whose main purpose it is to *kill humans*?"

"Did you know that vampire saliva acts as a coagulant?"

I grinned at that. "Um, no I didn't, but thank you for that totally random fact, Captain Irrelevant."

He chuckled and lightly swatted my butt, then said, "Vampires aren't killers by nature, and that proves it. After we feed from a human, all we have to do is lick the spot where we've bitten them and it closes up immediately. If we were meant to kill, why would our saliva and our blood heal? We *are* meant to feed on humans, obviously, but it's supposed to be a symbiotic relationship."

"Think so, huh?"

"I know so."

"Did you come up with this symbiotic theory on your own?"

"No. It used to be a cornerstone of vampire culture, many, many centuries ago. Since we were so much stronger, in return for your blood we defended the human race. That was the natural order."

"So, what happened?"

"Your kind tried to enslave us. We were always greatly outnumbered, even back then, and humankind began to see our strength as something to be exploited. Why send humans down into a mine, for example, when one vampire could do the work of fifty while surviving in toxic conditions? Eventually, of course, the vampires rebelled."

"So, it's all our fault."

"Well, a lot of it *is* humankind's fault, but not all. There have always been vampires unwilling to go along with the status quo, both then and now. Some believed we were superior to humans, meant to be the dominant race on this planet. Occasionally, one of those individuals would become a leader, attracting followers, gaining more and more momentum. But it always backfired. The humans rose up, organized, and learned to fight us. We have the strength, but they have the numbers. They've been winning the war for centuries now, and the result is the world we live in today – vampires forced to hide, to live in secret or risk execution."

My eyelids were getting heavy and I settled into Bane's arms as I said, "What's happening right now with the vampires, the way they're organizing – that's not just random. They have a leader, don't they?" He didn't answer me, so I muttered, "I mean, they would have to. They didn't all just happen to run into each other at Costco one day and say, 'hey, I know, let's team up, start hunting in packs and go after the hunters.' There has to be someone behind all of that."

"Get some sleep, Tinder."

I really didn't have a choice, I was already drifting off. He got up, pulling the covers over me, and I murmured, "What are you doing? Come back to bed."

"I have things I need to do, love," he said, scooping up his clothes. "I need to find out where my men are on tracking down the vampires that came after you. I'll be back in a few hours."

"You're dodging my question. You know who's leading the vamps, don't you?"

"We'll talk later."

"No we won't. You'll just dodge again." He sighed and headed for the door, and I murmured as I drifted off, "Be careful."

When I awoke several hours later, I called Bane's name, even though there was really no need to do that. The apartment felt empty, somehow. I knew he wasn't here.

I stared at the ceiling for a while, thinking back over the past few earthshattering hours. I felt amazingly good. Which is to say, my body ached in a hundred places, but it was the best kind of ache, one that reminded me I'd been well and thoroughly fucked. I grinned and played the highlight reel over in my mind a few times.

But then, gradually, a bit of doubt began to creep in as my afterglow receded. It had meant so much to me when Bane told me he loved me. I hadn't even realized how much I needed to hear someone say that to me, until someone finally did. Deep down though, I wasn't sure I believed him.

Those magic words weren't the reason I'd had sex with him again, by the way. I'd always been incredibly attracted to Bane, no matter how much I tried to fight it, and had been looking for an excuse to let my guard down and sleep with him again. But now what? Were we on the brink of an actual relationship? I couldn't imagine myself in a relationship with anyone, let alone a vampire. How was that supposed to work? How could I live with the hypocrisy of hunting vamps day in and day out, then coming home to one in my bed?

Even if I could come to grips with that and somehow learn to separate Bane from my job, there was still the issue of trust. I wanted to believe him when he said he had my back, and when he claimed to care about me. But how could I ever really trust a vampire?

There were too damn many questions, and no real answers.

Eventually, I rolled out of bed, feeling slightly deflated. I showered and got dressed, and wondered if I should wait for Bane to return. But there were things I really needed to do, so I headed for the front door. When the alarm went off, I jumped back, completely startled. What the hell? I pressed my hands over my ears and hurried to the elevator. It was still disabled. I ran over to the stairway, and found that the big metal fire door was still locked.

Seriously? After everything that had just happened between us, he was still locking me up against my will? And why was that so surprising to me?

Once again, the alarm didn't stop until I was back in the apartment with the door closed. A phone began to ring in the bedroom, and I ran to it and answered it with, "Are you kidding me?"

"You need to stay put, love," Bane told me. "I'm getting close to tracking down that group of vampires. Shouldn't be much longer, maybe only a day or two."

"Oh come on!"

"It's for your own good."

I felt betrayed. I really didn't know why I'd expected things to be different now, why I'd expected him to stop treating me like a child...but I had. As I sank down onto the edge of the mattress, I said, "I can't believe you locked me up again, after what just happened between us. After you told me you loved me."

"I do love you. That's why I need to keep you safe."

"You're not keeping me safe, you're keeping me prisoner!"

"Well, that wouldn't be necessary if you'd simply agree to hide out for a few days. I knew you'd never cooperate, though."

"Sane people don't hold their loved ones captive. You know that, right?"

"In your case, extreme measures are often necessary. It's not easy keeping you alive, you know, given how stubborn you are."

Anger boiled over in me and I yelled, "And now you're somehow making this my fault!"

"It is!"

"Damn it, Bane! Come back here and let me out."

"No."

"Christ, and I was actually contemplating having a relationship with you! I was willing to forgive you for so much, including staking me to a wall, for God's sake! But how can I forgive someone that treats me this way?"

"Treats you this way! Oh yeah, what a villain, providing you with a safe and comfortable penthouse apartment, in order to prevent a gang of murderous thugs from ripping you to shreds!" Bane was apparently behind the wheel, because there was the faint sound of tires squealing in the background, followed by some elaborate cursing on his part.

I got off the bed and paced around the apartment, eventually ending up in the kitchen as I said, "I don't believe that you love me. No way would someone lock up a person they love, under the guise of it being in their best interest."

"I've had to make hard choices with you, Tinder. Like I said, it's not exactly easy keeping you alive."

"So *stop trying*! I don't need your help. I'm more than capable of looking after myself, and I really don't appreciate you treating me like I'm a fragile little egg!"

"Excellent analogy, Humpty Dumpty, because without my help you'd be splattered all over a back alley in the warehouse district!"

"Yeah, you know what? If you didn't constantly feel the need to keep me in the dark about everything, I wouldn't have even *been* in the warehouse district! You could have told me what was going on with all those vamps in that warehouse, so I could stop digging for answers. Oh, and you might also have mentioned that my name was at the top of a damn hit list, so I would have known that I was about to go from hunter to hunted!"

"Even if you'd known about the list, you would have still been out there putting yourself in danger. You know that as well as I do!" Bane yelled. "Let's not forget though, *your* name isn't at the top of that list, *mine* is. And I sure as hell didn't get myself put on death row to then sit back and watch you get yourself killed. If I can do something to save your life, I'm damn well going to do it, whether or not you approve of my methods!"

I sighed in exasperation and pushed my hair back from my face. "I need answers from you, Bane. If you're really on my side, then prove it. Give me the name of the vampire that put the hit list together. It's the same person that's been getting the vamps to organize, isn't it?" I waited for a response, and when he didn't say anything, I yelled, "See? There you go again, withholding information!"

"If I did give you a name, you know what would happen? You'd go after him recklessly, totally undermanned, and you'd be dead before you got within fifty yards of him!"

"So in other words, you *do* know his name, and you're intentionally keeping it from me!"

"Of course!"

"You don't trust me, that's the bottom line. You don't trust my judgment, or my ability, or anything about me, really. And you know what? I don't trust you, either, Bane. Whatever the hell this thing is between us, it's never going to work out. It can't. Because without basic trust, we have absolutely nothing."

Instead of waiting for his response, I turned off the phone, set it on the kitchen counter, and looked around me. I had to get out of here. There was so much I needed to do, and I couldn't sit around until Bane arbitrarily decided to let me go.

In a flash of inspiration, a plan of escape occurred to me. I turned all four burners of the electric stovetop on high, found four big pots in the cabinet (why did a vampire have pots?) and set them on the burners.

When the bottoms of the cookware glowed red-hot, I picked up a big stock pot and pressed it against a corner of the thick plexiglass, holding it there for a couple minutes. When I pulled it away, I grinned with satisfaction. The window was slightly warped and melted. Just a bit, but it was a start.

I repeated the process again and again, switching out the pots, returning them to the stovetop when each one cooled. Some of the plastic began to stick to them and the apartment filled with a nasty smell when it burned off. I really hoped the fumes weren't toxic.

It took a while, but eventually I melted through the panel enough to kick out a section. I grabbed Bane's laptop and the note pads and zipped them up inside my jacket, then tried to squeeze through the opening I'd created. It was a tight fit, but I'd already spent way too much time on this. If Bane came back he'd stop me, so I had to hurry.

Ha! I was out!

And now I was on a six inch-wide ledge twelve stories up, and had to creep around the corner of the building, which made me nervous. I'd contemplated melting out a window closer to the fire escape, but figured the pots would cool down too much by the time I carried them across the apartment. This tightrope act was the price for that decision.

No one had to tell me that looking down was a bad idea. I looked straight up instead and tried not to think about where I was. It was predawn, and I concentrated on the faint grey light beginning to seep through the clouds. There was a breeze coming off the Pacific, the smell sharp and briny, its force strong enough to make me feel a little unsteady up here. Awesome. I inched along on the tips of my toes, trying to use my fingertips to somehow cling to the plaster façade, eventually rounding the corner of the building.

When I finally reached the fire escape, I exhaled slowly and eased myself onto the metal platform, then rushed down the ladder. If Bane was waiting for me at the bottom, I was going to be *so* pissed, because that would mean this had all been for nothing. But there was no sign of my captor as I hit the ground and started running.

It took over an hour to make it home on foot, my senses on high alert the whole way. At least most other vamps weren't a threat right now, not with the sun coming up.

If he was looking for me to lock me up again, Bane would of course go straight to my rental. Just in case he was already out front waiting for me, I approached the house from the rear, hopping my neighbor's side gate, then the fence between our yards. I stayed low as I crossed my dead lawn, picked the lock on the back door and let myself in.

I had taken half a step into the kitchen when Lee leapt out at me and yelled, "Freeze, motherfucker!" He was dressed only in boxers, a gun in one hand and a frying pan in the other, his short golden-blond hair sticking up in every direction.

"You really should have gone into law enforcement," I told him. "But I have to question your choice of weapons. With everything in your arsenal, *that's* what you went for? You planning to sauté an intruder to death?"

His body language relaxed immediately. "Holy hell, Tinder, you startled me. I just woke up, I ain't exactly thinkin' clearly. Where you been, anyway?"

"Long story. We need to get out of here, so get dressed and pack your things. I'll meet you in the living room in five minutes."

Lee did as I asked without question or comment. Meanwhile, I went to my bedroom, grabbed a duffle bag, and put Bane's laptop in it (yes, I was going to return it to him, just as soon as I copied all the files). The legal pads full of the notes I'd been taking went in the bag too, and I packed my few clothes before slinging it over my shoulder. I grabbed a second bag, which already held weapons and my books on witchcraft, and took a handgun from the top shelf of my closet, checking to confirm that the clip was full on the way to the living room. My roommate joined me thirty seconds later. We went out the front door (which wasn't an issue now that I had a loaded gun) and I locked up behind us before we ran for Lee's truck.

He drove us to a strip of seedy motels a few miles from the house and parked two blocks over to avoid totally giving away our location. We chose a motel at random. Apparently we woke up the desk clerk, and he handed us a key without bothering to count the cash I tossed on the counter. He was on his way back to bed before we'd even left the lobby.

Finally, when we were sitting on the sagging queen bed in the musty little motel room, Lee asked, "So, who we runnin' from, exactly?"

"Both Bane and a big vamp gang that might track me to the house." I filled him in on all that had happened over the last couple days, leaving out the part about sleeping with Bane. No hunter would understand something like that. Hell, I could barely understand it myself.

I pulled out the laptop and showed him the hit list, and Lee exclaimed, "Number seventeen! Screw that! I *know* I'm better than this yahoo in the number twelve position! And don't even get me started on number fifteen, she couldn't hit a vamp with a truck, let alone a stake! This list is downright insulting."

I had to grin at that. "So, you're upset because you're not higher on the list?"

"Damn straight. Plus, that's bullshit that only full-blooded hunters are in the top ten. My second sight is plenty strong enough to get the job done, I tell you what. It don't matter that I'm not a full-blood like you. No way should you be at number two, with me stuck way the hell down at freakin' seventeen!"

"Lee, this is a kill list, not a ranking for the hunter of the year award. Let's try to stay focused."

He frowned at me, but after a few moments said, "Yeah, okay."

"It sounds like you know some of these hunters. Do you have a way of getting in touch with them?"

"I have phone numbers for a few of 'em and I'll bet each one has the number for a couple more. We'll probably be able to get the word out to most of the people on this list."

"I want to arrange a meeting with as many hunters as possible," I said. "The vamps are organizing and we should, too. Maybe we can convince the hunters to start working in groups, or at least pairs, since that's what the vamps are doing. That'll improve our chances of survival."

"Good idea."

"It'd also be useful to swap information. Maybe someone's heard about the vamps' leader, the bloodsucker that made this list and that's getting them to work together. If we take him out, things might go back to normal."

Lee climbed up onto the bed and rested his head on a pillow. "Okay. We'll start making calls first thing in the morning."

"It *is* first thing in the morning."

"Not to our kind it ain't. Most hunters would've been out all night and will just be climbing into bed. They wouldn't be too receptive to anything we had to say right now, so let's just give it a few hours."

"Okay, you're right."

He held his arms out to me. "Come here, Tinder. You look as wore out as a flat tire on the side of a highway."

"I'm way too tired to fuck right now, Lee."

"I didn't say anythin' about fuckin'. Just come here."

After a moment's hesitation, I climbed up onto the bed and let Lee hold me, my head on his chest. It felt really good. It felt...*normal*.

What the hell had I been thinking, letting myself get close to Bane? To a damn *vampire*? I'd let lust and animal attraction take the place of logic and common sense, not once, but twice. I'd been an idiot.

Thinking about him was upsetting, so to distract myself I asked, "Do you really think the other hunters on that list will take us seriously and agree to team up?

Or are they just going to dismiss us as a couple dumb kids?"

"Hunters are a pig-headed bunch, that's for sure. But they'll listen to you, Tinder."

"What makes you say that?"

"Because you're a Reynolds, and a Sousa. Both sides of your family are legendary, no other hunter can boast that kind of lineage. I mean, hell, you're the closest thing we got to royalty," Lee told me.

"Oh, come on."

"I mean it. You're the real deal, Tinder. If anyone was in a position to step forward as our leader, it'd be you."

"Yeah, I don't think so. I'm no leader," I said.

"Not yet, but you could be. I really believe that."

After a while, Lee drifted off to sleep, still holding me. I tilted my head up and watched him, resting a hand on his chest, his heartbeat steady and reassuring beneath my palm. I'd always kept Lee at arm's length, afraid of getting too attached to him. Maybe that was because I'd already lost way too many people that I cared about and I knew I'd inevitably lose him, too.

But maybe I should stop pushing him away. Lee was already a friend, probably more than that, despite my efforts at keeping a barrier between us. He obviously trusted me. Hell, he'd packed up and left his home without so much as a single question, just trusting that I knew what was best. And he believed in me, he even thought I had it in me to be a leader. Maybe Lee should be a part of what little future I had ahead of me.

And Bane should remain firmly in the past.

Book Three: Destined

"Tinder!"

I rolled across the wet pavement, gasping for breath, and turned my head toward the sound of Lee's voice. He threw a stake to me and I grabbed it a split second before a big vampire landed on top of me. Instinctively, I lined it up with the vamp's heart. The fact that the pointy end faced up was dumb luck.

I turned my head quickly and pressed my eyes shut as the vampire disintegrated all over me. So gross! Because I was damp, it stuck to me in an ashy, nasty layer. If I lived through tonight, I was going to need a two hour shower.

There wasn't time to dwell on that though, because three more vamps were running at me. Lee had recovered his shotgun and managed to hit two of them, slowing them down a bit. They reeled from the impact, then turned and went after him. He was out of ammo and tossed the gun aside, so I yelled to him and threw the stake back. Lee grabbed it as the vamps closed in.

Meanwhile, I pushed the dusted vamp's clothes off me and scrambled gracelessly on my hands and knees toward my crossbow, which was maybe fifteen feet away. Before I could reach it, a hand clamped down on my ankle. I kicked as hard as I could with my free foot, making contact with the vamp's face. He yelled but didn't let go of me.

As he dragged me toward him, I searched my pockets frantically. Over the course of the last hour as we battled vamp after vamp, every one of my weapons had been used up, broken, left behind or forcibly removed from me. I kicked at the vamp again as he flipped me over roughly, his fangs bared, his eyes completely wild as blood ran down his face from his broken nose. I struggled with everything I had as he went in for the kill.

In the next instant, I was once again coated in a layer of creepy greyish residue. Lee stood over me, the big stake in his hand as the vamps' clothes settled on my legs, and said, "Dude, why'd you throw the stake back to me? You left yourself defenseless."

"You had two vamps coming after you and I only had one. You needed it more."

As he held his hand out to me and hauled me to my feet, he asked, "Do you think that's all of them?"

"Hell, I don't know. I thought we got them all after the first ten."

A pretty girl with short blonde hair jogged up to us and asked, "You both alright?"

"We're okay, Kira," Lee told her. "How about you?"

"I'm fine," she said, even though she had a huge gash on her left forearm that had been hurriedly bandaged with a bandana. "Either of you seen Stevie?"

"We thought he was with you," Lee told her.

"Come on, let's go look for my brother," she said. "He's probably with Rider." We recovered the few weapons we had left and ran through the dark, back into the heart of Griffith Park as it started to sprinkle again.

A few weeks ago, we'd managed to bring together twenty hunters from around the state for a strategy meeting. After that, some returned to the Bay Area to deal with hot spots that needed attention. Of the sixteen that stayed to work with Lee and me, three had gotten murdered last week, so now just over a dozen true hunters were trying to cover a huge area, from San

Diego to Santa Barbara. It was an impossible task. We'd begun nightly patrols in groups of four or five because hunting alone was suicide these days, and that meant we covered even less ground. Even working in groups, we still usually found ourselves outnumbered.

It was starting to feel so hopeless. No matter how many vamps we took out, it made no difference. The dynamic had totally shifted, too. It was no longer a matter of us trying to find them. Instead, they were coming after us.

The one positive was that it didn't seem like a lot of new vamps were being made. Instead, they were just converging here from all over. In the months after a vampire was first turned, they were far more animal than human: savage, uncontrollable and totally ruled by bloodlust. I was glad that wasn't what we were seeing, because newlies were a true nightmare.

"Stevie!" Kira dashed ahead of us. There were two humans up ahead, on the ground in a little clearing near the jogging path.

Kira's kid brother Stevie was battered and bloody but still breathing. The sixteen-year-old's head rested in the crook of Rider's arm, and he was brushing Stevie's hair back from his forehead. At twenty-five, Rider was a scarred, cynical veteran of the vampire wars. It was surprising to see him looking upset.

"He'll be okay," Rider murmured as Kira dropped to her knees and picked up her brother's hand. "I thought he was a goner for a few minutes there, but the kid's got a lot of grit."

A feeling of unease washed over me and I scanned the surrounding area. The park was heavily wooded in this section with a wide paved trail slicing through it. A flash of white caught my eye, way off through the trees, and I yelled, "Incoming!"

Rider leapt to his feet, stake drawn, and Kira threw herself down over her unconscious brother like a human shield. For just a moment a memory clouded my thoughts. I'd been five years old. My older brother Eddie had protected me just like that when our family was under attack, even though he'd been just a kid too. Somehow Eddie and I survived, but our older sister Jules wasn't so lucky. She'd bled out right beside us as I held her hand.

I shook my head to force myself to focus and grabbed a fallen tree branch, snapping it over my knee.

The end wasn't terribly sharp, especially since it was wet, but it was better than nothing. I also had one small stake left in my crossbow and I was going to make it count.

We formed a ring around the injured hunter and braced ourselves. My heart was thudding in my ears, my breath fast and ragged. I jerked my head to the left as another flash of white caught my eye. And another. And another.

They were close enough now so that the other hunters could see them and Rider muttered, "Oh shit."

Lee said, "Fuck, I count at least ten incoming. We're dead meat."

In the next instant, all of us were fighting for our lives. I took out the biggest vamp with my crossbow, then swung it like a bat and clocked another one with it. When he staggered a bit, Lee staked him, then ducked under the arms of a vamp that lunged at him.

It was total chaos. The entire clearing lit up like midday from my second sight. Rider dusted three vamps in quick succession, but more and more just kept coming. The first few we'd encountered earlier tonight must have put out a call, told their buddies where to find us. Fuck!

Kira was down in a low crouch with a stake in each hand, still trying to shield her brother, fighting with hell-bent determination and taking out vamps left and right. Rider, Lee and I were also fighting well despite our exhaustion, bringing down vamp after vamp. It didn't make a difference. They just kept coming, ten turning to fifteen, then to more than twenty.

I knew it was hopeless, but I didn't have it in me to give up. When both the makeshift stake and the crossbow were wrenched from my hands, I kicked and punched and scratched. A vamp grabbed my neck and I bit his hand, which made him yelp and punch me in the face. My vision faltered for a moment as I reeled from the impact and two vamps grabbed my arms. Oh shit, I was going to go out like a wishbone. I struggled wildly as they started to pull me apart, pain shooting through my body.

Abruptly, I fell to the ground with my limbs still intact and looked around. The vamps that had been about to kill me were nothing more than piles of clothing now and a new brand of chaos had broken out in the clearing. The vamps were falling, one and two at a time, the area getting darker and darker as they met their second death. I struggled to my feet shakily and we again surrounded Stevie, trying to make sense of what was happening around us.

Vampires were incredibly fast, but something even faster was moving among them. I caught a glimpse of a big, dark shape as two more vampires dropped, then two more. I didn't understand how something could give off no light at all.

The remaining vamps had forgotten about my little group of hunters and were trying to converge on the dark figure, which cried out in pain as they attacked it. There was something familiar in that cry and my heart leapt. I grabbed the big stake from Lee's hand, jumped over Stevie's prone body, and pushed my way into the fray.

I couldn't really see Bane, not even in the light cast by the other vamps, but by the way his dark silhouette was hunched over, I knew he was hurt. He was still fighting though, dropping vamp after vamp, right up until the moment he finally collapsed.

They swarmed him like piranhas on a sirloin. I staked my way through the remaining half dozen vamps in seconds, finally landing on top of Bane as the clearing went dark around us. He dropped his stakes, bringing his right hand up to lightly rest on my lower back as I put my head on his chest and struggled to catch my breath. "Ello, Tinder," he said. "I'd say you're looking well, but I'd be lying."

"Oh, because you look freaking awesome right now. Also, how the hell are you doing this dark shadow thing and holding back your light? It's really creepy."

"A little parlor trick I picked up somewhere along the way. Glad you like it. It's taking a hell of a lot of energy though so I need to let it go and concentrate on not bleeding out instead." His left hand clutched his rib cage.

"Am I hurting you by laying on you?"

"Like I'd tell you if you were." He relaxed a bit and gradually lit up beneath me with pure, white light. I disengaged my second sight and let my eyes slide shut.

That lasted about oh-point-two seconds. I'd actually forgotten for just a moment that there were other people in the clearing with Bane and me. Their startled yells brought me right back to reality, though.

I launched to my feet and grabbed Rider's arm as he lunged forward, stake at the ready. "Why are you stopping me, Tinder? That's a fuckin' vamp! Get out of the way!"

"No! This one's on our side," I told him. Lee and Kira flanked Rider, all three of them looking totally confused.

"On our side? What are you, high?" Kira asked.

"That's fuckin' *Bane*, Tinder," Lee said. "You been tryin' to kill him for years! I think maybe he found a way to compel you, 'cause you're actin' super weird right now."

I shook my head. "I can't be compelled, you know that."

"Then what the hell are you doing?"

"Didn't you see what just happened here?" I asked. "He saved our lives, every one of us! We'd be dead for sure if he hadn't shown up."

"We would have fought our way out," Rider said cockily. "We didn't need a damn vamp to save us."

"Uh, yeah, we did," I told him. "I was a nanosecond from getting ripped in half and the rest of you weren't doing much better."

"Bullshit." Rider started to go after Bane again. I pushed him back hard and he yelled, "What the fuck, Tinder?"

"Go back to the lodge, all of you. I'll meet you there later."

"We ain't leavin' you here, Tinder," Lee said. "It's not safe. You need to come with us."

He kind of had a point. I sighed and said, "Fine. Get Stevie back to the SUV, it looks like he's starting to wake up. I'll be there in a minute." Lee and Kira went to pick up her brother, but Rider still looked like he was itching for a fight. "I said *go*," I growled at him, staring him down. He clearly wanted to deck me, but after a few seconds Rider joined the others and they took off through the trees.

I returned to Bane and knelt down beside him. "Why aren't you healing?"

"Because I haven't fed in far too long."

"How come?"

"I'm on a diet. Wouldn't want to spoil my girlish figure."

I rolled my eyes at that and held my wrist to his lips as I said, "Try not to take too much. I might have to fight again tonight."

He took my hand in his and bit down. It only hurt for a second. I watched him as he drank from me. I wasn't used to seeing Bane like this, broken and vulnerable. He always seemed so invincible.

"Thanks for coming to help," I said quietly. "I owe you my life, and I know that's true for far more than just today. You've had my back for a really long time and I'm grateful for it."

He stopped drinking and frowned at me. "What the hell's wrong with you?"

"What do you mean?"

"You seem entirely unlike yourself."

I scowled at him and said, "Just shut up and drink." He was still frowning, but did as I said. After a minute I admitted, "I'm so damn tired, Bane. The situation with the vamps is totally out of control, and now I have this group of hunters expecting me to lead them. Me! As if I have a fucking clue what I'm doing! Stevie almost died tonight and he's only sixteen. Hell, we all almost died! If you hadn't shown up when you did, it would have been a massacre."

Bane licked my wrist to stop the bleeding, then sat up. He still held my hand. I didn't try to take it away. "I'm sorry I haven't been more help lately," he said. "I've been having a few difficulties. Somehow the Order gained access to my financial records, which led them to not only my home but also to all the safe-houses I maintained." The Order was the name the newly organized vamps had adopted.

"You *have* been helping, though. I know you have. You've just made sure I didn't know about it."

This was the first time I'd actually spoken to Bane in nearly two months, even though I often sensed him nearby and knew he was forever finding ways to help me. So much had changed during that time. The last few weeks had taken their toll on me, emotionally as well as physically, and given me a really different perspective on things. When life became distilled to nothing more than surviving and trying to keep the people that counted on you safe, there was no room left for pettiness and hurt feelings. That was why I just didn't have it in me to keep being mad at Bane.

When he didn't respond, I asked, "So where have you been living if your home was compromised?"

"Random hotels. I've been moving around a lot, every day or two."

"Bane, you need to get out of southern California. It's only a matter of time before the Order finds you and kills you."

"The only way I'd leave is if you came with me, and I know you'd never agree to that."

I sighed as I scooped up my crossbow and got to my feet. He stood up too as I said, "I don't suppose you're willing to tell me who's organizing the vamps yet."

"What makes you think I know?"

"I've heard the name Lucian a couple times. Does that mean anything to you?"

"No. Should it?"

"That's a hell of a poker face. But then, you've had five hundred and sixty-three years to perfect it." We stared at each other for a long moment before he finally broke eye contact.

"It's nice that you're speaking to me again," he said as he bent to pick up his stakes.

"I don't have the energy to be mad at you. I still don't appreciate you locking me up in the Tower of Beige though, in your misguided attempt at keeping me safe. And see? It wasn't as secure as you thought it was. The Order managed to find out about your safe-houses, so it's a damn good thing I got my ass out of there."

"You're right."

I cupped my ear with my hand and said, "Can you say that again? I didn't quite hear you."

He smirked at that, then fell into step with me as I headed back to the parking lot at the south end of the huge park. After a while I asked, "You're always watching me, aren't you? I feel you, you know, whenever you're nearby. I don't know how or why, but I do. I don't have a clue how you always find me, either. I've been through everything I own with a fine-tooth comb, there are no tracking devices. Whenever the other hunters and I change locations, we're so careful about covering our tracks. But no matter what, you're always close by. How do you do that?" We were a few hundred yards from the parking lot now and I stopped walking and turned to look at him. Any closer and the other hunters would see his energy signature and probably think they were being attacked again.

He turned toward me and just watched me for a long moment. Only a couple inches separated us. I took a deep breath, which caught a bit. My pulse picked up and I immediately began to get aroused, just from his proximity. His voice was low and seductive as he said, "Do you really wonder how I find you, Tinder, when the heat between us is this strong?"

Bane leaned in, his body now barely touching mine. It was hard to think, because my cock had cancelled out my higher brain functions. I balled my hands into fists to keep from grabbing him, but I couldn't quite stop myself from tilting my head forward and resting it against his broad chest.

God he felt good. Strong. Solid. I closed my eyes and breathed in his scent. All of Bane totally enveloped me and I let myself give in to it, just for a moment, feeling the attraction between us crackle and spark.

My breath was fast and shallow, my heart pounding as I whispered, "Really? This is how you find me?"

"No." He sounded amused. When I looked up at him, he smirked at me, his eyes sparkling mischievously. "What, you think you put out a sex beacon, like the bat signal or some such? What a completely daft notion!" He chuckled at that.

"Ugh!" I tried to push him away with both hands, but it was like shoving an oak tree. "You are *so* annoying!"

"I can just picture it. Your beacon could be in the shape of your cute little arse, silhouetted against the night sky. Instead of the bat signal it would be the butt signal!" He pantomimed two round orbs with his hands as he grinned delightedly.

"I really hate you." I turned and started to walk away from him.

Bane grabbed my arm and pulled me to him. In the next moment he was kissing me, deeply, wildly, awakening every part of me, my heart racing and my cock swelling as I grabbed him desperately.

When he broke the kiss, he smirked at me again. "You *wish* you hated me, love." He let go of me and stepped back, winking at me before sauntering off into the darkness.

He was right.

!

Everyone was looking at me funny. You'd think I would have gotten used to this over the course of my life, since I always stuck out growing up in far-too-cheery southern California. But the people staring at me now were hunters, the one group on Earth I should actually be able to fit in with. This sucked ass.

It was early afternoon and I'd just woken up. Rider had apparently been up for a while though, and had wasted no time telling everyone about the way I'd defended a vamp the night before. If he only knew about Bane's and my history. Scratch that, thank God he didn't.

I tugged my leather jacket to straighten it out, staring down the six hunters in the lobby of the abandoned off-brand-Elks lodge where we were currently hiding out, and snapped, "Yeah. I spared a bloodsucker's life last night, after he saved our asses by single-handedly wiping out about twenty vamps. If he hadn't stepped in, Stevie, Kira, Rider, Lee and I would all be dead, and all of you would be fucked because you

291

would have just lost more than a third of your soldiers. Bane is the only exception to our mission and if any of you encounter him, I expect you to do the same thing I did. He got to the number one position on the vamps' hit list by being our ally, so if you have a problem with me sparing his life, get the fuck over it."

"Sparing his life is one thing," a nineteen-year-old African American hunter named Jeffrey said. "But Rider said you and the vamp were cuddling. If we run into him, are we supposed to cuddle him, too?" Jeffrey grinned as everyone in the room chuckled.

"I fucking landed on him after staking my way through a dogpile of vamps. Rider's just being a douche." I went back to the room I shared with Lee, my quest for coffee forgotten.

He'd just woken up and was sitting on the edge of our bedroll, dressed in nothing but a pair of jeans. "Tinder, we gotta talk," he said. Never in the history of the world had those words preceded something good. I slid down the wall until I was sitting on the floor and mentally prepared myself for whatever was about to come out of his mouth.

After a pause he asked, "What am I to you?"

I answered without hesitation. "My friend." I'd tried to let this develop into something more over the last few weeks, trying to convince myself that getting involved with Lee was what I wanted. But at the end of the day, I just didn't feel anything more than that for him.

"That's it?"

"What do you mean 'that's it'? I can count my friends on one hand with plenty of fingers left over. Do you somehow think that means nothing to me?"

His expression softened a little. "I know it means something. I just...I wanna be more than that to you, Tinder. Not just your friend, not just your fuck buddy. You know what I'm saying, right?"

"I know Lee. I always told you though that I can't give you more than that."

He watched me for a long moment before asking, "Are you in love with Bane?"

"Where the hell did that come from?"

"I saw you last night, Tinder, the way you fought your way to him with every ounce of strength you had left in ya. Then, when you finally reached him and collapsed on top of him, and he put his arm around you...." He looked away for a beat, then looked at me again and said, "Do you know how fuckin' many times I wished you'd let me do that? Hold you after a fight, I mean?"

"I don't need to be held after a fight, Lee."

"You ever think that sometimes I do?" Admitting that clearly embarrassed him, and he jumped up and started to leave the room. I leapt up too though and grabbed him in a fierce hug. He tried to pull away at first, but finally stopped struggling and put his arms around me. "Fuck, Tinder."

"I love you, Lee," I said quietly. "Not the way you need me to, but I do love you."

"As a friend."

"Please don't say that like it's a bad thing."

"I know it's not. I'm sorry." He let go of me and stepped back with an apologetic little grin, trying to back-pedal his way out of what had clearly become an uncomfortable conversation for him. "I don't mean to be layin' all of this on ya right now, I know you got a hell of a lot on your plate. I just...I got jealous last night. I know I'm bein' stupid, though. I mean, no way on earth would you fall for a fuckin' vamp! I mean, *you*, of all people! Tinder Sousa Reynolds, a seventh generation pure-blooded hunter!"

I frowned slightly and murmured, "That'd be insane."

He chuckled at that. "Totally."

I chewed on my lip for a moment before saying, "We need to stop sleeping together, Lee. It's really complicating things between us and with everything that's going on, well, I think we both just need to take a big step back."

Lee had a pretty decent poker face, but a little disappointment slipped through anyway. "Yeah, okay. I mean, you're totally right. We both don't need any more complications right now. Just staying alive is complicated enough." He tried on a little fake smile and abruptly added, "Come on, let's get some coffee." I stifled a sigh as I followed him from the room. That conversation had been long overdue, but I hated hurting him like that.

A few more hunters had gotten up by now and some of them were clustered around a map in what had been the lodge's former dining room. Liz, who was the elder statesman of our group at twenty-eight and

Jeffrey's big sister, called over to me, "Hey Tinder, come take a look at this. We think we found us a new place. It's an abandoned shoe factory in Bellflower. My team broke in last night and checked it out, the thing's built like a fortress. It's on this street here," she said, running a short fingernail over the map. "Most of the other businesses on the block are shut down too, so we probably wouldn't attract much attention coming and going."

"Sounds perfect. Let's move over there this afternoon."

"Don't you want to take a look at it first?" she asked, pushing her long dreadlocks back over her shoulder.

"Nah. I trust your judgment." I spoke a little louder to address all the hunters in the room as I said, "I want everyone packed up and ready to move out by four o'clock sharp."

"Four? Come on! That's in like an hour and a half." That was from Colby, the chronic complainer of the group. I forgave him a lot, since the skinny fourteen-year-old was remarkably skilled with a crossbow and kept his head in a fight.

"I want us settled into the new place well before sundown, so we need to get our asses in gear. The usual drill, you're responsible for packing your own weapons and gear, but everyone pitches in with the mess hall and the arsenal. Spread the word to the whole group, wake them up if anyone's still sleeping." Everyone scattered immediately. I was always surprised when people actually listened to me.

"You sure we should be moving into someplace sight unseen?" Lee asked as we went to the kitchen. He'd adopted an all-business tone, which was good. He wasn't the type of person to let what had just happened between us get in the way of the job.

"I trust Liz's judgment. She has more smarts than ten hunters rolled into one."

I downed some coffee, then began loading the rows of plastic milk crates that lined the long counter of the industrial kitchen. Our supplies were pretty no-nonsense, mostly consisting of a bunch of canned food and ways to heat it up. With two of us working on it, the entire kitchen was packed up quickly.

Just as we were finishing, Kira came into the kitchen. It was obvious she hadn't slept, and she was still dressed in the same bloody, mud-covered clothes from last night. "Hey. How's Stevie?" I asked her.

"I don't know. I mean, I set his broken arm and he has some cracked ribs. That's all pretty standard stuff. But in the last couple hours, he's just been becoming more and more sluggish. I don't know what's wrong."

"Come on, let's go take a look," I said.

When we reached their room, Stevie was unconscious and pale to the point of looking grey, a fine sheen of perspiration on his skin. He didn't respond when we tried to rouse him. "Shit," Kira said. "He was awake when I left the room not five minutes ago. I need to take him to the hospital."

"Lee will go with you."

"There's no need for that," she murmured as she pressed a palm to her brother's forehead.

"I don't want any hunters out on their own. You might be there late and could run into trouble," I said. She was too distracted to argue. "We're moving, I don't know if you heard. I'll pack your stuff and ours. Get dressed, Lee, and meet us at Kira's SUV."

Lee bolted from the room and I gingerly lifted Stevie and his sleeping bag as Kira slung a backpack over her shoulder. By the time we reached the shed out back where her old Bronco was concealed and got Stevie settled on the back seat, Lee was at our side. "Call me when you hear anything," I told him, and he nodded as he jumped in the passenger seat.

After they pulled away, I closed my eyes and took a few deep breaths. Every time something happened to one of the hunters in my unit, I felt personally responsible. It was especially painful when it was one of the young ones.

"You look like you have the weight of the world on your shoulders, love."

I jumped a bit at the sound of Bane's voice. He was leaning against the far corner of the shed, out of sight of the lodge, dressed in a form-fitting black t-shirt and jeans. Every part of me took notice of his muscular body. "Even though I know you have a daylight talisman, seeing you out here like this still kind of throws me off." I walked up to him and added, "Would it be rude of me to ask what your talisman is?"

"I could show you if you'd like."

"Really? You'd trust me with that kind of information?"

He shrugged his big shoulders. "Why not? You can't take it from me, so what's the harm?"

Bane started to unfasten his belt and I raised an eyebrow. "What the hell are you doing? If you have a bespelled cock ring, I really don't want to know about it."

He chuckled as he finished unbuckling his belt and popped the button. "How would that even occur to you?"

"Hey, you're the one out here pulling your pants down in public. What am I supposed to think?"

He slid his zipper down, revealing a pair of little black briefs sexy enough to literally make me salivate. Then he pushed the right side of his jeans and the underwear down to just below his hip and said, "Give me your hand."

I had to grin. "As old as you are, let's hope this isn't your super-smooth attempt at trying to get a back-alley hand job. You really should have developed more game by now."

"I'm so sorry I told you my age. I should have lied, claimed to be a spry hundred and eighty-two. Though

300

clearly I have plenty of game, because you got turned on even before the pants went down."

"Well, hell, have you seen you? You're far too hot for your own good. You obviously know it, too. Just look at what you're wearing!"

"What about it?"

"Could that t-shirt *be* any tighter? Wait, let me answer that for you. No. No it couldn't, not even if it was applied with a can of spray paint!"

"It shrank in the dryer," he said.

"It did not."

"Okay, it didn't, but it could have." I rolled my eyes at that, and he unleashed his trademark smirk. "So sue me for trying to look sexy for you."

"For me? Come on."

"Who else do you think I'm trying to look good for?"

"How would I know? I have no idea what you do in your personal life. Maybe you keep a harem of sexy little twinks for your amusement and were trying to look hot for them. In fact, maybe you put on one of their little t-shirts this morning by mistake."

He stared at me like I was insane. "Because that's bloody likely!"

"It would explain the shirt in size elfin."

Bane stared at me for another long moment and finally said, "Do you want to see the talisman or not?"

"Yes please."

He picked up my hand, slapped it unceremoniously onto his hip, and muttered a few words in Varsrecht. Light spilled out between my fingers and when I took my hand away, I revealed a round tattoo about two-and-a-half inches wide. It was artfully done, four smaller symbols interweaving gracefully to make up one larger icon. "You're shitting me," I murmured.

He clicked his tongue and said, "I thought we already established that that's a vulgar expression."

"We did. Doesn't mean I'm going to stop using it." I looked up at Bane as he got dressed again and said, "I always thought a daylight talisman had to be an object, something like a coin or a ring."

"Usually."

"You're incredibly dangerous," I told him.

"Why? Because I might suddenly snap and tattoo up an entire army of daylight-walking vamps?"

"Exactly."

"I have no aspirations for world domination, love."

"You're also in all likelihood the only full-blooded warlock left in existence. The things you must be capable of!"

"Then it's a damn good thing I'm not a complete arse, now isn't it?"

"It's really irresponsible of me not to stake you."

"You know you don't want to. You could have killed me so easily last night when all those vamps overpowered me. Instead, you saved me." He gave me a big grin and quipped in a falsetto, "My hero."

I frowned at him and said, "I forgot to ask. Is there some reason you're lurking out here?"

"Indeed there is. The Order has begun compelling humans to seek out hunters for them, which means they have eyes everywhere both night and day now. That's why I'm watching your hideout, to make sure no one's sneaking about."

I leaned on the old wooden shed and thudded the back of my head against it. "We're so fucked."

"You're overlooking one incredibly powerful weapon in your arsenal, though."

"Do you mean you?"

Bane bowed at the waist with an elaborate flourish. "The world's last full-blooded warlock, at your service."

I chewed on my lip as I watched him for a moment, then said, "You know, you kind of have a point. But how the hell am I supposed to convince a pack of hunters to trust a vampire so you can work with us? There's no freaking way."

"The offer is there. Whether or not you choose to avail yourself of it is your call, of course. Now, aren't you supposed to be packing?"

I knit my brows. "How do you know about that?"

Bane smiled at me cheerfully. "It's so cute when you act like I don't know everything."

"I'm turning and walking away from you now, and I'm giving you fair warning. If you grab me again and plant one on me like you did last night, I'm going to punch you."

"Given the fact that our days are clearly numbered, are you really going to keep pretending you don't want me as much as I want you? Wouldn't it be so much better to give in to your desires and enjoy what little time we have left?"

"No."

"Get that punch ready."

"Don't do it, Bane," I said, taking a step back.

"And if I do?" There was that smirk I knew so well, paired with enough smolder to spontaneously combust a lesser man.

"I mean it. I have to get back inside. People are probably waiting on me, and—"

When his lips met mine, I practically climbed him. One moment I was talking, and in the next my arms and legs were wrapped around him as I sucked his tongue, my cock swelling and rubbing against his through our clothes.

Seconds later, I was being pushed up against the wall inside the old shed. I splayed my hands out and rested my forehead against the worn wood, bracing myself because I knew this wasn't going to be gentle. I grinned as heat and lust shot through me.

Bane managed not to tear my Levis off of me, but just barely. He got them unbuttoned and down around my knees in the time it took me to draw a single breath.

After pulling something from his pocket, he pushed two slick fingers inside me and prepped me roughly. "You were carrying lube? Presumptuous much?" I managed as I tried not to moan.

"Not presumptuous. Optimistic. There's a difference."

He freed his cock from his jeans and drove his length into me. His palm clamped down over my mouth a second before my yell of ecstasy went off like a tsunami siren. With his lube-slicked hand, he began to stroke my cock hard and fast, matching the rhythm of his thrusts into me.

Sex with Bane was all-consuming. Everything in the world fell away, except for him and me and the insanely intense pleasure he created. All I could do was brace myself against the wall to keep from getting driven through it and give myself over entirely.

Even though Bane was like a force of nature, that wild and powerful, he was also careful with me. Once he was sure I wasn't going to yell and bring all the hunters down on us, his big arm slid down around my shoulders, clutching me to him as his thrusts rocked me. He took us right to the edge of violence and held us there, ramming into me so hard, but not crossing the line and really hurting me. It was perfection.

"Oh fuck, Tinder. I love you so fucking much." Bane's voice was deep, rough. He pulled out of me and flipped me around like I weighed nothing, pressing my back to the wall and yanking my jeans off of me, right over my boots, which I wouldn't have thought possible. Then he pushed into me again, all the way to his balls, and claimed my mouth like he was claiming the rest of me. I clung to him as he fucked me and I came a few minutes later, my cock sandwiched between us, pressing my face into his shoulder to smother my cries.

He pounded me as I rode out that intense orgasm, my entire body shaking. Then it was his turn to muffle a yell against my shoulder. The sound he made was almost like a sob as he came in me, his arms wrapped around me tightly as he pushed into me again and again, filling me.

Bane was shaking too by the time he finished in me. He spun us around and sat down, leaning against the wall. I was curled up on his lap, his cock still deep in me, my arms and legs wound around him as he held me. God it felt good.

After a minute or two, I whispered, "Can you reach my jeans, Bane?"

"Not yet. Please? Don't get dressed yet."

"I'm not. I just need my phone." He pulled the Levis over to us by the cuff and I fished a small black phone out of my pocket. I'd gotten it for myself when I'd started working with the other hunters. There'd been no one to call before that.

I hit a number in my speed dial and when someone answered, I said, "Hey Liz. I decided to do some recon around our new neighborhood. Is everyone packed and ready?"

"Yeah," she said. "We're all good to go here."

"Move out in small groups as usual. Take Kira and Stevie's things with you, they had to go to the hospital. Leave the stuff that's in Lee's and my room. I'll swing back by for it and will meet you at the new place this evening."

"Not a problem."

"I want everyone to hang tight once they're set up in the new place, no one goes out hunting until I say so. When I get there, we're going to talk strategy."

"I'll let 'em know."

"Thanks, Liz." When we disconnected, I tossed the phone onto my jeans and put my head back on Bane's shoulder.

"Bet she'd love it if she knew you were talking to her with a vamp's dick up your arse." He tried to keep his tone light, but there was some hurt there.

"She'll never see that you're so much more than just some vamp. None of them will," I murmured.

We stayed right where we were as my team vacated the lodge. They were quiet and efficient, carrying our supplies out and loading their vehicles in a just a few quick trips. Bane got hard again as the hunters passed right by the shed, and he slid his hands down my back. He cupped my ass and began raising and lowering me on his cock, as if I was a sex toy. I fought back a moan, my eyes sliding shut.

He fucked me like this for several minutes as the hunters finished their tasks around us. One by one, their cars and trucks pulled out of the alley. When it was clear they'd all gone, Bane flipped me onto my back on the dusty cement floor and began moving in me, his face close to mine.

"I feel guilty for lying to them," I said softly as I looked up into his eyes.

"I know." He raised himself up a little and pulled off his t-shirt, then began undressing me, sliding my heavy jacket off my shoulders, still thrusting into me. When he pulled my t-shirt off though, he went still and whispered, "Oh hell, Tinder."

My body was a mass of bruises and there was a deep gash on my right bicep, held together with butterfly bandages. "Last night was a bad one," I told him quietly. "So was the one before that. Several vamps got a piece of me before I took them down. I'm really surprised I'm still alive."

He pulled out of me and sat up, gathering me onto his lap. "It has to stop, Tinder. You can't keep going out every night and facing down impossible odds. I'm doing all I can to protect you, but it isn't enough."

"Did you bespell me?"

"Yes."

"Thought so. Something felt different. What was the spell supposed to do?"

"There were two of them and they were meant to speed up your reflexes and make you more resistant to

310

injury. I'm still looking for spells to make you stronger and faster but I haven't found any that work on humans, only vampires."

"That explains a lot. I'd caught a few too many lucky breaks lately, surviving things that should have killed me."

He ran a fingertip lightly over a huge bruise on my collarbone and said, "I wish to God my blood would heal you without making you violently ill. I can't stand seeing you like this."

"It's okay. I'm used to pain." I relaxed in his arms as I said that, letting him hold me.

"I'm surprised you're allowing me to do this," he said softly, brushing his cheek against my hair.

"I seriously doubt I'm going to live to see next week, Bane. The way things have been going, I'm shocked as hell every morning when I'm still around for the sunrise. Don't get me wrong, I'm not giving up and I'm not going down without a fight. But in my final days or hours, I guess...well, I guess I'm cutting myself some slack. Instead of beating myself up over wanting you so badly, I made the decision to let myself have you, even if it's just this one afternoon."

He kissed me gently, then said, "Let's move inside now that the lodge is empty. That seems safer to me than our current location."

I got up, my legs a bit shaky, and Bane got dressed and gathered my clothes. Instead of giving them to me, he draped them over his arm, mischief in his eyes, and indicated the door to the shed with a 'you first' gesture. I wore nothing but my boots, and I said, "Really? You want me to parade around buck naked?"

"Most definitely. No one's in the alley, and it's only a few yards to the back door of the lodge." He flashed me a brilliant smile.

"You're sure we're alone?"

Bane nodded, still smiling at me, and I grinned a little and led the way out of the shed. When we got to the back door, I pushed it open, then turned to him. "I almost forgot, you won't be able to come in. I warded the building against—" he stepped over the threshold and I said, "vampires."

"I know."

"How do you walk through my spells like that?"

"By understanding where the loopholes are."

I shook my head, then led him upstairs to my room. When I reached the doorway, I stopped short. With his hugely heightened senses, the fact that Lee and I had had sex here as recently as a couple days ago must be screaming in his face. I turned to Bane and said, "I told Lee today that I'm not sleeping with him anymore."

His green eyes searched my face as he reached up and lightly traced my jaw. "I won't pretend I'm sorry to hear that."

Bane laid me on my bedroll and worked both of us back up gradually, exploring my body with his fingers and lips and tongue. I let myself remain perfectly passive, parting my legs for him, giving him whatever he wanted. I had this need to show him how much I trusted him, to at least give him that, after everything he'd given me.

Bane mounted me with one long, hard push. I winced, just a little, and he whispered, "Sorry, love," then held still inside me until he saw me relax. I locked eyes with him and gave him a smile, and he murmured, "My beautiful, beautiful boy." He began moving in me slowly, wrapping his arms around my shoulders, again holding me securely.

313

As his thrusts ramped up, I moaned and rocked my hips under him, trying to take his cock even deeper in me as I rubbed my straining hard-on against him. He fucked me hard and fast, until finally he threw his head back and roared, fangs bared, then bit my shoulder as he began to cum in me. I bit down on him too, totally by reflex, and that made him cry out against my skin and just pound me.

I rode him as he came and once he finished, he flipped us over so he was on his back and looked up at me, his eyes still wild. "Fuck me, Tinder," he ground out, his voice rough. I didn't need to be told twice.

I grabbed a bottle of lube from my backpack and prepped him quickly, then pushed into him as he grunted and spread his legs wide. I'd never topped before and it was disorienting and thrilling and it felt so damn good. I pistoned into him wildly, my body slapping his as I grasped his shoulders. I was already so far gone that it didn't take long for a massive orgasm to tear from me. I cried out as Bane moaned underneath me, grabbing my butt, pulling me into him as I came.

Finally I collapsed on top of him, exhausted. My sweat-drenched body trembled as my heart raced, and I used the last of my strength to wrap my arms around his shoulders. "I can't believe you let me do that," I murmured.

"Why not? I figured we'd both enjoy it." He pulled my old blanket over us and hugged me to him.

"Sorry I bit you. I don't know what keeps possessing me to do that," I told him.

"I can't even begin to tell you how much I love that. It feels like you're staking a claim to me."

I grinned and said, "Plus that makes us, what was it? Three-quarters married under vampire law?"

"Indeed. Just a couple lines of verse are all that's standing between you and me enjoying a lovely Niagara Falls honeymoon."

I chuckled at that. "Why Niagara Falls?"

He shrugged. "That used to be the thing you humans did. I'm not sure why."

"What are the two lines of verse?" I shifted a bit, settling more comfortably onto his broad chest.

He spoke in Varsrecht, and even though the language was inherently harsh and guttural, the lines had a nice cadence to them. I started to repeat them automatically, like I did any time I encountered a

315

foreign language, and he pressed a fingertip to my lips with an amused expression. "Didn't I just tell you what it means if you repeat that?"

"So to you, if I say those words, we're married. Just like that?"

"Just like that," he agreed.

"I want to learn Varsrecht. Will you teach me?"

"Why?"

"Because it's a part of you."

"I wonder if you realize how deeply you touch my heart at times." He sounded odd, and when I looked up at him there was sadness in his eyes. He pulled me close to him, his hand on the back of my head. "I love you so much, Tyler. Please forgive me," he whispered in my ear.

"For what?"

I didn't hear his answer as unconsciousness crashed into me from all sides.

"Get Tinder out of here!"

I heard Bane yelling that as I drifted out of a thick fog. My cheek was pressed against rough asphalt and as my vision came into focus I realized I was laying in the parking lot behind the lodge. Around me, people were fighting. I engaged my second sight to try to make sense of it all. A vamp landed right beside me and immediately turned to dust, the human who'd staked him jumping back into the fray.

Bane and two other vamps were fighting almost a dozen humans. It was still daylight, how were there so many vampires out here? The humans were built like the defensive line of an NFL team and didn't seem to be hunters since their attacks were all wrong. What the hell was happening? I tried to move, which was when I realized I was tightly bound from shoulders to ankles.

"I can't just leave you!" I tilted my head to look up at the vamp who'd just yelled to Bane. He was a stunningly handsome Latino with shoulder-length black hair, and he was crouched in a fighting position right beside me.

"That's an order, Allie! Go!" Bane bellowed that as he punched a huge guy in the stomach. Apparently killing these humans wasn't the goal, given the way he was fighting.

The vampire he'd called Allie scooped me up and threw me over his shoulder in a fireman's carry, cursing vividly. I felt like a football on the way to the end zone as he bobbed and weaved and several of the giant humans tried to tackle him. Finally we reached a black sedan and he chucked me roughly into the backseat. "Hey!" I yelled as I bounced off the door on the other side.

Allie got behind the wheel and floored it, the sedan launching forward with a squeal of rubber. I sat up and yelled, "What the hell are you doing? Get back there and help Bane!"

"Shut up," he growled, taking a wild turn that threw me against the door.

"Ow! Fuck! If you're going to drive like a maniac, at least untie me so I can put a seatbelt on!"

"I said *shut up*!"

"Are you seriously leaving him there? He's outnumbered!"

"I don't have a choice!"

"I'm staking the shit out of you when I get free, Al." I struggled wildly, looking down at the relatively thin silver chains that were wrapped several times around my torso and legs, pinning my arms to my sides. There was a very faint blue glow to them that was visible with my second sight, meaning they'd been bespelled. Fucking awesome. I also noticed I smelled like soap, was dressed in a clean t-shirt and jeans along with my boots, and my hair was slightly damp. What the hell?

He took another wild turn, knocking me over again. I wedged myself into the space on the floor behind the passenger seat and racked my brain for a spell to get free as the vamp shot me a look over his shoulder, then another one a few moments later. "How the hell can you be Tinder?" he asked.

"What were you expecting?"

"I don't know. A Greek god maybe, given the way August talks about you. Someone impressive, not a frail

319

little half-starved man-child. What did you do to get my maker to fall in love with you?"

"Your maker, awesome. And I didn't do a damn thing. Bane did that all on his own." I closed my eyes and began reciting a Hebrew incantation under my breath, over and over.

"What are you doing? Stop it!" Al sounded concerned.

"Fuck you." I went right back to the spell.

"I mean it, stop!" When I kept reciting he said, "Don't make me knock you out!"

"Bane will kill you if you hurt me." Again with the incantation.

"Son of a bitch," he muttered, then took a series of quick turns. I could hear tires squealing behind us. We were being followed.

The chains on my body loosened ever so slightly and I looked down at them. The blue light was gone, but I was still bound snugly. Damn it!

A couple sirens joined the party. "This is going to look awesome when the police catch you," I said, struggling against the chains. "Enjoy your prison term for kidnapping, Al."

"My name's not Al."

"I know, it's Allie. That's super butch, by the way. Don't let anyone tell you different."

"It's Alejandro, jackass."

"Nice to meet you, Alejandro Jackass. I'm just going to call you Jackass for short, m'kay?"

"God give me strength," he muttered.

By now, several more sirens had joined the procession. "What's the plan here, Jackass? Drive until you run out of road, then Thelma and Louise it off a cliff? If so, count me out. I'm not your Thelma."

"Would you please *shut up*? I'm trying to think and you're not helping!"

"I'm going to guess that's a bit challenging for you at the best of times."

"Oh shit! Brace for impact," he yelled as the car skidded. Before I could ask what the hell was happening, the sedan crashed into something. I was thrown around roughly as the front windshield shattered and the airbags deployed. "Fuck," he muttered as we landed with a sharp jolt.

Not two seconds later, he'd pulled me out of the car, thrown me over his shoulder again and taken off in a stunningly fast sprint. By the time I raised my head, we were halfway down the block. I caught a glimpse of the crumpled sedan inside the store front of an abandoned gas station. Four police cars skidded to a halt around the building and a black sports car stopped right behind the sedan.

Jackass kept sprinting for several more blocks before finally ducking into a garage with a broken-down truck off to one side, sunlight filtering in through one dirty window. When he set me down unceremoniously, I tipped over onto my ass. "We need to go back and help Bane," I told him as I struggled with the chains and managed to get one hand out from under them. It was easier now that they weren't bespelled to hold fast.

"I can't. Besides, without you there he can concentrate on defending himself instead of trying to keep you alive." As he was pacing around, he pulled a phone from his pocket, looked at it, and put it back where he found it.

He kind of had a point, but still I said, "I want to help him."

"August never needs help."

"You didn't seem too sure of that during the fight," I pointed out as I worked my arm out of the chains.

"That was a weird circumstance."

"What the hell was happening back there?"

"We were ambushed by several compelled humans with the goal, apparently, of taking August prisoner. He told us we couldn't kill them because they were just being used as puppets by the Order. That made it pretty tough to fight them, especially since they had no qualms about killing our men." Jackass stopped pacing and began to chew on the edge of his thumbnail.

"Take him prisoner?"

"Their leader pointed to August when they surrounded us and said, 'That's the one we bring back alive. Kill the rest.' In a way, that's good news. It means he probably isn't dead."

"How did I get chained up?"

"A much better question is, how the hell are you awake already? You were supposed to be out for hours."

I stopped fighting the chains for a moment and looked up at Jackass. "Bane did this to me, didn't he?" When he nodded, I asked, "Why?"

"He wanted to get you out of the country to keep you safe until he could neutralize the situation here in California."

"He wasn't coming with me?"

"No. I was supposed to take you, along with that contingent of bodyguards back there."

"Was he then going to work on taking out Lucian?" That was a wild guess. I'd heard the name before, but Bane would never tell me anything about him.

"Yeah. August thinks that once Lucian falls, the Order will unravel. He was going to try to find and then infiltrate his headquarters. I told him it was suicide, but he never listens." He pulled out his phone again, looked at it, and put it back in his pocket.

"Do you keep checking to see if he's called?"

He nodded, then looked at me. "I thought you didn't know about Lucian."

"I'd only heard the name. You just confirmed for me that he's the leader of the Order."

Jackass sighed at that, then took his phone out again and dialed a number. When someone answered, he asked, "Have you heard from August?" After a pause he told the person on the line, "We were ambushed by the Order and since he hasn't checked in, I assume they took him prisoner. You need to send all available personnel to comb the remaining neighborhoods in the hills immediately, and have an extraction team ready to go the minute we find their headquarters. Also, I need a car to take Tinder and me to the airport. I doubt the rest of our team survived. Send a driver to pick us up behind the old bottling plant off East Adams and Markley, I want to put some more distance between us and the people that were in pursuit." He listened for a moment, then hung up.

Meanwhile, I'd started fighting my chains wildly. When he tried to stop me, I kicked him in the leg as hard as I could and he yelped and stumbled back. I yelled, "We're not going to the airport! We need to rescue Bane!"

"I have my orders."

"I don't give a shit about your orders! Even though I'm totally pissed at him for trying to ship me off against my will, there is no fucking way on Earth I'm just leaving him in the hands of the enemy. I'm just not going to do it!" I finally got one arm free and as soon as I did that, I was able to wriggle out of the chains.

Without the spell binding them, they really weren't much of a challenge. I leapt to my feet and stared him down.

He watched me for a long moment, then said quietly, "You love him as much as he loves you, don't you? He said you didn't, but it looks like he was wrong about that."

I ignored that and said, "You need to help me save him, Alejandro. I've heard about the control makers have over their progeny, so I know you're bound to do exactly what he tells you. But if you're able to exert even a little free will, now would be the time."

"What I need to do is get you to safety, not just because August ordered me to, but because I know how important that is to him."

"But he didn't know he'd wind up in the hands of the Order! The vamps have branded him a traitor and if they're bringing him in alive, it has to be because they plan to torture him, to make him pay for turning on his own kind. We can't let that happen!"

"That's why I'm having his men set up an extraction team."

"I'm not letting you take me out of the country. I'll kill you if that's what it takes to prevent it, but I really don't want to."

"As if you could." He tried to sound cocky, even though I could see his resolve wavering.

"Everything that's happening to Bane is because of me and I'm getting him back," I said. "Instead of making this harder, help me save him, Alejandro. Do you know where they might have taken him?"

"We have it narrowed down and as I said, a team of our best people is preparing to go in after August the moment we pinpoint his location."

"Can any of them work a spell?"

"Well, no. Only my maker can do that."

"And me. Bane told you that, didn't he? I'm not in his league, but I can do things other people can't."

"Yeah, but—"

"What's your team's plan, to barrel through the front door when you find this place, guns blazing? That's not going to save your maker, because no matter how many people you have, I guarantee the Order has more. But when you figure out his location I might be able to slip in and get him out, right under their noses."

"You really think you'd be able to do that?" I nodded, even though I knew that was a hell of a long shot. Alejandro pressed his eyes shut for a few moments. Finally he sighed and shot me a look. "Come with me."

"What are we doing?"

"Covering my ass." He scooped up the chains that had been binding me, poked his head out of the side door to the garage and looked both ways, then stepped outside and started walking east. I fell into step beside him.

"Where are we going?"

"To meet the driver that's being sent to take us to the airport."

"No fucking way are you getting me on a plane."

"I know. Before the driver gets there, I'm going to let you knock me out. That way I can claim you escaped and August won't hate me for letting you go."

"I like that plan."

As we walked, keeping to back alleys and side streets in the run-down industrial neighborhood, he told me, "I think it's likely that they took August to Lucian's private residence, which from what we've heard is also H.Q. for the Order's lieutenants. I bet Lucian himself will want to be involved in August's torture."

"Where do you think this place is?" I asked as we cut down a narrow passageway between buildings.

"I don't know exactly, only that it's in the Hollywood Hills. We'd already been systematically searching every probable neighborhood and have it narrowed down. People are on their way now to search what's left. I'll let you know as soon as they find something."

"Thank you, Alejandro."

"I love him too, you know. Not the same way you do, and not just because he made me and that means I'm bonded to him. August is like a father to me and if there's even a chance you can get him out, well, it's worth a shot."

"When did he sire you?"

"It's been almost ten years. I'd been attacked by another vamp and left for dead. August found me and turned me to save my life."

As we stood behind a van and waited for a break in traffic so we could cross a busy street, I just had to ask. "So, do you and Bane sleep together?"

Alejandro turned to me with a raised eyebrow. "Dude, gross! Didn't I just say he's like a dad to me?"

"Well yeah, but—"

"I'm not even gay."

"You're not?"

"Do you really have to sound that surprised?"

"I think it's the hair," I told him. "It made me reach conclusions." He rolled his eyes at that.

After we darted across the street, I told him, "I like you a lot better now that I know you're not doing my...." I didn't know how to finish that sentence.

"Boyfriend?"

"That really doesn't explain what he is to me."

"Yeah, I know."

I sighed and said, "He drives me insane sometimes. Don't even get me started on this totally aggravating plan of his to try to ship me out of the country against my will. But he's a part of me. No one's ever cared about me that much, not even my own family. And I...well, I care about him, too."

"Is it really that difficult to say you love him?"

I thought about that for a while as we walked beneath a heavily graffitied overpass and finally said, "It's been hard for me to admit just what he means to me, because it kind of shows that my whole life has been one huge mistake. I've been killing vamps since I was a kid, just like generations of my family before me. I killed indiscriminately. I didn't stop and ask, is this a good vamp or a bad one? I really believed there was only one kind. So see, I'm not just admitting I have feelings for a vampire. I'm also coming to terms with the fact that some of you are good, because no way is Bane the sole exception. That means I must have killed countless innocents in my lifetime, just because they happened to be vampires. What do I even begin to do with that kind of guilt?"

"I see your point."

As we neared the old bottling plant, Alejandro pulled out his phone. "Let me have your number." After I recited it and he typed it in, he pulled out a business card and wrote his cell number on the back. "I'll call you the moment I hear anything, so only use this in a dire emergency. I'm going to really try to maintain the illusion that you escaped, so I don't bring the wrath of my maker down on me."

"What do you think he'd do to you if he knew you let me go?"

"We already have a strained relationship. I think this might be enough to make him disown me once and for all."

I thought about that as I turned the business card over in my hand. It was for an investment firm called APM and at the bottom it said Alejandro Vela, Vice President. The card was adorned with a minimalistic icon that sort of looked like a flower and I asked, "What is that?"

"It's a primrose, the logo for August's company. APM stands for August Pemberton Mayes."

A light bulb went off all of a sudden. "Bane's been sending me money for years, hasn't he? I thought they were coming from my benefactor, but I just realized my checks are signed by someone with the initials A.P.M., whose middle name is Primrose. That's no coincidence."

Alejandro grinned at me. "Took you long enough to figure that one out. I'm sure August left that clue on purpose. I think he always wanted you to realize he'd been taking care of you."

"What happened to the people that used to fund the war on vampires?"

"From what I've heard, all your backer organizations were infiltrated and brought down over three years ago. Some vampires believe that was Lucian's first great victory, but that's kind of an urban legend. Who knows if it can really be attributed to him?"

I asked, "If you had to guess, what would you say is Lucian's end game? Is it just to wipe out all the hunters, or does he have bigger aspirations?"

"I have no idea."

"What else can you tell me about him?"

"Not much, I've just heard a handful of rumors. Those who've seen him say he's huge with eerie silver eyes. They say he wasn't human before he was turned into a vampire."

"Not human? What the hell would that make him?"

"One theory is that he's a werewolf-vampire hybrid."

"Weres have been extinct for well over a century. And even if he's older than that, I thought werewolves couldn't be turned into vamps."

"I'm just repeating what I've heard, I have no idea if any of it's true."

I mulled that over for a while before asking, "Did Bane tell you about that warehouse by the Port of Long Beach? What was that supposed to be?"

Alejandro shook his head. "August was so pissed when you stumbled across that place. He thinks that was going to be Lucian's miniature Ellis Island. The Order has been bringing in vamps from not only all over the country but all over the world, some of them possibly slipping in quietly on cargo ships through the port. My maker's theory is that they wanted a nondescript location to use as a feeding station and maybe an orientation center for the newly arriving vamps, and you just happened to go bursting in when they were still setting up the place. You'd probably already been on Lucian's radar before that, but it put an extra-large target on your back."

"Thanks for telling me all of this. It drives me crazy that Bane feels the need to keep me in the dark all the time."

"That's him, though. He'd much rather try to take on the world all by himself, rather than risk endangering the people he cares about."

We'd reached the old bottling plant by now and as we circled around back, I asked, "You sure you want me to knock you out? Wouldn't it be easier to just talk to Bane after I save him and explain that you were doing what you thought was right?"

He picked up a three-foot length of old metal pipe from a stack beside the building and knit his brows. "No. Now make this count and then get out of here fast. The driver might bring reinforcements and it would be really annoying if they immediately recapture you. It would mean I got my skull bashed in for nothing."

I sighed and took the pipe from his hand as he tossed the chains on the ground beside him. Then he got on his knees facing away from me and I told him, "Thank you, Alejandro, for everything."

"Just save him."

"That's the plan." I swung the pipe like a baseball bat.

"Where have you been?" Lee asked as I entered the main floor of the former shoe factory that was our new hunter base camp. Everyone stopped what they were doing and looked up at me.

"Long story," I said as I piled his things and mine on a long table. "How's Stevie?"

"He needed surgery, he was bleeding internally. Kira called a few minutes ago. He's in recovery now, the doctors told her it went well."

I nodded at that as I slung my backpack off my shoulder. "Everyone, listen up," I said loudly. "The Order is compelling humans now to be their eyes during the day and look for us. They're also using them to do their dirty work. Several of them showed up at the lodge, prepared to do battle. If you encounter them, go for a knock out, not a kill. They're not the enemy."

"Fucking awesome," Jeffrey muttered. "Like we don't have enough to deal with, now we got zombie humans, too."

"Our approach of going out in groups and fighting vamps every night isn't working," I continued. "There are just too many of them. Even if we killed a hundred a night, it wouldn't make a difference."

"So, are we just giving up? Fuck that," Colby exclaimed.

"Hell no, we're not giving up. We're just going to try a different approach. We need to concentrate on finding out who the leaders of the Order are and taking them out. Nightly street fighting is only going to get us all killed, and once we're dead, the general population is fucked. So tonight we regroup, restock our weapons, and heal up a bit since we're all beat to shit. Then tomorrow, during the day, we're going to go out in small teams and start asking questions. I know that none of us has a very high opinion of the wanna-be hunters, but maybe it's time we start talking to them and finding out what they know."

"You're actually suggestin' we take a night off? Are you kidding?" Lee said. "With all those vamps out there, we're supposed to just sit back and relax?"

"Where the hell did you hear sit back and relax in any of that?" I asked him. "We've all been taking a beating and we'll be better able to go after the heads of the Order if we take a night or two to build our strength back up. Plus, our weapons cache is dwindling, we need time to address that."

"A night *or two*? Fuck that," Rider said, glaring at me from the corner.

I was in no mood for his attitude, and I yelled as I pointed across the room, "You don't like my ideas? Then there's the fucking door! If you want to go out and get yourself slaughtered, be my guest. But if you choose to stay here and be a part of this unit, then you fucking do as you're told! That goes for all of you!"

Everyone in the room seemed to hold their breath as they watched Rider and me. I knew I could lose all of them in the next minute or two. They could choose to leave, which would get every last one of them killed sooner rather than later. I stared Rider down, and he held my stare for a long moment. Finally he relented, relaxing his posture slightly as he said, "I guess we can take tonight to get our shit together. But I ain't gonna be benched longer than that. Come tomorrow night, I'll be back out there doing my job."

I unzipped my duffle bag and started arming myself with everything I had as I said, "Fine. I'm going out to do some recon, I'll see you in the morning."

"That doesn't look like recon," Liz pointed out, gesturing at my weapons. "That looks like you're preparing to take down a shitload of vamps without us."

"I'm just making sure I'm prepared in case I get jumped. I don't have to tell you it's dangerous out there for a lone hunter."

"Lone hunter? What the fuck are you talkin' about?" Lee wanted to know. "I thought we were stayin' in tonight and gettin' our shit together."

"You are. I'm not."

"Screw that. If you're goin' out, I'm goin' with you. In fact, we should probably take a couple more hunters along, too. Don't matter if all we're doin' is askin' questions. You know that trouble could find you no matter what."

"No. I told you to stay put." I was gearing up to rescue Bane the moment Alejandro called, and no way was I going to take other hunters with me on a mission that dangerous. This was personal. We could go back afterwards and take down the Order, once I'd not only

340

saved Bane but also gotten a look at their operations and identified their weaknesses.

For now I said, "The vamps found us at the lodge, so they could find us here, too." Maybe they'd just tracked Bane there, but still. "I need everyone to work together here. Set up round-the-clock lookouts, stay strong. I'm going to set up a perimeter for you, same as always, but it might not be enough."

There was some general grumbling, but like most hunters, these individuals had been raised to be soldiers. And soldiers knew to follow orders.

I pulled some chalk out of my bag and went to work bespelling every door and window in the old factory. It took a while, and as usual I got plenty of surreptitious glances from just about everyone as I did this, reminding me yet again that I couldn't blend in anywhere. Not even with hunters.

When I finished, I snuck a look at my phone (no messages) and slipped a small spell book into an inner pocket of my jacket, then turned and started to leave through the side entrance. Lee was right on my heels. He waited until we got outside and the door swung shut behind us before he said, "That was a good speech and all, but how about tellin' me what the fuck you're really fixin' to go do? You don't need your spell book to do recon, and you just put nearly every weapon you own on your body. What the fuck's goin' on, Tinder?"

Instead of answering him, I said, "In case I don't come back, I want you to know something, Lee. You're one of the best friends I ever had and one hell of a skilled hunter. I'm honored to have fought at your side."

When I turned to leave, he caught my arm and said, "Oh *hell* no. I'm definitely not lettin' you go off on some sort of crazy-ass suicide mission after that. What are you doing? Did you find out where the Order is headquartered and are ya fixin' on takin' 'em down yourself so you don't get the rest of us killed?"

"No. I just have something I need to do, that's all."

He stared at me for a long moment, then guessed, "Does it have somethin' to do with Bane?"

"What makes you say that?" I hedged.

"Because, Tinder, you told us we couldn't kill him and no matter what you say, I could tell there was somethin' between the two of you when I saw you together."

Finally I admitted, "He's in trouble and I'm going to go help him, just as soon as I find out where he is. Don't tell the others, okay? They won't understand."

"Hell no they won't understand! You're obviously puttin' yourself in all kinds of danger, given the shit you're packin' to go after him, and for what? For a fuckin' vamp, just 'cause he stepped in and helped us at the park? That's pretty fuckin' insane, Tinder."

"That's not why I'm helping him, Lee."

His brown eyes narrowed. "Are you in love with him? Are you in love with a goddamn vamp?" I sighed and turned away from him, but he grabbed me by my jacket and spun me around. "Please tell me that ain't what's happenin' here!"

"Let go of me, Lee."

"I will, right after you look me in the eye and tell me you're not in love with him."

I tried to look Lee in the eye. I really did. I just couldn't do it, though.

Lee punched me in the jaw, so hard that my vision faltered for a moment. He grabbed me by the shoulders and hissed, "I *knew* it! I bet you're lettin' him fuck you too, aren't you? That's why you said you and me

343

couldn't do it no more, ain't it? You sick son of a bitch! How the fuck could you choose a bloodsucker over your own people, Tinder?"

"They're not all bad, Lee. I used to think they were, but I was wrong. He's such a good man."

"He's not a man at all, he's a fuckin' monster! Did you forget how he staked you to a wall a few months back? Because I sure as hell didn't!"

"He was just trying to keep me safe."

"You're totally fuckin' insane!"

Lee shoved me away from him and I straightened up and squared my shoulders. "I know you can't understand this," I said. "I used to think the same way you did, I saw everything in black and white, and back then I wouldn't have understood it, either. But we've been wrong about so much."

There was barely contained rage in Lee's eyes as he said, "Don't come back, Tinder. I'll make an excuse to the others and I'll leave the rest of your shit behind the dumpster over there so you can get it later. I won't tell them the truth, because it'll shake 'em up too much and they don't need that right now. They don't need to know they've been following a sick fuck that'd actually allow himself to become some monster's bitch."

I watched him as he turned and went back inside, then sighed quietly and walked down the alley. I felt incredibly alone just then. It was a feeling I was used to.

*****

I decided sitting around waiting for Alejandro's call was going to make me insane, so I drove to the Hollywood Hills and began to meander around in my rental car. I really didn't know why Alejandro thought his people would even find this place in time to save Bane, considering the fact that they'd been looking for days or weeks already with no luck. I really didn't know how I expected to find it, either.

I pulled to the side of the road in a quiet residential neighborhood and racked my brain. I couldn't use a locator spell to find Bane, because he'd completely warded himself against that sort of thing. But then, a thought occurred to me. I turned on the dome light and fished around under my seat, then pulled out the big, old-fashioned spiral bound map book that this rental company inexplicably supplied with all their cars, as if its customers might be driving back in time to the land without GPS. I flipped to the page for the Hollywood Hills and set it on my lap, then pulled out my spell book and searched its pages. I had a weird theory, and I wanted to test it out.

I found several locator spells, and tried to figure out how to make them work for me. I had this idea that if I couldn't find Bane, maybe I could find everything that *wasn't* him. Whatever was left after that would be his location. Yeah, I know, it was kind of convoluted, but I didn't have any better ideas.

To manage even that though, I was going to have to tweak one of these spells a bit, and that was supposed to be impossible. Only a tiny, now-extinct sect of witches and warlocks had ever been gifted with the power to be the architects of spells, to build them from the ground up. The rest of us could only use what they'd written, which was why we spent so much time searching old archives and dusty, hand-written journals. Some crazy little part of me was encouraging me to give it a shot, though.

I read the locator spell and made the adjustment I needed. It was designed to work in conjunction with a map, and the one in my lap lit up vividly. I turned off the overhead light and held the map close to my face. Every street on the map appeared to glow. I scanned it carefully, inch by inch, and then something caught my eye.

One little half-inch of street high up in the hills wasn't lit. I'd asked the spell to show me where Bane wasn't, instead of showing me where he was (since he was warded against being found). The part that had lit up showed me where he wasn't. The dark part had to be his location.

I tossed the map aside and put the car in gear. I was maybe five miles from the dark spot. As I wound my way through the hills, I contemplated the fact that I had apparently just done the impossible. I'd altered a spell. I had no idea what this meant. It wasn't something I'd ever tried to do before, because I'd always been told it couldn't be done. This wasn't the time for deep contemplation though, because I had a job to do.

I parked a few blocks down the hill from the section of street the map had shown me, or rather, not

347

shown me, and stuck to the shadows as I proceeded on foot. It was maybe an hour past sundown, but nowhere in L.A. was it ever really all that dark.

I knew I'd found the right place as soon as I rounded a bend in the road, and I ducked into some bushes as I got a good look at it. The residence at the very top of Skyview Drive was far more fortress than house. I was on an incline above it, so I could see past the high masonry fence blocking off the front of the imposing concrete structure. The place looked a bit like a prison, even though the architect had probably been going for 1960s modern. Big, burly vamps patrolled the perimeter, adding to the prison vibe. I'd driven up through a swanky residential neighborhood to get here, but the houses thinned out the higher I went. This place sat by itself among minimalist landscaping dotted with artfully placed boulders. Behind it was a sheer cliff face, offering a view of all of Los Angeles in the distance.

No one would be patrolling the steep drop-off, so that was my ticket in.

I went back down the hill a bit, then used two of my wooden stakes the way I assumed a mountain climber might use a pick and approached the house from the end of the block, out of sight of the patrols. Carefully, I made my way over the vegetation and rough terrain, driving the stakes into loose pockets of soil while trying to keep a toe-hold on the rocks. The cliff face was incredibly steep, and one slip would probably end me. I tried not to dwell on that thought and I sure as hell didn't look down as I made agonizingly slow progress.

Eventually, I worked my way behind the house. I whispered a spell to conceal my scent, just to be paranoid because I already bore a tattooed symbol that did exactly that, then began climbing the fifteen feet or so to the patio above me. I lost my footing at one point and slipped down five or six feet before catching myself on a rock with my fingertips, dropping one of my stakes in the process. It bounced off a rock forty feet below me before continuing its descent. My heart was pounding as I waited and listened, wondering if anyone had heard me.

When no one came running to intercept me, I resumed my climb. By the time I reached the lip of the patio I was exhausted, which sucked because the hard

349

part was still ahead of me. I raised my head up slowly and took a look at the back of the house.

Unlike the front, the back was all glass to take in the million dollar view. The house was huge and only part of it was visible through the windows. From my vantage point I could see three vampires sitting in the living room and two more coming up a set of stairs off the kitchen. The two climbing the stairs were covered in blood.

I reached out with every one of my senses, trying to somehow determine if Bane was downstairs. I often felt him when he was near me...or I thought I did. Now I felt nothing. I was starting to wonder if I'd come to the wrong place when a yell of pure agony made all the hairs on the back of my neck stand on end.

Bane.

The cry had been muffled, but I just knew it was him. Another yell soon followed. What the hell were they doing to him?

And how the hell did I think I was going to waltz in there and get him out?

I ducked back down below the edge of the patio and perched precariously on a rock as I pulled my spell book from my pocket. I accidentally glanced down, which made everything sway and lurch as my fear of heights tried to overwhelm me. I pressed the back of my head against the hillside and took a couple deep breaths, then forced my attention to the little leather-bound book in my hand.

It had been in my mother's family for over two hundred years, and most of the spells were in Portuguese. Not a problem. What *was* a problem was the fact that for the most part, the spells simply served to protect a hunter. I didn't need defense, I needed offense. I needed shock and awe. I needed....

I slipped the book into my pocket and decided to try my luck again with assembling my own spell. I reached down deep, calling on the part of me that I often tried to ignore, the part that I'd inherited from the witches and warlocks in my family history. By embellishing on a couple spells I already knew and combining them in a unique way, I built the spell's foundation. And then I gave it teeth.

A surge of power shot through me and I gasped. I had no idea how effective this was going to be, but I also didn't know how long it would last, so I didn't waste any time. With one leap I was up on the patio. Then I was sprinting toward the house, moving incredibly fast, faster even than a vampire. I pulled two stakes from my jacket and leveled every vamp in my path, reducing them to dust before they could even turn their heads to look at me. I bolted down the stairs beside the kitchen, then hesitated for a moment.

The house was a fucking iceberg.

Only about ten percent of it was visible above ground. The rest of the structure had been built several stories down into the hillside. Well, hell.

Bane had fallen silent, so I just had to pick a direction at random and search for him. By now, all the vamps in the building knew an invader was in their midst, and they'd all gone into high alert, and they were all coming for me. I dodged hands and knives and fangs as I took out vamp after vamp. They just kept coming.

The spell and the effort of moving like this was draining my energy in a big way, but I couldn't stop now. If I did, both Bane and I would be dead. I kept fighting my way down hallway after hallway, searching each room. My right arm took a hit, re-opening the big gash on my bicep. A knife was thrown at me and I lunged out of the way, but it still caught me below my ribcage. I was bleeding now, gasping for breath and shaking with the effort of maintaining the spell. But I wasn't giving up.

I dropped the last vampire in the latest group that had been attacking me and yelled August's name.

His voice was weak, but close. "Tinder!"

I burst into a large office, ran through it and kicked open a door at the back of the room, then dusted two vamps in the span of a second. And there he was. I ran to Bane's side and when I got a good look at him, I whispered, "Oh God." He'd been chained to a metal gurney, naked from the waist up. He was beaten and bloody and cut and torn, but I realized right away that something far more sinister had been done to him.

"They injected you with colloidal silver," I murmured as my heart ached, tracing the fiery path of the poison under his pale skin. It left red and black trails as it burned through him.

"You should be halfway to Portugal by now, Tinder. What are you doing here?" His voice was raspy, his eyes pools of pain.

"Saving you." Or trying to. I pushed down my grief and searched all around for the keys to unlock the big padlocks fastening the chains to the table.

"Bloody hell," he muttered as I dove onto the piles of clothes on the floor and went through the pockets of the vamps that had been hurting him. I found a couple sets of keys and brought them both to the table, trying key after key. Finally, I got both locks open and put my arm around Bane as he got up shakily.

"You shouldn't have come, Tinder. We'll never make it out alive."

"If the situation were reversed, if I was the one that had been captured by the Order, would you have left me here?"

"No, of course not. But—"

"But nothing. I *had* to come for you, Bane. Just like you would have come for me."

"How did you get away from Allie? You didn't kill him, did you?"

"I may have fractured his skull. He'll be fine." As we were talking, we left the office and began making our way down the long hallway toward the stairs. Bane

354

leaned on me heavily, his body shaking from the effort of propelling himself forward.

From everything I'd heard about injecting silver into a vamp, he had to be in excruciating agony right now. It was burning him up from the inside and killing him, slowly but steadily. There was no cure as far as I knew, but I couldn't let myself get crushed under the weight of that reality right now. Not when a far more immediate death was about to come for both of us.

I could hear a lot of commotion above us and pulled a gun from inside my jacket, handing it to Bane. "Sounds like we're not just going to stroll out of here. I may have to let go of you when they start coming at us so I can fight with both hands, so use this to defend yourself. Don't worry about defending me."

He took the gun with a shaking hand and I looked up at him, holding his gaze for a moment before I put a hand on the back of his neck, pulled him down to me, and kissed him. When we broke apart I told him, "I love you, August."

His reaction wasn't exactly what I'd been expecting. He rolled his eyes and said, "Oh great, *now* you decide you love me! Right in time to come barreling in here and get yourself merked."

"Merked?"

"Killed. Murdered. Dispatched. Bumped off."

I sighed as I pulled a big stake out of my waistband and began to climb the stairs with him. "I didn't just *decide it*."

"I'm a dead man walking, love," he said as I struggled to keep him upright on the stairs. "With the silver in my system, I have two or three days at best before it kills me. You'd be much better off leaving me here and saving yourself."

"Not happening."

"Do you always have to argue?"

"Yes."

When we finally reached the top of the stairs, we found about two dozen vamps waiting for us with murder in their eyes. "Howdy, boys," I said, wielding the stake like a fencer's foil. "If you think you have safety in numbers, you're sadly mistaken. I'm going to do to you what I did to all your little dust-bunnied playmates. Now, who wants to go first?"

The sound of the shotgun blast behind me made my ears pop as the round tore into my spine. It knocked me onto my stomach as pain swallowed me whole.

I regained consciousness slowly. Pain radiated not only from my lower back, but from my wrists. My head lolled to the side and I looked up. I was hanging from the ceiling by a pair of metal manacles, which were tearing into my flesh. I tried to shift to take some of the pressure off of them, which was when I realized I couldn't feel my legs.

I tilted my head and looked down at myself. I'd been stripped of everything except my jeans, my bare feet dangling several inches above the floor. There was a pool of blood beneath me. It was hard to think, hard to focus on anything except the overwhelming pain, but I realized after a while that the pool was coming from me. I was bleeding out.

All I could do was just keep breathing. It took so much effort. It produced an odd sound, too, a whistling rasp.

A moan from across the room pulled me out of my slow collapse into myself. I raised my head and tried to focus. Bane was hung from his wrists like I was on the other side of the room, blood running down both arms as he lapsed into unconsciousness. I tried to speak, tried to call his name, but I just didn't have the strength.

"Where is that little fucker?" Loud voices and footsteps were approaching. A moment later, a big, red-headed vampire I'd met before was standing right in front of me, flanked by two other vamps and grinning delightedly. "I've waited way too long for this, Tinder." He hauled his fist back and punched me, shattering my ribs. My body jerked and swung from the chains. Suddenly breathing became infinitely harder, panic flooding me as I struggled to get air into my lungs. One of them had probably collapsed. Oh God.

The red-headed vamp leaned in close. "It's a damn shame that Lucian wants to speak to you before he kills you. I would have fucking loved doing the honors, flaying your skin from your body and making you suffer like no hunter has ever suffered before. He'll probably be pissed off that you're this far gone. He's just pulling up out front, be a pal and try to stay alive long enough for Lucian to have the satisfaction of killing you."

The fight to pull air into my lungs took the very last of my strength. The room went in and out of focus as some sort of activity went on around me. A huge figure appeared right before me, a hand lifting my chin. I looked up into silver eyes. Not human. So beautiful. For some reason, a sense of peace settled over me. I began to drift....

"Get out of here Sean," the figure told the red-haired vamp. He had an English accent. "Clear the building, take every soldier with you!"

"Why, Lucian?"

"Are you questioning me? I want this building cleared in the next ninety seconds. Now go!"

"Yes, sir." The vamps took off like a shot and Lucian slammed the door behind them.

An instant later, he was in front of me again. He pulled his collar aside and produced a small knife, which he used to cut himself at the spot where his neck met his shoulder. He put his hand on the back of my head and positioned me to drink from him. I barely had the strength to swallow.

"How the fuck can this be happening?" he muttered as he wrapped his free arm around me, lifting me to take the weight off my wrists. Exactly. I had absolutely no explanation for what he was doing right now.

Somehow I managed a sip, then another. Immediately, strength and energy began pouring into me. I began to drink desperately. I knew it was going to make me violently ill, but I also knew I'd been moments from death and this would save me before the nausea levelled me.

He let me drink for a long time. I could actually feel my body healing itself. When the feeling returned to my legs, I wanted to sob with relief.

Finally, I tilted my head back and looked up at the stranger who'd saved me. Lucian was enormous, maybe six-four and solid muscle. Long black hair fell almost to his waist and thick lashes emphasized those otherworldly liquid silver eyes. When he opened his mouth to speak, particularly sharp fangs made me flinch a little. "You alright?" he asked, his voice clipped.

"Yeah. Why'd you help me?"

He frowned as he said, "Because you're my mate."

"What are you talking about? Only shifters have mates." He just went on staring at me, so I asked, "Were you a werewolf before you were turned?" He nodded. "But shifters only mate with other shifters, not with humans."

"You have werewolf blood in you. Not a lot, but enough for me to recognize you."

"No way."

He let go of me and lowered the chains that suspended me from the ceiling until my feet were flat on the ground. Then he began pacing around the room, looking at me every few seconds. "How am I supposed to explain this to my troops, that I'm mated to a hunter? Not just any hunter either, but the big prize, the one they've all been gunning for! Do you know how fast my own men will turn on me when they find out we're mated? Hell, they'll probably turn on me just for saving your life!"

"But we're not mated. We can't be," I insisted.

He came close again, stopping a couple feet from me. Something strange stirred deep inside me. It felt a little like déjà vu. Without conscious thought, I tried to lean toward him, as much as my chains would allow.

"That's your shifter blood responding to me. The draw is far worse for me, since I was a half-blood werewolf before I was turned. You must be no more than an eighth." Lucian tried to step away from me, even as one hand reached out and gently touched my chest.

"What are you going to do about this?"

"There's nothing to be done. Now that we've met, our fates are sealed. We're destined to be together."

"I don't believe in destiny. I believe in free will," I insisted, even as my body responded to his touch, a weird euphoria blooming inside my chest.

"Doesn't make a bit of difference what you believe in."

"You don't even know if I'm gay," I hedged.

"Of course you are. The reason you're gay is because I am. You were born to be mine, my perfect mate."

"Wow. Because that's not completely creepy."

He pushed his long hair back with both hands, conflict spelled out all over his handsome face. "Nearly eight hundred of my people are waiting for me to lead them, but all I can think about is carrying you to my bed and making love to you for days on end. You! A bleedin' hunter!"

"Let me help you out a bit there: no fucking way am I going to bed with you."

He had stepped back a few feet again, but now he surged forward, so quickly that I caught my breath. I thought he was going to hurt me, but instead he just gathered me in his arms and held me for a long moment. It felt good. Fuck!

Lucian murmured, "I'd given up on ever finding you. Almost all our people are dead, so I figured my mate was probably killed long before I ever met him. The second I caught your scent though, everything changed. Everything. And I have absolutely no idea what I'm going to do about it."

He let go of me and went to the tie-down on a far wall, then lowered me even further so that I was in a seated position. He didn't unchain me, though. "I need to get out of here and try to clear my head. I've sent all my soldiers away, so no one will hurt you while I'm gone. I just...I need to figure this out." Lucian turned and left the room. He didn't just walk away from me, he ran.

I watched him go, then exclaimed, "Seriously?" I actually missed him. There had to be a way to break a shifter bond, because this was some majorly fucked up shit.

I got up and turned to Bane, who was stirring but just barely. He didn't respond when I called his name, though. I stretched as far as I could, trying to reach some implements in the basement-turned-torture-chamber so I could pick the locks on my manacles.

Failing that, I chewed on a thumbnail as I tried to figure out how to escape, then climbed one of the chains hand over hand until I was at the pulley on the ceiling. This didn't actually help me, though. Since I couldn't break it loose from its mooring or get the chain free, it didn't give me any more slack.

I let go of it and dropped back onto the concrete floor with a splash. There was still a big pool of my blood beneath my feet. I went back to analyzing my surroundings, but then spun around when Bane said my name. "Hang on," I told him. "I'm working on getting us out of here." I immediately realized the stupidity of saying 'hang on' to someone suspended from a ceiling, and sighed.

"How are you okay? You were shot in the spine."
Bane seemed to have rallied a bit, his voice stronger.

I told him what had just happened as concisely as
possible, then said, "It's all completely insane, though. I
can trace my bloodline back for centuries on both sides.
I'd know if there were werewolves in my family tree."

"Not werewolves, *werewolf*. Just the one."

"Wait a minute. There really was a shifter among
my ancestors?" When he nodded I said, "And you knew
that but never thought to tell me? Really?"

"It hardly seemed relevant, at least until your
boyfriend showed up."

I knit my brows at him. "You actually sound
jealous."

"You think?"

"How can you be jealous? I didn't choose this! I
don't know why any of that just happened, or if there's
even a shred of reality behind it. I don't even know why
his blood didn't make me violently ill like yours did."

"Because he's your fucking *mate*." There was
some bite to that. "That's why your system rejected my
blood, because it wasn't *his*. Your body chemistry and
his are linked."

"Well, that's not my fault. Stop acting like it is!" I turned back to the tools again. They were on a couple wide shelves spanning one wall, and even when I stretched as far as I could, they were still out of reach.

An idea occurred to me then, and I peeled off my bloody Levis. Since I didn't wear underwear, and since the vamps had been nice enough to remove the rest of my clothing, I was now buck naked. "Interesting distraction technique," Bane said.

"I had an idea."

"About how to shut me up? It's working."

"No." I tied the cuffs of the pant legs together, then held on to the waistband and threw the knotted cuffs onto the shelf, like a crude lasso. It landed among the tools and I yanked it back quickly. The shelf had a little lip on it though, so it didn't knock down a tool like I'd hoped it would.

When I'd done this half a dozen times with no success, Bane sighed and said, "Would you hurry up? Your lupine lover is probably going to be back soon."

"Christ," I muttered. On the next throw, I finally pulled a sinister-looking rusty ice pick to the floor, then hooked it with the jeans and dragged it over to me.

Once it was in my hands, I dropped down on one knee and went to work trying to pick the lock on the cuff around my left wrist.

Several minutes later, I had to admit it really wasn't going well. "For fuck's sake," Bane muttered. "Is it really that hard to pick a damn lock?"

"With an ice pick? Yeah, it is! You wouldn't be able to do any better." I tried for a few more minutes, before finally yelling, "Fuck!"

Some kind of movement in my peripheral vision caught my attention, and I whipped my head around to peer out the door that Lucian had left open. The office on the other side of it was dark, but the hallway beyond that was lit. Something moved in the shadows and when I engaged my sight a small figure lit up, white in the darkness. I was surprised to see someone I recognized. "Ty?"

The little blond vamp hesitantly approached the door and stopped outside it. A delicate hand came up to grasp the doorframe as he peered around it and said softly, "You remember me?"

"Of course I do."

"You told me your name was Tyler," he said. "But the other vamps were calling you Tinder. Is that you? Are you the vamp that murdered my maker?" His blue eyes were wide and frightened.

"I'm sorry, Ty. I didn't know then what I do now. I didn't know some vamps were good, not until I fell in love with one and had to face the truth. It was a mistake to kill your maker when he wasn't doing anything wrong."

He stepped just inside the doorway, fidgeting nervously with the hem of his white t-shirt. He wore only that and a little pair of white shorts, his feet bare. "That vampire over there," he said, tilting his head toward Bane, "is that who you love?" When I nodded, he said, "I heard him screaming your name when they were torturing him."

"Ty, can you help us get out of here? If the other vamps come back, Bane and I are both dead."

He took two more steps into the room, looking around fearfully. His thin fingers still twisted and tugged at his hem. Finally he looked at me and said softly, "I'll help you under one condition."

"Anything."

"Keep me."

"Wait, what?"

"If I help you escape, take me with you and keep me."

"Keep you?"

"Remember when we met? I told you I hated being on my own, that I needed to belong to someone. I gave myself to a vampire shortly after that, and then Sean brought me here to be a sex toy for the others." His gaze dropped to the floor. "I can't keep letting them hurt me."

"Why don't you just leave?"

"Sean swore he'd find me and kill me if I did that. I believe him."

"Can we hurry this along?" Bane asked. "We're all dead if the Order returns."

Even though Bane had a point, I had to ask. "Why would you try to give yourself to a hunter, especially now that you know I killed your maker?"

He shrugged his thin shoulders and said, "I guess because I know you could keep me safe if you wanted to. You could stop Sean from finding me and hurting me. And I don't think you'd kill me yourself. You could have done that easily when you were at my apartment, but you chose to let me live. I've thought about that every day since then."

"Okay. Just get us out of here and I promise to keep you safe." I would have agreed to just about anything at that point.

He ran over to the tie-down on the wall and released my chains, and then he and I ransacked the place looking for keys. Ty finally found them in the adjoining office, and as soon as he freed me, I ran to Bane and did the same. While Ty helped him to the door, I untangled and pulled on the bloody jeans, threw on my coat, which had been discarded in a corner, and stuffed my feet into my boots as I felt my pockets. My weapons and spell book were still in place, but my wallet was missing. Awesome.

I caught up with my companions as they made their way down the hall and supported Bane on his right side while Ty supported him on the left. "There's an underground garage this way," the little blond explained. "If you two stay out of sight, I can probably drive us out of here. There are still guards outside the front gate, but I don't think they'll bother to stop me."

The garage housed three vehicles, though it was big enough to hold more than a dozen. Ty grabbed some keys off a hook and jogged toward a large SUV. I popped the back hatch and Bane got in first, then I gingerly settled in around him and pulled the door shut before tugging the cargo cover over the top of us.

I slid my arm beneath his head, leaned in close and pushed my jacket off my bare shoulder. "Drink from me. Your injuries are taking too long to heal so you obviously need to feed." It wouldn't help with the silver poisoning his system, but it would keep the rest of him as strong as possible. He cradled me in his arms and bit down on my shoulder. I liked knowing my body was nourishing his and I kissed the side of his head as he drank.

Ty started the engine and pulled forward, climbing a ramp. A clanging sound indicated some sort of garage door opening. When we got outside, a guard barked, "What are you doing?" The SUV came to a stop and I held my breath.

"Joining Sean at the barracks. I got left behind and he wants me to meet him there." Ty kept his voice level.

"Yeah, okay." It sounded like a gate was opening mechanically, and then the big SUV rolled forward once more.

After we took a couple turns and I knew we were out of earshot of the guards, I called to Ty, "There's a white compact car parked on the street at the third intersection. Pull up behind it. I want us to switch vehicles in case Lucian keeps trackers in his fleet."

I got behind the wheel when we traded out to the rental car. Bane curled up on the back seat and shut his eyes and Ty sat beside me, hugging his knees to his chest. He glanced at me a couple times as I wound down the hillside and finally asked softly, "You won't forget your promise, will you?"

"Nope. I told you I'd take care of you and I meant it."

He leaned over and rested his head on my arm. "I'm glad I belong to you," he whispered as he curled up against me, tucking his feet under him. I suppressed a sigh and draped my arm around him. Even knowing he was a vampire and so much stronger than he looked, there was a vulnerability to Ty that brought out a

373

paternal instinct I never knew I had. I hoped I'd be able to make good on my promise to keep him safe.

I took a quick detour past the old shoe factory when we got out of the hills. Lee had left my stuff by the dumpster, just like he said he would. I wanted the rest of my books of spells and alchemy, just in case there was something in there about how to help Bane, in addition to my crossbow and other large weapons that hadn't come with me tonight. I knew we'd need them.

As I put my stuff in the trunk, I glanced up at the old building. The hunters were doing a good job of remaining inconspicuous. From here, there was no way of knowing the building was occupied. I didn't see anyone until I engaged my second sight and caught a couple pink glows through the cracks of the boarded-up windows. I'd already known they were watching me before I spotted them though, and knew they'd be picking up the two vampire signatures coming from my car. I didn't stick around long enough to find out what my former team had to say on that subject.

After I pulled away down the alley, Ty snuggled against my side again and asked, "You okay? You seem sad."

I tried to shrug it off. "I'm fine. There's just a group of people back there that I used to be a part of. It kind of...well, it felt like a family for a while. But I'm not welcome there anymore."

He thought about that for a while, his thin arm sliding around my waist. Then he said, "Maybe Bane and I could be your family instead. And you could be mine."

The old me would have made some kind of snide remark about not really being in the market to adopt a vamp, but I'd changed a lot in the last few weeks. I put my arm around Ty and held him securely as I told him, "I like that idea."

I drove north with no real plan, other than putting distance between myself and Lucian. We only had a couple hours to get Ty someplace light-tight before sunrise. "Bane, do you have your wallet on you?" I asked as I contemplated motel options.

"No. It's somewhere back at the compound with the rest of my clothes," he murmured. It sounded like he was falling asleep.

Without cash or credit cards, we were screwed. I glanced at the gas gauge. At least the tank was nearly full. I debated with myself for a while and eventually took the exit for Santa Barbara. I only had one friend left now that the hunters had disowned me and as much as I hated to potentially put Nate in danger, I really needed his help right now.

His husband Nikolai answered the door when I knocked. He was dressed only in pajama pants, his necklace with the silver cross resting between his pecs. He tensed up when he saw me and asked, "What are you doing here, Tinder?" Then he took a look at my companions and his forehead creased with concern. "What happened to Bane?"

"He's been poisoned. Can we please come in? We really need a place to stay. This is Ty, by the way. He doesn't have a daylight talisman and I can see dawn just starting to break over the horizon, so I'm kind of really hoping you say yes here."

Nikolai stepped back and held the door open. "Come in."

Nate wandered out of the bedroom looking adorably rumpled and exclaimed, "Tinder!" I helped Bane into a chair and set down my duffle bag, then embraced my friend.

"It's good to see you, Nate. I'm really sorry for barging in at this hour. I just didn't know where else to go."

"Are you in some kind of trouble?" When I nodded, he said, "Come sit down and tell me what's going on." He and I sat on the couch, his husband right beside him. Ty followed us and sat at my feet, resting his head on my thigh. Without even thinking about it, I put a protective hand on his shoulder.

I filled Nate and Nikolai in on the events of the last day. They both glanced worriedly at Bane when I got to the part about what had been done to him. He was dozing in their large upholstered chair, his hand propping up his head. "I thought the silver thing was a myth," Nate said. "Nicky's wearing a silver necklace right now. Except for the fact that part of it is in the shape of a crucifix, it isn't hurting him."

"It doesn't cause harm until it's introduced into the body. It's kind of like a human holding a cyanide capsule. It doesn't hurt us until we ingest it."

"Can we help him?" Nikolai asked, watching Bane with a concerned expression.

"We're sure as hell going to try. I have my alchemy books and Bane's laptop with me. I'm hoping something in there will tell me how to get the poison out of his system."

"What about a blood transfusion?" Ty asked. His voice rarely rose above a whisper. He'd raised his head from my leg and was looking up at me with puppy dog eyes. He was holding on to my leg now with one delicate hand, as if he was afraid to lose contact with me.

Absolutely everything about him made me want to take care of Ty. I brushed his hair back gently from his eyes and told him, "We can definitely try that."

"What, um...what's the situation here exactly?" Nate asked, gesturing at Ty and me.

"Ty was at the house where we were being held prisoner and helped us escape from the Order. In return, I promised to take care of him. We first met several weeks ago. I should have taken him in back then, but I wasn't in the same place I am now."

"No offense Ty," Nikolai said, "but Tinder, are you sure you can trust him? You brought a vampire with you that was at the Order's compound. What if he's working with them? He could call Lucian and tell him where to find you. If the Order showed up here, that would be incredibly bad for all of us."

Ty's big blue eyes filled with fear. "I would never do that, I swear! Please believe me, Tinder."

Here was yet another indicator of just how much had changed in me over the last few weeks. I trusted Ty with my life, because my gut told me he was a good person. The fact that he was a vampire didn't even factor into it. "I know," I told him.

379

He looked like he wanted to cry with relief and climbed onto my lap, putting his arms around me and burying his face in my shoulder. "Oh hell," I muttered as I put my arm around him. "It's like having a ninety pound cat."

Nate and Nick obviously thought what was happening in front of them was odd...and okay, they kind of had a point. But I didn't care. It was nice to feel needed. I shot them a look and said, "Don't judge."

"No judging here," Nate said. "Just, you know, last time I saw you, you'd come here to kill Nicky. It seems your stance on vampires has softened a bit lately."

"It has." I let my eyes slide shut and rested my head on the back of the couch for a moment.

"You must be exhausted. Why don't you try to get some sleep?" Nate said.

I nodded and sat up. "Could I use your shower first? My jeans have dried to my legs and it feels really gross."

"Of course. Whose blood is that?" Nate asked as he and his husband got up.

"It's his," Nikolai told him.

380

"I don't know why that gunshot blast didn't kill me," I said as Ty slid off my lap and stood up. "The only explanation I can come up with is the spell Bane used on me to make me more resilient. He probably saved my life. Again."

I retrieved the rest of my stuff from the car, then made up a bed for Bane on the couch. Once he'd settled in, immediately falling asleep, I set up my bedroll for Ty, then made sure there were no gaps around any of the curtains. He fell asleep quickly, curled up in a little ball under my old blanket.

I had to cut through Nate and Nick's bedroom on the way to the shower. Nate was asleep in his husband's arms, but the big vamp was awake and watching me, his expression grave. I paused and said, "Thanks for letting me stay here, Nikolai." I shifted my weight from one foot to the other and added, "I owe you an apology. I've always treated you like a monster, and, well, I get it now. I know I was wrong to do that."

His expression softened a bit. "I never thought you'd change."

"Me neither."

"Does Bane know you're in love with him?" I hadn't told Nate and Nikolai that, but apparently I didn't need to.

"Yeah. I finally admitted it to him. And to myself."

"I'm glad."

"I wish he never met me," I murmured, looking at the carpet.

"Why would you say that?"

I lowered my voice to a whisper and said, "You get what they did to him, right? And why? That's the worst thing you can do to a vamp, the most insidious form of torture possible. The only reason he's not screaming in agony every minute is because of sheer force of will. That was all because of me. He turned on his own race in his efforts to keep me safe. This is what loving me did to him."

"We're going to figure out a way to save him, Tinder."

"God I hope so. I was told that silver poisoning can't be reversed. But...well, the people who taught me were wrong about a lot of things. Maybe they were wrong about that, too." There was so much sympathy in Nikolai's eyes that I could barely stand it. I murmured,

"Anyway, thanks again for helping us," then continued on to the bathroom.

When I returned to the living room a few minutes later dressed in a clean t-shirt and jeans, everyone was still asleep. I pulled Bane's thin, silver laptop out of my duffle bag and settled onto the big upholstered chair with my feet tucked under me. Even though I was exhausted, I couldn't stand the thought of sleeping away precious hours. Not when a time bomb was ticking inside the man I loved.

As the laptop powered up, I watched Bane. His forehead was creased, his jaw set. Even though he'd managed to fall asleep, the pain obviously still had him in a vice grip. His face was covered in dirt and dried blood, but even with all of that he was still beautiful. He was so much more than that, too. He was kind and loyal and smart and a million other good things. What the hell had I ever done to make a man like that fall in love with me?

My gaze lingered on his full lips for a while. I was surprised when they curved in a little smile and I glanced up at his eyes, which were open now and watching me. He held a hand out to me and I set the computer aside and crossed the room to him. As I snuggled against him and pulled the blanket over both of us he murmured, "You were a million miles away, love. What were you thinking about?"

"You."

"What about me?"

"I know so little about you."

"I'll tell you anything. What do you want to know?"

"Everything."

I was tucked under his chin, so I could hear his smile in his voice rather than see it. "That might take a while. We'd best block off the weekend." My heart clenched up at that. I didn't know if he'd live that long.

I pushed that thought down and interlaced my fingers with his, our hands between us as I asked quietly, "What do you like about me, August?"

"Everything."

I tilted my head back and smiled up at him. "No you don't. I drive you insane at least half the time."

He grinned and said, "That stubbornness is part of what's so great about you, though."

"I was just sitting there wondering what I'd ever done to get you to fall in love with me."

Bane gave me the sweetest smile. "Were you now?" I nodded and he said, "I can pinpoint the exact moment it happened."

"Really?"

He nodded. "It was a little over three years ago, the night your brother Eddie died in your arms. You and he were fighting vampires in that burned out department store and had been completely outnumbered. It was rare to see vampires team up like that back then, but these had fancied themselves as a street gang of sorts."

"I remember," I whispered.

August touched my cheek gently. "When your brother's life left his body, you threw your head back and yelled. I'll never forget that sound of such all-consuming anguish. You set Eddie down gently and then you got up and pulled two stakes from your jacket. You were barely eighteen then, just this fragile little slip of a boy. But you proceeded to take out six huge vampires singlehandedly, even as tears streamed down your face. It was the only time I've ever seen you cry, and heaven knows you've had plenty of reason to. You

385

fought with so much heart and with such focused determination. You were savage and beautiful, unlike anything I'd ever seen in over five centuries. Even though the odds were hopelessly against you, you stood strong and you triumphed." He cupped my face in his hand and whispered, "As I watched you avenge the death of your brother, I fell hopelessly in love with you."

The memory of that day still shook me to my core. I pushed it back down, like so many other things, and asked, "Where were you while this was happening? Why were you even in that building?"

"I was on the second floor gallery above you, looking for Allie. He'd been dating this gorgeous blonde vamp that was pure trouble. She often talked about a vampire uprising and about targeting the hunters. I'd heard a gang had formed and found out where they'd be that night. I was afraid she'd dragged him into that mess, but they weren't there."

We fell silent for a while, just watching each other. Finally I brought August's hand to my lips and kissed it, then said, "I should get back to the computer. Any idea where I should start looking for a way to cure you?"

"There is no cure, Tyler," he whispered.

I shook my head and told him, "There has to be a cure, and if not then we'll invent one ourselves."

He smiled at that. "There's the guy I fell in love with, a fighter no matter the odds."

"Damn right. I'll fight to save you with everything I have."

He leaned in and kissed me, so gently. "I appreciate that, love. But what's happening to me right now has one inevitable conclusion."

"I don't accept that."

He grinned and said, "Of course not. You wouldn't be Tyler Sousa Reynolds if you did." August kissed me again, tenderly, lovingly, his lips a soft caress against mine. He held me carefully, as if I was the most precious thing in all the world to him, and made me feel cherished more than I never even imagined was possible.

"I love you more than anything, August," I told him, looking deep into his beautiful eyes.

"That's the greatest gift I could possibly imagine," he whispered, then went back to kissing me.

I awoke to the hum of my tattoo gun and raised one eyelid. I was tucked in on the couch and on the floor in front of me, Ty lay on his left side, his shorts pushed down a few inches to reveal his bony hip. August sat cross-legged right behind him, a look of concentration on his handsome face as he drew on the exposed skin.

Ty smiled at me when he saw I was awake and said, "I'm getting a daylight tattoo! I can't believe it! I haven't seen the sun in over four years. It's going to be amazing to get to feel it on my skin again!"

As I sat up August told me, "I'm planning to do Nikolai next. Every time I see that cross around his neck, it makes me flinch. Do you realize how much it must hurt him to wear that against his skin?" He was freshly showered, his dark hair still a bit damp, and was dressed in a pair of jeans and a black t-shirt that must have been on loan from Nick. The pain of the cross pendant was nothing compared to the pain August must have been in right at that moment, but he was doing such an admirable job of trying to hide it. He'd even cast a spell to conceal the burning trails the silver left all over his body, probably because he knew how much seeing them upset me. It broke my heart that he was still trying so hard to make things good for me, even while suffering terribly.

"How long was I asleep?" I murmured, pushing my hair out of my face.

"Not nearly long enough," he replied, not looking up from his task.

I watched what he was doing for a while as I tried to wake up, then asked, "Is there some reason you're putting that in the exact same spot as your daylight tattoo?"

"Indeed there is. Symbols are always most effective when aligned with the body's energy centers. There are three more tattoos that go with this one, I've already inked them onto Ty. If they weren't positioned properly they wouldn't do their job, and this is one you really don't want to get wrong."

"Oh. I pretty much just slap my tattoos wherever."

He knit his brows and said, "I know."

"It's not like I knew better. But whatever. It's a done deal now, not like I can rearrange them."

"I could if you'd let me." August raised the gun from Ty's hip, took a look at his handiwork, and said, "You're done, kiddo. Let's see how the others have healed up."

Ty hopped up onto his knees and pulled down his t-shirt at the nape of his neck. "Does it look okay?" he asked.

"Perfect." August checked the small of Ty's back and his other hip, then said, "Sit tight for just two more minutes while I hide them."

Ty looked over his shoulder at August and asked, "Do you have to? They're so pretty."

"I'm afraid so. You know what I told you about this."

"That it has to remain a secret."

August nodded, then put his hands on Ty's narrow hips, each of which was marked with an identical tattoo. He cast a spell in Varsrecht, chanting quietly for a while. When he pulled his hands away, Ty's pale skin was pristine once again. August stood up and said, "Want to go outside and try it out?"

Ty stood up too, tugging his shorts back up as he asked, "Are you sure it worked?" August nodded, and

Ty turned to look at me nervously. "Will you come with me, Tinder?"

"Sure, just give me a minute." I made a quick pit stop in the bathroom, then led the way through the small house to the back door, just because a frolicking vampire really didn't seem like a front yard sort of thing. "Where are Nate and Nick?" I asked as I flipped the deadbolt.

"Nate's at work and Nick is off trying to find me some sort of solution at the library. I told him not to bother," August said. I sighed at that.

When I opened the door, Ty dove behind me with a gasp. Not that any sunlight spilled in. The back of the house was in shadow, so we'd actually have to cross the small deck and venture onto the lawn before he was in direct light. August and I stepped out onto the deck, but Ty hung back and admitted, "This is terrifying. Every part of me is telling me not to do this."

"That's your natural survival instinct," August told him. "You're going to find that, even though you can go out in daylight now, you're really not going to feel like sunbathing or anything. Being out in the day will always feel a bit off to you. You'll also realize though, that not having to worry about being caught without shelter and bursting into flames is a tremendous load off."

Slowly, Ty walked outside. He came up to me and took my hand, and he and I went to the edge of the shadows together. "Is this really going to be okay?" he asked, his eyes wide as he looked up at me. When I nodded, he looked out into the yard. He took a deep breath and held it, then thrust his hand into the sunlight. Nothing happened.

He pulled his hand back and remained rooted to the spot. After a few moments, I said, "Count of three, let's do this." He looked at me with so much trust in his eyes and nodded. We counted together, then took a big step into the sunlight.

Ty closed his eyes and tilted his face up into the light. A huge smile spread across his face. "This is amazing!" he yelled, and grabbed me in a hug before running to August and taking his hand. "It's working!" Ty towed him out onto the lawn.

As the little blond laughed and ran and spun around the yard, August draped his arm around my shoulders and said, "I always wondered what it would be like to be a parent. And right now, I feel like I know."

"What about Allie? Isn't he like a son to you?"

"Not really. He was twenty-eight when I sired him and has always been fiercely independent. The only way he's like a son is that we spend most of our time arguing."

"Oh." That actually made me feel bad for Allie.

I wondered how old Ty had been when he was turned. Surprisingly, August answered my unspoken question. "Ty was only seventeen when he was made. He was telling me about his life when you were sleeping. It's tragic, really. He'd been in and out of foster homes before his maker abducted him."

"Abducted him? He talked about his maker like he was sired by a saint."

"I know. I hope now that he's in your care, you'll help him have a little bit of the childhood he missed. Technically, you and he are the same age since he was turned four years ago, so...I don't know. Maybe you can figure out a way for both of you to enjoy at least a little of the childhood you were denied."

I didn't bother telling August that as soon as I found a way to heal him, I was going to be right back on the front lines, trying to take down Lucian and dismantle the Order. If he wanted a fantasy of Ty and me watching sports and playing videogames, acting the way twenty-one-year-olds were supposed to act, I'd let him have it.

But for now, I rested my head on August's shoulder and I let myself pretend, too. I pretended that the man I loved wasn't dying, and that he and I and the little blond boy dancing on the lawn were a real family. I pretended that this was our home, and it was safe and secure, a place where nothing could ever hurt us. I pretended that we'd have more days just like this one, and that they'd stretch into years. August and I would watch the seasons change back here in the little yard after Ty found someone of his own. We'd spend evenings in front of the fireplace and curl up in bed each night in each other's arms. We'd have a real life. We'd be together.

I was suddenly so overcome with emotion that I grabbed August in a fierce hug and exclaimed, "I can't fucking lose you! I just got you! How the fuck am I supposed to do this, August? How am I supposed to watch you die and then go on living?"

"That's exactly what you have to do, love," he said softly, his cheek against my hair. "I need you to go on living for both of us, instead of throwing your life away by trying to stop the Order. It's too late, that dam's about to break and when it does there won't be a hunter left standing. That's why I'm begging you to save yourself. Once I'm gone, let Allie take you out of the country. Start a new life. You've been fighting an unwinnable war since you were a child and it's time to retire, Tyler. Please! Go against every one of your natural impulses and *just walk away*. For me."

I couldn't tell him no. How could I hurt him like that? But he and I both knew I couldn't walk away. I was born a hunter, and I was destined to die as one.

I took a few deep breaths and half-turned from August as I tried to pull myself back together. Ty was standing a few feet away, nervously fidgeting with the hem of his t-shirt. I held out a hand to him and he rushed forward and took it. "Do you want to stay out here a bit longer?" I asked him, changing the subject. "Or are you ready to go back inside?"

"A little longer please," he said.

"Okay."

"Do you think maybe we could move the patio chairs into the sun and sit back here together?"

"Being out here doesn't bother you?"

He shrugged and said, "A little I guess. But being in sunlight again is way more good than bad."

"Maybe you and August can sit back here for a while. I should really get to work. I need to go through all my books on alchemy and—"

August cupped my chin and turned my face toward him as he said gently, "I'm telling you Tinder, you won't find anything in those books that will help. Please, just spend some time with me. That's all I really need." He looked at me so imploringly that I relented, taking him in my arms and stretching up to kiss his lips.

There were only two chairs, so August pulled me onto his lap after we'd carried them onto the lawn. He then proceeded to make Ty and me laugh with some completely outlandish stories about living in San Francisco in the 1970s. He was trying so hard to keep my mind off our troubles and it actually worked for a while. "Oh man," I said with a smile, "I'd give anything to see you back then! I'm picturing polyester bell-bottoms, huge mutton chop sideburns, and a great big porn 'stache. Am I right?"

"No," he said, shifting his gaze with an embarrassed grin.

"Oh, I'm totally right! What I wouldn't give for a scrapbook of August Pemberton Mayes through the centuries."

He grinned at that. "Had such a thing existed, I would have burned it long ago. And I didn't realize you know my full name."

"That reminds me." I kissed him and rested my forehead against his. "Thank you for the years of financial support. I would have been really lost without those checks."

"I always thought you'd be so angry when you found out that was me."

"A few months ago I would have been. Not now."

August raised an eyebrow at me. "You didn't escape from Allie, did you? He let you go, but not before you had a nice, long chat. That's how you know all of this, isn't it?"

"You have no proof of that," I said as I draped my arms around his shoulders and settled in comfortably.

"He had one job!"

I pressed a fingertip to his lips. "He loves you like a father. You should consider cutting him some slack."

"Bloody hell. You two really did bond, didn't you?"

"Don't be mad at him. Please?"

"Too late."

We sat outside for maybe another hour before Ty finally had enough. Most of the yard was in shadow by that point anyway. Once back inside, he asked to watch TV. We left him with the remote and went off to borrow Nate and Nick's bedroom for a while. "This is bad parenting," August joked, "letting the television babysit the kid while we sneak off for a little afternoon delight."

"That's not what we're doing. We're just going to lie down for a few minutes because you must be exhausted."

"I'm perfectly fine, Tinder."

"Liar."

"Okay, I'm not. But I refuse to act like an invalid."

We closed the bedroom door behind us and August stripped off my t-shirt and jeans, then picked me up and carried me to the bed. When we reached it, he tossed me onto it playfully and bent to kiss my stomach. "Won't you be joining me?" I asked when he straightened up and tapped his chin with a fingertip.

"Not yet. I need to do a bit of manscaping first."

"Meaning what, exactly? You're going to go off and groom your pubes?"

He grinned at that. "Why are you talking about pubic hair?"

"You brought it up with that manscaping comment."

August raised a brow at me. "Are you telling me that's a real word? I thought I just made it up. I was trying to be funny."

I smiled at that as August ran both his hands over my torso. "You've done quite a number on yourself with all of these tattoos. It's going to be a bit like working a jigsaw puzzle, trying to get them to the spots where they'll do the most good. Also, some of these are utterly useless. I'm removing them."

"Oh, we're doing that now?"

400

"Yes."

"I still don't see how you're going to relocate ink on skin."

He smiled at me cheerfully. "Magic."

"Well yeah, but still."

He proceeded to chant softly in Varsrecht while basically giving me a massage. It felt really nice, actually. I let myself relax as his strong hands ran over my body, my eyes sliding shut. Automatically, I whispered the spell as he worked on me, committing it to memory. "Does this spell only work on tattoos?" I asked after a while.

"Yes. It was designed for exactly this purpose, to move protection symbols that had been put in the wrong place. What else did you think it might work on?"

"I don't know. Rearranging words on paper, maybe."

"There's a different spell for that. I can't quite recall it, though."

"Do you ever try to come up with your own spells?"

"I can't. You know that only a certain extinct sect of witches and warlocks, the Bauschaft, ever had the power to create spells. All the rest of us can do is utilize them. That's why we're forever digging through the archives and looking for spells to suit our needs. Be a hell of a lot easier if we could just make up our own. My mother actually had some Bauschaft blood in her by the way, but she didn't pass the gene on to me. Instead, I took after my father."

"But, I think I did that yesterday. That's how I was able to find you and then get through all those vamps to reach you, by combining and altering existing spells."

"That's not possible. Your warlock ancestors were Willenschaft like I am. Workers of spells, not architects."

"Maybe I just stumbled on a couple existing spell by accident, then," I murmured as his hands swept down my right leg. I really didn't think that was the case, but right now I had no other explanation for what had happened. "Speaking of my ancestors, I'd really like to know about this werewolf that apparently climbed into my family tree. How did you know about that?"

"Like I told you before, I was an acquaintance of Duarte Sousa, your great, great grandfather. He had one daughter, Beatrice. She'd been forced to marry another full-blood hunter to keep the bloodline pure, but her husband was a miserable brute. I totally understood why Beatrice snuck off behind his back and had an affair with Dimas, a lovely, dirt-poor fisherman."

"Who, don't tell me, let me guess. Also happened to be a werewolf."

"And a nicer werewolf you'd never hope to meet."

"So she got knocked up by the dog boy. Great."

August clicked his tongue. "You're failing to see the beauty and romance of it. Two young people with a forbidden love which could really only end tragically. It's the stuff of poetry."

"It's also what got me mated to a sociopath."

"Well, there is that."

"How do you know all of this?"

"Because her father and I were in the same guild, as I'd said. He found out about his daughter's indiscretion and needed my help to cover it up, since I was the strongest warlock he knew."

"Really? He helped her? Given the day and age, I'd have expected him to disown her or worse."

"Well, he was less than thrilled, of course. But maybe he understood why she'd done it, given the poor woman's husband."

"So, how did you cover it up?"

"We bespelled the baby. He was only half werewolf, so we didn't have to worry about him shifting. But he was born into a family of hunters, so we had to conceal his...lack of humanness from the rest of the family. Otherwise, they would have killed him."

"Well, kudos. That was a hell of a concealment job. Right up until the moment my, what did you call him? Oh yeah, lupine lover showed up, I didn't have a damn clue that I had werewolf blood in me."

August's hands continued to caress me. After a while he said, "Done. Take a look and tell me what you think."

I sat up and looked down at myself, then murmured, "Holy shit."

I slid out of bed and went into the bathroom so I could look at myself in the big mirror over the sink. After August had relocated my tattoos, he'd concealed most of them. "You left three. Why is that?" I asked. I still had a circular symbol above my right nipple and lines of text down the inside of each arm.

"Because they're sexy as hell," he said with a grin. "Also, purely ornamental."

"Ornamental?"

"None of the three do a damn thing. I just like them."

"You hid all my scars, too. I don't even look like myself."

"Indulge me on that one, will you? I always hated the history of pain and suffering written across your body in all of those scars. Now there's not that constant reminder of all you've been forced to endure."

I thought about that for a few moments, then turned to August and said, "Thank you."

"Really? You're okay with it? I thought you'd argue. It always seemed like you wore those scars as a badge of honor."

I shrugged and said, "If this makes you happy, hell, why not."

"Agreeable Tinder is a strange beast. I don't quite know what to make of him."

"Just enjoy it," I told him as I picked up his hand. "Now come on, let's lay down and rest."

"I'm all for laying down, but resting is not on the agenda."

When we got back to the bed he scooped me up and laid me on my back, then ran his eyes down my naked body as he undressed himself. His chest was perfectly, flawlessly smooth. He'd hidden the damage being done to him completely, creating this illusion for me. "How bad has it gotten?" I asked quietly.

"We're not going to talk about that right now, Tinder."

"But I need to know."

"No you don't," he said as he climbed up on the bed and pushed my legs apart. "This is all about living in the moment. Life never comes with any guarantees, you know. None of us has any idea if this is our last day on the planet, even at the best of times. All we can do is enjoy the present." He climbed on top of me, supporting himself on his knees and elbows, and kissed me deeply before murmuring, "I'm so damn grateful to get to have today with you."

When he kissed me again all of me responded. He rubbed his growing erection against mine and nipped my bottom lip, and I moaned as he slid down my body and deep-throated my cock. He wrapped his lips around it tightly and pulled up slowly as I went rock hard in his mouth, his eyes locked with mine. As he repeated that several more times, I arched up off the mattress, heat shooting up my spine.

He slipped an index finger between my lips, and after I sucked it he slid it inside me until his hand was cupping my ass. I fought back a yell of pure pleasure as he fingered me, all the while continuing that intense blow job. By the time he sat up, I was wild with need.

He murmured, "Sorry Nate and Nick for the invasion of privacy," and pulled open the drawer of their nightstand, then grabbed a bottle of lube and slicked himself quickly.

Instead of just pushing into me, he picked me up and sat me on his lap, burying his cock in me to the hilt. He held me tightly as he thrust up into me and I wrapped my arms around him, my forehead against his. "God I love you," I murmured.

"I love you too, Tyler. More than life itself."

I bounced on his cock as he thrust up into me, pulling back a couple inches to look deep into his eyes. "Tell me," I whispered.

He didn't need to ask what I meant. "You're mine, Tyler. And I'm yours, too."

I kissed him with everything I had, fiercely, passionately, trying to show him how much he meant to me. He laid me on my back, his arms still around me, and began to thrust into me hard and fast, eyes locked with mine. I cried out when I came, my cock pressed between us, and as my body clenched around him August came too, deep in me, and then he murmured again, "I love you more than anything."

We stayed there for a long time afterwards, kissing and touching each other. I wanted it to go on forever, to never stop holding him and to never stop being held. But of course, forever wasn't an option.

Finally August got out of bed, standing beside it and caressing my cheek as he tried on a grin. It was almost convincing, though the pain had to be eating him alive. To keep us from getting swallowed up by the thought that that might have been the last time we'd ever make love, he said lightly, "We're officially the worst houseguests ever. Come on love, let's wash our hosts' bedding before they get home." I pushed down the heartache and got up, taking his hand.

*****

Nate and Nick arrived home together in their old Jeep maybe an hour later. They found Ty, August and me all lined up on the couch. Ty and I were going through my alchemy books while August played with my hair, my leg draped over his. He refused to help look for solutions because he insisted there were none to be found.

Nikolai said, "I didn't turn up anything at the library. Silver poisoning usually isn't fatal in humans so there was nothing much on how to treat it. I tried to relate it to other forms of toxicity, but I didn't find anything we could use."

"Tried to tell you that, mate. I appreciate the effort, though," August said.

"You hungry?" Nate asked me, and when I nodded he said, "Come into the kitchen, let's see about some dinner."

While Nate and I put a meal together, August fired up my tattoo gun again and went to work on Nikolai's daylight symbols. I knew why he wanted to get that taken care of as soon as possible. He didn't think he'd be around much longer.

"How are you holding up?" Nate asked as he put some rice in a pot.

"I almost lost it at one point today, but fortunately I got my shit together quickly. That's just not helpful."

"I think we need to take Bane to a hospital and have him compel a doctor into giving him a blood transfusion."

"He and I talked about that, but he says the silver's not just in his blood. He says it's burned into his tissues, so a transfusion wouldn't help."

"Do you think he's in a lot of pain?"

"Yeah. Every now and then, I see glimpses of it in his eyes," I said, "but he's trying so hard to hide it."

"He doesn't want to worry you."

"You're right."

As I helped chop some vegetables I said, "Thank you again for letting us stay with you. I really love it here. This house feels so comfortable, like a home, I guess. I never felt that anywhere but here. I wish I could stay longer, but we need to leave in the morning. We can't keep putting you and your husband in danger like this."

"The Order will never find you here."

"Probably not, but then again, who knows what they're capable of?"

"Where will you go?"

"I have no idea."

"Just stay, Tinder. Bane shouldn't be out on the road, not now. Let us help you."

"You've always been such a good friend to me," I said quietly as I set down the knife and rested my hands on the counter. "All I've ever done is make things difficult for you, but still, you've shown me nothing but kindness. I don't know what's going to happen to me after I leave here, but I want you to know your friendship has meant so much to me."

He drew me into a hug. "I hate how much that sounds like goodbye."

When I let go of him I pulled up a little smile. "Nah. Not goodbye. Just...thanks."

We went back to cooking. There was so much comfort in this, just the simple act of preparing a meal that didn't come from a can. When we finished, Nate and I carried our plates into the living room and ate as August worked. Nikolai had stripped to the waist and was leaning forward, forearms on his knees, as he told the story of his maker, who'd sired him to be a soldier. Ty was curled up on the couch beside them, knees drawn to his chest as he listened closely to Nick's tale. He glanced at me when I finished eating, some kind of need in his blue eyes.

"Are you hungry?" I asked him. When he nodded I said, "Come here." Nate took my empty plate from me and I murmured, "Thanks," as Ty hurried across the room and climbed onto my lap. I was struck again by how incredibly childlike and innocent he was, despite all that had been done to him in his short life. "Go ahead and drink from me." I stretched the neck of my t-shirt out to the side, exposing some skin for him.

He put his thin arms around me and bit my shoulder. His maker had filed down his fangs, so he had to bite pretty hard to draw blood. "Sorry," he murmured, then drank from me hungrily. I wondered

412

how long it had been since those fuckers that had kept him as a toy had bothered to feed him.

Ty stayed on my lap after he finished eating. "Thank you," he said softly.

"You're welcome."

"I was so right to give myself to you," he whispered, his cheek against my chest. "This is all I ever wanted, just someone to take care of me."

I couldn't imagine a worse choice. After killing all those vamps and escaping from their headquarters, I knew the Order had to be gunning for us with a vengeance. It was only a matter of time before we were spotted and they closed in. When that happened I'd try to keep Ty safe, but I'd probably fail him, just like I'd failed all the members of my family. The face of my brother Eddie flashed though my memories, the way he'd looked when he was dying in my arms. I took a deep breath to calm myself and hugged Ty a little tighter.

When the tattoos were done, Nikolai removed the daylight talisman he wore around his neck and set it on the coffee table, rubbing the spot on his chest where the crucifix had ached and burned for decades. "I'm going to bury that up on the hillside tomorrow morning," I said, "so no other vamp can ever find it and use it." It was kind of a waste, since the thing really belonged in a museum. It was finely made and looked like it had probably come out of the Italian Renaissance. But I didn't know of a way to remove the spell that had been cast on it, so it had to go. I could just imagine it falling into the hands of someone like Lucian.

"Be my guest," Nikolai said.

Nate proposed a movie night and we all agreed. August curled up in a corner of the couch and I leaned against him, his arm around me and his computer on my lap. I'd decided to search his archives trying a different approach. Instead of looking for a way to cure silver poisoning, I was now trying to find something that would purify the body. If I found something even close, I was going to try to build on it like I did yesterday. I still didn't know what had happened back there, but on the off chance I was capable of coming up with a new spell, I had to try to use it to help August.

We were watching Star Wars because somehow Ty had never seen it. He was curled up on the couch beside us, his head on my thigh. I glanced over at my friends.

414

They shared the big upholstered chair, Nate on Nikolai's lap, their arms around each other. They weren't even pretending to watch the movie, even though I knew it was one of Nate's favorites. Instead, they were kissing each other tenderly, so totally wrapped up in one another. The love between them was incredibly intense and truly beautiful. I was so fucking glad I hadn't gone through with killing Nikolai, back when I thought the world was black and white.

August hugged me a little tighter and I tilted my head back to look up at him. I was surprised to see him looking drawn, strain clearly visible around his eyes. The pain was taking its toll on him. I reached up and touched his face gently.

Suddenly, every vampire in the room went on alert. August opened his mouth to say something. I never heard it though, because a fraction of a second later, the front door splintered inward with a huge crash.

All of us were up in an instant as Sean and a dozen more vamps barreled into the house. Nate was standing closest to the door, and the huge red-haired vampire backhanded him so hard that my friend flew across the room. He hit the far wall hard enough to crack the plaster and crumpled to the floor as I screamed his name. He wasn't moving.

"Tinder!" I turned to look at Ty, who threw me my double-sided crossbow before rushing to the corner and crouching down, terror in his eyes.

I spun around and took out two vamps, then ducked another's grasp and kicked him in the kneecap with the heel of my bare foot. I realized I was still moving much faster than usual. Apparently whatever I'd done to myself earlier hadn't worn off yet.

I was quick enough to reach my weapons bag and load two more stakes in my crossbow. A vamp grabbed me from behind, but August pulled him off me and staked him with what must have been a piece of the splintered front door. Two more vamps grabbed him, but I took them both out easily with my crossbow and turned to reload again.

I was oddly clear-headed during all of this, my focus unlike anything I'd ever experienced. I guessed that was because of the way August had fine-tuned my protection symbols. I spun around again and assessed the situation in a fraction of a second. August was holding his own against one vamp and three more were trying to attack Nikolai, stakes drawn back as they tried to find an opening. Nick was fighting like a demon, totally given over to his vampire side, rage just radiating from him. I took out two of the three vamps attacking him to help his odds. My aim was perfect. Another upshot of what August had done for me, no doubt.

Two more vamps ran at me. I was moving and thinking so fast that it was almost like watching them in slow motion. I pulled a gun from my bag and emptied my clip, which slowed them down even more before August engaged them. When the gun was empty, I threw it aside and went to reload my crossbow again, but I had to dig down in my bag to find more of the thin stakes it fired.

I was picked up all of a sudden and propelled across the room where I was slammed into a wall, my feet way up off the floor. Sean held me by my throat and yelled, "Why the fuck does Lucian want you alive? It can't just be because he wants to kill you himself, because he had every opportunity to do that before you gave him the slip. What the fuck are you to him?" He slammed me against the wall a couple times in frustration.

"How did you find us here?" My voice was all rasp, since he was right on the verge of crushing my windpipe. I was stalling for time, and just knew Sean was arrogant enough to take the bait and brag about how brilliant he was.

"One of your little playmates was dumb enough to go to a public library and research silver poisoning. We have eyes and ears all over southern California and some compelled human spotted what your pal was doing. From there it was just a simple matter of writing down his license plate and sending the information to me." He looked incredibly smug.

"Great. You got me. Go ahead and take me to Lucian." I was helpless as long as I was pinned to this wall, but the moment he let me down I was going to end this fucker.

"Lucian's on his way here, but it'll take him a while to reach us. He'd gone running after a red herring that sent him all the way down to San Diego looking for you. Now I wonder who could have gotten him out of the way like that?" His gloating grin made the answer pretty obvious.

"Why'd you throw him off my scent?"

"So I could get here first and do what he's somehow unwilling to. I'm going to thoroughly enjoy killing you, you little shit."

"But Lucian wants me alive," I said as he drew an enormous blade from a sheath at his hip.

"I know. But what could I do? My men went crazy and sliced you up before I could stop them – at least as far as Lucian will ever know. You've already managed to dust most of them and I'll take care of the rest. Dead men tell no tales, or so I've heard." His smile made my blood run cold.

I gasped and struggled with everything in me as he tightened his grip on my throat and raised the knife to my eye, my hands clawing wildly at the one that was about to cut off my air supply. In the next instant, I fell to the floor beside Sean's clothes, little bits of him still swirling in the air. I looked up at Ty, who grasped a huge stake in both hands, and said, "Thank you." My voice was scratchy.

He burst into tears and I leapt up and grabbed him in a hug as I quickly assessed the room. August had been grappling with a vamp that was built like a Viking, and just then managed to stake the big blond. That had been the last of the invaders. I looked for Nate and Nick and realized they were behind the overturned upholstered chair. A moment later, I heard Nikolai sobbing.

I let go of Ty and ran to where Nick cradled his husband's lifeless body in his arms, yelling, "No!" as I dropped to my knees and touched my friend's face.

August dragged himself over to us. He was bleeding in several places and he'd had to drop the veil he'd been maintaining, so I could see that his entire body was crisscrossed with a web of red and black burn marks, just below the surface of his skin. "Nikolai," he exclaimed, his voice rough with pain. "What are you waiting for? Turn him! It's your only chance to save your husband!"

"It's too late. He's already dead." Nick's voice was pure heartbreak.

"He just passed moments ago. There's still time, but you have to do it now!"

Nikolai looked up at him with wild desperation in his eyes. "How?"

"Mix your blood with his. He won't be able to swallow it, but you can still get it in him." August used the stake he was holding to pierce Nate's wrist, then did the same to Nikolai. Nick didn't hesitate. He pressed his wrist to his husband's and held them together with his free hand as tears streamed down his face.

"This doesn't always take since he'd already died," August said, dragging himself into a seated position, "but I know how to give you some extra insurance. With this, he'll probably be reborn." *Probably*. He put one hand on Nikolai's forehead, the other on Nate's, then closed his eyes and began to chant in Varsrecht.

Several minutes went by. Ty knelt down and put his arms around me and I clutched him tightly. Eventually, August leaned back against the wall, his voice weak as he said, "It's done. Your wrist has probably healed up by now Nikolai, so you can go ahead and remove it. Make sure you completely seal Nathaniel's wound to keep your blood in him." I held Nate's arm as Nick ran for a medical kit, then quickly wrapped his husband's wrist with first aid tape. He sat back when it was done and tenderly brushed Nate's hair from his forehead.

"Do you think it worked?" I asked August.

"There's one way to be sure. What do you see when you use your sight?"

When I engaged it, the three vampires around me lit up immediately. But when I looked at Nate I murmured, "I don't see anything."

"Ty, turn the lights off and Tinder, look again."

Ty rushed to do as he'd been told and I leaned over Nate, staring at him long and hard. "I don't know," I said. "All I see is Nikolai's light."

August shakily pushed himself to his feet. "Come here for a moment, mate. Let's let Tinder get a good look." All three vampires stepped back from us.

I leaned in close, touching my friend's cheek. "This has to work," I whispered. "I can't lose you,

Nathaniel. You're the best friend I've ever had." I looked for even the faintest glimmer of light. There was nothing, though. Nothing at all. I sat up and yelled, slamming my fists into the floor. It was my fault he was dead. Everything was *all my fucking fault*.

August pulled me to my feet and clutched me against him. "I know what you're thinking," he said, "but you didn't do this."

"Of course I did! I never should have come here!"

"You didn't know this would happen. The Order shouldn't have been able to find us here."

I turned my head and looked back at my friend's body. Nikolai was standing over him and sobbing, his body shaking. And then I whispered, "Oh my God."

I let go of August and dropped to my knees again, leaning in close to Nate and staring at his profile. The palest white light radiated from him. A peal of laughter burst from me and I looked up at Nikolai. "I can see it! Just barely, but it's there. He's turning!"

Nick fell to his knees, still sobbing but this time with relief. He grabbed his husband and hugged him tightly as I got up and flipped the lights back on, his tears soaking into Nate's sun-streaked hair. August righted the chair and sank into it as he said, "You need to get him out of here, Nikolai. I heard Sean say Lucian is headed this way, although it sounded like he's a fair distance out. Also, you know how wild Nathaniel will be when he wakes up in a couple days, and he'll stay that way for months. You'll have to take him someplace isolated."

"I have a place we can go, a lake house," Nick said. "It's really remote."

"That's perfect, mate." August hesitated before saying, "There's one other thing. You know he might not recognize you when he wakes up."

Nikolai looked up at him with a stricken expression. "Oh God, that's right. That happened to me. I forgot everything about my human life after I was turned."

"That only happens about half the time," August told him. "And if it does, well, you'll just make him fall in love with you all over again."

"But he has a family, too, a mom and stepdad and little brothers."

August said, "We don't know yet if he'll forget them." He leaned back in the chair with a wince.

424

"Regardless, you'll need to tell them he's going away for a while until you can get Nathaniel to the point where he can be around people again." Nikolai nodded in agreement and August told him, "Right. Well, why don't you pack some clothes while Ty and Tinder secure your house? Maybe they can use the bedroom door to close up the gaping hole where your front door used to be. Best be quick about it."

Nick carried his husband to the couch, where he set him down gently. He seemed reluctant to leave his side, but Ty approached them and said, "I'll stay with your husband while you pack." He knelt on the floor beside Nate and picked up his hand, which he held between both of his. Nick hurried to grab a few things.

August closed his eyes, a tremor going through his body. "Before we do anything else, you need to drink from me," I told him.

"There's really no point, love," he said. "I'm way too far gone."

"Don't say that." I sat on the arm of his chair and held my wrist out to him. "Just drink."

"Draining your blood also drains your energy. I'd rather keep you strong, since I'm a lost cause anyway."

Another tremor racked his body and he sharply drew in a breath.

"No! There has to be a way to reverse what's been done to you. I just need a little more time to figure out what to do!"

"I'm out of time, Tyler. I can feel it, I'm starting to go. Just come here." He held his arms out to me. They were shaking. I climbed into his lap, straddling him, and clutched him to me.

"I love you so much, August. You have to fight to stay alive!"

"I love you too, Tyler. More than anything. But we have to accept this."

"I can't! Don't just give up!"

"It's inevitable, love." Pain creased his forehead and he cried out, grabbing onto me. Whatever was going on inside him was happening so damn fast all of a sudden!

"No!" I sat up and cupped his face in my hands. Quickly, desperately, I tried to cobble a spell together. When it did nothing, I tried another. And another.

"Please, Tyler. Keep yourself safe. For me. That's what I want, more than anything in all the world."

Talking seemed to become a huge effort, and there was no more hiding the pain. His eyes filled with agony as his body trembled, a sheen of perspiration breaking out on his brow. He started to slip in and out of consciousness.

"Please don't die. Please!" My voice sounded so small and childlike. He passed out, even though his body still twitched and shook as if he was having a seizure.

A deep voice said, "I know how to save him." My heart leapt in my chest as I looked up at Lucian, who filled the doorway. "But it'll come at a price."

"Do it," I exclaimed. "Hurry! He doesn't have much time."

"Don't you want to know what the price will be?" Lucian asked as he approached me slowly.

"I can guess. I'm the price, right?" He nodded, and I exclaimed, "Fine. Just save him!"

"Do you understand what you're agreeing to? I'll save his life only if you promise not to run away again."

I wanted to punch him in the face. "How the fuck can you give me ultimatums at a time like this?"

"I have no choice. You'll always run from me otherwise, and I don't want to drag you out of here and keep you in chains. That would just make you resent me."

As desperate as I was to save August, I suddenly saw an opportunity to save a lot of lives. "If I go with you, not only will you save August, you'll take him off your hit list. In fact, I want you to do away with your hit list altogether. I want the Order to stop going after the hunters."

His knit his brows and crossed his arms over his massive chest. "Really? You're negotiating at a time like this?"

"Not much point in saving August tonight if you just turn around and kill him tomorrow."

He ground his teeth. "Is that it?"

"Actually no. You also have to leave every vampire in this room unharmed."

"Why do you think I'd agree to any of this?"

"Because I have something you want."

"You *are* something I want."

"Same difference. Do we have a deal?"

He stared at me long and hard, his eyes flashing with anger. Finally he muttered, "Fine."

"Fine what? Say it."

"As long as you promise not to run away, Bane, the hunters on my hit list, and every vampire here will be safe from the Order and from me. You have my word."

"Do it," I murmured.

"Swear to me too, Tinder," Lucian said. "Swear you'll keep your end of the agreement."

I looked in his eyes. "I swear I won't run away."

He immediately became all business. "Help me lay him down." I leapt up and we moved August onto the floor, and then Lucian tore the bloody t-shirt off of him. "This will be quickest if you and I work together," the big vampire said and we knelt on opposite sides of August. Lucian picked up my left hand and rested his other one on August's stomach. "Do everything I do."

I put my free hand on August's midsection as Lucian started chanting in Latin. After he went through it twice, I started chanting in unison with him. A shock like static electricity passed between our joined hands. The burned out tracts under August's skin swelled and rolled, as if the silver was boiling under his skin. We repeated the chant over and over, then Lucian said, "After one final recital, pull your right hand up as fast as you can."

We ran through it one more time, then yanked our hands away from August. The skin across his stomach tore open as a stream of blood shot out, spattering the ceiling. Lucian quickly shielded the wound with his body as a little of the blood dripped back down, and it landed on his back instead of on August. After a moment, he picked August up and dragged him across

430

the room to keep him from getting re-infected by the dripping blood.

"Are you sure that's all of it? It wasn't just in his blood, it was in his tissues, too," I said.

"I drew all the silver back into his blood before concentrating it and expelling it from his body."

"Thank you," I murmured.

Lucian looked into my eyes. "Go ahead and feed him, then say goodbye once he wakes up. I'll be waiting out front." He got up and left without another word.

I picked up a stake and gouged my wrist with a slight wince, then pried August's mouth open and let my blood run between his lips. It was almost a minute before he swallowed. A couple minutes after that he regained consciousness, taking hold of my arm and drinking deeply.

Finally he sat up, all of his injuries completely healed, and asked, "What happened?"

"I made a deal to save you."

"With who, the devil?" he asked as he looked down at himself. There was absolutely no sign of the silver poisoning.

"Yeah, pretty much." My heart ached as I leaned in and kissed him, then whispered, "I have to go." This wasn't goodbye forever, it was goodbye for now. I wasn't going to say that with Lucian in earshot though, and it still hurt, even if it was just temporary. I knew that August would do what he always did. He'd find me, somehow. He'd fix this. I just didn't know how long that was going to take, or what would happen to me in the meantime...though I could probably guess what Lucian would do to me.

"What do you mean? Go where?"

"I love you more than anything, August. That's why I just couldn't let you die, no matter the cost." I kissed him again and said, "Take care of Ty, okay? And help Nate and Nick, they're going to need it."

"I don't understand what's happening."

I got up and he did, too, and then I drew him into my arms and held him tightly. "I know. Nikolai and Ty can explain it to you after I'm gone. Just know I chose this because you mean more to me than anything, August."

I let go of him and gave Ty a hug. Tears were streaming down his face. "I'm sorry that I have to go.

August will take good care of you, though." He just nodded, looking up at me like a lost puppy. To Nikolai I said, "Please tell Nate I said goodbye. I know you're going to have a few rough months ahead, and wish you both all the luck in the world."

August followed me out the gaping hole where the front door used to be, immediately going into fight mode when he saw Lucian on the sidewalk beside a midnight blue coupe. "It's alright," I told him, putting a hand on his arm. "I just need to go with him now. Remember I love you, okay?"

"What are you talking about? You can't go with him!" August exclaimed.

"You'll always be the love of my life. Only you, August. Now and forever." I stretched up and kissed him again. "Thank you for loving me and taking care of me, even when I was totally unlovable."

I turned and started to walk away, my heart aching as August tried to come after me. *This is just for now. It's not forever,* I thought, wishing he could read my mind. I hated that I was hurting him.

Lucian raised one hand, just a little, and I felt a shockwave roll past me. It didn't affect me at all, but it pushed August back, then held him there. When I stopped in front of Lucian, he reached into my pocket, pulled out my phone, and tossed it onto the lawn. Then he opened the passenger door for me and closed it once I climbed inside. He came around and got behind the wheel as I pressed my eyes shut. August was yelling for me, so much anguish in his voice.

As he pulled away from the curb, I told Lucian, my voice tight, "I hate you. I will *always* hate you. And there's not a single fucking thing you can do about it."

"I know." He said that so softly.

We drove north up the coast, leaving Santa Barbara behind us. "Where the hell are you taking me?" I asked after a while.

"I have absolutely no idea."

"Seriously?"

"I can't bring you back to my home, not with so many of my men coming and going from there all the time. They'd never understand that we're mated, they would just see it as a betrayal." I didn't say anything. After a pause, he asked, "Is Sean dead, the vampire with long, red hair?"

"Yeah, he and the rest of his death squad."

434

"He tried to kill you?"

"Newsflash: you really don't have much control over your troops. He was going to dice me up and claim it was done by another vamp that had already been dusted."

"Sean was always a loose cannon."

We drove in silence for maybe an hour, until Lucian abruptly turned down a private drive. He parked in front of an impressive, contemporary beach house that was off by itself among some low dunes and went up to the door. An annoyed middle-aged yuppie in loud red, white and blue striped silk pajamas answered his insistent knocking after a couple minutes.

"Do you know what time it is, asshole?" the homeowner demanded in a nasal voice. "I don't give a shit about your broken down car, or whatever personal crisis you're having that you somehow think justifies waking me up and—" the vampire glamoured him with a single word and asked who else was in the house. "No one. I live alone," the man replied.

"Well there's a shocker, given that charming personality," Lucian muttered, then sent him on vacation for a week, with instructions to call after daybreak and cancel the cleaning service and anyone else that might be coming to the house for the next seven days. The man grabbed his keys and drove off in his pajamas, and Lucian parked in the garage, then shut the door behind us with a switch on the wall.

We went through to the large, obviously professionally decorated pale blue living room. Lucian picked up the house phone and crushed it effortlessly, then pulled his phone out and dialed a number. When someone answered, he said, "Sean's dead, along with his team. I'm taking a couple days to regroup. You're to cease all strikes immediately. Bane and the hunters on our list are no longer targets. Is that clear?" He paused for a moment to listen, then said, "Until I return, you're in charge, but are to do absolutely nothing without my approval. Do you understand?" Apparently whoever was on the line answered in the affirmative, and Lucian shut off the phone and told me, "Wait here." He went upstairs, then came back down a minute later.

"What did you just do?"

"Hid my cellphone and car keys, in case you get any ideas."

"That was pointless. I could just walk away if I decided to renege on our agreement. Are you going to hide my legs, too? Actually, ew. Don't answer that."

He watched me for a moment, then headed down a hallway to my right as he said, "Come with me."

When we reached the dark master bedroom, Lucian took his jacket off and tossed it over a chair, then began unbuttoning the cuffs of his black dress shirt. He looked at me and said, "Get in bed."

"No."

A muscle twitched in his jaw. "I said, *get in that fucking bed*, Tinder."

"And I said no."

He lunged at me with a growl, baring his fangs, those otherworldly silver eyes flashing with anger as he towered over me. For reasons I couldn't explain, I cowered instead of fighting, casting my gaze to the floor. What the fuck? Lucian hesitated, then reached out and touched my hair gently. I shrank away from him, which made him sigh quietly.

His voice was low and calm when he said, "I'm not going to rape you, Tinder. But I am going to sleep in the same bed as my mate, and I'm going to hold you, whether you like it or not. I'm not doing that to torture you. I'm doing it because I need to touch you so desperately that I feel like my insides are being ripped to shreds." He lowered his voice further and said, "Now please get in that bed."

Fear coursed through my system as I did as I was told. Why the fuck was I obeying him? Lucian stripped down to just his briefs and climbed under the covers, then pulled my t-shirt off before laying down and drawing me into his arms. My hands were balled into fists and pressed to my chest like a shield, but even so he sighed with relief as our skin made contact.

I lay there in the darkness with my heart racing, preparing to fight him off the moment he tried to take this further. After a few minutes, during which absolutely nothing happened, I asked, "Is this really it? Only this? You're not going to try to have sex with me?"

"I love you," he said quietly. "That's not a choice, it's just an inescapable fact of this damn bond between us. Even though I'd give anything to make love to you, I meant it when I said I wasn't going to rape you. I would never hurt you like that."

I took that in for a while, then asked, "What kind of hold do you have over me? Why couldn't I look you in the eye when you were yelling?"

"I'm your alpha. It's hardwired into you to submit to me."

"Fucking great," I muttered.

After a pause he said, "I'm sorry I yelled. This whole situation is throwing me completely off kilter. I've never felt my wolf side so strongly before, that's what came out earlier. I didn't even recognize myself."

He fell asleep eventually and only then did I let myself relax a little. I should have been slipping out of bed and finding something to use as a stake, but somehow I just couldn't. It didn't matter that I hated Lucian. I just didn't have it in me to end him. In fact, I actually felt a little protective of him.

"Fuck my life," I whispered as I closed my eyes.

"Is that breakfast?"

"No. This is," I said as I flipped Lucian off.

I crossed my bare feet, which were up on the yuppie's coffee table, and took a long drink from the bottle of Jack in my other hand as he said, "You're going to give yourself liver poisoning."

"Totally worth it." A thought occurred to me and I raised an eyebrow at him. "You don't have some fucked up idea about turning me into a vampire, do you? Because I did not sign on for that shit! If you try to turn me, the deal is off and I am *staking* your ass!" My words slurred a bit and I added, "Well, technically, your heart. Staking your ass wouldn't actually be effective."

"I have to change you, otherwise I'll outlive you by centuries. I wouldn't be able to stand it."

"So why didn't you do that first thing? I mean, I would have stopped you, but why haven't you tried yet?"

He pushed his long hair back from his face and sighed in exasperation. "Because of this accursed mate bond! It makes me care about your feelings, and I know you don't want to be turned. Clearly I need to get over that."

"Is this the first time you've ever cared about somebody else?"

"To this extent, yes."

"Newsflash. That's not because you're a vampire. It's because you're a douche." I took another long drink, then added, "Besides, if you really cared about my feelings, you wouldn't have taken me away from the man I love."

Lucian narrowed his eyes. "Do you have any idea how much I hate Bane? But I saved his life *for you!*"

"You know what August's crime was? Falling in love with me. He turned on his people so he could help me and keep me alive. Ironically, here you are, going behind the backs of your fellow vampires and betraying their trust, for the exact same reason!"

"But I didn't choose to fall in love with you!"

"Do you think August did? Do you think *anyone* ever makes a conscious decision to fall in love? Let me answer that for you. Hell no! It just happened to him, the same way this mate bond happened to you!"

"Okay, maybe. There are plenty more reasons to hate him, though." He started to leave the living room, but I jumped up and followed him.

"What's the plan here, Lou? Do you mind if I call you Lou?"

"Yes."

"Tough!" I took another drink and he spun on me, grabbed the bottle from my hand, and threw it across the room, where it shattered against the wall. I didn't even react to that. Instead I said, "You got what you wanted, me as your totally ungrateful and super pissed off house pet. Now what? Are we just going to hide out here until the vamps that were dumb enough to follow you decide they're okay with their leader being mated to a hunter? I'm going to guess there isn't another vamp-werewolf hybrid in the lot of them, right? That's too bad, because they would've been the only ones that might have even sort of understood the mate thing. The rest of them are just going to regard you as a traitor for being with me, which means you're utterly fucked."

"Do you think any of that is news to me?"

I flashed him a big smile. "No, but it's fun to remind you. Over and over and over."

"If you think being incredibly annoying is going to get me to release you from the oath you took, you're sadly mistaken."

"Oh I'm not acting like this to get you to release me. I'm doing it because making your life a living hell is the only way I can possibly endure being saddled with you."

"I hate the fact that you're only an eighth shifter. If you were half-blooded like me, you and I would be on even footing. You'd be aching with need just like I was, instead of endlessly harassing me."

"Aching with need. Ugh, TMI."

He frowned at me. "I don't mean that in a sexual sense, although the urge to breed you is quite powerful. My need for you is so much deeper than that, though."

"Right. You need me in a nonsexual sense. Why don't I believe that?" Lucian grabbed me suddenly, pressing my back to his chest. As he clamped his hand down on my forehead, I struggled and yelled, "What the fuck are you doing? Let go of me!"

"You need a lesson in empathy, so I'm letting you in." Some kind of energy surged from him. It kind of felt like a huge truck rushing past on the highway. In the next instant, I could feel him, as if I was living his emotions. A yearning so intense, so all-consuming flooded me that I cried out. Yes, there was a sexual component to it, but he'd been telling the truth. There was so much more there, including pure love and profound sadness, brought on by a mate that didn't love him in return.

When he finally let go of me, I tried to shove him and only ended up driving myself back a few feet. "Fuck! You just made me care about you, you asshole!"

"Is that really such a horrible thing?"

"Yes, considering you're a total sociopath!"

"I'm hardly a sociopath. I'm trying to lead my people out of oppression. We don't deserve to be hunted like animals, Tinder. You've condemned my entire race based on the actions of a few. What your kind has been doing is nothing short of genocide."

"And vampires are so innocent."

"I know not all of us are, but look at the facts. In the last few months, the number of vampires in Los

Angeles has more than quadrupled, and yet the murder rate has remained constant. Doesn't that tell you something?"

"Why are you gathering vamps from all over? Are you planning to overthrow the government or something?"

"If we were, why would we be headquartered in Los Angeles? It's hardly militarily strategic."

"Why are you in L.A. then?"

"Large numbers of vampires require equally large numbers of humans to sustain us. Southern California has a huge population base."

"Why are you building an army?"

"I'm not building an army, I'm rebuilding a peaceful civilization," he said. "Our history, language and culture has been all but lost over the centuries. I'm trying to piece at least some of it back together."

"That's an awesome first step to your peaceful utopia, trying to wipe out all of *my* people, all the true hunters. Irony much?"

"*Your* people have been systematically trying to bring about our extinction!"

"Are you going to put down any vamp that doesn't go along with your new world order?"

"Of course not!"

"You've been trying to kill August, though."

"He became a hunter when he sided with you and started killing our kind. When your own brother betrays your entire race, it's pretty hard to just look the other way," Lucian said. "Though of course, that was only the latest in an incredibly long list of atrocities."

I raised a brow at that. "Brother? Were you two sired by the same maker?"

"No. We had the same birth mother."

"You're kidding."

"I'm not. Her name was Sarah and she was a witch. August and I had different fathers, obviously, mine a werewolf and his a warlock."

"Sarah could really pick 'em."

He frowned at me and added, "Since neither of our fathers stuck around and our mother died young, August raised me."

I stared at Lucian. "There's no way." He held my gaze steadily and I asked, "You're serious? Why the fuck would you put your own flesh and blood at the top of a kill list?"

"In addition to betraying his people, how about the fact that he's pure evil? The man you think you know isn't even sort of the real August. He's left a trail of carnage behind him unmatched by any vampire in history."

"If you honestly believed that and it concerned you enough to put him on your hit list, you never would have saved his life last night."

"I needed to use that as leverage or you never would have agreed to go with me."

"Is that the only reason you saved him?"

He sighed and admitted, "No. When I saw him like that, burning up from the inside, I felt sorry for him. All of a sudden I was seeing my brother there, instead of the beast that he'd become. It probably helped that he wasn't actually saying anything. Every time he'd open his mouth, he would infuriate me."

"August is a good man. That's such bullshit, *the beast that he'd become.*"

"You don't know him, Tinder. Not really. His name's not even August, it's Alexander," he said with a humorless smile. "He adopted that new name a couple centuries ago. Granted, Lucian isn't my birth name either. But in my case, I didn't change it to hide centuries of murder and destruction. You should read up on the vampire Alexander sometime. It'll give you nightmares."

I knew of Alexander, of course. All hunters had heard the tales of the most bloodthirsty vampire to ever walk the Earth. I always figured they were just campfire stories to scare the crap out of young hunters, especially because so little was known about him. There wasn't even a drawing or photograph of this creature, he was like the boogeyman. Not only couldn't that thing be August, it also couldn't possibly be real.

"You're just trying to make me doubt the man I love," I said. "I don't believe those lies about him. I don't believe that bullshit about you trying to build a peaceful vampire society, either."

"Aside from going after my brother and the hunters in order to keep my people safe, what have I ever done that would make you doubt me?"

"What about Ty? You let your men sexually abuse an innocent little vampire!"

448

"What the bloody hell are you talking about?"

"That thin blond back at the house in Santa Barbara. Sean, your right-hand man, brought him to your compound to be a sex toy for your men."

He looked distraught. "I had no idea that was going on."

"Yeah, right!"

"It's the truth. I always kept myself separate from my lieutenants. If I had known, I would have stopped it immediately!"

"I don't believe you. I also don't believe you didn't take advantage of him yourself!"

"I swear I didn't know. And as for the latter, I've been celibate for the last two decades, Tinder."

"Really? Why?"

"Because no one was ever *you*." He turned and walked away from me. I didn't try to stop him.

*****

We avoided each other for the next couple hours. Eventually though, Lucian gravitated out to the deck where I was and sat on a low wooden chair in one corner. I idly wondered what his daylight talisman was, or if he had a tattoo.

"You're going to get sunburned. You should come inside," he said after a while.

I was flat on my back on the deck, staring up at the sky, arms flung out to the sides with a bottle of Jameson in my hand. The booze and the constant sound of the waves breaking on the shore had lulled me into a stupor. "Don't even think about giving me advice. I'm not interested in being tended to by a vampire nursemaid."

"If you come inside, I'll teach you how to build a spell. I saw you when you were trying to save August. Clearly, you've never had any training."

I sat up and looked at him over my shoulder. "I think I did that successfully when I raided your compound, but I shouldn't have been able to. My family is the wrong flavor of warlock." Yeah, definitely a bit drunk. Good.

"But since you're my mate, your magic dovetails with mine. Because I'm Bauschaft, you are, too."

450

I rolled my eyes. "Oh yeah. Same reason I'm gay. It's really special to know I was custom-made for an asshole."

He grinned a little. "We mirror each other, Tinder. So if I'm an asshole, well, right back at you." Lucian got up and headed for the sliding glass door. "I'll be on the couch if you decide you want to learn what you're capable of." I chewed my lower lip and stared out at the ocean for a couple minutes before finally taking the bait and following him inside.

"Alright, I'm here," I said, dropping onto the couch, liquor bottle still in hand. "Go ahead and dazzle me with your mad skills."

"Hold out your hand," he said. I stuck out my left hand, palm up, and he hovered his right hand about six inches above it. "Hold really still for this. I don't want you to get burned."

"Burned by what exactly?" Suddenly a bright ball of light appeared between our hands, pulsing with energy. "Holy shit, what is that?"

"A weapon for when you find yourself unarmed and need to defend yourself. You don't need a spell for this one, you just call it up from within. It takes a lot of

451

energy, so you can only do this once or twice in a twenty-four hour period. But it can be very useful."

"So, you're telling me I can call up atomic fireballs at will. That would have been pretty freaking good to know a lot sooner. How exactly are you doing it, though?"

"We're both doing it. Relax and feel where it's coming from."

"It's not coming from anywhere."

Lucian took the bottle from me and set it aside, then widened the gap between our palms as he picked up my free hand. The fireball doubled in size with a surge of power. "Sure it is. Feel it."

"Feel the fireball. *Be* the fireball," I quipped. "Yeah, no. I don't feel anything, aside from way too much heat on my palm."

He flicked his wrist and launched the ball across the room. It crashed into the open fireplace and exploded, shooting flames several feet back before extinguishing itself. "You really didn't feel where that was coming from?"

"No. Not at all."

He considered that and asked, "When you work a spell, do you feel the place within you that gives it power?"

"No. And if you told me this was going to be a new-agey bullshit session, I would have stayed on the deck." I started to get up, but he kept hold of my hand.

"Come on." He grinned just a little and said, "You know you want to be able to smite your enemies with an atomic fireball. Isn't that a kind of candy, by the way?"

"Yes. And you're the only enemy I'd like to smite. But I seem incapable of doing that, which sucks."

"Speaking of which, thanks for not murdering me in my sleep." That little grin still lingered.

"Oh, it was tempting, believe me. You're oddly jolly right now, by the way. What's up with that?"

"I'm happy because I'm holding your hand. Even if you don't feel our bond as strongly as I do, you still have to admit that it feels incredible."

"I'm in love with your brother. I will *always* be in love with your brother. Someday, I'm going to marry him, no matter how much you try to fuck that up for us. That'll make you my brother-in-law. And holding

453

hands with my future brother-in-law will never be anything short of totally freaking weird."

He let go of my hand, a little frown line appearing between his brows. "Way to suck the joy out of that."

"You're welcome." I watched him for a moment, then added, "Can we continue this without it turning into 'use the force, Luke' or do we need to just give up now?"

"I'll try my best not to Yoda the hell out of this lesson," he said, a little cheer returning to his eyes.

We spent the next couple hours trying to upgrade my abilities. Lucian was patient, even when I didn't quite get the whole drawing from within thing. When it came to constructing spells though, that I picked up immediately.

Around dinnertime, I raided the well-stocked refrigerator. I felt a bit bad about eating this stranger's food, but then again, Lucian had sent him away for a week. It was all going to spoil anyway. I had no justification for drinking his booze, but whatever.

As I made myself a sandwich, Lucian came into the kitchen and sat on one of the barstools at the wide granite island. After a while he said, "I wouldn't have chosen it either, you know."

"Chosen what?" I stuffed the sandwich in my mouth and took a huge bite.

"The mate bond. It's completely consumed me. Since the moment I caught your scent, I could think of nothing but you. Everything else just fell away, including my life's work. I've become this love-struck puppy dog, following you around, hoping for a scrap of your attention. And there's not a damn thing I can do about it."

I considered that, then swallowed and said, "Why not? I mean, you can design your own spells, and the two of us working in unison can probably pull off some pretty impressive shit. Can't we just break our bond?"

He shook his head. "It's in our DNA. There's no way to pluck it out of there."

"So, once a werewolf meets his or her mate, they're just destined to a life of obsession? That's kind of ridiculous. How did your race ever even function, given that?"

"It's only this all-consuming in the very beginning. After a couple mates, the intensity levels out. The two still need to be together, a werewolf can never be happy without his other half, but it doesn't stay intense like this. The longer a couple goes without consummating their relationship though, the more overwhelming the obsession."

I raised an eyebrow at him. "We're not having sex. No way, no how."

He sighed and said, "I wish I was more of an arse. Then I'd just order you to sleep with me and you'd have to comply. Once we had sex, you wouldn't be the only thing I could think about anymore."

"Well, yay to you not being that much of an ass. Only enough of one to force me to go with you and leave the love of my life behind."

"I'm glad that I took you away from August. He had you so fooled with that good guy routine. But people don't really change, not on such a fundamental level." He was leaning on the kitchen island as he said that, idly tracing a vein of dark brown in the light brown granite.

I watched him for a while before asking, "So, as time goes on and I continue to not sleep with you, is your obsession going to get so out of hand that you will eventually order me to put out? Because just so you know, that'll make you *such* a fucking asshole."

Lucian glanced up at me. "Remember when I let you feel what this is like for me? Mating with you is critical, but that's tempered by love and concern for your well-being. That said...I don't know. It's manageable now. I mean, sure, I think about ripping your clothes off and making love to you every second of every day, but I don't have to act on it. A few days or weeks down the road as this continues to consume me, who knows? Maybe my wolf will just take over, and ordering you to mate with me will become as involuntary as the rest of this." He returned his gaze to the counter.

"This whole situation is completely fucked. And apparently I will be too at some point. That's just awesome," I muttered.

"You know you'll be feeling the same things though, just on a smaller scale. The urge to mate will build in you, just like it's building in me. It might not even be necessary to order you to consummate our relationship, because you yourself might instigate it."

"What about free will? What about choosing to be faithful to the man I love? Does none of that even sort of factor in to this fucked up mate bond?"

"No. Not at all," Lucian said. "This is our most primitive animal nature at work, not our rational brain."

I pushed the sandwich away and went to find the bottle of whiskey.

*****

August's super butch commando-style rescue later that night was well-intentioned, if a bit over the top. A dozen huge guys with automatic weapons burst through the front and back doors and a couple of the windows, then lost a bit of momentum when they discovered Lucian and me sitting on opposite ends of the living room watching reruns of Star Trek, The Next Generation. They looked around in muscle-bound confusion, then turned to August, who was dressed in head-to-toe black including a painted-on t-shirt, cargo pants and some stylin' combat boots.

"Well damn," I exclaimed. "Check you out, all Rambo and shit."

"What the fuck, Tinder?" He actually looked a little pissed off.

"Wait a minute. Are you mad because I wasn't in jeopardy? Should I have been in more peril for you, maybe hanging from the ceiling in some kind of leather S and M harness?"

"I'm totally picturing that," Lucian said cheerfully.

August was right on the verge of glaring at me, so I said, "Why don't you go back outside and we'll try this again? Maybe Lou can go out and find a section of a railroad track and tie me to it. Then you can burst in again and save me all proper-like."

Lucian chuckled while August lowered his assault rifle and put his hands on his hips. "Why are you acting pissy, Tinder?"

"Because you are!"

"Well, color me sorry, mate! I just didn't expect to find you two cozy in front of the telly!"

"Okay, could you not make it sound like I was sitting on his lap feeding him grapes? We're on opposite sides of the room!"

"If he wasn't actually keeping you prisoner, did it maybe occur to you to pick up a fucking *phone* and let me know you were alright? I've been sick with worry for the past twenty-two hours!"

"First of all, I didn't have access to a phone. Secondly, this is kind of a delicate situation, so I really wasn't going to piss him off on day one by begging to call you!"

"Oh, 'eaven forbid!" August was so mad that his accent went full cockney. "Wouldn't want you to ruffle the feathers of your one true mate!"

I crossed my arms and stared at him. "You were a lot nicer when you thought you were dying, but now you're back to this bizarre jealousy thing again. You're welcome for saving your life, by the way!"

"Saving my life and then immediately breaking my heart by walking out on me!"

"I made *a deal*! My life for yours, basically. Do you think I wanted to leave you, Bane? Is that what you think?"

"So I'm back to being Bane again, am I?"

"Right now, yes. You're acting like your old self, after all."

"You know, Tinder didn't really—" Lucian had been on his feet during all of this, staring down the barrel of an AK-47. Another 'roid monster directly behind him with an even bigger assault rifle swung it around and bashed the stock against Lucian's skull, cutting him off in mid-sentence.

"Quit it!" I yelled, propelling myself toward Lucian as he dropped to one knee. Without even thinking about it, I wrapped myself around him and shielded him with my body. His arms went around me as he rested his forehead on my chest, blood trickling from the back of his head.

"Oh for fuck's sake," Bane exclaimed. "Would you look at yourself, Tinder? I get that there's a smidgen of werewolf blood in you that makes you think that blighter is your mate, but do you really need to cuddle him right in front of me?"

"I'm not cuddling him, I'm keeping your goons from bashing his brains out!"

"Why? You would have loved the opportunity to do the same, all those months when he was hunting you like an animal!" Bane's green eyes flashed with anger.

"I get why he was targeting the hunters. He stopped doing that, by the way. He made a deal with me and as far as I know he's upheld his end of it. He actually seems like a pretty decent guy."

"Decent guy! He's a ridiculous, arrogant, self-deluded, pompous git and I can't believe you're falling for his bullshit, mate bond or not!"

"Hell of a way to talk about your own brother," I told him.

Bane paused, staring at me for a long moment. Then he said, more calmly, "Told you that, did he?"

"Yeah. Were you ever going to?"

"No. He stopped being my brother a very long time ago." I straightened up and so did Lucian, who kept a wary eye on the mercenaries as Bane said, "Are you so overcome with love for your one true mate that you've forgotten what his men did to us in the torture chamber in his basement? Oh and by the way, how many *decent guys* do you know that have torture chambers, Tinder?"

"That house belonged to a sadistic gang leader. We compelled it out from under him, torture chamber included, not that I expect you to believe me," Lucian said. "And for the record, I had no idea my men were going to silver you. I never would have condoned that."

"Oh no, you'd never let them silver me. But killing me *humanely*, that was fine."

"That's what has to be done with rabid *animals*, Alexander!"

Bane flinched a little at the name, but then covered it with a smirk. "Tell me, *Lucian*. Brilliant moniker, by the way. Watched Underworld one too many times, did we?" Bane raised an eyebrow at him and said, "Are you starting to believe your own lies? You sound so convincing! And yet you and I both know you're full of shite."

"That's rich coming from you, *August*!" Lucian stepped forward, as if he meant to get in Bane's face. Immediately half a dozen mercenaries closed in around him, guns pointed at his head. Now it was Lucian's turn to smirk. "Hiding behind your toy soldiers, big brother? Among your many flaws, I had never pegged you as a coward. My mistake."

Bane pushed past his men and punched his brother in the jaw. Lucian's head whipped to the side, but then he straightened up and smiled, his eyes lit with menace. In the next instant they were completely brawling. The miniature army tried to intervene, but Bane ordered them back.

The siblings were really evenly matched. They both moved incredibly fast, landing and ducking brutal punches and kicks, busting walls, furniture and anything else in their wake. It was absolutely ridiculous. When Bane threw Lucian through a window and jumped out after him, I'd finally had enough.

I snatched an AK from a soldier that had been watching the action like a prize fight and fired a few rounds over the brothers' heads. That got their attention. I yelled, "I'm about to die of testosterone poisoning from the cloud of macho coming off you two. Knock it off!"

"You're coming with me, asshole," Bane said, yanking Lucian to his feet by his hair.

"Like hell I am!"

"Oh, I'd say you are. I'm the one with all the men and all the guns for a change. All you have is a dumb haircut."

"And Tinder," Lucian said smugly. Bane sucker punched him in the jaw, then grinned as his brother clutched his face and yelled, "Ow!"

"Couple of overgrown children," I muttered as I turned and picked my way carefully around all the broken glass.

Four huge SUVs were parked halfway down the private drive. I left through the front door and got in the passenger seat of the lead Range Rover, and after a few moments Bane slid behind the wheel. Lucian meanwhile had been chained and stuffed unceremoniously into the back of the vehicle right behind us.

Bane ground his teeth as he pulled onto the highway and turned right, heading south. "Do you feel better now that you smacked your brother around?" I asked him.

"A little. I would have liked to smack him around more, except you threatened to riddle us with bullets."

"What a lame way to settle your differences! At least you were both totally holding back, but it was still ridiculous."

"I was not holding back."

"Of course you were. If you really wanted to hurt your brother, or if he really wanted to hurt you, one or both of you would be dead right now. You could have just plucked his head like a grape and been done with it."

"Thank you for that charming visual."

"You know I'm right. You obviously both care about each other, or else you wouldn't have engaged in that pathetic slap-fight."

"My fractured collarbone says that was no slap-fight."

"Whatever."

"Also, he put me on a bleedin' kill list! Interesting way of caring about me."

"For some reason, he thought you were a monster. When was the last time you actually spoke to your brother?"

"September."

"Oh yeah?"

"1754."

"You haven't spoken to your brother in two hundred and sixty years? Seriously?"

"Wish it was longer."

I watched his profile for a while. He was still grinding his teeth. Eventually I asked, "How do you always find me, Bane?"

"I use a tracking device."

"Where is it?"

"Between your shoulder blades."

"Oh my God. You microchipped me like a cocker spaniel!"

"I didn't!"

I narrowed my eyes at him. "Did you mark me with a tattoo and then hide it?"

"Okay, that I may have done."

"When?"

"A while back."

"How? I think I'd remember being tattooed."

"You may not technically have been conscious...."

"Oh, because that's okay!"

"It was just to keep you safe."

"Wait. If I'm basically carrying around a homing beacon, why did it take you almost a day to come after me?"

"The silver poisoning ended up really throwing me out of whack. Even after it left my system, it still took hours to regain the use of my extra senses so I could cast a spell to track that beacon. At least that gave me time to assemble a strike force, though."

"Super butch, by the way."

"Thank you. Again, just trying to keep you safe. That's what I do, you know."

"Yeah, you know what? When I made a deal with Lucian and left with him, I was doing the exact same thing: saving you, and then keeping you safe."

"It's my job to keep *you* safe Tinder, not vice versa. I never would have wanted you to make that deal and to put yourself in the hands of Lucian! I'd much rather have died than let you sacrifice yourself for me."

"That right there is a fundamental flaw in our relationship. I'm not your ward, August. I'm supposed to be your partner. When two people are in love, they take care of each other. Granted, we're operating with a few glaring discrepancies that make you believe you're supposed to be my protector. Like, don't even get me started on our age gap! Daddy complex? Uh, try forefather complex!"

"Definitely should have lied about my age." He glanced at me and finally offered me a little grin. "I'm sorry that I'm being an arse about the thing between you and Lucian. I do get that you didn't choose it. But somehow, knowing that doesn't stop me from being consumed with jealousy."

"There has to be a way to break that mate bond. It's making Lucian crazy, too. I bet he'd actually help us if we could figure out how to sever it."

"The bond is a 'til death you do part deal. It's not going anywhere as long as you're both still kicking."

"I don't accept that. There has to be a loophole somewhere, or a thread to pull to get the whole thing to unravel."

We both pondered that as he kept driving down the coast. After a while I said, "I don't suppose there's any news about Nate yet."

"There won't be for a while. He'll probably be unconscious for a solid forty-eight hours. Sometimes the change takes even longer. Nikolai took him to the lake house last night. I couldn't tattoo Nate's daylight symbols before they left because my magic was still offline, so they'll have to use the cross pendant until I see them again."

"And where's Ty?"

"I made him wait at the house Alejandro rented for you today."

"Why'd you rent a house?"

"Because you and Ty need a home base. He's incredibly attached to you, by the way. He really wanted to come along tonight, but I told him it wasn't safe."

"The only reason he's so attached to me is because he doesn't have anyone else. Which is actually my fault," I murmured.

"He's very sweet, I'm glad you took him under your wing. Well, and then handed him off on me. That was fine, though. He really does make me want to take care of him."

"So, this rental house. Will you be living there, too?"

"Would you want me to?"

"Yes."

"That's kind of a big step, don't you think?" He grinned a little.

"Well, it's not like you and I just met."

"No. But you only very recently decided you loved me."

"I did not suddenly decide that! I've felt it for ages. It just took me a while to actually say it."

"Good to know."

"We'd all been moving around before this to stay safe," I said. "You think it's a good idea to stay in one location now?"

"I knew I'd find Lucian when I found you. I'd planned to kill him, which would have brought the Order to its knees. That would have eliminated the need to keep hiding."

"But you can't kill him, can you?" I asked and he sighed and shook his head no. "I knew you two still care about each other, despite it all."

"I don't know when I became so bleeding sentimental," he muttered.

A fog bank was rolling in off the Pacific, reducing our visibility to a few feet in front of us. "I missed you." I said that quietly as I picked up his free hand.

"Missed you too, love." After a pause he asked, "Out of curiosity, how long were you planning to make good on your promise to stay with Lucian?"

"Until you rescued my ass," I said with a grin. "I knew you'd come for me, and I only promised not to run from him. I didn't promise not to be taken from

471

him. It still really hurt to say goodbye to you, though. I didn't know how long it'd be before I saw you again."

"I'm sorry it was even that long."

"Out of curiosity, where'd you get the platoon of steroid-guzzling semper fi wanna-bes?"

"Craigslist."

"Really?"

August grinned and said, "No, not really! There's no category for soldiers of fortune! I just went to a couple gun clubs and compelled the biggest blokes I could find. I did pretty well, I think."

"You compelled them? That's kind of unethical."

"Desperate times."

After another pause, I said, "Aren't you going to ask?"

"No."

"You don't want to know if Lucian and I slept together?"

"You would have had to. Even if you're only part-shifter, the pull had to have been overwhelming."

"We didn't. He insisted that we slept in the same bed, but all he did was hold me."

"He didn't force himself on you?"

"No."

"Surprising," August murmured, then flicked on the windshield wipers to clear away the fine mist that had accumulated.

"It wasn't just because the bond makes him care about me. There's good in your brother."

"Please don't call him that."

I frowned at his profile. "How long have you known that the person who is in fact still your brother and the leader of the Order were one and the same?"

"Last month, I finally obtained a physical description of their leader and realized that had to be him. Not a lot of huge, black-haired vampires with silver eyes mucking about."

"What are you going to do with him, now that the tables are turned?"

"I'll try to get him to dismantle the Order, for starters," August said.

"He claims his goal is to rebuild a peaceful vampire society. Do you think he's telling the truth?"

"Actually, I could see him coming up with a daft notion like that. And here in L.A. Brilliant."

"It makes sense that they'd need to be around a lot of humans. They'll have to eat."

"Of course they will, and it's just a matter of time before a large group of vampires draws the attention of the general population. That's what got us hunted nearly to extinction in the first place," he told me. "You can compel the person you drink from and any witnesses you're aware of, but you can't be certain that you took care of everyone that might have seen something. In this day and age especially, there are eyes everywhere: security cameras, people with cell phones ready to snap a picture at a moment's notice, traffic cams. We only survive by remaining invisible. How does he not understand that?"

"So you think he might be telling the truth about rebuilding your culture and trying to save your language and traditions and all that? Or is he trying to do what you said leaders have attempted in the past, leading his people out of hiding and making a play for dominant race on the planet?"

"He always was an idealist, so he really might be trying to rebuild our society. But he's also incredibly short-sighted." August shook his head. "He probably thinks that all he has to do is take out the hunters, that they're the only thing standing in the way of his utopia. But he's failing to grasp a bigger problem, besides the inevitable discovery by the human race. There have always been a few among our people who are perfectly willing to kill humans because they regard them as nothing more than livestock. So far, he's managed to keep a lid on that problem, since the murder rate in L.A. hasn't skyrocketed. It's just a matter of time though before some rogues move in to his allegedly peaceable society and throw a wrench in the works. I don't know how he expects to deal with that."

"I don't either. Overall though I have to say, aside from the part where he decided to wipe out all the hunters, I think what he's trying to do is actually kind of noble."

"Still daft, though," August muttered.

*****

The house August had rented was a little north of Pacific Palisades, nestled between the ocean and the foot of the Santa Monica Mountains, where residential area gave way to open space. The moment I stepped in the door, I was tackled by a skinny little blond who didn't know his own strength. "Hey there, Ty. You're kind of crushing my ribs. Can you dial it back just a smidge?"

He loosened his grip slightly and murmured, "I'm so glad you're back."

"Me too."

"Are you okay? Did Lucian hurt you?"

"I'm perfectly fine." I just had to ask, because I really didn't know how much of what Lucian had told me was bullshit. "When you were staying at his house, did he ever hurt you?"

"No. I almost never saw him. He isolated himself most of the time and left his lieutenants to run things."

"Do you think he knew how his men were treating you?"

"I don't think he even knew I was there."

I looked down at him and brushed his soft blond hair back from his eyes, then changed the subject by asking, "Are you hungry? Do you want me to feed you?"

"Thanks, but I'm fine. You just fed me last night."

"Oh, right. Feels like a long time ago."

He led me inside and showed me around. The house was Spanish style, with arched doorways, white stucco walls and tile floors. It was a really beautiful home. I'd be willing to bet that aesthetics hadn't factored into Allie's decision to rent it though, so much as where it was situated. You really had to get out to the fringes of L.A. like this to find a place without nosy neighbors right on top of you.

August came up behind me and scooped me up, tossing me over his shoulder in a fireman's carry. To Ty he said, "We're going to be very busy for the next couple hours. You might want to go watch a movie or something down in the basement rec room."

"What are you doing?" I asked as Bane headed for the staircase. "Oh man, you're going caveman on me, aren't you? Do you have some idea of fucking that mate bond right out of me?"

"Ah, if only it were that simple," he said as he carried me up the stairs. I raised my head and looked back at Ty, who was grinning at me.

"So what are you doing then?"

477

"I may not be able to fuck the bond out of you. But I sure as hell can remind you, graphically and vividly, that you do, in fact, belong to me." I grinned at that as my cock stirred. Since it was pressed against his shoulder, I knew he felt me starting to get hard. "So you like that idea." I could hear him smiling, even if I couldn't see it.

Most of the house was unfurnished, but the large master suite had been outfitted with a king bed, all done up in indigo blue bedding with a pretty wrought iron bedframe. I laughed self-consciously as August tossed me onto the mattress, then stood back and watched me. The heat built in me and I bucked my hips and writhed a bit under his gaze.

His voice was low and seductive when he said, "Tell me you want me." Something wild stirred in his green eyes, making me draw in my breath as my heart rate sped up.

"I want you so fucking much, August. More than anything."

He climbed on top of me, pinning me beneath his big body. His lips hovered close to mine as he locked eyes with me. But instead of kissing me, he turned his head and licked me, from my neck to my ear. I shivered as lust shot through me.

He sat back a bit, grabbed my t-shirt and tore it in two, then discarded both halves. Next he pulled off my black leather belt and tossed it beside us on the mattress. The thick denim of my Levis offered no resistance when he ripped my jeans right off my body.

I found it deeply erotic that I was now totally naked and he was still clothed, especially in that commando gear. I ran my gaze over the tight t-shirt and the black cargo pants that hugged his lean hips, down to those sexy combat boots as my cock throbbed. I parted my legs and laid back, offering myself to him, my breath fast and shallow.

August licked his way down my body, swirling his tongue around each nipple, then biting them in turn, just hard enough to make me cry out in pleasure. When he got to my cock, he did something surprising and took the tip between his teeth, very lightly, right at the seam where it flared out from the shaft. His fangs nestled on either side of it.

Part of me couldn't help but squirm a bit at the thought of him biting down. But then he began to use his tongue on my cock head, lapping at it as he held it gently, then probing the hole a little. It felt so damn good. As he did that, both hands ran down my thighs in a gentle caress, followed by pushing them apart roughly and fondling my balls. I didn't dare move, not with his teeth holding me in place like that, and maybe that was the whole point of what he was doing.

When he let go of me abruptly and sat back, I almost begged him to take my cock between his teeth again. Being controlled like that had been far more exciting than I would have guessed. But August had other items on his agenda.

He flipped me onto my belly, then took hold of my wrists and wrapped them with the leather belt. He did this slowly, watching my reaction as he bound me. I just grinned at him.

That made him grin, too. He attached my wrists to the iron bars of the headboard with the loose ends of the belt and cinched it securely. I didn't argue, not when it made my cock throb and swell like that. I was completely at his mercy and it felt so fucking good.

He picked me up, then slid his knees beneath me and sat back on his haunches before lowering me onto his lap, bare ass up, my cock against his. "Seriously?" I murmured when I realized what he was planning.

"If you don't absolutely love it, we'll stop. But I'm guessing you'll be begging me to keep going." The rational part of my brain considered vetoing this idea, but my body had other ideas. I wiggled on his lap, rubbing my stiff dick against him as I waited for what I knew was coming.

When he brought his hand down on my ass with a resounding slap, I couldn't hold back my moan. I'd always liked giving up control during sex. In fact, I craved it. Suddenly I realized that letting him spank me was taking that to a whole new level for me. Besides the fact that it was incredibly erotic, it also felt *amazing*. Each slap was like a wake-up call to every nerve ending in my body, the sting a jolt of electricity that went straight to my throbbing cock. I bucked and squirmed as he worked my ass, smacking one cheek and then the other in a steady rhythm.

August reached under me with his free hand and took hold of my cock, which he angled downward between his thighs. He jerked me off for a few strokes, then coated his fingers in my precum and slid two of them into my exposed hole. "Oh fuck," I ground out, almost delirious with pleasure.

He fingered me deeply as he continued to spank my ass. I wanted to tell him I was his, but my words degenerated into wild cries and moans. I kept bucking on his lap, my cock rubbing against his inner thigh as I pulled at the bindings on my wrists. He turned his hand and began massaging my prostate, and I yelled and arched up as my orgasm tore from me. He kept spanking my ass as I came, all the while fingering me so deep that the rest of his hand cupped my ass with each push into me.

I came incredibly hard, dizzy from the force of it, my jizz shooting out in spurt after spurt as my whole body convulsed violently. He fingered me right through to the end of it, until I was a sweaty, shaking heap on his lap, gasping for breath. An aftershock ravaged my body and I shuddered.

When I eventually returned to myself, I realized August's fingers were still inside me, fucking me very gently. His other hand was massaging my butt, which felt warm and tingly. It throbbed a bit too, but it was definitely a satisfying ache. "So good," I murmured.

"I just knew you'd enjoy that." He sounded amused, but his voice was tender. "I hope you didn't fill up on the appetizer though, love. I have a big main course planned."

I turned my head and grinned at him over my shoulder. "Go right ahead and feast on me."

He smiled at that. "Hell of a thing to say to a vampire."

I winked at him, then said, "It may take me a few minutes to catch up to you since that orgasm almost blinded me. But what you're doing feels amazing."

He played with my butt a little longer as my heart rate and breathing leveled out. Then he eased his fingers out of me and said, "Be right back, love." August slid out from under me and went into the adjoining bathroom, where I could hear him washing his hands. He came back shirtless and carrying a little plastic bottle of lube.

Even though he freed me from the headboard, he kept my wrists tied together. "I really like that," I murmured as I rolled onto my side.

"Thanks for trusting me enough to let me tie you up."

"I trust you with my life, August."

He smiled at me, then scooped me up with one arm and cradled me to him as he pulled off the soiled top sheet and discarded it onto the floor. He rearranged the pillows and sat on the bed, propped up against the wrought iron headboard, still holding me in the crook of one arm. I snuggled against him, my bound hands brought up under my chin almost like I was praying. "I love seeing you like this," he said, so softly that it was almost a whisper.

I tilted my head back and gave him a goofy grin. "Partially unconscious from an earth-shattering orgasm?"

He smiled, too. "I meant how relaxed you are right now, and how you've let every one of your defenses fall away. I love the warrior in you, but I love this part, too, the part that lets you be so vulnerable during sex. I've always marveled at the way those two sides of you somehow coexist."

"I used to hate that about myself. I considered it a weakness. I just didn't understand why I was a bottom, or why I had this need to be really passive during sex. At some point though, sometime after you and I got involved, I guess it started to make sense to me. It's the one time I don't have to be in control. It's such a good feeling to let go, even just for a little while."

"Makes perfect sense to me." August's kiss was sweet and undemanding.

I broke eye contact, suddenly feeling a bit shy as I murmured, "Just so you know, I'm never going to have sex with anyone but you. Maybe it's kind of early to be making that kind of commitment...but, well, I wanted you to know. I don't like the way I used to be. I'm not proud of how I used to use anonymous sex as a coping mechanism. I was stupid and reckless, and I guess...I guess it was because I didn't think my life was worth anything. I'd always felt like I was born to die, so why take care of myself? I've changed a lot in these last few months, though. I'm just...I'm not that guy anymore." I felt the color rising in my cheeks as I added, "Geez, I really didn't plan on making a speech there. I don't know what happened."

"I love you, Tyler. And I actually made the same commitment to you a long time ago, way before it made any sense. I stopped sleeping with other people as soon as I fell in love with you. Maybe that was a bit daft, to be carrying on a monogamous relationship without us even really being involved. But, well, there you go."

I smiled at him. "That *is* crazy, but I like it."

"Just so you know," August said with a sparkle in his eye, "I'm going to fuck you senseless now."

My smile got even bigger. "Bring it."

He tossed me onto the bed face down, and I took hold of the iron footboard with my bound hands as he yanked my legs apart. He grasped my cheeks and spread me open, then pushed his face between them and ate me out voraciously, his tongue fucking me roughly as I moaned and my cock swelled.

By the time he drizzled lube between my cheeks and pulled his thick erection from the fly of his cargo pants, I was so turned on that I was thrusting against the comforter, trying to make myself cum in my desperate state of arousal. He picked me up with my back to him and got off the bed, then impaled me on his cock and began bouncing me up and down, fucking me so deep that he bottomed out in me on every upstroke. I absolutely loved it when he handled me like this, his strength and power so evident.

August swung us around after a few minutes and put me on the bedroom floor, and I rested my cheek against the smooth, cool tiles. I was on my knees, ass pointed up, and he stood over me and began pile driving down into me, hitting my pleasure spot again and again, my moans punctuated by the force of his thrusts.

The next time he picked me up, he swung me around so we were face to face and pushed into me again. We were close enough to the bed so that I could brace my feet against it and drive myself onto his cock, clutching him between my thighs. He held the belt that bound my wrists and I leaned back, pushing myself onto him over and over, as hard and as fast as I could.

Of course, that was nothing compared to how hard he could fuck me. The next time he shifted positions, I ended up on my back on the floor, folded in half under him, my bound wrists around the back of his neck. He was a lot heavier than me and I loved the feeling of being pinned under him as he slammed into my body. A thrill went through me as I looked into his eyes. There was nothing tame, nothing civilized left in the man that was fucking me. He was pure vampire, primal and lethal and gorgeous, taking what he needed.

He even sounded nothing like himself when he growled, "You're mine, Tinder. Not Lucian's, not anyone else's. Only mine. I'll fucking kill anyone that tries to take you from me." It was such a rush to hear those words, my body rocking from the force of his thrusts. I was going to be so damn sore in the morning. I really didn't care.

There was an odd kind of determination on his face when he started to cum in me sometime later. It was as if he was trying to breed me in a way, or at the very least push his seed so deep into me that it became a part of me. He wrapped his big arms around me, holding me to him as he pumped spurt after spurt of his cum into my body. It was so erotic that it set me off too, splashing our bellies as my cock twitched and my balls tightened up, releasing my load.

I cut off my yell by biting down on the top of his shoulder, almost as a way of grounding myself. I shook with pleasure, still cumming hard, then unclenched my jaw and rolled my head to the side, tipping it back to expose my throat to him. "I belong to you. Only you," I rasped. He bit me too, right at the spot where neck met shoulder, sinking his fangs deep and latching on, then holding me there. He didn't release me until we both finished cumming, then gently licked the twin punctures he'd left behind, healing them right up.

We came down from our orgasms slowly, both of us trembling. After a while, he pulled back a few inches and stared at me. "What?" I asked. My bound hands were still behind his head and I stroked his dark hair with my fingertips.

He grinned and said, "That was the first time I'd ever seen your wolf. It was really sexy."

"What are you talking about?"

"Your eyes changed when I was fucking you. I saw a wildness in you that I hadn't seen before, and it was like...like your monster and mine recognized each other or something. Right after that, you submitted to me. That was an incredible rush."

"Submitted to you?"

He nodded. "That's what that was, when you tilted your head back and exposed your jugular. You offered me your life, or your wolf did."

"You're reading a lot into a head tilt."

"I'm not. Your wolf was on full display right when you did that. And when a werewolf exposes his neck like that, it's the ultimate gift. It says, 'I'm yours. Do with me what you will.' It shows trust and love and unparalleled devotion. A werewolf only ever gives that gift to one person: his mate."

I smiled at that. "Oh yeah?"

August smiled too. "You may have a biological attachment to Lucian, but you've chosen me as your mate regardless. You didn't choose me because of DNA, you chose me with this." He placed his palm over my heart.

"I could have told you that," I said as I relaxed under him and wrapped my legs around his waist.

"You just did." He leaned in and kissed me, then nuzzled the side of my head and nipped my earlobe before saying, "That's no small thing, overcoming biology and choosing your own destiny. It takes a pretty extraordinary individual to be able to do that. But then, I always knew how incredibly special you are."

"I'm glad you think so."

He eased his cock from me carefully, then slid out from under my arms and unbound my wrists. After massaging them gently, he stripped himself naked, scooped me up and said, "Let me show you the best feature of this house." I was all too happy to let him carry me across the room, since my legs were jelly. He pulled back the sheer white curtains and slid open a glass door, then stepped out onto a wide balcony. A table and chairs were at one end, a compact hot tub at the other. He pulled off the hot tub's cover with one hand, then pushed a button to start the jets before lowering us both into the warm, soothing water.

"This feels wonderful," I murmured, wrapping my arms around his shoulders again and snuggling against him.

"I was fairly rough with you, hopefully this helps soothe some of your aches."

I grinned and shut my eyes as I relaxed in his arms. "I love it when I still feel it long after you fuck me, I love that constant reminder of what we did."

I was almost to the point of dozing when August said, so quietly, "Aren't you going to ask? I know my brother must have brought up my past. It's the reason he hates me so much. Don't you want to ask me if he was telling the truth?"

"I didn't believe him."

"But...what if what he told you was true?"

I sat up and looked into his eyes, straddling his lap as the steamy water swirled around us. "You're not Alexander. There's no way."

"The man you know...I wasn't always this person, Tinder. I earned the nickname Bane, and before that...before that I—"

I pressed two fingers to his lips. "It doesn't matter."

He gently pulled my hand away. "But it does, love. You need to know the whole story, who and what I really am."

"But I do know you," I insisted.

"You know August. But you never knew me when I was Alexander. Back then...." He broke eye contact for just a moment, then looked up and held my gaze steadily. "Back then I wouldn't have just killed you if we'd crossed paths. I'd have made you suffer terribly as I did it. There was no humanity in me whatsoever, only bloodlust and hate and the need to destroy. I've spent over two centuries trying to come to terms with the things I did, the things that made the name Alexander the stuff of nightmares."

"How can you possibly be Alexander? How can he even be real? I grew up on the stories, they were worse than any horror movie. I figured they either had to be either hugely exaggerated or made up entirely."

He leaned his head back against the edge of the Jacuzzi and looked up at me. "I don't know what you were told, but I doubt there was much exaggeration. There was no need for that. I left a wake of death and destruction everywhere I went. I had a burning hatred for all of the human race and killed people by the hundreds."

"Why did you hate us so much?"

"I watched what they did to my mother when I was just a boy. I watched them stone her to death just on the suspicion that she was a witch. They killed her, brutally and violently, just because she seemed a bit different. And they *enjoyed it*, Tinder. Two big brutes held my brother and me down as the entire village, people we'd known all our lives, took pleasure in killing her. They were laughing and joking as they threw the stones. Their eyes gleamed with excitement." He paused for a while, reliving the memory, no doubt, then said quietly, "I learned to hate that day."

"Oh God," I whispered.

"I bit the man holding onto me and then clawed at the man restraining my little brother. When they let go of us, we ran. Otherwise, we'd have been next, since we were the spawn of a suspected witch. I was just eight, Laurie was four. Over the next two decades, as we struggled to survive out on our own in the world, the anger and hatred in me festered, poisoning me from the inside out. When we were caught by a vampire and turned, that flipped a switch in me. I shed my humanity willingly. *Gladly*. I became my hate and my anger and I made every human pay for what those villagers had done."

"I'm so sorry about what happened to your mom."

"Thanks. As horrible as it was though, it didn't justify what I became. I slaughtered indiscriminately. I became so much worse than the people who'd killed my mother."

"What finally brought you out of it?"

"You did."

"That's not possible."

"About ten years before I moved to Portugal and met your great, great grandfather, I had a vision. It came to me in the form of a dream. That happens sometimes with warlocks, maybe you've experienced it yourself." August cupped my face in his hands. "In my dream, I saw a beautiful, human boy, around twenty years old with black hair and pale skin and eyes like the sky right after a storm. I saw *you*, Tyler. I didn't know who you were then, and would have to wait over two hundred years to actually meet you. But I knew that I would love you with all my heart and that you'd love me in return. It was enough to make me flip the switch and reawaken my long-dormant humanity. I stopped killing humans after that, then gradually became the man I am now. I still had to learn to let go of my anger, though. It was during that time that I earned the nickname Bane. I was pretty insufferable."

"You chose to reclaim your humanity just because of a dream?"

"I chose to reclaim my humanity because of *love*. It's the most powerful, beautiful, unstoppable force in all the world, sweetness. Don't underestimate it." I smiled at him and he said, "I awoke from that dream on a gorgeous summer morning and the whole world looked different. It was early August. That's why I took this name, in your honor." That touched me so deeply that I couldn't even reply. I put my head on his chest again and he kissed my hair and wrapped his arms around me.

We held each other for a long time. Eventually something occurred to me, and I said, "I don't think it's a coincidence that your brother is bonded to me. He's a part of you, you share half his DNA. I think I was always meant to belong to you, but because he was the one with wolf blood, the mate bond found him instead of you."

"That's an interesting theory."

"It kind of makes sense, you have to admit."

"In a way." He smiled and wrapped his arms around me a little more snugly, nuzzling my hair. After a while, he whispered, "You're still here."

"Why wouldn't I be?"

"I always thought you'd run from me when you found out I was Alexander, or, more likely, stake me. But you're still right here in my arms."

"That's because I get it," I told him. "I know exactly what it feels like to be fueled by hate and anger. Why do you think I killed so many vampires all those years and did it with such determination? I hated all of them because a few had killed my family. I wanted the entire vampire race to pay. It's the same as what you went through, only I didn't have the excuse of my humanity being switched off. I killed because I wanted to."

"You thought you were doing the right thing. It was what you'd been taught since birth."

"Still. I feel so guilty. You must feel the same way."

"Oh, I do. You did a lot of good though, too. You saved countless human lives."

"I know. But that doesn't justify the rest." I sighed and said, "I can't change the past, but I'm going to try so hard from now on to atone for those wrongdoings."

"I guess that helps explain why you take care of Ty like you do," he mused.

We held each other as the hot tub whirled and bubbled around us, and I told him, "Just like I was your turning point, you were mine, too, you know. I changed because loving you opened my eyes. When I finally let myself acknowledge the truth, that there was so much good in you, everything changed. The world stopped being black and white."

He kissed me gently, then picked up my hand and kissed it. When he noticed my wrinkly fingertips August said, "Come on, love. Let's move to dry land."

We showered off the chlorine in the spacious master bath, then took turns drying each other before climbing under the covers. August reached up and turned off the overhead light, bathing the room in moonlight before gathering me in his arms. "I'm grateful for every moment I have with you, Tyler," he whispered. "Thank you for doing what you had to in order to save my life. I should have said that sooner. I was just so distraught about being what sent you into Lucian's arms and I know I didn't deal with it very well."

"I love you, August. I'd do anything for you," I murmured as sleep closed in, so secure as he held me close.

The urgent knocking at the door the next morning made me sit bolt upright in bed, my heart racing. Alejandro called out, "August? You in there? I need to talk to you. Something's happened."

"Come in." August sat up in bed, pushing his hair back, and I pulled the blanket over my naked body as Allie burst into the room. "What's going on?"

"There was a raid this morning, about an hour after sunrise. The hunters that Tinder used to lead found the old barracks the Order was using as a home base. Hundreds of vampires were sleeping inside, when...." Allie's voice caught, raw agony on his face. "They burned it down, August. The hunters burned the barracks to the ground. They killed everyone inside, hundreds and hundreds of our people."

"How do you know this?" August asked.

"Because I was there, only I was on the northern edge of the air field since I checked the wrong set of buildings first. I'd been talking to Lucian last night, after you brought him back here. I wanted to see what he was trying to do for myself. I didn't know if I could believe him, but I thought, if he really was trying to rebuild our society, then I was going to talk to you about it and try to convince you to let him go." Allie paused and drew in his breath. "I got there just as the barracks went up. The hunters used explosives and the old wooden building ignited in more than a dozen spots all at once. A few people managed to run outside. Those without talismans burned in the sun. The hunters fired on the rest and killed them with crossbows."

"Oh God," I whispered.

"The whole structure was consumed by flames in a matter of seconds. The sounds of people screaming as they burned alive – I'll never forget it. Never." Alejandro's hand was shaking as he ran it over his forehead.

"Does Laurie know what happened?" August asked.

"Laurie?" Alejandro echoed.

"Lucian, I mean. Does Lucian know?"

Allie shook his head. "I came straight here."

August gritted his teeth and looked at the floor for a few moments, then muttered, "Give us a minute to get dressed. We'll meet you downstairs."

"I don't have any clothes," I murmured as August swung out of bed. He crossed the room and pulled open the double doors to the closet, then scooped up my duffle bag and brought it to me. I was surprised that he'd thought to bring it from Nate's house and thanked him as I pulled open the zipper.

He paced around, a muscle working in his jaw as I put on a pair of jeans. Finally he went to the closet and pulled on a t-shirt and briefs from a duffle bag of his own. "You okay?" I asked quietly.

"Yeah. I mean, it's a hell of a thing, all those lives lost. I don't know how I'm going to tell Laurie. He'll be utterly devastated."

"Is that your brother's real name?"

"Yeah. Laurence. I always called him Laurie," he muttered distractedly.

"Maybe I should be the one to tell him," I said as I pulled a worn black t-shirt over my head.

"I hate to put that on you. Still, I can't imagine I'd be the ideal messenger." August stepped into a pair of

501

dark jeans as I stuffed my feet into my boots and tugged on the laces.

"It'll be better coming from me."

When we were dressed, we met Allie downstairs. Ty must have heard what happened. He hung back in a corner, his eyes pools of heartbreak, and when I held a hand out to him he ran to me and embraced me. I noticed someone had bought him new clothes, but had underestimated just how slight he was. The pale blue t-shirt and jeans hung loosely off his slender frame. "I need to talk to Lucian," I told him. "Want to come along?"

"I want to be wherever you are," he said softly.

August led the way out the back door and across a fairly overgrown lawn. There was a three-car garage at the edge of the property. As soon as we stepped into the little mud room at one end of the structure, Lucian called out, "Tinder!"

"I had him chained up," August said as he took a set of keys off a hook inside the door and handed them to me. "I thought I was going to need to force him to cooperate with dismantling the Order, and I didn't want him to flee. Or worse, kidnap you and then run."

When we went through a doorway into the main part of the garage, I caught my breath. Lucian's body was bruised and bloody, his clothes torn. He hadn't been beat up. He'd done the damage on his own by fighting against the thick chains that bound him to a central cement pillar. "Oh God Lucian, what have you done to yourself?" I asked as I let go of Ty and rushed across the room.

"I had to try to get to you. I couldn't stand us being apart. This bond is killing me, Tinder. It's only getting stronger with each passing hour." When I unfastened his chains, he leapt to his feet and threw his arms around me, his body shuddering with relief. "Thank you for coming," he said. "I needed this so much."

I returned his hug, feeling him tremble. After a minute I said softly, "Lucian, I have to tell you something."

He pulled back a little, his silver eyes searching mine. "Are you okay? What's wrong?"

"I'm fine. I have bad news, though." I relayed everything that Alejandro had told us and when I finished, Lucian looked like he was in shock.

"But those were just innocent civilians. They never harmed anybody." He looked at me and said, his voice a hoarse whisper, "I need to go there. I need to see it for myself. Maybe...maybe a few of them survived somehow. They'll need me...."

Allie spoke up. He'd been hanging back by the doorway, but now he took a few steps into the garage. "No one could have survived it, Lucian. I was there, I watched it happen. The hunters were too thorough. Everyone burned, either from the fires or sunlight, except for the few that made it out with daylight talismans. They were picked off with crossbows."

"How'd you get away?" I asked him.

"By being almost half a mile away and able to take cover," Allie said. "All their attention was on the barracks, I'm damn lucky they didn't notice me."

Lucian said, "I need to see it. I need to see what happened to my people."

"I'll go with you," I told him.

"We all will. Come on, Laurie. My car's out front." August headed out of the garage.

Lucian paused in front of my companion and said quietly, "You're Ty, aren't you?" When the little blond nodded, Lucian touched his arm hesitantly, almost as if he was trying to comfort him. "I didn't protect you, either. I found out from Tinder that my men had hurt you. I'm so sorry. I didn't know."

"It's my fault," Ty said in his whisper of a voice. "I never tried to stop those men and I was too scared to run away. You didn't have any part in that."

"I'm still sorry," Lucian said.

Ty looked down at his new sneakers and said shyly, "It's okay." Lucian paused for a moment, watching Ty with an unreadable expression, then headed out of the garage with Alejandro right behind him.

"You should stay here," I told Ty. "This is going to be bad."

"I want to come along."

"Why?"

"I don't want to be alone."

"It'll just be for a little while," I said, but there was such pleading desperation in his eyes when he looked up at me that I relented, despite my better judgment. "Okay, you can come. But when we get there, I want you to wait in the car, okay?" He nodded and took my hand.

The five of us were tense and quiet on the long drive. When we reached the decommissioned air base at the south end of town, we found the place swarming with police, firefighters, and EMTs. The huge barracks had collapsed inward and the fire had more or less burned itself out, reduced to just a thick plume of smoke by this point.

August compelled our way through every roadblock and when we parked a hundred yards from the wreckage, Lucian murmured a spell that glamoured everyone in the immediate vicinity all at once. I swallowed hard at the lump in my throat. The scene of destruction before us was utterly overwhelming. "Wait here, Ty," I said.

"I'll stay with him," Alejandro murmured, and the rest of us got out of the SUV.

Because of Lucian's spell, the rescue workers didn't even glance at us as we took in the scene before us. A police officer standing nearby was handed a message from a firefighter, then spoke into the radio on his shoulder. He said, "There are four confirmed fatalities so far, but the center of the structure is completely inaccessible, so expect that count to go up."

That didn't make sense to me, since all the vampires would have turned to dust as they died. I asked Lucian, "Why are there bodies?"

He muttered, "Some of the vampires were married to humans."

I wondered how the hunters would feel when they found out they'd killed humans. There were hordes of reporters outside the airfield, this story was going to be all over the news so the hunters would learn the full extent of what they'd done. They obviously weren't going to lose any sleep over slaughtering hundreds of vampires, but the loss of human life would be another story.

"I couldn't believe it was true, not until I saw it for myself, but they really are gone. All those people. And it's my fault," Lucian said after a while, his voice tight. "I brought all these people here with promises of utopia, of rebuilding a grand society. But I failed to keep them safe and now they're all dead."

"Now that you've seen it, we should go," August said. "There's nothing to be done here."

Lucian went on as if his brother hadn't spoken, his eyes on the smoking ruin before us. "I thought this building was far enough off the radar. No one ever comes out here, aside from a few security guards who we'd compelled to leave us alone. I warded the building to keep the hunters out, but I should have done more. It just never occurred to me that they'd do this."

"No one could have predicted it," I told him.

He said, "I was refurbishing a huge ranch for all of us outside Santa Clarita, it was almost completed. We were going to be moving in next week. But that probably wouldn't have been safe either. I guess no place is."

"August is right, we should go," I said gently.

Lucian stared at the burned out barracks for another minute before saying in a low voice, "I was right to target the hunters. I knew they posed a huge threat, though I never imagined they'd pull off something like this. Every life that was lost this morning is on their heads. And they're going to fucking *pay*." He growled the last word.

"That's not the answer." I tried to touch Lucian's arm, but he shook me off. "There's been too much violence, too much killing. It has to stop."

When he looked at me there was a dangerous glint in his eyes. I didn't know if it was his wolf or his vampire I was seeing. Either way, there wasn't a trace of humanity in him when he hissed, "It'll stop when every last hunter is dead."

August must have thought his brother was about to turn on me, because he quickly put himself between us. Lucian shoved him so hard that August flew back several yards and crashed into the side of an ambulance, rocking the vehicle and leaving a big dent. Before he hit the ground, Lucian was gone, running off so fast that I couldn't even register it.

"Shit," I muttered.

August brushed himself off and returned to my side as a bunch of EMTs gathered around the ambulance. They may have been compelled not to notice us, but the huge dent was another story. "We need to go," he said, and we hurried back to the Land Rover.

"What are we going to do about Lucian?" I asked as August started the engine.

"If he just went completely feral," he muttered as he threw the SUV into reverse, "we'll probably have to kill him."

When we returned to the house, August said he had to make some calls and left Alejandro, Ty and me in the kitchen. I sank down on one of the stools at the breakfast bar and leaned forward, splaying my arms out across the granite surface. Ty sat right beside me and rested his head on my shoulder.

The entire drive back had been spent debating what to do about Lucian. If he had just switched off his humanity, no one was safe around him. I maintained that there had to be a way to capture him and talk him down, but between Lucian's strength and his ability to work magic, that wasn't going to be easy. The only reason we'd been able to bring him to the rental house in the first place was because he'd allowed it to happen in order to remain close to me.

One thing I knew for a fact: sooner or later he'd come for me. He was distracted by thoughts of revenge now, but even with that, he wouldn't be able to help it. In fact, if his wolf was in control now instead of his rational side, the mate bond would probably be pulling at him more than ever. With his humanity shut off, there was absolutely nothing preventing him from taking what he wanted once he came after me.

"I don't know if I should stay here or try to go back to work," Alejandro said, snapping me out of my thoughts and shifting his weight from one foot to the other as he looked in the direction that his maker had gone. "I don't know what August wants me to do."

I sat up and took Ty's hand. He'd been silent since the air field, obviously processing what he'd witnessed. To Allie I said, "Why don't you stick around? August might want to talk strategy when he gets back out here."

"He doesn't involve me in decisions. He just gives orders."

"Are you two okay? I really didn't mean to make things bad between you."

Alejandro leaned his hip against the kitchen island. "Things have never been great. It's even more strained now because I failed to follow orders and take you out of the country, but I'm glad I disobeyed him. He was wrong to try to ship you off without your permission."

Ty said softly, "I didn't know things could be bad between a maker and his progeny. I thought you had to love each other no matter what, that it was just built into your bond."

"It's not. I love him like a father and want to obey him, but he doesn't have to feel anything at all toward me, maybe apart from a sense of obligation. He never wanted this. He purposely avoided turning anyone for more than five centuries. When he turned me, it wasn't because he wanted me. He was good friends with my mother and she begged him to turn me because I'd been attacked by another vampire and was dying."

"Where's your mom now?" Ty asked.

"She's dead. She came to see me too soon after I was turned and I killed her. I was completely consumed with bloodlust. Yet another reason why August hates me. And why I hate myself." Alejandro turned his head and looked out the patio door across the room, his dark eyes bright with unshed tears.

August said, "That's what you think? That I hate you?" He'd come into the hallway at the far side of the big living room, where he would have heard everything Allie had said.

Alejandro glanced at his maker. "It's pretty fucking obvious."

His maker approached him and stood there for a long moment looking down at him. Allie, though a good four inches shorter, squared his shoulders and raised his chin, meeting his maker's gaze defiantly, as if to say *I dare you to deny it.* But instead of saying anything, August just drew him into a hug.

Alejandro remained completely rigid, arms at his sides. August finally exclaimed, "Oh for fuck's sake! Meet me half-way, would you? I'm not going to quit this bleeding hug until you reciprocate, so you might as well just stop being completely pig-headed and give in!"

"Fine." He returned the hug awkwardly, and when August finally let go of him he said, "Can we never do that again? It was just weird."

"It was weird because you made it weird! I'm going to hug you every day from this point on," his maker told him. I had to grin at that.

"Please don't."

"You brought it on yourself," August said. "I'm going to hug the shite out of you until you finally grasp the fact that I love you like a son. I always have. Yes, you drive me insane half the time, but that just reinforces the fact that you and I are family."

Allie frowned at him and said, "Can I go back to work? The whole world's falling apart right now and it'd be kind of nice if our livelihood didn't follow suit."

"Fine, but I want you back here tonight. In fact, pack a bag because you'll be staying here indefinitely."

"Why?"

"Because I said so!" August exclaimed and I covered a laugh by coughing into my hand. He really was such a dad.

A few minutes after Allie left, Ty told me, "Your phone's ringing." He dashed upstairs and was back with it before it clicked over to voicemail. I was surprised to see Lee's name on the screen.

I answered by muttering, "Hey," as I got up and wandered into the living room.

"So, I just thought I'd let you know you don't have to worry about the Order anymore. We took care of 'em." Oh God, he was actually calling to brag.

"I know."

"You do?"

"Yeah."

"Oh." After a pause he said, "I'm sorry that I hit you. I don't know what the fuck's going on with you right now, but I know that wasn't how I should've handled it. You're a damn fine hunter, and you were a good friend, and...well, I just hope you figure out whatever messed up shit is going on between you and Bane, because I know that ain't really you, Tinder."

I repressed a sigh and said, "Think so, huh?"

"I know so. Anyway, I gotta go. Kira and I are headed north. There's been some vamp activity in Sacramento, we're gonna go straighten it out."

"How's Stevie?"

"Doing better. He's still benched for the next few weeks, but he should make a full recovery."

"I'm glad." I leaned against the glass patio door and looked out at the mountains as I asked, "What happened to the rest of the hunters?"

"After this morning they're all packin' up and headin' back to their home turf."

"But you and Kira are sticking together?"

"She and I are gettin' married, so yeah. We'll be stickin' together from this point out."

"You two barely know each other!"

"We're gettin' married because we need to continue the bloodline. There ain't many true hunters left, so we need to do what we can to make sure our kind don't go extinct. Since you're a full-blood I really hope you do the same someday. I mean, I know you're gay and all, but at least father some kids. It's your duty."

Wow, was that ever not going to happen. Instead of trying to explain all that was wrong with that statement, I just left it at, "Take care of yourself, Lee."

"You too, Tinder. I'm gonna be prayin' for ya." Awesome. When he disconnected, I sighed and slid the phone into my pocket, then raised my arms over my head and leaned them and my forehead against the glass door.

August had told me once that the only reason my parents had me and the rest of my brothers and sisters was because they wanted soldiers to fight in their war on vampires. I'd been so mad when he said that, even though I knew deep down that he was absolutely right. My parents hadn't gotten married out of love, they did it because they were both pure-bloods and wanted to

517

make pure-blood children. They never loved any of us. If they had, they'd have tried to protect us and keep us safe. Instead, they threw us in harm's way as soon as we were old enough to hold a stake. Every one of my brothers and sisters had died fighting a war they never chose to be a part of. If it wasn't for August, that would have been my fate, too. It was a hell of a thing, knowing you were born to die.

"You didn't tell him about the humans that were killed back at the barracks."

I turned my head to look at Ty. He stood a few feet behind me, fidgeting with the hem of his shirt. "I know. He'll find out soon enough when he hears it on the news. I wonder if he'll be upset, or if he'll just consider it collateral damage."

"You didn't tell him Lucian's gunning for him and his group, either. Didn't you want to warn them?" Ty's hearing was good enough to have heard both sides of that conversation, so he knew exactly who I'd been talking to.

"No need. The hunters are scattering far and wide, I doubt he'll be able to find them. Even when the Order was at its strongest, Lucian still had trouble tracking them down. Hunters are always careful. They know to fly beneath the radar."

"Don't you mean we?"

"What?"

"You keep referring to the hunters as 'they.' Don't you consider yourself one of them anymore?"

I turned to face him and leaned against the glass door. "No. I'll fight if I'm attacked or if I need to protect someone, but that's different than what I was before. I won't just kill indiscriminately anymore."

"Does it feel weird, not being a hunter after all that time?"

I considered the question, then told him, "Yeah, but it's a good thing. I was always told who and what I was, my life wasn't my own. It feels strange not having that sense of purpose, but at the same time, I can see a future now, one where I get to make my own choices. That's pretty awesome. I always felt like I was living on borrowed time, like every single day would probably be my last. That's why I was always so reckless with sex and everything else, because I was a dead man walking anyway, so what did it matter what I did? But now, everything's different."

Ty dropped his gaze and said, "I'm not going to hold you to your promise anymore. You have much bigger things to worry about besides taking care of me. You've got your whole life to figure out, and you have your new relationship with August, and the bond with Lucian to deal with, and I know I'm just a burden. I don't know why I'm like this, why I'm so needy and so afraid of being alone. But it's my problem, not yours, and—"

I cut him off by gathering him into my arms. "I'm so glad you're a part of my life Ty. And for the record, it feels good to be needed."

"Really?"

"You're right that I have a lot to figure out. We all do. But we're going to figure it out together, because that's what families do."

Over the next week, we settled into a routine at the house beside the mountains. August hired a battalion of armed guards, humans for daytime, vampires at night, who patrolled the property and kept an eye out for Lucian. We had no idea where he was, but we knew it was just a matter of time before the mate bond pulled him back to me. Leaving here and trying to hide wasn't an option, either. No matter where I went, Lucian would be drawn right to me. The opposite wasn't true, though: my bond to him just wasn't strong enough to be able to find him. And of course he'd thoroughly bespelled himself to make locater spells useless.

Instead of just waiting for him to come for me, August sent people all over the state looking for his brother. He also checked the news repeatedly, expecting to hear about a gruesome killing spree that would point the way to Lucian. That hadn't happened, though. I wanted to believe it was because Lucian had re-engaged his humanity, but somehow I doubted it.

521

He'd been far too angry to just let go of his need for revenge.

As we waited for Lucian to make his location known, August, Allie, Ty and I really did form a family unit of sorts, even if it was a pretty dysfunctional one. August felt the need to keep all of us close after witnessing the massacre at the air field. Not that he thought anything would happen, it just made him feel more secure to know everyone he cared about was under his watchful eye.

Allie resented being told what to do, and the two constantly got on each other's nerves. We all grew closer though, too. Most evenings were spent in long conversations in the spacious living room, which August had outfitted with comfortable sofas. He loved telling stories about the late, great vampire civilization and passing on some of the language and lore. I realized he was as passionate about not forgetting their heritage as his brother was, only Lucian had taken it to the extreme of trying to rebuild what once was.

Ty was endlessly fascinated by this subject, and began transcribing all that August told us. He felt strongly that there should be a written record, something that could be passed from vampire to vampire. August wasn't so sure. One of the first things his people had done when they went into hiding was destroy all written records so they could disappear from history. But Ty maintained that humans wouldn't believe it was real if they somehow got their hands on it, especially if it was written to sound like mythology.

As he took on the task of recording his people's history, Ty grew more confident. I bought him a laptop to help him with what he was trying to do, and he used it not only to record the stories August told him, but also to search the internet to see if any more vampire history had been recorded under the guise of legend or fiction.

One afternoon when I complimented him on how dedicated he'd become, Ty admitted, "I used to love school. I only made it to the start of my junior year, but this reminds me of when I'd do research and write papers."

"What do you think about the idea of getting your G.E.D.? I bet you can study for the test online. Once you had that, you could take college classes."

His eyes lit up. "Really?"

"Sure. I'll help you any way I can."

From across the room, August looked up from his newspaper and said, "I wholeheartedly support that idea. In fact, if you decide you want to go to school, Ty, I'll pay for it."

"Thank you," Ty said softly. "That's incredibly generous."

"The same goes for you, Tinder," August told me.

"Thanks, but no thanks. I'm not the classroom type, never have been," I said. "But Ty, I really think you should pursue this since you said you loved school."

"It would be a dream come true," Ty murmured. He immediately began researching high school equivalency testing and by that afternoon had signed up for online coursework. I admired the fact that he took the ball and ran with it like that. I also kind of wished my life was that easy to figure out.

That same afternoon, I went up to August, plucked his laptop from his grasp, and set it aside. Even though he wouldn't admit it, I knew he was worried about his brother. But if Lucian hadn't publicly and spectacularly gone off the rails in a week, he probably wasn't going to, so there was no need to keep combing the news for clues to his location.

I sat on his lap sideways, so that my bare feet were hanging over the armrest of the club chair, and kissed August. "Hi," I said with a grin, putting my arms around his shoulders.

"Hello, love." He brushed my hair from my eyes as he smiled at me, his left arm coming up to hold me gently.

"I wish we could go for a walk," I said. "I'm going stir crazy. I don't know how much longer I can take being under house arrest."

"I know, but it's too dangerous to be out in public right now. No matter how much I arm myself, Lucian could still overpower me and take you. Once he has you, there's absolutely nothing to stop him from raping you this time."

"*I'd* stop him."

"He's far more powerful than any opponent you've ever faced, though. His strength and speed are already off the charts, even before you factor in his ability to conjure virtually any spell he can dream up. I also know you don't have it in you to kill him, and nothing short

525

of that would prevent him from consummating your bond."

"I still like my idea of working a spell to bring him to us. That way it takes away the element of surprise." August and I had already worked a series of spells to make me stronger than any human, taking both the magic and my body to its absolute limit. But of course, Lucian had done the same thing to himself long ago. And even if we'd both, let's say, quadrupled our strength, he was still going to be infinitely stronger, given the fact that his starting point had been a werewolf/vampire hybrid.

"I'm completely opposed to the idea of drawing him to you on purpose. It's just too dangerous, whether or not we think we're ready for him. Besides, he'd probably be able to counteract any spell we put together."

I sighed and leaned back against his arm, looking up at August. We'd have variations of this discussion every day this week, so I'd known it wasn't going to go anywhere. "You're right."

He flashed a brilliant smile at me. "I never get tired of hearing you say that." His kiss was loving and tender.

I glanced across the room and saw that Ty and his laptop had cleared out. He was good about giving us privacy, and we in turn were bad about making out all over the house. I reached up and traced the curve of August's jawline as I asked randomly, "How many times have you been in love? There must have been a lot of men in your life over five and a half centuries."

"Counting you?" I nodded and he grinned at me. "Once."

"Oh, come on!"

"While my humanity was switched off, love wasn't actually a possibility. I'd fuck other vampires and had a few regular partners over the centuries, but that was just sex. After that, I was just waiting for you to come along."

We kissed for a long time, his hands caressing my body gently, and next time we broke apart I asked, "Do you ever think about turning me?"

"All the time."

I searched his eyes as I asked quietly, "Is that something you want?"

"It doesn't matter what I want. That decision would have to come from you alone, Tinder. It's one thing to accept the fact that you're in love with a vampire. It's another thing entirely to decide to become one."

"But if you don't turn me, you'll outlive me by centuries. You'll wind up alone."

"It's still not my choice. And of course you have to consider the ramifications," he said. "It's a coin toss as to whether you'd even remember me after you were turned, along with the rest of your life. You could forget your family, your brothers and sisters, everyone that ever mattered to you."

"Plenty of my life would be worth forgetting," I murmured.

"But not all of it. Not your brother Eddie."

"You could remind me."

"But that's not the same as remembering for yourself," he told me.

"There are even odds I'd remember. I bet we could even figure out how to bespell me and increase the chances of coming through with my memories intact."

"Possibly, but there are other problems, too. You'd be completely consumed by bloodlust for months afterwards. I'd basically have to keep you prisoner to prevent you from going out and murdering half of Los Angeles."

"I know. But I also know you'd take good care of me and make sure I didn't hurt anyone."

He watched me for a moment before saying, "Okay, maybe there are ways to mitigate those concerns. But you know you're not addressing the main problem with being turned, and you also know there's just no way around it. You really think you could face feeding from humans for all of eternity?" I tried to suppress a shudder, but August felt it anyway. His expression became sympathetic as he said, "It wasn't my choice when I was turned into a vampire. My maker never asked if that's what I wanted, he just took my brother and me against our will. If someone had asked me, even someone I cared about, I couldn't have said yes to it, either."

"But I *am* saying yes," I told him. "I love you and I can't stand the thought of you being all alone after I die. I know there's going to be a hell of a lot to adapt to, but

I'll get forever with you in return and that's worth any price."

He kissed me again, then stood up and deposited me on the chair. "It's far too soon to be having this discussion, love. Maybe years down the road, but not weeks into our relationship."

I stared after him as he went upstairs. Okay, yeah, maybe this discussion was way premature, but his reaction was surprising. I thought he'd be happy that I was willing to be turned for him.

Thinking about being turned reminded me of my friend Nate, so I pulled out my phone and dialed his number yet again. I'd already left two messages earlier this week, even though Nikolai had told August there was no cell phone reception at the lake house. Sooner or later he or his husband would probably go into town though, presumably to feed. I wondered how my friend was doing and if he remembered me, or anything at all about his former life. After I left yet another message, I set the phone on the little table beside me.

I glanced at the staircase and considered going after August. But then, since I was a bit thrown off by his reaction to the idea of turning me, I thought it was best to give us both some space. I decided to sit right outside the patio door on the little wooden deck to get a little fresh air, because I really was getting cabin fever. What harm would it do to be a mere twelve inches from the living room?

Plenty, it turned out.

Lucian came out of absolutely nowhere. One moment I was sitting on a wooden chair out on the deck, just inches from the open patio door, and the next I was a hundred yards from the house, then two hundred, then five hundred. By the time a startled yelp left my lips, I couldn't even see the house anymore.

He clutched me tightly against his big body, moving at speeds that should have been absolutely impossible, no matter how much magic you conjured or how unique the mix of supernatural blood that ran in your veins. No way should this be happening. And no way was August or anyone else ever going to catch him.

By the time he slowed to a walk, we were miles and miles away. He was slightly fatigued, which was unusual for a vamp. But then, so was running at supersonic speed. I was actually kind of dizzy from how fast we'd been moving, so it took a minute or two before I could attempt to break free of his grasp. Even though I was much stronger than I had been, it was still no contest. He just adjusted his grip on me slightly. Even though his hold was gentle, his arms were like steel bars.

"Lucian, please don't do this," I said as I struggled. My head was firmly against his shoulder, his big hand on the back of my head so I couldn't even look at him. "Please take me back to the house. This isn't what I want and if you can somehow look past the mate bond, you'll see that you really don't want this either." He didn't reply.

He'd taken us into the mountains behind the house, and when we came to a kind of generic grey sedan he loaded me in the passenger seat, chained me to it quickly and efficiently, then got behind the wheel and started driving. I glanced up at the ceiling, where a large symbol had been drawn with a thick, black marker. It was used for concealment. I wondered if it would be enough to counteract the locater mark on my back.

I turned my head to look at my captor. His jaw was set as he stared straight ahead. I tried again. "I know you don't want to hurt me, Lucian. I also know you really don't want to be mated to me. Let's work together and figure out how to break this bond. There has to be a way."

His silence was really unnerving. He was taking me someplace to rape me and consummate our bond, I knew this for a fact. With his humanity switched off, there was absolutely nothing to prevent him from taking what he wanted.

We drove for over an hour, finally pulling up in front of a ranch house in the middle of nowhere. I could tell as soon as he opened the passenger door that the house was heavily warded. It practically thrummed with energy. I'd been counting on August to track me down, but Lucian was obviously prepared for that this time.

I yelled and cussed and fought with everything I had as he removed my chains, then carried me into the house and down a long hallway. When I saw the large bed outfitted with shackles, my cursing turned to begging. "Please Lucian, don't do this. You'll hate yourself for it. You're just not this person, you're not a rapist! Even if your humanity's switched off, this still can't be what you want!"

He threw me on the bed and ripped my t-shirt and jeans from me, then quickly chained my wrists and ankles. Even though I was naked and spread-eagled on the big mattress, I wasn't done fighting. I began speaking in Latin, cobbling a spell together as fast as I could as he took off his shirt, then his boots. My heart was racing and it was hard to think clearly with fear coursing through me, but I managed to do something right. I knew this because Lucian was suddenly pushed back two of three feet, as if he'd just been struck by an invisible force.

When he met my eyes, I saw pure, animalistic rage. He growled, baring his fangs, and lunged at me. My spell held for a few seconds, but soon he pushed through it with sheer force of will, his big body landing on top of mine.

The tension left him immediately. A warm sense of contentment filled me now that we were skin on skin, which must have been amplified many times over for him. He threaded his arms under me and clutched me to him, breathing in my scent. He kissed my shoulder, then my neck, and nuzzled against me. This would have been reassuring if it wasn't for the huge erection pressed against my thigh. "Please, Lucian," I whispered. "Please don't do this. I belong to your brother. I love him with all my heart, and he loves me too. If you care about him even a little, then you can't rape me. It'll ruin everything between you for all time."

I was surprised when he spoke, his voice deep and emotionless. "He's nothing to me."

"That's not true. I know you love each other, even if you're both too stubborn to admit it. Please, Lucian, let me go, then work with me to break this bond. Do that not only for my sake and August's, but yours as well. You don't want to be saddled with me as your mate. You know you don't."

"I love you."

"But you don't, not really. The mate bond is making you feel things you normally wouldn't. Those feelings aren't real. Given a choice, you'd never select me as your mate, would you?"

He pulled back to look into my eyes for a very long moment, some kind of battle raging within him. When he finally spoke, he said, so quietly, "No. I'd choose Ty."

"Oh! You have feelings for him?"

"I didn't protect him, though. I didn't know what was happening to him, right under my roof. He must hate me."

"Ty doesn't have it in him to hate. He should hate me more than anything because I killed his maker, but he doesn't."

Lucian rolled off me and sat on the edge of the bed facing away from me, but he kept one of his palms on my bare chest. "I felt something when I looked into his eyes, the day my people died."

"What did you feel?"

"Hope." He whispered the word.

"We can fix this Laurie, it's not too late. We can break this bond that's imprisoning you, so you and I can both be with the people we were meant to love." I added quietly, "Unchain me. Let's find a solution together."

He turned and looked at me for a long moment. Then he got up and crossed the room, picked up a little wooden chair that was beside a dressing table, and smashed it to pieces. I drew in a startled breath. He picked something up from the floor and turned to me, and I saw that he was holding one splintered chair leg like a long, sharp stake. I panicked a little as he returned to my bedside and stood over me with the weapon.

"You don't know how difficult this is," he said quietly. "Every fiber of my being is driving me to mate with you, to seal our bond. This past week, I've been driven nearly insane with my need for you. I can't live like this."

He moved the hand holding the stake and I braced myself. Killing me would break our bond, it would rid him of me. Oh God.

But in the next moment, he pressed the handle of the stake into my palm and my hand closed around it. He said, "I'm just barely in control of my werewolf side. I still might try to consummate our bond, even though the tiny part of me that remains rational really doesn't want this. You may need to defend yourself." He broke the thick metal cuffs around my wrists and ankles and I sat up.

"When did you turn your humanity back on?" I asked, covering up self-consciously with a corner of the sheet.

"I never turned it off. I was sorely tempted when I saw those burned out barracks, because the pain was so overwhelming and I wanted to make it stop. But I didn't do it."

"So, wanting to track down and kill the hunters...."

"That was all me."

"But you didn't go after them, did you?"

"You were right, there had been enough killing. I thought I wanted revenge, but I didn't have the stomach for it. Not after witnessing so much tragic loss of life. As soon as I calmed down a bit, I realized this. After that I just needed to be alone so I could grieve. But this mate bond kept consuming me. Finally I couldn't take it anymore. I had to come for you."

"Laurie," I said. "I think I just figured out how to break this bond and free us both."

"How?"

"It's simple, really," I said, swinging out of bed. "I just have to die."

I tugged at the tight t-shirt I was wearing, trying to stretch it out a bit. Since my clothes had been destroyed, I was forced to borrow some things from the closet of the clearly gay teenage boy (or possibly straight teenage girl) who'd been sent out of the house that Lucian had occupied. "Promise me," I told my companion as I fidgeted on the crinkly paper covering the examination table, "that if this doesn't go as planned, you'll bury me in my own clothes. No way do I want to go to my final resting place in turquoise skinny jeans and a One Direction t-shirt."

Lucian grinned at that and squeezed my hand. He found he was better able to cope with the pull of the bond when we were touching, hence the hand-holding. "I'm not going to promise that, because this isn't going to go wrong. If for some reason the doctor can't restart your heart again, I'm going to turn you, just like we discussed. That's still what you want, right?"

"Yeah. But you also have to swear to release me from the maker bond if you do end up turning me. I want to spend eternity with August, not sired to you."

"You have my word." Lucian watched me for a moment, then said, "I really hope my brother appreciates you. I'd give anything to be loved the way you love him."

"I tell him all the time that I love him, but it's almost like he doesn't believe me. Right before you abducted me, he and I were talking about turning me and he seemed way less than thrilled with the idea."

"I overheard that conversation when I was out on the edge of the property," Lucian said. "I think my brother just wants you to be absolutely certain of your feelings for him before taking such a huge, irreversible step."

"But I've loved him forever, long before I even admitted it to myself. He *knows* I love him too, because he saw it in a vision he had over two centuries ago!"

"Just give him time, Tinder."

"Speaking of time, that doctor you compelled needs to get her butt in gear." August was probably on his way here and would definitely try to stop what we were doing. I didn't want to hide from him, which was why my location wasn't concealed. But I only wanted him to get here after this was a done deal.

"This really is such a bad idea," Lucian said.

"I really think it's going to work. The mate bond is severed when one partner dies. So stopping my heart for a minute or two, in effect killing me, should do it."

"I wish I could be the one to do this. I hate that we're gambling with your life."

"You can only be killed a few specific ways as a vampire, all of them irreversible."

"I know, but still. It's taking everything I have not to grab you and carry you to safety." Lucian gathered me in a hug, and I rested my head against his chest.

"You're going to be so happy when you don't have to care about me anymore," I told him.

"I can't even imagine it. From the moment you were born twenty-one years ago and our mate bond came into being, I continually felt like a piece of me was missing. It wasn't until I met you that I finally felt whole."

"But you'll have a chance of finding a lover of your own choosing now, and it'll feel just like that," I said.

"I hope so."

"Laurie, once the bond is broken, make sure Ty's what you really want before you start something with him, okay? He'll probably get really attached to you and it would be way too easy to break his heart."

"I promise I won't hurt him." He was still holding me, and he rubbed his cheek lightly against my hair. "I like it when you call me Laurie, by the way."

"Why'd you ever change it?" I murmured. Cuddling like this was going to seem so weird after the bond was broken. For now though, it was incredibly calming and comforting.

"I was tired of being Laurence. Over all those centuries, he never did anything that really mattered. When I finally decided to make a difference and rebuild my race's proud heritage, I decided a new name was in order to reflect the new me."

"Did you choose your new name by watching a movie?" I asked with a grin.

"Worse. I picked up a book of baby names in a shop, flipped randomly to a page and jabbed a name with my finger."

"Seriously?"

He leaned back a bit and grinned at me. "I'm afraid so."

"Well, you're damn lucky you didn't end up with something truly insane, given that method."

"Oh, I did," he said. "I didn't realize the girls' names were in the front half of the book, so the first name I came up with was Helen." I chuckled at that and he added, "Lucian was the fourth name I landed on, once I found the boys' section. The first three needed to be vetoed."

"Do you remember what they were?"

"The first was Horatio. That was *not* going to happen. The next was Dwayne. I couldn't see that inspiring much confidence. After that was Ulysses, which seemed a bit much." He smiled self-consciously.

I watched him for a while before saying, "You're alright, Laurie. I hope it works out between you and Ty."

"Thank you for the vote of confidence. I really don't deserve it though, given the fact that I kidnapped you just a couple hours ago with far less than noble intentions."

"But that was the mate bond. I totally get what it's doing to you. That's why I'm willing to go to such drastic lengths to break it, because I know it's completely overwhelming you."

"It hasn't had much effect on you at all, has it?"

"Well, it's had some. I don't like the fact that I take comfort in your touch. It makes me feel disloyal to August."

"So really, you're doing this for me and for him, more than for yourself."

"It's for me, too. It'll be nice to not have to worry about being abducted by your wolf." I grinned at him and he looked embarrassed.

The doctor that Lucian had compelled finally returned, pushing a big crash cart. "I thought we could do this with adenosine," she said, "but I reviewed the drug's efficacy and it will only stop your heart for less than a minute. You said you wanted to stop it longer than that, so we're going to have to go with an electric shock."

"Bloody hell," Lucian muttered. He turned to me with worry in his eyes. "We can't do this, Tinder. We need to think of something else. It sounds far too risky."

"We're doing it," I said as I stripped off the t-shirt. "Can I borrow your phone?" He handed it to me and as the doctor plugged in the cart and flipped some switches, I dialed August's number.

He answered on the first ring with, "Tinder? Are you alright?"

"I'm fine," I said.

"No you're not. He hurt you, didn't he? That must be why you're in a hospital."

"How'd you know I'm in a hospital?"

"Because Ty and I are pulling into the parking lot right now."

"Wow, that was really quick. I thought I'd have more time."

"What are you talking about?"

"Just stay in the car. Okay? I'll be out to see you in about fifteen minutes."

"What's going on?"

546

Instead of answering, I said, "I need you to know something, August. I need you to know I love you more than anything in the world."

"Tyler, what's happening?"

"I'll talk to you in a few minutes. Please stay in the car." I disconnected just as he was starting to yell, then shut the phone off and handed it back to Lucian. To the doctor I said, "We need to hurry. Do you know what you're doing?"

She picked up a set of paddles as I stretched out on my back on the exam table. "In theory. Obviously I've never intentionally stopped a heart before. Doctors are generally in the business of trying to keep those going."

"Let's do this," I said, and gave Lucian a reassuring smile.

A split second before the paddles touched my bare chest, the door to the exam room was flung open. August and Ty both looked completely panicked. Electricity shot through my body as the paddles made contact.

The pain was horrible. Terrifying. Incredibly intense. It lasted just a moment before everything went black.

*****

When I awoke I was staring into beautiful green eyes. I felt cold, clammy, and a lot like I'd been hit by a truck. What the hell was going on?

"Love, are you okay?"

I tried to sit up but the room swayed so violently that I immediately had to lay back down. "August," I whispered.

"Fuck, Tyler." He gathered me into his arms and crushed me in a hug. "What the hell were you thinking?"

My head was clearing a bit by now and I murmured, "Did it work? Did we break the bond?"

"It worked," Lucian said. "I don't know how to thank you for what you did. You freed us."

"That's good," I murmured, licking my dry lips as I let my eyes slide shut.

"We'll leave you two alone," Lucian said as the doctor wheeled the cart out of the room. "Ty, will you take a walk with me?"

I couldn't see Ty since I was pressed to August's chest, but I heard his soft, "Sure," before the two of them left the room.

"I'm so fucking furious with you," August said as he stroked my hair. "Do you know what that felt like, watching the man I love die, then be riddled with electric shock? It didn't work right away, either. The doctor had to shock you several times before your heart started beating again."

"You weren't supposed to see that," I told him. "I was just going to tell you about it afterwards, so you wouldn't have to worry."

He climbed up on the exam table and pulled me onto his lap, clutching me to him. "Remember when you said you and I were supposed to be partners? What happened to that idea? Didn't you think I'd want to be involved in this decision?"

"I knew you'd be afraid for me, so you'd try to prevent it. But it had to be done, it was the only way to break the bond. And until it was broken, none of us could get on with our lives, Lucian especially."

"So you did this for him?"

"I did it for all of us, for Lucian and you and me and Ty."

"But what if it didn't work? What if the doctor couldn't bring you back? You had to know there was a chance of that. You were gambling with your life!"

"If I died, Lucian was going to turn me," I admitted, even though I knew how that'd go over. August's body went rigid, his jaw setting in a firm line. "He promised to break the maker bond afterwards," I added. "I wouldn't have ended up tied to him yet again."

He set me down on the exam table, the paper crinkling beneath me, and handed me my t-shirt. "Get dressed, Tyler." Then he left the room, the door swinging shut behind him.

I pulled the shirt on and stood up, but immediately dropped to my knees. I was weak and shaky, and I ached like I'd taken a few hard punches to the chest. As I tried to catch my breath, Lucian and Ty came into the room. "Let me help you," Lucian said, and scooped me into his arms.

I grinned at him and said, "This feels awkward." The bond was definitely broken.

"I know. It's fabulous! Come on, let's get you home."

As we left the hospital I asked, "What happened to August?"

"He left in a huff after first punching me in the stomach," Lucian said. "He's furious that I let you risk your life like that. Apparently he wasn't too keen on our contingency plan of turning you, either."

"He asked us to take you home." Ty added, "He's really mad, but he's still concerned for your well-being. That's a good sign."

Possibly. Or maybe I'd finally pushed him too far.

*****

I slept in the back seat of Lucian's sedan on the long drive to the Spanish-style house beside the mountains. By the time we got there, I felt well enough to head indoors on my own two feet. Lucian walked us to the door and as I went inside he said, "Ty, can I speak to you a moment?"

"Sure."

I made my way to the kitchen slowly as I heard Lucian say, sounding as nervous as a teenager asking someone to prom, "Would it be alright if I called on you tomorrow night?"

Called on him. That made me grin. I opened the cabinet and took out a glass as Ty stammered, "Oh! Yes. I'd like that."

"Terrific. Is eight o'clock okay?"

"Perfect."

"That's great. Well, goodbye for now, then," Lucian said. I heard him walk away. It was a long moment before Ty closed the door behind him.

I was sitting at the kitchen island sipping some water when Ty came in and said, "Did you hear what just happened?" He looked a bit dazed.

"Yup. Sorry, I didn't mean to eavesdrop."

"What do you think it means?" He sank onto an accompanying barstool and blinked at me.

"I think it means you have a date tomorrow night."

"It couldn't possibly be that. Why would a man like Lucian ask someone like me on a date?"

"Because you're sweet and kind and beautiful," I told him, "and because he has a huge crush on you."

Ty stared at me incredulously. "He does?"

"Yup."

"Oh. Wow." He tucked a lock of his soft, blond hair behind his ear as he said, "I had a crush on him from the moment I first saw him, but I figured I didn't have a chance in hell with Lucian. And now...he knows I let myself get used by anyone that wanted me back at his house in the hills. What must he think of me?"

"He obviously doesn't judge you for that. I don't either."

"You don't? But you know how I used to be. You remember what I was doing when you first found me."

"I totally understand why you used to do that, and you know I used to do the same thing. I understand better than anyone what it means to be lonely and desperate for a little human contact."

"Or vampire contact," he said with a grin.

I smiled and said, "That too. But you and I have both come such a long way. I can't go on punishing myself for the mistakes of my past, not if I expect to have any kind of future, and you shouldn't punish yourself either."

He chewed on his full lower lip for a while before saying, "I still just find it beyond comprehension that a man like that would want me."

"Did you hear how nervous he was? He probably can't imagine why *you* would want *him*." He smiled shyly at that and lowered his gaze, and I added, "You're a total catch, Ty."

"Thank you for saying that." He folded and unfolded his hands, then looked up at me again. "There's something else that worries me too, though. Are we sure Lucian is trustworthy? I mean, he targeted his own brother for assassination."

"For over three centuries, August shut off his humanity and was a complete terror. At some point they lost contact, so Lucian didn't know he'd changed. He believed his brother was not only evil, but that he'd turned on the vampire race. Given all of that, I get it."

"You're really convinced Lucian's a good guy, even after everything."

"Yeah, I am. I mean, you'll have to use your own judgment and see what your gut tells you about him, but I tend to believe he tries to do the right thing." I pushed myself to my feet and said, "I need to go and collapse now. If anyone wants me, I'll be asleep on the couch. The stairs just seem like way too much effort."

*****

I was awakened by the sound of keys in the lock the next morning and sat up to find Alejandro pushing open the front door dressed in an expensive suit, carrying several bags of groceries. "Hey Allie. What're you doing?" I asked, rubbing my eyes.

He frowned at me and said, "August wanted me to drop off a few things for you before work."

"Where is he?"

"No idea."

"Is he still mad at me?" Someone, presumably Ty, had covered me with a blanket, which I set aside as I stood up.

He glared at me and snapped, "What do you think?"

"Why the hell are *you* mad at me?"

Allie dumped the bags on the kitchen island and asked, "What the fuck did you do to him, Tinder?"

"Nothing!"

"Yeah, right!"

"Well, okay, maybe not *nothing*."

I quickly relayed the story of how I broke the mate bond. When I finished, Allie relaxed his stiff posture a bit and said, "Oh. Well, shit. I thought you cheated on him or something from the way he was acting."

"Hardly. I just did something reckless, and because I knew he'd stop me, I didn't tell him about it ahead of time."

"That's a guaranteed recipe for pissing off August. The two things he absolutely can't stand are not being consulted on big decisions and the people he cares about endangering themselves." He watched me for a moment before asking, "Are you okay? I should have asked sooner, but I didn't know you died yesterday."

"I'm fine. I was only dead for maybe ninety seconds."

"Well, while I'm glad you're okay, you really did some damage where August is concerned."

"I did?"

Allie pulled a couple folders out of one of the grocery sacks and said, "He had me place a bunch of calls first thing this morning. He paid the rent on this house a few months out and instructed me to bring you all the information on your investment accounts. That's what this paperwork is."

"He has investment accounts for me?"

"Of course. He set them up years ago. Taking care of you was always vitally important to him."

"So...what exactly is happening here? Is August planning on sulking for *months*, because of what I did?"

"I wouldn't put it past him."

I crossed my arms over my chest and said, "That's ridiculous. I need to go talk to him. Where is he?"

"Like I said, I have no idea."

"Bullshit. He probably told you not to tell me. We both know you suck at keeping secrets though, so why don't you just go ahead and spill? It'll save me the trouble of coercing it out of you."

Allie rolled his eyes. "Yeah, good luck with that. I need to get to the office. He wanted me to stock your pantry too, that's what all this crap is. I think you can put it away yourself."

"He is *such* a caretaker, even when he's pissed off at me."

"No shit." Alejandro started to head for the front door, but I muttered something in Latin and he bounced off an invisible barrier, landing on his ass and then exclaiming, "What the fuck was that?"

"Me coercing you."

He stood up and groped at the wall I'd conjured, then muttered, "When the hell did you go full Harry Potter, exactly?"

"Turns out there's more to my ability to work magic than I ever realized. Don't make me show you the atomic fireball, even though it's totally badass. Just play nice and tell me where to find August."

"Is it your goal in life to make him hate me? I can't tell you. He's still fuming from the last time I disobeyed him!"

"He loves you. He'll get over it."

Allie raised an eyebrow at me and said, "I think it's a good idea for you two to spend some time apart. He's pissed and you're annoying. It's a bad combination."

"You're right, I am annoying. *And*, I can conjure spells at will. You so don't want me to torture this information out of you. Think the invisible wall was annoying? How about trapping you in an invisible box like a mime and then blasting accordion music at you night and day? There is literally no limit to how annoying I can be." I smiled at him pleasantly.

He narrowed his eyes at me and we stared each other down for several moments. Finally he sighed dramatically and said, "Fine. I really hate you, by the way."

"No you don't."

"Keep up this Vegas magician shit and I will."

"So where's August?"

He pulled a pen and business card holder from his pocket and removed a card from the case, then scribbled something on the back of it. "I'm pretty sure this is where he went. All of his properties were compromised when he was hiding from the Order, but there's no reason he wouldn't be using them again. In the past, this was his destination of choice when he was really ticked off about something and just needed to stew." He slid the card across the kitchen island and I took it and glanced at the Big Sur address, then wedged it in the pocket of those annoying skinny jeans. "What the fuck are you wearing, by the way?"

"I've decided to become a fashion trendsetter. Don't be hating."

He stared at me for a beat, then said, "Can I go to work now?"

I frowned at my handiwork and said, "I don't actually know how to take the barriers down. You'll have to go around them." Since I'd blocked off both ends of the kitchen, the only way for Alejandro to get out was to crawl gracelessly over the center island in his expensive suit, which made me chuckle. I pulled a Sharpie from one of the drawers and wrote the word "wall" on both sections in big letters. They appeared to just hang in the air. It was cool. "So people don't keep running into them," I explained.

He rolled his eyes at that. "Brilliant."

"Do you think I can bum a ride?" I asked him. "Now that I'm not hiding from half the world, I want to go get my car."

"Fine."

"I'll be ready to go in ten minutes." He pulled out his cell phone and began flipping through messages as I dashed upstairs to shower and change, then grabbed my duffle bag and went to find Ty.

He was in the large basement rec room, studying for his high school equivalency test. I said, "Hey. So, I need to go apologize to August. I may stay in Big Sur awhile, depending on how long it takes to talk him down from being totally pissed off at me. You okay hanging out here?"

I was kind of surprised when he grinned and nodded. "I'll be fine. I'm trying to work on not being so clingy, so it's good practice."

I gave him a hug and said, "Good luck on your date tonight."

"Thank you. Good luck with August."

"Thanks, I'll need it. By the way, careful if you go into the kitchen. Mistakes were made."

*****

Allie drove me to the garage where I'd stashed my Camaro weeks ago, when I was trying to lay low and avoid detection by the Order. "Thanks," I said, "I appreciate the lift."

"It was on my way."

"Really?"

"No." I smiled at that and climbed out of his car, but then he called, "Hey Tinder?"

"Yeah?"

"August is stubborn as they come, but he needs you. Try your damnedest to make things right with him, okay?"

"That's the plan."

The drive from L.A. to Big Sur was a solid six hours, but it was nice once I got out of the congestion of southern California. I put on some classic rock and relaxed a bit as I wound my way up the coast. It was good to have some time to think. There was a lot I needed to sort out, in addition to this current situation.

For one thing, there was the question of what I was going to do with my life now. I'd known I needed to retire from hunting as soon as I fell in love with August and realized not all vampires were bad. It had taken so much from me, twenty-one years of my life and every member of my family. Being a hunter had been the sum total of my identity and it came with generations of family history. It felt like casting off a huge piece of myself. But letting go was the right thing.

Yes, there were still vampires who killed humans, and yes, they needed to be stopped. But there were plenty of hunters to deal with that, it didn't have to be me. It was actually a good thing that most of the remaining hunters out there were just regular people without the sight. They could only target vampires that they actually witnessed harming humans, as opposed to randomly killing everyone that happened to be a vampire.

As I approached Big Sur, I focused on the task at hand and cast a concealment spell on both myself and my car, just in case August was angry enough to go storming off if he sensed me coming. I found the address Allie had given me and parked at the side of the private drive as soon as I pulled off the main road. It was a quarter-mile walk to the house, the hilly terrain dotted with manzanita, tall grasses, and clumps of yellow mustard flowers.

I could smell and hear the ocean ahead of me, but couldn't see it until I came to the crest of a hill. A hundred feet ahead, central California's rocky terrain crumbled into the blue Pacific, giant boulders punctuating the tide. Fifty yards to my right, an artfully designed house was nestled into its environment, almost disappearing into the landscaping. The home was made up of dark timber, and lots of glass that reflected the sea and sky.

I spotted a tall figure off to my left at the very edge of the cliff face, looking out over the ocean. I cut along the dirt footpath, finally stopping maybe fifteen feet behind August. My concealment spell was working awfully well. Normally it was absolutely impossible to sneak up on a vampire.

When I tried to drop the spell, I got stuck again, just like I had with the barrier in the kitchen. I frowned at myself and said aloud, "There's a lot of stuff I'm not very good at."

August flinched at the sound of my voice and spun around, staring at me in confusion. I continued, "For one thing, I don't know how to undo the spells that I create from scratch. I didn't want you to see me coming and run from me, so I conjured a way to go unnoticed. But then I didn't know how to shut it off. I'm glad I didn't startle you right off that cliff."

I stepped just a little closer, stopping maybe four or five feet away as I told him, "Another thing I'm not very good at is being in a relationship. Even when I was part of a family, I was taught to be self-reliant above all else. I think my parents knew eventually there would only be one of us left, and that the last kid standing would have to be really good at fending for himself."

I said softly, "I have a lot of flaws, which I know isn't news to you. But I also have the ability to change and to grow. I can learn to be the kind of partner you need me to be, to consider opinions other than my own and to be more cautious. You're probably stuck with my stubbornness, that's pretty much who I am. But the rest of it I can work on. Please, just give me another chance, August, and—"

I didn't get to finish my sentence. August closed the distance between us and took me in his arms. He kissed me passionately as I clutched him to me, then pulled back a few inches to look into my eyes. "I'm so sorry, Tyler. I got mad at you for being the man I fell in love with, for being brave and self-sacrificing and decisive. Before you got here, I was berating myself for having gone storming off like this. It was incredibly childish of me. Both of us need to learn how to be in a relationship, not just you."

"I'm sorry, too. I should have told you what I was planning. "

He grinned a little. "I would have stopped you."

"I know, and I totally get how much that scared you. I'm sorry for that too. It was a calculated risk though, it's not like I just jumped in front of a bus. I really did think through all my options and there wasn't another solution."

He cupped my face with one hand. "That's so you. Always more concerned for the greater good than your own safety."

"It seemed like you were especially mad at the contingency plan of Lucian changing me."

"Of course I was. I was already insanely jealous of my brother because he had that mate bond with you. Then when I heard you asked him to change you, I felt like you'd just be swapping out the mate bond for the maker bond. You'd still be his and not mine."

"But August, he was willing to change me *for you*. He and I don't want each other, we never have. He was willing to turn me as an absolute last resort, only if it was between that and death, and he was willing to do that for just one reason: so you and I could be together."

"I know. I really do. And I know it's ridiculous to be jealous, just like it's ridiculous to be so overprotective of you. I used to be far more rational before I fell in love with you, you know. But now, my world revolves around you, around this fragile, breakable, unbelievably precious little human, and it's just making me crazy. What if something happens to you? How would I bear it?"

"That's why I want you to turn me, because I can't stand the thought of you alone for centuries after I die."

"It's still far too soon for that discussion, love."

"I know, and I'm not saying we do it in the next five minutes," I said. "But you should know that I love you with all my heart, August. And you know what? I've loved you for *years*, far longer than I was ever willing to admit to myself. Back when I thought all vampires were evil, I tried to fight and deny my love for you, because it went against everything I'd ever been taught. But I still loved you, even while I tried to tell myself otherwise."

He smiled at me, his eyes sparkling as he said, "I'm so glad you finally got a clue."

I burst out laughing at that. "Me too"

He kissed me tenderly, then said, "Thanks for coming after me. I was just about to drive back to L.A. to see you, so it's lucky we didn't miss each other."

"Very lucky." The breeze picked up, which made me shiver a little in my thin t-shirt.

"Come on, love. The view's nice from inside, too." He took my hand and led me down the narrow path to the house. Once in the living room, he tossed a bunch of pillows in front of a big river rock fireplace, then got the fire going as I settled in comfortably on the area rug. Once the fire was crackling and warming the large living room, he pulled a blanket off the back of the couch and draped it over me, then settled in behind me, spooning my body as he kissed my shoulder.

After a while, he whispered, "Are you sure I'm really what you want, Tyler?" He sounded so uncertain when he asked that, and I turned around so I was facing him.

"Do you really have to ask? You must know how I feel about you. I mean, you even saw it in that vision centuries ago."

"But what if that was just wishful thinking? I've wanted you for so long Tyler, and I guess...I guess I have a hard time believing you'd want me in return."

"Why?"

"Because I'm a monster." He said that so quietly. "The things I've done...there's so much blood on my hands. I know you said you understood, but how could you love me, knowing what I am? Knowing the things I've done?"

I never would have guessed a man like August could be so insecure. I pulled the blanket up so it covered him too and took him in my arms as I said, "I know what you did in the past, but I also know who you really are. You show me every day that you're kind and decent and loving. You're such a good man, August, and I love you with all my heart."

"And you'd really be willing to be turned for me?"

"Absolutely."

His eyes searched mine, and he said softly, "That's just astonishing, that you'd actually be willing to give up your human life for me."

"Should tell you something."

"It does." He smiled at me and relaxed in my arms a bit. "Tells me you're a bit daft."

I grinned at him and said, "You say that like it's a bad thing."

"Oh no, not at all. I've always liked that about you, actually."

I kissed him again and we ended up making out for a while before I told him, "So, starting today, no more running away when things get complicated, and no more major decisions without consulting one another."

"Agreed."

"We have a lot to figure out, August. I have absolutely no idea what path my life will take from here, but I do know one thing. Whatever happens, I need you right there beside me."

He smiled at me and pulled me close. "I will be, love. That's a promise."

December, Eighteen Months Later

August and I got married at Christmastime, about a year and a half after that day. We had a small ceremony in front of the fireplace at the house in Big Sur with a justice of the peace and our family. I say family because they'd all become so much more than friends.

Nate was my best man. It had taken him almost five months to come back to himself after being turned. Fortunately, he'd come through with his memories intact. We visited him and his husband frequently (and yes, August had tattooed Nate's daylight symbols just as soon as he was calm enough to sit still for that). Nate had returned to school and his family was back in his life now (after being told a story of a fictitious extended backpacking trip through Europe).

I was surprised how much Nate still seemed like his old self. I'd never known anyone both before and after the transition and had assumed it would really alter his personality, but that wasn't the case. He was the same sweet, considerate, happy guy he'd always been, and he and Nikolai seemed even closer and more in love than ever.

Alejandro was August's best man. His current girlfriend, a pretty redheaded vampire named Lorelai, also attended the wedding. He and August still had some issues, but they always would. They were too much like father and son not to bicker and argue. Allie had taken over as president of August's investment company when August decided to focus on other things. We saw him a couple times a month. He and I were becoming really good friends and I teased him mercilessly about becoming his stepdad.

Another couple attended our ceremony, too. Laurie and Ty had built a relationship slowly over the course of a year and married six months ago in a small, gorgeous summer wedding. They clearly adored each other and spent almost every moment of every day together.

Both of them had dedicated themselves full time to the task of recording the history of the vampire race. They'd recently published the first in a series of books that was billed as fiction to the general populace, but vampires knew the truth. August and I had joined them in their quest to gather information. We'd taken several trips to Europe, South America and Asia over the last year and a half to locate other vampires and record their stories of the lost vampire civilization. Laurie and Ty would sometimes travel with us. Gradually, the two brothers were learning to trust one another. It was obvious that they really did love each other, despite their turbulent history.

Our wedding ceremony was simple but beautiful. After the justice of the peace declared us married and took off, we all settled in around the living room and talked and laughed well into the night. Eventually, our guests departed. We'd put all of them up in a local B and B, because we needed privacy for what was coming next.

August led me to the bedroom, where we took turns undressing each other. He made love to me tenderly in our big, warm bed and bit me and drank from me right before we both came. I did the same thing. I looked into his eyes and recited two lines in Varsrecht that I'd wanted to say for a very long time. Then I asked, "Did I say that right?"

"Perfect, love. Do you know what you just said?"

I nodded. "I said I'm yours for all of eternity and you're mine. I'll give my life to protect you and I know you'll do the same for me. I love you with every part of me, just like you love me, not just today and tomorrow but until the end of time." I grinned at him and said, "That's actually pretty romantic, considering the fact that vampires get married while having sex."

"I love you, Tyler," he said, and then he repeated the two lines of verse that married us under vampire custom.

After that, we went back to the living room. He held me on his lap as he settled onto the big couch, which we'd moved right in front of the warm, cozy fireplace. Our Christmas tree twinkled with white lights off to our left in front of the big windows, which reflected its light.

"Are you sure about this next part?" August asked, cradling me as carefully as if I was made of glass.

"Absolutely positive. This is going to be fine, you and I both know that. We've been casting spells for weeks to eliminate the chances of anything going wrong."

There was still worry in his eyes, but he drew in a breath and said, "Alright. Just like we planned, then."

"Just like we planned," I agreed.

He picked up a long, slim dagger that we'd left beside the couch, its polished blade reflecting the firelight. After he cut his shoulder with it, I sat up to drink deeply from him. I'd gotten surprisingly used to this, so it didn't faze me in the slightest.

When I finished, I leaned back in his arms and smiled up at him. "I love you more than anything. See you on the other side, hubby."

"Please remember me," he whispered, raising the blade. "I love you so much."

August said that a moment before he plunged the dagger into my heart.

I awoke suddenly with a gasp, pulling air into my lungs automatically. There was such a loud ringing in my ears. Deafening.

Where was I? There were thick covers on me and I pushed them off as I jumped out of a big bed and looked all around me. There were heavy curtains on the wall of windows, but I could tell it was light outside. A shudder went through me.

I looked down at myself. I was naked. I held up my own hands and stared at them as if they were foreign to me.

Movement to my left caught my eye and I spun on the tall figure beside me. Fear and panic and something else, something *strong*, flooded me. Need. I needed...I needed *something*, desperately, *right now*. I stared at the big man who was slowly approaching me. His lips were moving, he was saying something. I couldn't hear him over the ringing in my ears. His hands were raised, palms toward me as if he was trying to calm me.

I bared my teeth automatically as he got closer and crouched a bit, ready to attack if he kept coming closer. I cut my tongue on something, then ran it over my teeth. Fangs, long and sharp, were in my mouth. Had they always been there?

Still the man approached. I caught his scent all of a sudden. *Him.* He was what I needed!

I picked him up and threw him onto the bed effortlessly, even though he was bigger than me. Was I always this strong? I couldn't remember.

I tore his shirt off him, then his jeans and underwear. He didn't fight me. He just watched me closely, his brows knit with concern as he laid back against the mattress.

Instinct drove me to bite him, and I sunk my teeth into the spot where his neck and shoulder met. As soon as his blood filled my mouth, I moaned with pleasure and calmed, just a bit. I drank from him deeply, and right away that need in me started to ebb. But there was something else I needed, too.

I released his neck and sat up. I was so disoriented, my head swimming with so many sensations, all of them overwhelming. I was straddling the man's body and I understood that I'd just fed on him, but somehow, he didn't look afraid. Instead, he smiled at me and ran his hand down my chest, then lightly skimmed my swelling cock. *Yes.* That was what I needed now.

He pulled a small bottle from under the pillow and applied something cold and wet to my cock. Did he want me to fuck him? I needed sex, I needed it more than anything right now, but somehow I didn't think I wanted what he seemed to be offering. I wished my ears weren't ringing so loudly, it was impossible to think....

I realized what I needed all of a sudden and reached behind me. His big cock was swelling, too. He held up the bottle for me and I took it from him, accidentally crushing it as I tried to squeeze out some of the liquid and getting it all over my hand. I shook off the excess and grabbed his cock quickly, rubbing it to make it hard, then aiming it at my ass and sitting down on it.

I threw my head back and moaned. It felt *so good*. I needed this as desperately as I'd needed to feed. I rode his cock feverishly as he stroked mine. After a few minutes of this I felt him cumming deep inside me, which triggered my own release.

I understood now. This man was my mate, I was sure of that. He belonged to me.

We belonged to each other.

"August," I whispered. His face erupted into the most glorious smile.

My body was shaking as I laid down on top of him. Gradually, the ringing in my ears ebbed. He held me tightly. I could hear him now. "Welcome back, Tyler."

With each passing minute, my head became clearer and clearer. Finally I sat up a bit and looked at him as I asked, "What the hell did you do with Allie when you sired him? I never realized vampires wake up completely horny."

He burst out laughing at that. "Oh my God, you really *are* back! How are you even talking right now? You should be pure animal!"

"Answer the question. Please tell me you didn't fuck Alejandro when you turned him, because that's going to seriously gross me out."

"Of course not! Vampires don't always wake up randy, only those that are mated." He stared at me incredulously and added, "I still don't see how you can be so rational right now."

"I don't feel rational, I feel like fucking you for days. I'm also hungry again."

"The fridge is full of bags from a blood bank, you can drink your fill. As far as sex goes, I have absolutely no problem with you using me however you need." August flashed me a big smile.

I leaned down and kissed him, but ended up nicking his lip with one of my new, sharp canines. I licked the blood away and his lip healed instantly. "The teeth are going to take some getting used to," I said as I propped myself up a bit. Then I noticed the big pile of heavy restraints on the bedside table and asked, "Why hadn't you used the chains on me like we discussed?"

"You were only out about thirty-two hours and I didn't expect you to wake up so soon. I did get your daylight tattoos done last night, though."

"Thank you."

He put a hand behind his head and studied me as he said, "I wonder if it has something to do with the unique combination of elements that comprise you, the dash of werewolf and the generous helping of warlock mixed in with your human genes? Or maybe your hunter blood that gave you the gift of your second sight had something to do with you waking up quickly and being so lucid."

"No idea." I leaned over and picked up one of the heavy iron manacles, then gave him a flirtatious smile. "These shouldn't go to waste though, just because I didn't wake up wild. What do you say, want to chain me up and spend the next day or month or year fucking me senseless?"

"As if I'd say no to that! But first, come here." I set the manacle aside and he pulled me close and kissed me for a long time before murmuring, "I love you so much, Tyler."

"I love you too, August. Thank you for turning me, I know you were worried."

"I always worry about you, love."

"But it worked out better than we could have hoped for," I said as I nestled against his chest.

"It really did."

"Now that it's done and I've come out the other side, I just feel...*right*. I kind of feel like I was always destined to wind up just like this."

August kissed the top of my head and said softly, "Maybe you were."

The End

Thank you for reading!

For more by Alexa Land, please visit

http://alexalandwrites.blogspot.com/

Books by Alexa Land Include:

Feral (prequel to The Tinder Chronicles)

The Tinder Chronicles (Tinder, Hunted and Destined)

And the Firsts and Forever Series:

Way Off Plan

All In

In Pieces

Gathering Storm

Salvation

Skye Blue

Made in the USA
San Bernardino, CA
19 December 2018